A SUMMER WITH THE
DEAD

A Summer With the Dead is published by Elder Signs Press, Inc.
All rights reserved.
The content in this book is © 2017 Sherry Decker

Design by Deborah Robbins.
Cover by Zagladko Sergei Petrovich.
Edited by Charles P. Zaglanis.

FIRST EDITION
10 9 8 7 6 5 4 3 2 1
Published in May 2017
ISBN: 9781934501696
Printed in the U.S.A.
Published by Elder Signs Press
P.O. Box 389
Lake Orion, MI 48361-0389
www.eldersignspress.com

A SUMMER WITH THE DEAD

BY SHERRY DECKER

Sherry Decker

Elder Signs Press
2017

Special thanks to Kaaron Warren for allowing *Tool 4* to be reprinted here.

Tool 4

He was a handsome man. When he danced (traditional, wild, subtle or worshipful, there was nothing he couldn't do) you'd think he was a god. But you don't know what's in a person until you bury them. Leave them ten years. Then dig them up and see what they've become.

A good man is rot and bone.

A bad man stays solid, hoping for a second chance.

The god of dance was turned to iron, frozen in a dance move that used to work for him.

–Kaaron Warren

Chapter One

CEMETERY LANE. THE STREET sign leaned at a crazy angle toward a weedy drainage ditch. Some homeowners living along the lane had complained to the City Council. They wanted the name changed to Memorial Boulevard, insisting it sounded less morbid. After all, the cemetery was another mile and half down the road, around the landmark boulder and past the grove of quaking aspens. It wasn't a *lane*, really, they insisted. It was a road, or at least an avenue.

Cemetery Lane was where Maya grew up. It had a median down its center covered with wild grass, dandelions, and a giant maple tree. The maple shaded the street, sidewalk, and the yard in front of her house. She often played in the shade of that tree with her dolls and tea set. She carved her initials into the bark on her tenth birthday. M.E.P. Maya Elenore Pederson.

That was the day Maya's father walked down to the corner where the city was putting up the new street sign and asked them if he could have the old sign. The foreman shrugged and handed it over.

Twenty years later that sign still hung over her father's workbench in the old garage. Maya never understood why he wanted it or why he kept it. She never asked him, and she couldn't ask him now, because he was dead. Maya's mother said, "I have absolutely no idea why your father wanted that sign. He acted as if it protected him from something."

Memorial Boulevard aged gracefully over the years. The craftsman style homes with their level front yards were considered quaint and charming. Every homeowner in the development kept his lawn mowed and his house painted. The street had a manicured appearance. Tidy. Conservative. Orderly.

Maya rolled to a stop in front of her childhood home and sat at the curb, chewing a bloody hangnail. She checked her face in the rearview mirror. Her brown hair was pulled high into a ponytail, the way her mother always fixed it for school. Never mind that she was now thirty and educated. She would always be Mama's little girl. Mama made sure Maya remembered that.

A bottle of store-bought water helped moisten Maya's dry mouth before she opened her car door, crossed the sidewalk, and climbed the brick front steps. By the time she reached the screen door, her mouth was dry again. She dreaded this visit. Mama would not understand.

As always, her mother followed the tradition of steeping a pot of tea and having a cookie or sharing a slice of cinnamon toast. She and Maya sat in the peach colored dining room on ivory silk upholstered chairs with clear vinyl covers and a lace tablecloth and two matching napkins. It was something they both relished, those small niceties. Mama enjoyed entertaining, even if it was just for the two of them. No one else ever came much anymore, Mama said.

"How's your job going, dear?" Mama leaned forward and shoved a stray hair from Maya's face, tucking it behind her ear, in with all the obedient hairs.

"I resigned last week," Maya said. "I'm taking a sabbatical."

"What does Benson have to say about that?"

"Nothing. I'm divorcing Benson."

Mama's china teacup paused at her thin lips, and then rattled into the saucer. "You don't plan to move back home, do you? I'm putting this place up for sale, remember?"

"I remember, Mama. You told me." *Six times.*

"Then, where will you go? I never dreamed my college graduate might become a homeless person."

"Calm down, Mom."

"Please don't call me that and don't tell me to calm down."

"I'm not going to be homeless, Mama. I'm going to stay with Aunt Elly for the summer."

Mama dropped her napkin on the table beside her uneaten oatmeal cookie. "I see."

"Aunt Elly said she's looking forward to my visit. She said she could use some help around the farm. She's having back trouble . . . arthritis probably. I've always wanted to see her farm, remember?"

"That woman is unstable. I've often said that," Mama said. "She's never been . . . normal."

"Worse than me?"

"Oh, Maya. You've had problems, yes, but Dr. Conover has helped you, hasn't she? She's been there for you through tough childhood issues, and she continues to see you, even though I thought by now she would have referred you to someone who treats adults."

"Yes, I like Dr. Conover," Maya said. "I see her every other month now, instead of weekly."

"All psychiatrists suspect child abuse at first. She doesn't mention that anymore does she?"

"She decided my anxiety and depression are due to unresolved stress." Maya's mother sipped her tea. "Your father never hit you, did he?"

"No." Maya shook her head. "Daddy never did anything mean to me, ever."

"Your father was too quiet, too withdrawn. He held things in. He should have talked about his problems. It might have helped him."

"Yes, it might have. Talking helps."

"Does it, Maya? I'm glad. Taking you to Dr. Conover was the right thing to do then, wasn't it? I did the right thing?"

"In the long run."

"In the long run?"

"Well, dragging me there while I was crying and terrified was traumatic."

"I don't remember you crying. You were terrified?"

"Don't you remember me wetting my pants in the elevator?"

"But you also used to wet the bed, Maya. I didn't see any difference."

"Mama, you remember things that relieve you of any blame. You tend to forget unpleasant things you might have done."

"That's a mean thing to accuse me of, Maya. Is that the kind of thing you tell Dr. Conover?"

"Remember having my kitten put down because it cried all night the first night I had it?"

"What kitten?"

"I better go now, Mama. I promised Aunt Elly I'd be there by four o'clock this afternoon and it's a long drive."

"Do I have Elly's number?" Mama shoved her chair back from the table and headed for the kitchen. She yanked open a drawer. "There's paper and pencil in here somewhere."

"I'll have my cell phone, Mom."

"Please don't call me that."

"Mama, you have my cell phone number and you can reach me on that."

"I don't remember any kitten."

Maya kissed her mother's temple and headed for the door. At her car, she forced herself to smile and wave goodbye. Her mother stood on the front porch, biting her lower lip. Usually Mama was good at concealing her emotions, but not today. Maya had touched a nerve. For a second she felt guilty about that, but as she opened the car door, she decided, ***screw that.***

One more glance at the house, in case it was the last time she ever saw it, because, who knew? It might sell tomorrow. Mama would move out and it would be gone forever. It would be inhabited by another family. Normal people.

Good luck to them, whoever they are.

Maya's vision blurred. She blinked, cleared her eyes and focused on her mother again. Instead of a fifty-five year old woman in a yellow flowered dress and white, lace cardigan, Maya saw green, tattered rags draped around a gray corpse, its skull grinning, its bone fingers clawing the screen door, its moldy hair hanging in dull ringlets. The eye sockets were empty, deep, and black.

"Look away," Dr. Conover would advise. "What you see is not really there. How could it be?"

Chapter Two

THE FORD EDGE'S WINDSHIELD was dry and Maya took it as a positive omen. Sunlight glanced between racing clouds as seagulls swooped and dove in a gusty wind, easing Maya's earlier sense of disaster. She always anticipated obstacles and was seldom disappointed. She was accustomed to problems. Nothing she ever tried came easily so why should running away from Benson be any different?

Every night for the last month she dreamed about escaping and it would take more than foul weather to stop her. "Nothing will stop me," she said aloud. Nothing would make her go back to a life of fear. Nothing could be worse than that.

Behind her brown eyes and brown bangs, the westbound lanes of the Tacoma Narrows Bridge filled her rearview mirror. Over her right shoulder, Mt. Rainer jutted up through a gray cloudbank, its snowy glaciers glaring with sunlight. The harsh white slopes were blinding. She squinted, blinked, then looked away.

Miles ahead an adventure awaited. Maya believed it with all her heart. With the wide bridge stretched out ahead and her Ford Edge purring like a silver cat, it felt as if a gate had swung wide open, a giant gate of iron bars with spiked tops, and a lock the size of a gravestone. She pictured a weathered sign chained to that gate. NO RETURN.

Their marriage was over, along with Bensons tantrums. Last month, during one of his rages, he'd shoved her and she fell. His eyes held an odd light as he straddled her on the kitchen floor, trapping her arms against the cold tile with his knees. His hands on her throat squeezed off her air. Her eyes felt like they would pop from their sockets and the top of her head threatened to explode, but then Benson's expression changed. His grip on her throat loosened, most likely from a fear of consequences. Benson did foolish things all the time, but he was no fool. That was the moment she decided to leave him. She refused to believe his old, familiar promises, that he would never hit her again, that he could change. That he loved her. "He does love me," Maya said aloud. "But his temper will end up killing one of us."

Maya glanced in the mirror again and stretched her lower lip forward with the tip of her tongue. The red scar had faded to pink but the memory would last forever. The black eye and the red, swollen cheekbone were healed. He would never hit her again. She promised herself that.

• • •

The Ford Edge hummed past the airport exit as heavy raindrops hit the windshield, blurring the glass. The sign read Tacoma Narrows Airport, but when she'd lived here it was the Wollochet Airport, and as far as Maya was concerned, it would always be Wollochet.

Maya flipped on the wipers, twisting the dial until they swept back and forth fast enough to clear the windshield, but not so rapid the noise made her tense, like noises sometimes did. "One…two…three…four," she counted aloud as the wipers swept back and forth. Four was good. Four was her lucky number. It was an even number. Even numbers were safe.

She set her cruise control for sixty mph and zipped by Gig Harbor, through Purdy, past Port Orchard and around the tip of Sinclair Inlet at Gorst. She saluted the navy ships anchored in the deep green water outside Bremerton before she headed north. She drove out from under the dark clouds and the rain halted as abruptly as it'd started. Ahead, the highway was dry. She pulled into the Double-Decker Lunch in Poulsbo for a turkey sandwich and iced tea, visited the restroom and climbed back behind the wheel, noting the time. Two P.M. She was a bit ahead of schedule. Maya lowered her speed to fifty and cruised in the slow lane.

She heard Benson's voice inside her head; "I hate how you check your watch four times every hour."

"But you're glad I have dinner ready every day at 5:30. You like how I vacuum on Mondays, fold the clean laundry on Tuesdays and grocery shop on Wednesdays, don't you?"

"I can't complain about that, but it's irritating how you store all the canned goods in alphabetical order. Only people with emotional disorders do things like that."

Maya bit her tongue and said nothing after that. Arguing led to Benson losing his temper. He never complained that she paid bills and took care of the budget on Thursdays, cleaned the refrigerator, scoured the bathrooms, and changed the sheets on Fridays.

Maya arranged the bath towels inside the linen closet in the color spectrum, like an artist's palette. She remembered buying a peach colored towel for no reason except there was a gap between the yellow and red towels on the linen shelf.

"You're nuts," Benson said. "Normal people don't act the way you do."

"But I'm not hurting anything by doing this," Maya said. "The towel was under four dollars and I stayed within the budget. I like things to be tidy and in order, lined up in straight rows, and, I think being on time is important."

The last time she folded and organized Benson's clean socks and underwear in his top drawer he pulled the drawer back open and tossed them all like salad. In the pantry he rearranged the canned goods, switching the artichoke hearts to the end of the shelf, after zucchini. He moved all the baked, green, kidney, and navy beans behind the canned tomatoes. Sometimes he turned all the cans around so their labels faced the back wall of the pantry. Once, he super-glued a can of tomato sauce to the shelf. The scar remained, where the paint had torn away when she pried the can free. He did things like that for no reason other than to frustrate her.

Maya gave up folding Benson's underwear and socks and started dumping them straight from the laundry basket into his drawer. He didn't seem to notice, but for her it was difficult to leave them like that, all in a jumbled mess. It was a challenge to walk away.

"I know, I'm obsessive-compulsive," Maya told Benson. "I'm trying to change, Bens."

"Change faster!"

"Yelling at me doesn't help."

Benson held up his fist. "Would this help?"

• • •

At 2:40 PM Maya crossed the Hood Canal floating bridge near Port Gamble and headed northwest into the untamed Olympic Peninsula. The evergreen trees looked like they stretched on forever; so did the inlets of turquoise green water, rocky beaches, and snow-tipped Olympic Mountain peaks.

Maya felt a quiver of excitement in her chest. This was an exhilarating adventure already. It felt good to be starting over. It felt good to run away, to run away from Benson. She hoped he worried, but doubted he would.

"Sorry, Bens," Maya said. "I never loved you. That was wrong of me. I tried, though."

Maybe that was why he was so angry all the time. He knew she didn't love and admire him anymore.

Benson was handsome and he made a great first impression. His employer kept advancing him through the corporation. Benson had been a new member of the sales staff when she first met him. Today he was VP of Sales. At first he treated her well but that was seven years ago. "Damn, I was so naïve at twenty-three." Reaching the age of thirty was a wake-up call. Life was passing by at breakneck speed. Life was too precious to waste on a man who blamed her for everything wrong in his life. Why waste her life with a man who wanted her dead? And Benson did. Why else would he punch her in the face, straddle her on the kitchen floor, and choke her?

Maya checked her watch again. 3:15. She turned the radio on low. Classics from the seventies. One by one, Maya punched the delete button, erasing all the country-western radio channels.

Forty minutes later Maya crested a forested hill. She turned off the radio, pulled to the shoulder of a narrow blacktop road, and lowered her driver's side window. A cool breeze ruffled her bangs. She smelled fresh cut cedar and faint wood smoke, moss, and damp earth. A nearby alder groaned as it swayed back and forth in the wind. She'd missed the road sign at the last crossroads, but someone painted the name Pederson in blue paint on the rural white mailbox. Maya gazed across a valley to the opposite hillside.

Aunt Elly's farm surprised her. Maya always pictured a tidy, white farmhouse with window boxes full of colorful annuals, and a lush vegetable garden beside the house. Instead, the farm she saw was a sprawling, turn-of-the-century, three-story house built on a wide slope. The house stood as if shackled to the hillside by rusted barbwire fences. A neglected looking fruit orchard surrounded it on three sides. The fruit trees all wore dull gray bark; their limbs were bare. For a moment, Maya thought the place looked abandoned. Two, third-story windows faced the road. Their dark glass reflected the overcast sky and appeared to be staring at her in silence. The large picture window on the first floor formed a wide, rectangular, mouth. The placement of the windows made the front side of the house look like a screaming face; the tall brick chimney, like an off-center, rust colored scar.

Maya checked the address again. This had to be the place. There were no other mailboxes in sight. She studied the farm again and noticed thin smoke coiling from a rear chimney. "Someone's home." Maya rolled up her window.

As a child, she'd longed to see this farm. She begged her parents, but they said no.

She wanted to roam the fields, the hilltops, and the surrounding forest; to explore the barns, the streams, and trails that she'd heard about in her aunt's letters and birthday cards. She wanted to see this place in person, and now she finally would.

The late April sun burned a hole in the clouds and radiated a welcome warmth through the windshield. Maya coasted down the dirt driveway, across a wooden bridge and over a dark stream. On the stream's black banks, yellow skunk cabbage glowed like giant lemons squatting in mud. She accelerated upward into the shadows of giant evergreens. Enormous ferns brushed her car windows and the Ford's tires straddled a center line of chartreuse moss.

The driveway led up and around to the backside and then leveled out between the house and a low building with four, small, curtained windows. For a second, Maya thought she saw a blue curtain move, and suspected someone watched her.

"Maya?" A tiny woman stood on the back steps of the house. Her gray hair was pulled into a small chignon at the base of her head, and she wore long, loose blue pants and a dark gray cardigan buttoned up to her neck. Her bony hands squeezed the front of the cardigan together over her chest as if substituting the sweater for gloves.

"Aunt Elly." Maya climbed from the car and threw her arms around her aunt. "I'm so glad to see you. It's been such a long time!"

"Careful, honey," Elly said. "My back's been bad lately. Arthritis I think."

Maya released her aunt and stepped back. "This big old farm is a lot for you to manage all alone."

"Yes, it is. When Harlan was alive we had over fifteen hundred acres, but I've sold it off bit by bit, down to about five hundred acres now. I'm not the manager Harlan was. I've been thinking seriously about selling." Elly shivered. "Let's go inside, honey. This damp wind makes me ache."

"I'll get my luggage," Maya said.

"Naw, Coty'll get it."

"Who's Coty?"

"He's an old friend's nephew. He lives right there in the bunkhouse, other side of the driveway." Elly pointed toward the low building. "He's been a blessing these last few months."

"It's good that you have someone to help around here."

"Coty probably spotted you before you turned in the driveway, Maya. He don't miss a thing."

Once inside, Maya warmed herself by a wood stove in the corner of the kitchen while Elly made tea and put out paper napkins and a dish of cookies on the table. The round table and matching light green chairs fit the bay window with room to spare. A cream-colored doily centered the table and upon it stood an empty blue vase. The floor was aged yellow linoleum and the cupboards were lacquered pine with black hinges. It was a cozy room. Maya moved to a kitchen chair with her back to the sunshine.

"Are you always so punctual?" Elly asked. "You said four o'clock and, lookee there." Elly nodded at the vintage clock above the stove. "It's two minutes after."

"I try to be punctual, Aunt Elly. Thank you for inviting me. I've always wanted to see your farm. I almost didn't come, though." Maya said. "I had a job offer the other day. Not a great job, but a job. I don't want anyone to think I'm mooching off you. I'm planning to help out around here."

"I'm so glad you're here, Maya honey. I need someone to talk to, someone other than Coty. He's not much on conversation. He doesn't take after his aunt Judith at all. If she's awake, she's talkin.'"

"Maybe that's a blessing. Some people never get anything done, they talk so much. I've worked with people like that."

"True, but Coty . . . well, like I said, he's very quiet. I invited him to move in upstairs and eat his meals in here with me, but he shook his head. 'Bunkhouse is fine' he said, and I guess he's okay out there. He's got a potbellied stove and a sink and toilet. I guess he heats water and bathes in the old washtub. I noticed it was gone from the shed wall." And then, as if reading Maya's mind, "He just showed up at the door one day, about three months ago. Early February."

"Have you checked him out? Do you think you should let a stranger live on the farm with you?"

"Oh, Coty's not a stranger. I was talking to my friend, Judith one day, back around Thanksgiving. You remember Judith, my childhood friend? Anyway, I was complaining about all the physical labor and how my back's been hurting, and Judith said she'd send her out-of-work nephew over to help. She said his name was Coty."

Maya nodded, even though she didn't remember Judith. "So, this Coty fellow is handy with tools and making repairs?"

"He sure is. The first words out of his mouth were, 'Your front porch is rotten. I can fix that.' I told him I was well aware of this farm's neglected condition. Well, he fixed the porch with lumber that's been stored in the upper barn for years. He did a good job too. In February we had heavy rains and some flooding down in the fields and I was afraid to drive over that bridge. There were planks missing and a support timber had almost washed away, and he fixed those too. And just yesterday Coty said my roof has missing shakes. I heard him up there this morning, clomping around. I swear, if it weren't for him I'd already be living in that retirement place in Seattle where Judith lives. She sent me photos."

"I'm glad for the chance to see your farm before you sell it. I can help you get it ready, Aunt Elly. I can do minor repairs inside, and I can paint and clean and we can have a garage sale and–"

"Sweety, those are great ideas and even though I love this old place, I know it's time to move on. And I know your Uncle Harlan would understand, bless his soul."

"Have you told Coty you plan to sell and move away?"

"No. We haven't really talked at all. Sometimes he doesn't even answer when I speak to him, as if he's hard of hearing, but I'll write him a strong recommendation when the time comes." Elly took a sip of her tea. "Come on, baby girl. You've waited thirty years to see this place. Let me show you around. There's a lot to see."

Chapter Three

ELLY LED THE WAY through a narrow pantry and into an adjoining room that jutted out from the north side of the house. It resembled a glassed-in porch surrounded by overgrown rhododendrons. The shrubs blocked any view of the yard or fields. Overhead, a single skylight was covered with pine needles and moss and did little to lessen the gloom.

"It's always dark in here." Elly paused to turn on a lamp. "I hardly ever come in here anymore except to run the vacuum around and sometimes slap everything with a dust cloth. Seems a waste with all this great big furniture and nobody using it, doesn't it?"

Maya nodded. "It's beautiful furniture. An antiques dealer would probably buy it from you. It's in excellent condition."

"Harlan only wanted quality. He never settled for anything less."

"Of course," Maya said. "He married you."

"That's funny, you saying that. Harlan used to say the same thing. He was such a sweetheart."

They circled back into the kitchen through the same pantry hallway. Elly pointed into the dining room and headed toward a flight of stairs. "The bedrooms are all up here." At the top of the stairs she paused in an open door. "This is my room."

Elly's room was pale blue with cream wainscoting. A small, stone fireplace filled the opposite corner. Beside the bed stood a table and tarnished brass lamp. The room looked sparse and masculine, as if the room had not been redecorated since Uncle Harlan died.

Continuing down the hallway Elly opened storage closets, linen cupboards, and a bathroom door. Inside stood a claw foot tub, pillar sink, and a toilet. White tile covered the floor and walls.

"The medicine cabinet is empty because I bathe and keep my things in the downstairs bathroom. I got into that habit years ago when I'd come in from working outside in the garden. I'd just strip right in the kitchen and toss everything down the basement stairs to the washer and dryer. There's more bath soap and toilet paper in the hall cupboard if you need it, and towels and washcloths too."

Further along the upstairs hallway were three more bedrooms. They faced the back driveway. Elly paused long enough to open the doors. Inside were four-poster beds, rocking chairs, vanities, and tallboys, beneath ash-colored drop cloths.

Maya shivered. Peering into those rooms reminded her of when she was eleven years old and her father died. While her mother made arrangements for the funeral, Maya tiptoed around the quiet, carpeted hallways of the funeral parlor. She remembered parting a burgundy velvet curtain and meeting a yellow-faced woman in a green dress. The woman was stretched out inside a pearled silver casket with a white satin lining. The yellow woman wasn't breathing. Her lips looked like someone had glued them together with the same glue they used for her eyelids.

"I don't even heat these rooms anymore," Elly said. "I keep the furnace vents closed, and the doors shut." Elly opened one of the last two doors at the end of the hallway.

"Here's your room, sweety pie. I put you down here at the end because I thought you'd like having a fireplace too, and this room has the best view of the valley. Your window looks north."

Maya stepped into the room. There was the faint smell of fresh paint and paste wax. The hardwood floor gleamed. The walls were smooth, pale, pewter gray. The wainscoting and chenille bedspread were white. Everything looked new including the brown and gray braided rug beside the bed. A colorful patchwork quilt lay folded across the foot of the bed and white lace curtains filtered a view of the valley. Maya stepped closer and parted the curtains. The lower fields sloped away from the house. At the bottom of the slope were the stream and the bridge. From behind the crest of a distant hill, smoke trailed upward through the tops of emerald evergreen trees.

"This is cozy," Maya said, yet she shivered with a sense of déjàvu. She was certain she had seen this room once before, or a room exactly like it. Somewhere. Maybe in a dream?

"Harlan and I slept in this room when we first moved here," Elly said. "We liked the view too, but Harlan didn't like looking down on that mossy skylight. He said it kept reminding him of all the work that wasn't getting done. And, he said it was more important to have a view of the barns."

"You have a neighbor over the hill? I see smoke."

"Oh, that's Parker Ellroy's place. He's about a mile away as a crow flies."

"And what a wonderful little rock fireplace, just like the one in your room."

"Harlan's the one who enjoyed a friendly flame of an evening. He was always hauling in wood and I was always sweeping up behind him. The furnace in the basement is new. I had it installed five years ago. It struggles to heat the second floor though."

Maya said, "I just saw a shadow pass under the skylight."

"That's probably Coty. I asked him to bring a load of firewood up for you. I had him paint this room last week, and while he was working I told him that my blood-kin niece was coming to stay a while. He didn't say anything, but he sort of frowned and I got the impression he didn't approve."

"Why would he disapprove?"

"I don't know, honey. Like I said, he's different."

Maya stepped back into the hallway. "Where does this door lead?"

"Down into that skylight room behind the kitchen, but I never go that way. Those stairs are steep and dark and there's no hand railing. Let's go back the other way."

Maya's three-piece luggage sat in the middle of the kitchen floor. Elly opened the back door and leaned outside. "Coty?" she called and then shrugged. "I can't keep track of him."

Maya jumped. A man stood so close they bumped elbows when she turned around. He was a head taller than her. He was dressed in a thick black and red buffalo checked jacket and navy blue jeans. Beneath the jacket lay a black turtleneck and above the turtleneck jutted a square jaw with dark stubble. His cheeks looked ruddy from the brusque wind outside. He narrowed his brown eyes and assessed her. His bronze, windblown hair was streaked with silver at the temples. A short scar divided one eyebrow. He smelled like fresh split cedar. Maya stepped back.

"Coty! Don't sneak up on us like that," Elly said.

Coty's gaze darted from Maya to Elly and back again. "Didn't mean to startle you." His voice was deep.

"Coty, this is Maya, my niece. I told you she was coming, remember?"

He nodded. "You're why I painted the guest room."

Maya cleared her throat. "Hello." She knew she should have offered her hand, but by then it felt too late, and then awkward.

Coty said, "I'll take this luggage upstairs and come back for the big trunk in the back of your car. Then I'll get the firewood."

"I'll help," Maya reached for a suitcase.

"Naw, I got them." He was shoeless and wore wool socks. He didn't make a sound as he climbed the stairs carrying the two big suitcases and her cosmetics case under his arm. The smell of fresh-cut cedar faded.

"Thank you," Maya called, before saying to Elly, "I'm not sure why, but I pictured someone younger when you said he's your friend's nephew."

"That's funny, Maya, because before Coty showed up at my door I pictured someone older. Judith is seventy-six just like me and Coty is her oldest nephew. I'd say he's what, forty-five, forty-six?"

"I'm not a good judge of age," Maya said. "It doesn't matter anyway, I guess."

Elly and Maya sat at the kitchen table munching iced raisin cookies. Not just one cookie each, the way her mother doled them out. There was an entire plateful on the table.

Something about Coty made Maya nervous. Maybe it was his penetrating gaze. Was he judging her? Did he think she was taking advantage of Aunt Elly? That she was a freeloader? After an inheritance? Maya felt insulted, even though Coty'd said nothing to suggest he thought such things.

An upstairs door closed and the ceiling groaned. A minute later Coty strode into the kitchen. He jammed his feet into boots before exiting the back door.

"I guess it wasn't Coty I saw through the skylight," Maya said. "Why would he walk all the way around to the side of the house with my luggage when my car is right outside the back door?"

"It had to be him. There's no one else here," Elly said. "Maybe Coty was in the fields when he spotted you arriving. If so, he'd probably come in through the basement. The only other door is in the living room and no one uses that door. No one has used that door since . . . well, it's been so long I can't remember the last time. Maybe since Harlan was alive. I keep it locked at all times."

Coty entered the back door again, kicking off his boots on the porch. He hoisted her trunk to his shoulder, crossed through the kitchen and dining room and up the stairs without a word. The kitchen ceiling groaned again as he strode the length of the upstairs hallway. The smell of cedar came and went.

"I wish I could have visited the farm while Uncle Harlan was alive," Maya said. "I never got to meet him. Where did the two of you meet?"

"Heavens, Maya. I don't remember ever not knowing Harlan. We grew up in the same neighborhood. That was so many years ago, though, and I've forgotten more than half of what I ever knew. Sometimes, I could swear Harlan is still here with me. I see him sometimes, out of the corner of my eye, but when I look again, of course he's not there. It was just a shadow or something, but sometimes I'm convinced I hear his voice. He says my name and it wakes me up in the middle of the night, but when I call out to him, he doesn't answer. And sometimes in the bathroom, I'm certain I smell the soap he used. He never wore colognes or stuff like that, just that clean, soapy smell."

Poor Elly, Maya thought. She's lonely. "I always hoped you and Uncle Harlan would come for Easter, Thanksgiving, or Christmas."

"We wanted to, honey, and we would have, but back then we had animals here on the farm. A cow, a horse, and some chickens. We couldn't go off and leave them. Cows gotta be milked and chickens gotta be fed and watered. Besides, your mother never liked me. You knew that, didn't you?"

"Let's not talk about Mama. I'm so glad to be here and to see your face and hear your voice. Let's celebrate. I'd like to take you and Coty out for dinner. What do you say?"

Elly grinned. "I haven't gone out for dinner in years. Let's go find Coty and ask him."

Elly crossed to the base of the stairs. "Coty?" she called. He didn't answer.

Maya followed her aunt across the driveway to the bunkhouse. Elly knocked, opened the door and leaned inside. "Coty?" She closed the door again. "He's not in there. He wouldn't have gone with us anyway, Maya. He hardly ever leaves the farm."

"Should we search for him?" Maya glanced around the yard, wondering where to start. The sun was already low and the shadows were black beneath the surrounding trees. Again, Maya had the feeling someone watched her.

An alder tree groaned and creaked as the wind pushed against it. Green leaves fluttered overhead as last summer's leaves, with their points curled under, skittered along the driveway like brown crabs. Maya shivered. It was one of those moments she so often fought against, this sudden sense of déjà vu and dread. It always came with the sight and sound of rustling leaves or a wind bending the trees.

Sometimes by a hard rain. Sometimes it was other things. Maya looked away from the shadows.

"Let's go," Elly said. "Just you and me. The two of us need time for girl-talk, without Coty listening in."

Chapter Four

Maya drove five miles into town, over a stone bridge, its sides covered in moss, and past a sign that read, 'Welcome to Graceville—Population 1390.'

Elly pointed to the sign. "Someone should repaint that. There's only nine hundred eighty people here now. In the past few years families have just up and walked away from their homes."

Maya parked near the front door of the River Lodge Café. The three-story structure was built log cabin style, with a sizable front porch. Across the porch, a dozen unpainted cedar chairs faced the road. Behind the chairs, multi-paned windows caught the dusky evening light. Inside, customers were drinking, talking, and laughing. Miniature table lamps warmed their faces with golden light.

"This place looks cheerful and inviting," Maya said.

"I've always thought so too," Elly said.

A hostess led them to a booth in a back corner with a view of a stream. The evening sun turned the river water amber and the lawn lime green. Clumps of daffodils bobbed in the breeze as new aspen leaves quivered.

The booth's green vinyl seats felt warm, as if previous customers had left a moment earlier. The waitress slid two glasses of ice water and two menus on the table. "Be right back, ladies," she said and hurried away through double doors.

"Well look at that. There's chicken and dumplings on the menu," Elly said. "It's one of my favorites. We used to have chickens."

"Yes, you mentioned having chickens."

"Did I?"

"Yes, and a cow and a horse. If that's what you want, then order the chicken and dumplings. We're celebrating remember? I think I'll have the river trout. Benson didn't like me to cook fish. He said it made the house stink."

"What are we celebrating, Maya, other than getting together after such a long time and you finally getting to see the farm?"

"Freedom," Maya said. "I don't know if selling the farm makes you want to celebrate, Aunt Elly, but I'm relieved to be free of Benson. I think a party is in order."

"You're getting a divorce, Maya?"

Maya nodded. "Benson was served divorce papers yesterday, while he's in the hospital with both legs and one arm in a cast. He's so smashed up, he can't lay a finger on me, so it was perfect timing. I suppose that sounds harsh. Is that what you're thinking?"

"That depends. How'd he get so banged up?" Elly asked. "You take an iron skillet to him, honey?"

"Maybe I should have, but no. He was street-racing his car like a dumb kid. I'm just glad he didn't hurt anyone else before he flipped and crashed. I was always afraid he'd hit a young couple with a baby or some poor kid on a bicycle."

Elly shook her head. "Harlan was always so good to me. I've always said, there's no one like my sweet Harlan."

"I've never had good sense when it comes to men, Aunt Elly. Handsome men are my kryptonite. I've missed meeting some nice guys by marrying Benson. Benson was all gift wrapping and no gift."

"Let's not think about Benson then, honey. You've caught the attention of a good looking man here tonight," Elly said. "Over there in the opposite corner booth. He's glanced over here five times to check you out. He's quite attractive with his wavy blonde hair and blue eyes."

"I'm taking a break from men, *especially* the handsome ones." Maya dug into her shoulder bag. "Here's some hand sanitizer, Elly. I read an article that said menus are crawling with germs."

After ordering, the waitress brought their dinners. "Enjoy, ladies. Let me know if you need anything else."

Outside their window, a Canadian goose pecked along the banks of the stream. He raised his black beak toward the sky and honked as more geese circled and landed.

Maya's cell phone vibrated in her purse. She dug it out. "It's Mama," she said.

"You're not going to answer it?" Elly asked.

"I'll call her back later. Mom would just spoil our dinner with her questions and remarks."

Elly chuckled and turned her smile toward the man in the other booth. A moment later he passed by. Maya focused on the geese outside the window. She was serious about avoiding men for a while. *For a long while*. Maya made a point of studying her cell phone when the blond man exited the restroom door and returned to his own booth. He wore a pleasant cologne.

"Did you save room for dessert, ladies?" the waitress asked. "We have a special on spring rhubarb pie ala mode this evening. That, or chocolate mousse."

"I ate every bit of my dinner," Elly said. "No room for dessert."

"Nor for me." When Maya paid the bill she was surprised. It was rare these days for two people to have dinner in a restaurant for less than forty dollars, including tip. If Benson had been there, ordering cocktails and wine, the total would have doubled. An ever-climbing credit card balance never seemed to hold him back. Money was no issue with Benson.

Maya and Elly returned to the car. A bright half-moon shimmered above the peaks of the River Lodge's three dormers.

"There he is again," Elly said. "The man who was eyeing you inside the restaurant."

The blonde man exited the front doors as Maya backed out of her parking spot. He wore beige slacks and a dark leather jacket.

"He looks familiar to me," Elly said. "I'm pretty sure I've seen him before somewhere. Maybe he's a clothing model in a magazine. He could be, with those looks."

Maya drove back toward the farm through trails of thin fog. The fog blanketed the marshes, hollows, and bogs. At the two-mile post, the car's engine sputtered and died.

"Aw crap." Maya rolled to the shoulder and turned on the car's emergency flashers. "I can't imagine what's wrong, I had a mechanic go over this thing from top to bottom just two weeks ago when I told you I was coming." She dug in her handbag for her cell phone. "We're in a dead zone here. There's no signal."

Headlights appeared at the crest of the hill behind them. The driver flashed his lights and pulled up behind Maya's car. The blonde man from the restaurant climbed from a silver Audi and strode to Maya's lowered window.

"Car trouble?" he asked.

"Can't be anything too serious. I had everything checked out recently," Maya said.

"I'm no mechanic, but let's take a look."

Maya popped the hood. By the time she joined him at the front of the car, he had a flashlight shining into the engine compartment. He slid a screwdriver from his jacket pocket and tightened something in the shadows. "Try it now."

"Aunt Elly, turn the key," Maya said.

The engine roared to life and he wiped his hands on his handkerchief. "I'm Tony Bradley."

Maya shook his hand. "I'm Maya Pederson. Aunt Elly said you look familiar."

"Really? Can't imagine how, since I moved here just three weeks ago. I own Bradley Realty, on Main Street."

Elly lowered her window. "I'm Elly Pederson. I own the farm on Cemetery Road."

"The old place on the hillside above the stream?"

"That's the place," Elly said. "How'd you know that?"

"I'm already familiar with just about every bit of land for ten miles around. I'm building a photo album of properties." Tony Bradley lowered the hood of the car. "Maybe your aunt saw me taking pictures out along the road." His hair glowed silver in the moonlight.

Like kryptonite.

Aunt Elly called again. "How about a home-cooked dinner as our way of saying thanks?"

"I'd love it." He smiled.

"Saturday evening? Around six o'clock?" Elly suggested.

Tony Bradley headed toward his car. "Looking forward to it." He honked as he drove away.

"It's so much easier to meet someone nowadays, than when I was young," Elly said.

"You do realize you've invited a realtor to your house. He's a salesman. He'll want to list your property. He might become a pest about it."

"I have no problem getting rid of pests," Elly said.

"You sound very positive about that."

"I am."

Okay," Maya said. "Dinner it is."

"It has occurred to me on more than one occasion though, that I never dated anyone except Harlan. I never even talked to another man on the phone. Well, I did, but only for business. I just never met anyone else. It's so much easier these days."

"I don't know about that. You had no trouble flirting with Tony Bradley just now."

"Aw," Elly giggled. "He's too young for an old lady like me, but I've always been a sucker for blondes. Harlan was a blonde when he still had hair."

"It's a very modern thing for a woman to keep her maiden name after marriage, but you did that decades ago."

"Harlan didn't care. He said the only thing that mattered was that we were together."

"He was open-minded," Maya said. "I've petitioned to get my maiden name back. But I'm not waiting for it to be official. I'm already using the name Pederson again."

"I noticed that," Elly said.

"Until I heard you mention it to Mr. Bradley, I didn't realize you live on Cemetery Road," Maya said. "I grew up on Cemetery Lane. That's an odd coincidence isn't it?"

"When we moved here, fifty-five years ago, our address was just Cemetery Road Farm, Graceville WA. Simple as that. Problem is now, half the time the road sign is in the ditch because drunks keep knocking it down on Friday or Saturday nights." Elly straightened, leaned toward the dashboard and pointed. "Right there—see the tire marks in the dirt? And there's the sign—in the ditch. The county will send a crew out in a week or two and stand it back up. They had to replace it twice last month. I guess there's no hurry though. People around here know where the Cemetery is."

When they arrived at the farm, a dim light glowed through the curtains in the bunkhouse windows.

"Looks like Coty's up reading again. I saw boxes full of books when he moved in. Only one box of clothes, the rest was books and papers," Elly said. "Lots and lots of papers."

Upstairs, Maya found a dozen pieces of seasoned fir stacked beside the little fireplace in her room. Beside the hearth stood a bundle of kindling, a stack of old newspapers, and a box of wooden matches. Not a twig, leaf, or wood chip littered the floor. Maya's first impression of Coty had suggested he was rough and outdoorsy, not necessarily tidy. People often made the mistake of assuming Benson was neat and organized because he was a natty dresser. He kept his hair trimmed, his nails manicured and his shoes polished. Maya smirked, because Benson had been a slob around the house.

Maya twisted two sheets of newspaper and dropped them on the grate with a handful of kindling. She struck a match and flames crackled as they spread from the paper to the cedar. She added small pieces of fir and then wedged one log of madrona into the pile. After setting the screen across the hearth, Maya sat on the bed. Firelight danced on the floor and walls. The golden flicker drove away the lonely feeling she felt when Elly first showed her this room. Now the room felt cozy and she felt safe here. She felt no déjà vu or sense of dread.

Maya set her watch on the bedside table, undressed, and slipped into her robe and slippers. She pulled pajamas from a drawer and crossed the hall to the big bathroom. An old electric clock sat on the counter. 8:55 PM. She bathed in the claw foot tub and brushed her teeth in the pedestal sink. She returned to her room where the firelight had already slowed to a waltz on the walls and floor. She crawled into bed and pulled up the sheet, bedspread, and patchwork quilt. Reaching for the lamp switch, she noticed her watch was gone from the bedside table. She checked the floor and underneath the bed, inside the little drawer and behind the table, but it was gone.

Maya slapped the corner of the bedside table with frustration. "I left it right there . . . didn't I?"

One day, several months ago, she found the unopened mail in the freezer, but had no recollection of putting it there. Maybe that was why Benson's words stung so much: "You're nuts, you know." She felt a little better when Dr. Conover assured her, "We all do bizarre things when our minds are overwhelmed or we're feeling stressed."

Her day had been hectic, a little stressful, and it felt longer than most days did. Maya was tired. Packing her things into the Edge and escaping the condo felt like two or three days ago, not like this morning.

The sheets were crisp and smooth. "I'll find my watch in the morning." Maya turned off the light and opened the window a half-inch. Cool air puffed against the lace curtains. She smelled the green fields, fir trees, and moss. *Country smells.*

"Finally, I get to explore the farm," she whispered. A glimmer of excitement warmed her.

Maya pictured Benson's face, his sneering lips, his cold eyes. She heard his voice, as if her ears were scarred by the sound. "You're crazy."

"Benson, just . . . shut up. I'm not going to let you ruin this adventure for me. Dr. Conover said I'm doing great, and I've even cut down on my meds. I'm just stressed, not crazy."

In her rush to flee their condominium, Maya'd forgotten to request a refill on her Lorazapam before leaving Tacoma. She had sixteen pills left and would soon need to phone Dr. Conover to ask for more. She dreaded that, even though Dr. Conover'd always authorized the refills.

Maya closed her eyes and allowed the memories of the day to replay themselves, like scenes flashing across a bright screen. Again, she felt the panic to get away from the condo, experienced the tense drive across the Tacoma Narrows Bridge, was calmed by the country views between Purdy and Bremerton, and then felt the excitement build as she reached the Olympic Penninsula. Peaceful scenes slid across the backs of her eyelids. She smiled at the remembered image of Elly's farm from the road. She loved the way the driveway wound down one hillside, crossed the stream and climbed into the evergreens. She loved the way arriving at the house was like driving out from between velvet green curtains and across a sunlit stage. She liked the way the backdoor opened to a warm kitchen, and once inside, she liked how it took six steps to cross from one side of the kitchen to the dining room, another six steps to cross to the living room and the bottom of the stairs. There were eight stairs up to the landing, and fourteen stairs to the second floor. All even numbers. Plenty of even numbers here at the farm. That was good, very good. Even numbers were a protective sign.

Maya had been relieved after she saw Elly lock the back door when they retired for the evening. Security was a serious matter. It was important to double-check locks, the same way it was important to unplug small appliances before plugging them back in. Hair dryers, food processors, vacuums, curling irons, can openers, almost anything with an electrical cord. Dr. Conover called Maya's persistence to do these things an obsession. These were rituals, she said. Ceremonies. Good luck charms.

No, they're more than that. They're insurance.

"It bugs me, the way you organize all the drawers and cupboards, Maya," Benson often said. "I feel like a school child, the way everything is alphabetized in the pantry, with all the canned goods lined up so perfect and straight, as if they're on rails."

"It makes looking for something easier, Bens," Maya answered. "And making out a shopping list is easier too, because I can see what we're low on."

"And what's this?" Benson held up a pair of red, silk underwear. "I gave these to you on Valentine's Day. Why were they in the recycling bin?"

How did he find those, buried beneath a layer of junk mail?

Maya stammered, "Because blue is my luc . . . favorite color."

"But red is sexy."

I don't want to be sexy around you.

When Maya felt anxious or tense, she counted steps and stairs. Doing these things kept trouble away. If not four steps, then eight. If not eight, then twelve. Blue underwear had proven itself time and time again. She'd thrown away the red silk underwear because red was bad luck. So was black. Yellow was okay. Yellow was neutral. She liked yellow. It was cheerful, like daffodils. She loved daffodils.

Thinking about Benson made Maya tense. She took a deep breath, stretched her legs out as far as she could and opened and closed her hands several times. Muscle by muscle, she relaxed, starting with the arches in her feet and working upward. Calves, thighs, abdomen, neck and arms. The mattress and sheets were smooth and cool. The room was silent. The low fire flickered. It was quiet here in the country. It was calm. A distant owl hooted in the forest.

Maya heard someone whisper, "Don't leave me here."

Maya sat up. "Aunt Elly, is that you?"

Did I doze off? Maya waited but heard nothing else. *I must have fallen asleep and the whisper was the start of a dream.* She glanced toward the hearth. The fire was now a pile of glowing coals. *Yes, I was asleep.*

The lace curtains lifted and brushed against the windowsill, the only sound other than Maya's own breathing. She pushed the curtains aside and checked the roof outside. The silvery cedar shakes reflected moonlight like the edges of serrated knife blades.

The whisper was not repeated and an hour later, Maya slept.

Chapter Five

Maya phoned her mother and smiled when the answering machine picked up.

"Hi, Mama. Everything's fine. I had no trouble getting here. The farm is wonderful. I have a cozy room with a view of the valley and fields—and my own fireplace! Talk to you soon." Maya hung up. *Obligation met.*

Maya arrived downstairs in the kitchen, dressed in faded jeans and a flannel shirt, ready for whatever household chore Aunt Elly needed done. Seven straight hours of sleep helped, and she felt convinced the whispering at bedtime was the result of a long, stressful day. Dr. Conover's advice about hearing voices was always the same. "There's nothing there, Maya. It's just your imagination. What else could it be?" Those last words had become Maya's mantra. *What else could it be?*

Maya found her aunt squatting in front of the little wood stove, shoving split fir into the flames.

"Good morning, sunshine," Aunt Elly said. "Sleep okay?"

"I did. When did you get up?" Maya asked. "I thought I might make it down here ahead of you and fix breakfast for us both."

"I've gotten up at dawn for so long I doubt I'll ever break the habit, but I kept your breakfast warm in the oven."

Maya found a foil-covered plate of pancakes and sausage. She sat down at the table.

"Any ideas what kind of dinner we should fix for Tony Bradley on Saturday?" Elly asked.

"Something easy. How about roasted chicken?"

"Sounds good," Elly said. "And hot rolls, green beans and tossed salad. How about apple pie for dessert? Apple-walnut was always Harlan's favorite. And since we're having company, let's eat in the dining room. I'll have to remember to build the fire in the living room because the dining room stays cool even with the furnace turned up."

Elly opened a cupboard door in the sideboard and pulled out an ivory lace tablecloth and napkins. "These'll need to be laundered," she said. "They haven't been out of that drawer in decades. And I'll need to polish the silver too. It's awfully tarnished."

"I'll handle the tablecloth and napkins," Maya said. "I enjoy laundry anyway."

"I'm glad to hear that, because I've never been crazy about it, especially ironing. The washer and dryer are at the bottom of the basement stairs, honey. Soap's on the counter."

Maya smiled as she washed breakfast dishes. She noticed that Elly never wore things that needed ironing. Sweaters, sweatshirts, flannel shirts, jeans or polyester slacks—that's what Elly wore.

Maya gathered up the tablecloth and napkins and carried them into the basement. She stuffed them into the old pink Maytag and as the machine filled she studied the dark surroundings beneath the northern half the house. The basement had a dirt floor and was empty except for the washer, the dryer, the furnace, and nine support beams. The back wall had a door with a square window that stared outward at the lower fields like an etched, gray eye.

Maya stood on the bottom step beneath one dangling overhead bulb. The bulb hung straight down over the washer and dryer area and except for that, the etched window at the far end provided the only light. The distant corners refused to reveal themselves. They cloaked themselves in deep shadow.

A clothesline hung between two support timbers and a blue towel draped across the line. The towel was crooked, stiff, and dusty, as if it had been there for a very long time. Maya fought the impulse to throw it into the washing machine with the tablecloth and napkins. She struggled against the urge to at least straighten that towel. She counted to twenty and then repeated, *It's just an old towel, just an old towel, just an old towel.* The urge passed.

A smooth cement walkway cut across the dirt floor from the bottom of the steps to the faraway door. A square of newer concrete bore the weight of the furnace near the west wall, but what Maya noticed foremost was the smell. There was a familiar smell, like old basements often had—cool, dry. *Like a mausoleum.*

The Maytag finished filling and started chugging and sloshing. Every few seconds it made a sound like a man groaning in his sleep, either from pain or fear.

Maya's eyes returned to the farthest corner where no light penetrated. She squinted, peering into the shadows, shivering, not from cold but from the chilling suspicion that something peered back. She checked the temperature and water level in the Maytag before hurrying back upstairs and closing and locking the door behind her.

"Here's my old ceramic pie dish," Elly said. She stood at the entrance to the pantry with a bright blue baking dish in her hands. "It's one of the first things I bought after we moved here. It bakes a great crust."

"It's a pretty dish, too," Maya said. "Such a cheerful color."

"The reason I bought it was because of something Harlan said. He complained he was hungry for apple pie, so I said I'd make one. Later, he said it was the smell of that apple pie baking that called him inside. He opened the oven door and said, "Where's the pie?" I told him I didn't have a true pie plate, so I made flat apple pie. He looked at me with a confused expression and asked, "Where'd you get flat apples?" I almost died laughing, but Harlan took offense at that. I told him there were no flat apples, just a flat pie, baked in a jellyroll pan. "But, where'd you get flat apples?" he asked again, and I said again, it's just a flat pie, not flat apples, but he seemed to get even more confused, so I told him I'd get a real pie dish the next time we were in town. And this is it."

Maya grinned. Later, as she finished ironing the tablecloth in front of the dining room window, she spotted Coty climbing the hill from the lower fields. His black, knee-high boots were splattered with mud. His breath puffed into the cool air. As he approached the fence he slapped one gloved hand on the post and leaped over the gate, like a young man, like someone who pushed himself to stay fit. Maya doubted she could sail over a fence the way he just had.

You wouldn't like Coty, would you, Benson? You would consider leaping over fences, showing off. But Coty doesn't know I'm watching. So he isn't showing off for anybody.

Back in Tacoma, at the condo, Maya had worn makeup every day, in case Benson brought a client home for dinner, unannounced. "No ponytails," Benson insisted. "None of the upper management wives wear ponytails."

Maya stroked her clean face with her fingertips. She had not worn makeup since Benson's car accident two weeks ago, and there were four new, ponytail elastic bands in her cosmetic case.

Maya spread the tablecloth across the dining room table and smoothed it straight. As she placed the folded napkins at one end and centered the candlesticks, she spotted Elly on the lower landing, one hand on the newel post, eyes aimed toward the second floor as if mesmerized by something only she could see.

"Aunt Elly? Everything okay?"

Elly dragged her gaze away and stared at Maya for a full three seconds, as if she didn't recognize her. Finally she said, "Yes, baby girl. Everything is fine."

"If you don't need me for anything else today, I thought maybe I'd get some fresh air and stretch my legs. Exercise helps me sleep."

"Oh that's fine, honey. You go right ahead. I'm going to read my new retirement magazine. Judith sends them to me every month. She's such a dear."

"I won't be gone more than an hour." In the kitchen Maya slipped on her blue, hooded jacket, boots and gloves. She reached for the back door but spotted Coty through the window. His arms were loaded with firewood and he booted open his bunkhouse door, stepped inside and kicked it shut again.

Maya opened the yellow door and descended into the basement. She hurried along the cement walkway, her eyes avoiding the darkest corner. *There is nothing there. How could there be?* She reached the outside door, yanked it open and stepped through.

A gust of wind rattled dead leaves trapped in the corner of the foundation, spinning them around and around. Maya pulled her hood over her ears and trudged downhill, away from the house. She glanced back every other minute, determined to keep Elly's big farmhouse between her and the bunkhouse windows.

She couldn't figure out why Coty made her feel so edgy. Maybe it was his penetrating eyes, as if he could read her thoughts. He wasn't tall but he moved like a powerful man. He smelled of raw cedar, apples, and fresh air. Maya shook images of Coty from her mind and continued downhill. This was her first adventure at Aunt Elly's farm and she was determined to enjoy it.

The afternoon sun hovered near the tops of the trees and the temperature was already dropping. Maya cinched the hood tighter around her neck and ears. She entered a stand of alder trees and followed a narrow deer trail through mounds of naked blackberry vines. On the other side of the alders waited huckleberry bushes and ferns. Out of sight of the house now, she followed the deer trail as it angled left, toward a stand of Douglas fir, their massive trunks buried in Boston fern, salal, and Oregon grape. The wind was muffled by the giant trees. It was calm on this side of the hill.

Wild grass and dandelions in the adjacent field yielded to granite and paper-thin lichen that crunched underfoot. Five feet ahead, the granite dropped straight down into a round, black lake. Maya inched closer, pushing her hood back. She leaned forward and peered at the water at least a hundred feet below. Its smooth, dark surface reflected the pale clouds gliding by overhead. She shuddered, imagining how it would feel to fall into that black water from such a height, the terror for those few seconds of falling. A cold, damp wind whistled up over the edge of the cliff and into her face.

"Looks deep, doesn't it?"

Strong hands grabbed her shoulders from behind, trapping her at the cliff's edge. Maya felt paralyzed, unable to draw a breath. She recognized the sleeves of the black and red buffalo checked jacket.

"Coty?"

"It's an old granite quarry," he said. "Didn't Elly warn you that a fisherman drowned here two months ago? The sheriff said his men dragged the lake but didn't find anything except for his waders and one glove. Two weeks later they found his body downstream—washed down through the gorge and over the falls. The sheriff said they weren't sure, at first, if the remains were even human."

"Let me go." Maya struggled but Coty held her tight.

He said, "The poor old guy might have been standing right where you're standing. Maybe he climbed up here for the view, or to eat his lunch. We'll never know. Sheriff said he might have fallen, or maybe he just slipped on the rocks down there while fishing, and his waders filled up and pulled him under."

"Stop it!" Maya twisted, terrified of the cliff, terrified of Coty. "Let me go!"

"Maybe that old fisherman was snooping around. Maybe someone was afraid he saw something they didn't want him to see."

"Stop! I want to go back to the house," Maya said. "It's getting cold."

"It is cold, isn't it? We're at eleven hundred feet elevation here." Coty pulled her against him and held her tight against his chest. His breath was warm against her cheek, his stubble rough against her ear. "Especially after the sun goes down." His arms trapped her against him. He rested his chin on the top of her head. His breath smelled like winter apples and his jacket like autumn hay. "Warmer now?"

"Let me go!" Maya kicked backward, but her boots were heavy and awkward. She missed his shins.

"Don't go wandering around this place by yourself," Coty said. "There's rusty barbed wire, rotten old barns and abandoned wells. Or you might stumble and they'll find your body downstream, battered beyond recognition. Better hurry back to the house where it's warm and dry."

Coty swung Maya away from the cliff's edge and back toward the stand of trees. She stumbled, caught her balance and then she ran without looking back. She sprinted, racing uphill without pausing once to catch her breath. She reached the basement door with its gray, etched eye.

The leaves rattled and spun in the foundation corner as Maya shoved herself inside and slammed the door. She inched forward, hands out, blind in the darkness. To her left she heard something rattle. To her right, something growled. She saw a wide, glowing mouth and jagged teeth.

"Ohh . . ." Maya's legs buckled. She dropped to her knees, shaking. Her pulse pounded as she knelt there, eyes wide, dizzy with fear until she recognized the glowing flames in the mouth of the furnace. Not teeth. Her fingertips felt the concrete, new and rough to the touch. She pushed herself up and brushed the knees of her jeans. She glanced left but saw nothing in the deep shadows. The rattle she heard there must have been the echo of the furnace turning on. She followed the cement walkway and climbed the stairs on weak legs. Perspiration rolled down from under her bangs and stung her eyes.

The kitchen stove's little window glowed with a golden light. Maya locked the basement door behind her, turned, and leaned against it.

Elly needs to know Coty just scared the hell out of me. A moment later Maya shook her head. *He didn't hurt me . . . and he could have if he wanted to. All he did was tell me about the dangers of exploring the farm on my own. Damn.*

She and Coty were both there to help Aunt Elly, weren't they? They had that in common, didn't they? Maya didn't want to frighten Elly if there was no reason for it. Maybe she shouldn't say anything.

"How was your walk, honey?" Elly stood in the middle of the pantry hall between the kitchen and the skylight room with a steaming cup in her hands. Maya smelled tea.

"I walked clear to the granite cliff above the old quarry."

"You sound breathless, Maya."

"I ran all the way back. I wanted to get inside before dark."

"That's probably wise, since you're new to the farm and the trails around here. It's quite a view from the cliff, isn't it? I've always been scared of heights, though, so I don't go there."

Maya lifted the kettle with trembling fingers. "The water's hot. I'm going to have a cup of hot instant cocoa. It was cold outside."

● ● ●

It rained that night, tapping on Maya's bedroom window with sodden fingertips, sounding like pebbles rattling down the shake roof. She built a small fire and set the screen on the hearth. She crawled across the bed and parted the curtains, admiring the glistening roof outside. At the corner of the house a drainpipe funneled rainwater toward the ground. The sound reminded her of children, giggling. A gash in the clouds revealed the face of the moon and Maya spotted the bridge at the bottom of the hill and the dark stream gliding beneath it. *It's peaceful here. Except for Coty. I don't know what to think about him.*

It was a calm night with no wind moaning through the trees. After a while the rain let up. It grew silent as the fire died to coals.

"Don't leave me here." The whisper came from somewhere above or behind her. It was impossible to tell.

Maya sat up. "Hello?" she whispered. "Where are you?"

She listened for a full minute but heard nothing else.

Maya closed the curtains, laid back down and pulled the covers up to her chin. She felt childish, shivering in her bed like a schoolgirl. *I'm hearing voices again. First time since Benson's accident.*

"It's just your imagination," Dr. Conover would say.

Yes, I dozed off and the voice was the start of a dream. I think.

"I'm alone." There was no voice, no one there to whisper to her. No one else there at all. "It's just my imagination. What else could it be?"

Chapter Six

Maya drove into town with Elly and they bought groceries at the Red Apple. Maya filled her tank at the Graceville Gas-Up and they headed back toward the farm.

"Do you think Bentley will follow you here?" Aunt Elly asked. "I've been wondering about that."

"You mean Benson. I've wondered that myself. I suppose he could track me down if he's determined. There is a credit card trail. My Visa is under my name and he's not responsible for the debt, but since the divorce won't be final until he signs the papers, I suppose he has a legal right to trace my whereabouts."

"Is he dangerous, Maya?"

Maya frowned. "He's got a bad temper and he lashes out. He takes offense at the slightest thing. He picks fights with guys bigger than himself, but he usually wins those fights, oddly enough."

"Sort of like a banty rooster?"

"A what?"

"Banty roosters are small and they don't seem to realize they're no match for a bigger rooster," Elly said. "And sometimes they manage to bluff the big guys with their cockiness."

"Yeah, that sounds like Benson," Maya said.

"I'll tell Coty to keep an eye out for Benson."

"That might be a good idea. Coty looks like he can take care of himself."

They arrived home and carried the groceries inside.

"I'll put everything away," Elly said. "I know where things go and you cleaned house all morning. Why not take a break? Go lie down. Put your feet up. Do whatever you want."

"I'll take another walk, but before I do let me ask you something. Is there anything you haven't told me about the farm? Anything I need to be aware of? Any dangers? Like old wells or sink holes?"

"Well, I hadn't thought about that. Guess I should have. Harlan bought out some neighboring farms forty years ago and he bulldozed over their wells. We have a map here someplace that shows the old property lines and the location of those wells. I'll look around for it. The only thing that ever really scared me though was that old quarry. Someone drowned there not long ago. A fisherman I heard."

Maya said, "I'm heading uphill this time. I want to climb to the top of the ridge."

"I haven't been up there in thirty years. Harlan and I considered building a house on the ridge, but winters come early at higher elevations. Some years, it starts snowing as early as October up there."

After pulling on her hooded jacket and gloves Maya paused at the kitchen sink to check Coty's bunkhouse. Smoke coiled from his chimney and she remembered smelling something cooking when she and Elly returned from grocery shopping. She wanted to slip away from the farm without him noticing this time. He did seem to have a keen eye. What was it Elly said about Coty? *He don't miss a thing.*

Stepping on clumps of grass and moss to muffle the sound of her boots, Maya hurried across the driveway and into the trees. From there, Coty's back window was dark, the curtain drawn across the glass. She turned and strode up the trail.

Twenty minutes later Maya reached a field of wild grass. The remains of an ancient log cabin squatted in the center of the meadow, its roof blanketed by thick moss.

She paused to catch her breath and to check the wooded trail behind her. It was noon and the sparse clouds allowed sunlight down into the undergrowth. The spring leaves on the vine maples and dogwoods glowed like holiday lights and the tree's branches were so slender the leaf lights appeared to float in midair. Seeing no one on the trail behind her, Maya crossed the meadow and climbed the steep trail on the other side.

Soon, the forest floor leveled out again. She clambered up the side of a boulder beneath the branches of a cedar tree and sat down to admire the scene. A few moments later she heard the snap of a twig. A doe and her spotted fawn appeared, as silent as dappled sunlight. The doe raised her regal head and stared in Maya's direction. Maya held as motionless as she could. The fawn approached, reaching the base of the boulder. The doe must have spotted Maya because she flashed her white tail and stomped her feet. The fawn ran back to the doe and together they loped down the trail and into deep brush.

Something moved beside the trunk of a large Douglas fir. A minute later Coty stepped into sunlight and strode up the trail. He passed by the boulder where she sat and continued up the trail.

He's following me again?

Maya remained on the boulder and soon Coty returned. His boots thudded against the soft earth. He slapped a tan baseball cap against his thigh and then he halted, tilting his head the same way the doe had, as if listening with the ears of a wild creature. Then, as if the sound of her heartbeat drew his ear, he turned around. He jumped as if startled and frowned at her.

"I left my hat by the pond yesterday, while fishing," he said. "I just wanted to get it before it rained again." He held the hat up for her to see, as if it proved his words were true.

"If I take another walk and you show up, I'll suspect you're stalking me. I'll want to know why."

"Stalking you?" He jammed the cap on his head, jerked the brim down tight and stomped down the trail. The sound of his boots faded.

Maya jumped down from the boulder and continued her climb. At the next turn she came to a large fir log. The log spanned a small stream and the stream poured into a green pond. She crossed the log and followed the path around the water. Fat trout circled in the shadows.

Ahead, the trail divided. One path looped all the way around the pond and the other climbed higher into the forest. Maya continued upward. When she arrived at the top of the ridge she gasped at the view. To her right were the Olympic Mountains, looking as if she could hit them with a rock. To her left were the bays and inlets of Puget Sound dotted with islands and the floating bridge near Port Gamble. Looking further east over the tops of hills she spotted the Seattle skyline in miniature.

Maya heard someone clear his throat. She turned to find Coty behind her.

"Look," he said. "I was rude. I wasn't following you, but I owe you an apology for yesterday. You really do need to be cautious around here though. There are dangers."

Maya shrugged. "Okay, but if you had simply told me, I would have listened. It wasn't necessary to scare the hell out of me, and you did, you know."

"Sorry." After a moment of awkward silence Coty nodded and retreated down the trail. Maya waited five minutes before heading back down behind him. Halfway down, she paused on the path.

I should have told him about how for twenty-five years I've wanted to visit and explore this place.

When Maya arrived back at the farm she spotted Coty behind the shed, with an axe raised high over his shoulders. He drove the axe down into a thick round of maple. The maple split into two halves. His strength frightened her. He could have so easily tossed her into the quarry. With a shudder she stepped inside the kitchen door and locked it behind her. She drew the curtains across the window, overlapping them. She straightened them, adjusted the gathers, checked the lock again, unlocking it and then relocking it. She stepped to the sink, counting her steps aloud. "One . . . two . . . three . . . four." She drew the curtains shut behind the sink.

"Something wrong, Maya? You're so pale you look like the devil was chasing you." Elly entered the kitchen through the dining room.

"Not the devil." Maya took a shaky breath. "I should have told you yesterday, how Coty scared the bejeebers out of me at the quarry. He grabbed me and held me right at the edge and he told me frightening things about the farm."

Elly asked, "What did he say about the farm?"

"He said there's rusty barbed wire and abandoned wells and that a fisherman drowned in the quarry and how his body went over a waterfall and how he was unrecognizable when they found him. But the worst part was being held there—right at the cliff's edge above that horrible black water. I was so scared I could hardly breathe, and he wouldn't let me go!"

"Then what?"

"Then . . . I almost wet my pants!"

"What do you want me to do, honey? Coty is . . . well . . . he's Judith's nephew. I can't imagine what she'd say if I accused him of something." Elly lowered herself into a kitchen chair, twisting and worrying her hands together, her eyes fixed on Maya.

Maya pushed her bangs away from her sweaty forehead. "He did apologize a few minutes ago, but I don't understand what he's thinking. At first he seemed, you know, different, a little odd maybe, but now it seems like he doesn't want me around the farm. He insists there's dangers and that I could get hurt. He really scared me, Elly." Maya waved her hands, trying to erase the image of the black quarry water from her mind. "I could be wrong. I've been wrong before." She heard the tremble in her own voice.

Maya remembered all the times Benson accused her of being neurotic. "A basket case," he said, and even Dr. Conover told her to try looking at things from "someone else's perspective." Maya had Dr. Conover's phone number in the zippered pocket of her handbag. If things got worse, if all the counting didn't help, if she started hearing voices or if she saw things . . . things that weren't really there, she would phone Dr. Conover. She always felt better after hearing Dr. Conover's reassuring voice.

"Maybe I'm over-reacting," Maya said. "Boys like to scare girls. Maybe Coty has never outgrown that behavior."

"Harlan was never one for pranks or teasing. He didn't have time for silliness and he was impatient with people who were," Elly said.

"Impatient how?"

"Oh, you know . . . he'd separate himself from people like that."

"Like I've done with Benson," Maya said.

"Kind of."

"That reminds me, do you have any photos of Uncle Harlan?"

"Yes," Elly said. "But I'll have to remember where I put them. Too bad they're all from when we were both much younger. Harlan didn't hold still long enough to have his picture taken after we moved here. He kept so busy. He was a serious fellow. A hard worker. But I'll find those old photos. I'd like to see them again myself."

Chapter Seven

"The kitchen hasn't been this clean in decades." Elly stood in the center of the room and turned completely around, smiling. "I used to keep this whole house spotless but that was because Harlan took care of everything outside. He sometimes hired local help during haying season or when he needed help building a shed or a barn. Back then I was young and strong and enjoyed keeping everything tidy and in its place. Sometimes I even helped Harlan outside. I helped build that bridge over the stream and the chicken coop too."

"I hope you don't mind," Maya said. "I found some canned goods in the hall pantry with expired dates and I threw them out. I'll pay for replacing them."

"No, no, that's fine. Judith told me it's easier to sell a house with empty closets and cupboards. She said she got rid of everything she didn't absolutely need before putting her place up for sale and I plan to do the same."

"We'll sell a lot of stuff at your garage sale."

"Oh, that's right. I forgot about the garage sale. I appreciate your ideas, baby girl."

"My pleasure. I'll start cleaning the other downstairs rooms tomorrow," Maya said. She carried a basket of clean, folded laundry upstairs. She set Elly's things on the foot of her bed and then stored the clean towels and washcloths in the hall cupboard outside the bathroom before heading down the hall toward her room with the rest of the clean laundry.

Coty probably doesn't realize how terrified I was, and how menacing he sounded. Back in school several boys had been teasers. Some were rough or clumsy, not realizing their own size and strength. *Maybe Coty is like that.*

That evening, with the chicken roasting in the oven and the wild rice steaming, Maya wiped down the old Frigidaire, the cupboards and counters again. She wrung out the washcloth and tossed it to the bottom step of the basement stairs. Through the window above the sink she caught sight of Coty striding up the driveway toward the house. He wore a black stocking cap and had two day's growth of dark beard. His breath steamed in the chilly air as he passed the window. Maya stepped away before returning to draw the curtains closed. Coty entered his bunkhouse door and slam it shut.

He stays busy around here, I'll give him that. He's not a slacker. Maya was uncertain why her strongest instincts were to avoid Coty altogether. Something about him, in addition to the incident at the quarry, gave her chills. She found herself thinking about him often.

Across the driveway a blue curtain parted as an Audi rolled up and parked by the back door.

"Tony Bradley's here." Maya felt her cheeks grow warm. Tony was a good-looking guy.

"You and Tony are both prompt people. Promptness is a good sign." Elly opened the back door and Maya heard Tony's voice.

"Hello there, Elly," he said. "I brought both red and white wine. I wasn't sure what we're having for dinner."

"Let me take your coat, young man." Elly's cheeks were rosy and her pale blue eyes sparkled. "I'll get us some wine glasses."

Tony smiled at Maya as he stepped inside. He rubbed his hands together and glanced around. "This is a fabulous old kitchen. It reminds me of my uncle's farm in west Peoria."

"You're from Illinois?"

"Chicago actually, and that's about as Illinois as anyone can get."

"I'm helping Aunt Elly get this place ready to sell," Maya said. "There's a lot to do but we're making headway."

"Selling? Really? It's sad how old family farms keep disappearing." He stepped closer to the table and the bay window. "Great view of that gorgeous valley down there. Developers have been known to reroute streams, you know. It can be a tough battle with the EPA but eventually they succeed, because money talks. Money talks louder than anything else."

Elly wore a pensive expression. "I won't let that happen here, Mr. Bradley."

"I've heard people say that before, but within ten years I'll bet some developer has built a dozen houses on that field out there. And call me Tony. When people say 'Mr. Bradley' I expect to see my father, and he's been dead for thirty years."

Aunt Elly was quiet during dinner and Maya suspected the mention of Tony's father's death had reminded her of Uncle Harlan again. Elly seemed to brighten, though when Tony said, "This is the best apple pie I've ever eaten."

"Thank you. That recipe's been handed down through generations, except now days, instead of lard I use vegetable shortening for the crust," Elly said. "It's healthier."

After several more cups of coffee, Tony helped clear the table.

"You don't need to do that," Maya said. "We have a system, don't we Elly?"

Tony smiled. "My mother taught my brothers and me how to snuff out candles without splattering wax, how to scrape dishes, and stack them on the counter, and how to gather up the linens and put chairs back under the table."

"He's a keeper, Maya," Elly said. "Tony, if you don't mind, I'll be heading upstairs, but you stay as long as you want."

"Elly's back bothers her," Maya explained. "She needs to lie down."

"Oh, sorry to hear that." Tony said.

"Thank you for coming, Tony. It was a treat having you here." Elly said.

"The pleasure was all mine. I appreciate the home cooking and the lively conversation with two lovely ladies."

Maya heard a slow, drawn out lilt to the way he said, *lively conversation,* and *lovely ladies,* not at all like someone from Illinois. His off-center smile and genteel manners reminded her more like a character from *Gone With the Wind.*

"You go rest your back, Elly. I'll talk to you again soon, all right?" Tony said, and as Elly climbed the big stairwell, he added, "She's a sweet lady."

"I love her to pieces. She's made me feel right at home here."

"If it's all right, I'd like to explore this farm sometime soon, to get an idea of its size and value."

"I'll mention that to Elly in the morning. I have a feeling she'll want to list the place with you when the time comes. I can't say for sure, but I'm assuming."

Tony retrieved his coat from the row of hooks behind the back door and made a quick, informal bow.

"Maya, the meal was delicious. I'm openly hinting for another invitation."

"Do come again." Maya opened the door and was surprised by Tony's touch on her arm. His hand slid down to her hand. He lifted her fingers to his lips and kissed them.

Not at all like someone from Chicago, she thought.

He squeezed her hand and stood there for a few seconds, smiling. For a moment Maya thought he meant to kiss her. He leaned a couple inches closer, as if anticipating the same move from her, but then he straightened and stepped outside. The wind ruffled his pale hair as he opened his car door. He waved and a moment later his brake lights blinked as his Audi coasted down the driveway and into the trees.

"What just happened?" Maya shook her head as she strolled through the dining room and into the living room. She arrived beside the big picture window in time to see Tony's rear lights cross the bridge and climb the hill to the county road. Tony was so attractive he could have modeled men's clothing for Nordstrom. He could have made commercials, or movies. She felt her face grow warm again at the memory of the missed kiss. "Did I mess up?" *Probably.*

Maya returned to the kitchen. She locked, unlocked, and re-locked the back door. She filled the sink with hot, soapy water. Soon the dishes, flatware, and cookware, were draining in the rack. As she draped a towel over them and glanced up at the kitchen window, she jumped back. She flipped the light off.

A pale, shadowy face had loomed in the darkness outside, like an oval moon through fog. She looked again but saw nothing except a black treetop waving back and forth across the face of the moon. Was it the moon she had seen?

No, the moon I just saw—had eyes.

Maya checked the door again. Locked. She checked the yellow basement door. Locked. She stood in front of the aged and blistered, yellow door. There was always an odd smell by the door. Maya had examined the floor and the doorframe several times already, with no answer to the mystery of that smell.

Maya shrugged and then counted six steps across the kitchen to the dining room, six steps to the bottom of the stairs, eight steps to the landing and fourteen more to the second floor. Thirty-four. An even number.

And I'm wearing my lucky blue underwear.

On the wide upstairs landing a round window glowed with moonlight. *It's called a rose window.* This lavender, stained glass window, resembled the face of a morning glory.

The door at the far end of the hall was dulled by shadows. To its right, her bedroom door stood ajar. Her bedside lamp cast a golden wedge into hall. *Elly must have turned it on for me.*

Maya washed her face at the pedestal sink. She tilted her prescription bottle and rolled a Lorazapam into her palm. She swallowed it down by gulping tap water from the faucet.

Minutes after crawling between the sheets Maya was asleep. If anyone whispered to her from the darkness, she didn't hear him.

Chapter Eight

MAYA SPRAWLED ACROSS THE frigid bottom of a deep well, while far above a disk of pale light promised freedom. The light looked so very far away. This all felt familiar.

I know I'm asleep, on my back—my eyes are closed. She could not move or call out. She knew that ten feet away, Benson stood in her open bedroom door, glaring at her, squeezing his fists and clenching his jaw. She *felt* him in the doorway. She pictured his face, bloodless and pale. She felt his hate, knew he wanted her lungs to stop breathing, for her heart to stop beating, for her mouth to never utter another word. He wanted to be the last person she ever saw. He wanted to strangle her, to hear her choke, to feel her pulse flutter, for her to suffer at his touch.

Maya struggled against the paralysis, dreaming she had wings instead of arms. She rose, slow as smoke. High overhead, the light grew larger and brighter. She reached the top of the well and gasped awake. She sat straight up in bed and eyed her room. The door was closed. Benson was not there. Dr. Conover had warned her how Lorazapam made it easy to fall asleep but that it could be difficult to wake.

Her heart raced as she slipped from the covers and opened her bedroom door. The upstairs hall was bright with lavender moonlight through the morning glory window, its triangle panes meeting in the center like the heart of a blossom. Her heart calmed. She guessed it to be two, maybe three o'clock in the morning.

Today I'll search and find my watch.

There were only two clocks in this entire house, one in the kitchen and one in the upstairs bathroom. She needed her watch. Time was important.

Maya tiptoed down the hall. She eased the bathroom door closed behind her and flipped the light on. Two pink frosted glass sconces beside the medicine cabinet glowed. The clock on the counter said it was two forty-five. At the far end of the bathroom stood a full-length mirror and Maya studied her reflection. Her brown hair tangled around her oval face and across her shoulders. Her feet were bare. Her pajamas were lucky blue.

Benson hated pajamas. He nagged her to wear short nightgowns, or better yet, nothing.

"I can't sleep nude," she told him. "I keep waking up."

"You're a miserable prude."

"I don't nag you about what to sleep in, Bens. Naked or a snowsuit, I don't care."

The nightmare nagged Maya's mind. The image of Benson in her bedroom doorway refused to vanish. It was as if he *was* there, somewhere in the house at that moment, and the thought made her knees shake.

Maya drank from the faucet again and then, sitting on the side of the bathtub, she listened to the silence. *Benson isn't here. He's in St. Joseph's Hospital in Tacoma.* Maya turned off the light.

A pale green light shimmered in the hallway. It retreated, as if it had been waiting for her. It halted outside her bedroom. It formed a human shape, arms, shoulders, a blurry face with almost familiar, penetrating eyes.

Maya stepped back inside and closed the bathroom door. She backed up until her shoulders pressed against the cold mirror. She stared at the bathroom door, expecting the apparition to follow her, but it didn't. She tiptoed toward the door again. She paused and leaned against the sink. A moment passed and she opened the door, her breath shaky. The green apparition remained outside her bedroom. It resembled a boy about seventeen years of age with a black Mohawk, tattoos on his neck, a pierced nostril, pierced brow and right ear. He opened his mouth. His lips formed words but he made no sound. He raised one hand, motioning for her. Maya shook her head no.

The boy wore baggy, knee-length shorts and a hooded sweatshirt with a W on the front. He was transparent below his knees, his feet nonexistent. He raised both hands toward her, motioning again. His lips formed the words, *help me.*

"Maya?"

Maya jumped, a pain in her throat.

"What's wrong, honey?" Elly stood to the right of the bathroom door.

"That boy," Maya said.

"What boy?"

"At the end of the hall. He's inside a green swirling light."

"Are you awake, Maya, or having a nightmare?"

The boy was gone. Maya blinked three times. "I guess it was a dream. It seemed so real though."

"Come'on, honey. Let me fix you some warm cocoa," Elly said. "That always soothes me."

Maya hurried down the stairs behind her aunt, afraid to look behind her but glancing back twice. "What are you doing up this time of night, Elly?"

"Watching television. Sometimes I don't sleep straight through the night. The weatherman says a storm's coming our way. I've never liked storms. They always raised havoc with the animals, back when we had animals."

The kitchen light was already on and the woodstove radiating heat, and yet, Elly wore flannel pajamas beneath her wool robe and wool socks inside her slippers.

"Are you cold?" Maya asked.

"I woke up shivering and saw my breath in the air when I turned on the light. So I got up to make sure the furnace is working. No good reason for it not to work. It's only five years old."

"Did you check to see if your room's heater vents were open?"

"I did. The vents were shut, but I don't remember closing them This has happened before."

"Maybe when you vacuum, you accidentally rake the vents closed," Maya said.

"Maybe." But Elly's face looked doubtful.

"Aunt Elly?"

"Yes, baby girl?"

Maya wrapped her arms around Elly. "Thank you for inviting me here. Thank you for making me feel welcome. I needed a refuge. I won't let nightmares ruin this visit. It means too much to me."

Elly patted Maya's back. "Things are better now that you're here, honey. I needed someone like you in this house. I've never wanted to live alone with all these . . ."

"Sad memories?"

Elly nodded. She heated milk and made two mugs of cocoa. They carried them into the living room where the old tube television flickered black and white shadows around the room. An issue of Retirement Living lay open on the sofa. Maya eased into the armchair to the right of the stone fireplace. She sipped her cocoa. "It probably was just sleepwalking," she said. "But it seemed so real."

"I've had nightmares like that before," Elly said. "The other night I dreamed the house was sinking into a big hole, as if the earth wanted to swallow the entire place in one gulp. Maybe because you asked me about sink holes the other day. Remember? What was your nightmare about, sweety?"

"It started out with Benson standing in my bedroom doorway. He wanted to strangle me."

"He's sounding more and more like a no-good skunk," Elly said. "If he shows up here I'll show him my double-barrel shotgun. I keep it under my bed at night. Benson will see the deep, empty eyes of hell one second before I pull the trigger if he comes inside my house uninvited."

Maya swallowed an uncomfortably large amount of cocoa as she studied her aunt for a moment. She tried to picture Benson's astonished face, staring into the black barrels of a shotgun with such a tiny woman aiming it at him. "I can't picture Benson breaking and entering, Elly. He's more of the cussing and swearing, pound-on-the-door kind of guy. He'd throw a rock through your window and shout for me to come out, but I don't think he'd ever force his way in."

"He'd better not." Elly sounded dead serious.

"And while I have bad dreams about him wanting to throttle me, I don't think he really would. I think my subconscious is simply trying to finish divorcing him. My mind needs to justify my actions."

"Benson might have you rattled, Maya, but he don't scare me none."

"Have you ever killed anything, Aunt Elly?" Maya asked.

"Sure, honey. Chickens, a sick calf. Poor thing was suffering. A trout. Clubbed him on the head till' he stopped flopping around. A rat in the basement. I hit him with a shovel five times before he stopped squealing. A pigeon that was building a nest in the porch rafters. It kept shitting on my porch and front door so I blew it out of the sky one morning and tossed the carcass in the yard. I spotted a coyote running off with it later."

"Farm life is harsh. You can't get sentimental about farm animals, I guess," Maya said.

"Can't be sentimental about anything, two legged or four legged, except for those you can trust."

"Yes . . . well, we can't shoot *people* we don't trust," Maya said.

"It gets easier over time."

"What does?"

Elly pulled her eyes away from the flickering television. "What?"

"What gets easier over time?"

"Not sure what you mean, honey," Elly said.

"That's what you said."

"When?"

"Just now. We were talking about killing animals and about trusting people, and you said we can't be sentimental and that shooting those we don't trust gets easier over time."

"Gracious, baby girl. Farm life gets easier over time. Taking care of sick animals and getting rid of pests. Those things get easier over time."

Maya nodded, but she had an uncomfortable feeling. Aunt Elly didn't make sense sometimes, as if her thoughts were jumbled or like she didn't follow the logical progression of a discussion. Maya reminded herself that maybe this time next month, or the following month, Elly might be living in the retirement home. The caregivers there would not allow her to keep a shotgun under her bed, or to decide who was or wasn't trustworthy.

Benson's words continued to trouble Maya however, even though she told herself over and over again to stop thinking about him. Sometimes she believed she heard his voice, the actual words in the air—

"You're nuts, Maya." His voice was like a scar on her eardrums.

Mental illness can run in families.

She'd read that last month in a magazine in Dr. Conover's waiting room. Dr. Conover advised her to stop self-diagnosing, and Maya agreed it probably wasn't helping, but Elly was her father's older sister. He died of heart failure in a sanitarium years ago, but he wasn't there for heart trouble.

Chapter Nine

Maya spent the following three mornings cleaning the living room and dining room, digging into every crevice and corner with the vacuum nozzle or a damp cloth wrapped around the head of a screwdriver. Short of taking apart the television, everything was scrubbed, wiped down, inside and out. While Maya cleaned, Elly wrapped her knickknacks, vases, and collectables, with bubble wrap and packed them into various cardboard boxes. She taped the boxes shut and listed the contents on the cardboard with a permanent marker. "A few of these will go into the storage unit the retirement home provides. I know you said you don't want anything, Maya, but after I'm gone you might have second thoughts. If you still don't want any of it, maybe you can sell it all and buy yourself something nice."

"Okay, Elly," Maya said. "I'm positive you'll sell almost everything else at the garage sale."

"I've driven by garage sales before but never stopped. There were always too many people hanging around," Elly said. "I don't like crowds, or for that matter, people. I've met too many who were nothing but nasty."

"I found a Wedgwood vase at a yard sale once," Maya said. "I paid eight dollars for it and sold it to a collector for six hundred."

"What's the difference between a garage sale and a yard sale?"

"A yard sale means the sellers can't fit all the junk into their garage. They set stuff in the driveway and out across their yard. You can usually get the best deals at yard sales because they don't want to move it back inside again. Whatever they don't sell, they have to haul to the junkyard or to some charity. To get a good deal, you just need to make a reasonable offer."

"There's a lot of junk in this house and in the sheds and barns. We might need to have a yard sale then," Elly said.

"Good. That means more money for your retirement years."

"Look at that. It's already eleven-forty. I'll make lunch," Elly said. "How about a toasted cheese sandwich and a cup of tomato soup, honey?"

"Sounds fabulous. I'm almost done in here. I'll help you."

"Naw," Elly said. "I got it handled. It's hard to start up a cleaning project once you've sat down and rested. I remember how that goes."

"All right. Ten minutes and I'll be done." Maya raised a dust mop and knocked down a cobweb she'd missed in a high corner. She traveled around the room until she'd dusted the entire ceiling a second time. By then, her shoulders ached and the smell of frying bread and melting cheese made her mouth water.

"Lunch is ready," Elly called from the kitchen.

Maya gathered up the dust mop, cleaning rags, polishes, put them all into one big bucket, carried them through the back skylight room and through the pantry hall. The soiled rags she tossed down the steps and into the basement. Maya washed her hands in the kitchen sink and sat down at the table.

"Dig in, honey." Elly sipped her soup from a mug.

Maya bit into her sandwich. "This is how I like them, with the bread edges all crispy." Maya tasted the soup. "You put oregano in it?"

"And bits of grated cheese, do you like it?"

"It's delicious. I think this proves we're related, which reminds me. You find any photos of Uncle Harlan yet?"

"I'm pretty sure they're up in the attic. I just haven't wanted to climb those stairs yet.

None of them were taken around the farm here though. Before we moved here we knew a number of people and I remember posing for some group shots. I'll look for those."

"People you worked with, you mean?

Elly nodded. Her thin, silvery brows pinched together as if some memories were unpleasant.

"I'd love to see them. How old were you when you moved here?" Maya asked.

"We moved in the day before my twenty-first birthday. Harlan was almost twenty-nine."

"So, you've lived here—wow, fifty-five years."

"The years flew by, baby girl. Don't let your life fly by. Don't let people take things from you. Don't let anyone push you into corners where you don't want to go."

Maya nodded but was unsure what Elly meant, unless she meant Benson, and Benson was history.

After lunch, Maya washed the dishes, watching raindrops plop into the puddles in the driveway. As always, the woodstove was stoked and it was warm in the kitchen. She struggled to hold her eyelids open.

"Whew," Maya said. She dried the last utensil and slid it into the drawer. "I think I'll sit down for a while."

"Go on upstairs and take a proper nap, baby girl. You've been working since breakfast."

Maya said, "If I crawl into bed I might sleep the whole afternoon away."

"I'll wake you. What time?"

"Don't let me sleep any later than one-thirty or I won't be able to sleep tonight."

Maya climbed the stairs, dropped her jeans and shirt on the chair and crawled into bed. The sheets were cool against her bare skin, the pillow smooth and crisp against her cheek. The window was open and inch. The lace curtain swayed and a chickadee sang from the peak of the roof.

"Maya? Honey? Wake up. Wake up."

"What time is it?" Maya's voice sounded distant in her own ears. Her tongue was dry and stiff. It tasted sour.

"It's one thirty-five. I've been trying to wake you up for five minutes. Are you all right?"

Maya sat up, trying to work up saliva. "I must have slept with my mouth open. I'm all dried out."

"Come on downstairs. There's fresh lemonade."

When Maya entered the kitchen, Elly entered the back door, her arms loaded with firewood.

"The oddest thing," Elly said. "Just now, Coty asked me how well I know you. He asked me if I'm sure you're my niece."

Maya poured a tall glass full of lemonade. "He asked you if you really know me?"

"I said, of course you're my niece. You and I have exchanged cards, letters and photographs from the time you were five years old. Your first letter was written in blue crayon. I still have that letter somewhere."

"What did he say then?"

"He didn't say anything. He just shrugged, almost like he doubted me."

"This is kind of a coincidence, Elly. You know how your mind wanders while you're cleaning? I was thinking earlier this morning, maybe you should ask Judith to send a photo of her nephew, so we know for sure Coty is who he claims to be."

Elly faced the bay window and the fields. "Good idea. I'll ask Judith to send a photo the next time I talk to her. But then, she'll want to know why. She wants an explanation for everything. Some of my thoughts are private and I don't feel like telling her everything. If she wants to know what it's like here, why doesn't she come for a visit? She's not a prisoner over there in Seattle. It's a retirement home, not an asylum like that place where your father died." Elly wore a sudden, pained expression, as if she had bitten her tongue. "Oh dear. You already knew about that, didn't you Maya?"

"About Dad dying at Western State Hospital? Yes, Mom told me."

"You were just a little girl then. About ten years old?" Elly asked.

Maya nodded. "Almost eleven."

"That's too young to know about such morbid things. I hope you mother didn't tell you everything."

"She said Dad died of heart failure."

Elly's smile was sad. "We all die of heart failure, honey. That's how the doctors decide we're dead. No heartbeat. Did your mother tell you I went to see your father there? After all, Stephen was my little brother. How could I not go?"

"She refused to say anything about it."

"Of course not. Your mother would never tell you that I did something kind. I went three times. The first time they let me look through a little window into a cell with thick, white mattresses all over the floor and walls. Stephen crouched in a corner, hugging his knees, facing away from the door. I knocked and called his name but he never even looked in my direction."

"Mom never took me to see him," Maya said. "She was afraid it would frighten me."

"That was for the best, honey. Stephen wasn't himself. The second time I went," Elly said. "He was in a room full of people, some in wheelchairs, some on couches. A few were humming. Some drooling. Some walked in circles. Several stood in corners, swaying back and forth or bumping their heads against the wall." Elly's voice faded to nothing. She was someplace else, somewhere far away, someplace only she saw. A moment later she continued. "Stephen sat at a table covered with puzzle pieces. He'd pick them up, stare at them and then put them down again, one piece after another, never seeming to comprehend the pieces could be connected. I put my hand on his shoulder and he jumped. The table and puzzle pieces went flying everywhere. Stephen started crying and a nurse came and led him out of the room, so I left and came home. I waited a month before returning. That time, Stephen said my name. "Elly." He touched my hand and then tears rolled down his face like his heart was broken. "It's over, Elly," he said. 'All over.' I asked him what he meant but he just shook his head. I stayed for an hour. We sat side by side and nurses walked by and smiled. Finally one of them said visiting hours were over. The next day your mother phoned and told me what had happened."

"What did happen?" Maya said.

"I guess you're old enough to know now. Stephen hanged himself. He tore his pajama bottoms into strips and braided them into a cord—they found him hanging from a water pipe in the hallway."

Maya's stomach muscles quivered, as if her cheese sandwich and tomato soup might come back up. She sipped her tea, added sugar and stirred it with a spoon. "Mom never said anything about that."

"I'm sorry if that upsets you," Elly said.

"I knew there was more to the story than what Mom told me. Aunt Ruth always got so quiet when the subject of my father came up," Maya said.

"Who is Ruth?"

"My mother's older sister."

"Oh, her. Never liked her."

"She was outspoken and bossy, but she was always good to me," Maya said.

"That's because you were her sister's child. I wasn't a blood relative so she made it clear she didn't like me, but that's all water under the bridge now. Your father is gone and so is Ruth. Oh, look there . . . out the window. The storm has arrived."

A limp brown leaf hit the window like the palm of a hand, flattening itself against the glass. Raindrops followed, pounding the glass, pouring down, running in rivulets and smearing everything outside into a green and gray blur. The leaf slid down and caught on the windowpane. It quivered in the wind and then blew away. Wind whistled in the chimney and the rhododendrons thrashed back and forth as if in agony.

Chapter Ten

Monday morning, Maya woke at five and arrived in the kitchen ahead of Aunt Elly. She raked up hot coals in the stove, added kindling, small pieces of pitchy fir and one large piece of alder. When flames curled around the alder, she closed the door and filled the teakettle. She oiled the griddle and placed it across two burners on the electric range. She stirred pancake batter in a bright yellow bowl, filled a pot with water, and dropped in four eggs to hard boil.

"Morning." Elly stood at the bottom of the stairs wearing oversized jeans and a denim shirt. Her hair was gathered into a thin ponytail at the nape of her neck and the ponytail disappeared beneath her collar. Thick socks covered her tiny feet.

"You coming down with a cold? Your voice sounds a raspy," Maya said.

"I'm fine, thank you."

"The tea is ready and there will be eggs and pancakes soon," Maya said.

"I never eat pancakes."

Maya frowned and studied her aunt. "You ate them last Thursday morning."

"I never eat pancakes. I'll take a cup of tea, though and I'll be back for a couple'a those eggs after I get more firewood from the shed. Wouldn't mind a piece of toast, dry."

Maya stepped back as Elly shoved her stocking feet into boots, slipped on the flannel-lined denim jacket from a hook beside the door and grabbed the leather gloves from the windowsill. "Go ahead with your own breakfast, young lady. I don't require conversation with mine."

Maya shivered. It wasn't Elly's voice. It wasn't Elly's clothes or Elly's petite, upright posture. It was as if someone else stood in the kitchen with her at that moment. Maya chewed her lower lip in silence as her aunt opened the back door and exited. Even Elly's walk had changed.

This person strode, leaning forward at the hips, arms swinging loose.

Determined. Masculine.

"What the hell," Maya whispered.

A tap on the window above the sink startled her. She recognized Coty, and for the first time, she was glad to see him. She motioned for him to come inside.

He opened the back door and stepped inside, arriving with the smell of crisp spring morning air and pine pitch.

"What's Mr. Elly up to this morning?" he said.

"Who? What are you talking about?"

"Elly has done this before. This is the third time since I arrived. One moment she's Elly and the next moment, she's . . . someone with a gruff voice and a swagger. I call him Mr. Elly."

"Well, Elly ate pancakes last Thursday morning, but now she almost snapped my head off because, she 'never eats pancakes.'"

Coty nodded. "That sounds like Mr. Elly all right. I had to introduce myself a second time because Mr. Elly didn't seem to know who the heck I was just two weeks after I got here." Coty shook his head. "She's nuts, you know."

"Don't say that, Coty. She's just having a hard time remembering things. She has signs of dementia, that's all."

"If you insist."

"I do."

"Okay." Coty raised his brows and exited.

Maya shelled two eggs, put them on a plate beside two pancakes and sat down at the table. Her hands trembled as she poured warmed syrup from a small blue pitcher. *She's nuts, you know.* The words hurt almost as much as when Benson said the same thing about her.

Maya'd never told Benson about her father, but somehow he found out. Maya suspected her mother revealed the secret. One evening, when Benson's friends came over to watch a Seahawks game on the big screen, Benson blurted out how Maya's father, Stephen Pederson had died in Western State Hospital. "Maya's old man was batshit loony." Benson described to their friends how her father'd spent two days laced in a straitjacket and in a padded cell for three weeks before finally being assigned a regular room. "It's a good thing I decided not to have kids," Benson added. "Can you imagine raising a pack of psychos?"

Maya'd felt embarrassed, humiliated, wishing she could dissolve into the sofa cushions all the way through to the condo below theirs. Her face burned when Benson's friends laughed out loud. Benson's buddy, Fred, called her the next day.

"Hey Maya. I think Bens was wrong to say those things in front of everyone. If you ever get tired of his bullshit, just let me know. I'd treat you a lot better than Bens does. Our secret, of course."

Maya finished eating and washed her dish and utensils at the sink.

Elly returned from the shed, the two-wheel pushcart loaded with firewood. She rolled the cart up on the back porch.

Maya opened the door. "Why didn't you have Coty get the wood?"

"Who?"

"The handyman . . . lives out in the bunkhouse."

Elly tossed a disapproving glance across the driveway. "Oh, him. I got him busy doing other chores. Sides' that, I don't want him inside the house."

Maya brought in six pieces for the wood box in the kitchen while Elly stacked the rest outside on the porch.

"One cartload is usually three day's worth of wood. Let me know when you need more," Elly's voice sounded even deeper than before.

As Elly washed up at the kitchen sink, Maya shelled the other two eggs and made toast while the tea steeped. Then she sat down at the table across from Elly. After a few bites of toast, Elly paused. She leaned forward, holding her head in her palms.

"Elly? You okay?" Maya asked.

Elly didn't answer. Her right hand dropped to the table, sending the fork flying and bouncing across the floor. As if dizzy, she swayed back and forth in her chair and then she straightened.

"Oh dear," Elly said, her voice back to normal. "I'm dropping things again."

"Wait. I'll get another one." Maya hurried across the kitchen, opened the drawer, and returned with a clean fork. She picked up the other one and tossed it in the sink.

"Mama used to scold me for dropping things or for spilling my milk. I think of her every time it happens," Elly said. "She said I was a clumsy child, more like a boy than a girl."

"What was your mother's name?" Maya asked. It was a relief to hear Elly's normal voice.

"Her name was Eunice but I don't remember much about her. I remember thinking she was pretty. She died when I was eight. Didn't Stephen tell you anything about our mother?"

"Daddy said she wouldn't ever let the neighbor kids inside to play."

"Mom was always cleaning. She was so afraid of germs she boiled our laundry in a big pot over an outside fire. She was raised during a flu epidemic. We had to change our bedding every day."

"Want some pancakes with your eggs?" Maya asked.

"I thought I smelled pancakes. I'd love some, baby girl."

• • •

Maya strolled the backyard after breakfast. She picked a bouquet of daffodils for the dining room table because that room needed color, something cheerful to brighten the gloom. The dining room was always chilly, even though it was adjacent to the kitchen, the warmest room in the house. The dining room had one south-facing window, the sunny side. Even so, the room always felt cold.

It's all that dark wainscoting. Maya centered the vase of daffodils on the dining room table and stepped back to weigh the effect. Instead of the flowers brightening the shadowy room, the room grayed down the bright yellow blossoms to a mustard color. Sunlight cut into the room through the window and painted a golden square on the hardwood floor, but it failed to warm the room. More than once, while passing through, Maya shivered. The dining room felt thirty degrees cooler than the kitchen. Sometimes in the evening she saw her breath in that room.

Heading upstairs, Maya met Aunt Elly on the landing.

"Gonna shoot them llamas if that bastard Karl Schaff doesn't get 'em off'n my land," Elly growled.

"Llamas?"

"Ain't ye seen 'em, girl? Over the hill there? Eight llamas grazing on my property. I told Schaff more'n once to get'em out'a there, but he hasn't done it yet. I'll bet when he finds one of them ugly beasts dead, he'll listen to me then."

"I didn't see any llamas, Aunt Elly." Maya spoke before noticing the change in Elly's voice. Elly was gone and in her place, Mr. Elly stood, bending forward at the waist, his brows cinched together.

"Hmph," Mr. Elly snorted. "I should've bought Karl Schaff's land when I had the chance.

I wouldn't be havin' trouble with them llamas now if'n I had." Mr. Elly stomped into the kitchen and pulled an aged phonebook from a drawer. "Maybe I'll call the sheriff." He thumbed through the pages. "Schaff wanted way more'n his place was worth. He said my offer was 'insultin.'" Mr. Elly's thumb halted halfway down a page. "Here's the Sheriff's number."

"How about you and I take a walk over the hill and you show me the llamas," Maya said.

Mr. Elly glanced up with a scowl. "What fer?"

"I was there just yesterday, remember? When I went for a walk over the hill? There were no llamas."

"You callin' me a liar, girl?"

"Of course not, but I think we should make sure before calling the sheriff. It would be embarrassing to accuse your neighbor and then have the sheriff show up and say those llamas aren't on your property."

"But I seen'em. Go take a look, girl. I know Karl Schaff's llamas are on my land. If the sheriff won't do nothin', then I'll load up my shotgun and . . ."

"I'm heading up over hill right now. Let me get my boots and jacket on and I'll check on those llamas, okay? Before you phone anyone, or load that gun?"

Mr. Elly shook his head back and forth like an angry bull. "I'll be wait'n right here in my own kitchen. At the age of eighty-four, one trip over the hill and back is enough for one day."

"I thought you said you're seventy-six." Maya clamped her mouth shut. "I'll be right back." Maya hurried out the door and along the driveway toward the upper pasture. At the woodshed Coty wedged the axe into the chopping block and hurried to join her.

"Where we going?" he said, matching her stride.

"I'm glad you didn't sneak up on me this time," Maya said. "I have enough problems."

"I never did sneak up on you. Both occasions were strictly coincidence. What's the dilemma?"

"Mr. Elly insists Karl Schaff's llamas are grazing on his land and he's threatening to shoot them."

"What llamas?"

"Eight llamas, he said, and if Karl Schaff doesn't get them out, Mr. Elly is going hunting."

"We can't let that happen," Coty said. "I like llamas."

Ten minutes later they reached the top of the hill and paused to catch their breath. They stood side by side on a ridge above a neighboring valley. Forested foothills back dropped the pastures and rail fences followed the rollercoaster tree line.

"I was almost hoping we'd find some llamas up here. I have an apple in my pocket," Coty said. "Do llamas like apples?"

"I don't know, but I wish we would have found some llamas too," Maya said. "I dread telling Mr. Elly there are none. He was getting angry when I doubted him."

"I'll go back inside with you. Maybe if there's two of us, he won't be so irritable."

Maya nodded. "By the way, Mr. Elly doesn't like you," Maya said. "I mean, judging by his expression when your name came up."

"I know."

They headed back downhill.

"What are you working on?" Maya asked.

Coty stubbed his toe on a clump of grass and almost fell before regaining his footing. "Working on?"

"Around the farm. Building fences, repairing the roof, digging a drainage ditch, stuff like that? Elly said you were handy."

"Oh!" Coty sounded relieved and Maya wondered what he'd thought she meant. "I'm replacing the toilet in the bunkhouse, along with new floorboards and support timbers. The old john was about ready to drop right through the rotten floor into the crawlspace underneath, and let's face it, the timing could be uncomfortable, if not dangerous."

Maya grinned, picturing the bunkhouse toilet collapsing the floor in the middle of a rainy, blustery night.

Coty opened the back door and they stepped inside. The kitchen felt like an oven compared to outside. Maya unbuttoned her jacket and slid free.

"There's tea." Elly stood beside the woodstove, kettle in hand. Her voice sounded normal.

"No llamas," Maya reported.

"What, dear?"

"You said Karl Schaff's llamas were on your property," Coty said. "We went to check."

Maya added, "Coty and I just walked up there and there's no llamas in sight."

"Well, heavens no," Elly said. "There's been no llamas on Karl Schaff's land since nineteen seventy-five when Karl died and his son, Eddy, took over running the place. Eddy sold all the llamas to Franny Linderman next county over." Elly picked up the teakettle. "Did you say you wanted tea?"

Chapter Eleven

MAYA SPOTTED COTY THROUGH the kitchen window. This time she didn't duck out of sight. Instead, her neck and ears grew warm. She waited to see if he looked in her direction, her hand raised, ready to wave, but he swung the long handle of a shovel over his shoulder and headed uphill toward the barns.

She hated admitting she was attracted to him, especially after accusing him of stalking her. Her face burned at the thought. He'd followed her all the way to the top of the ridge and apologized, and she knew face-to-face apologies were not easy.

She liked the way he looked and the way he moved. He had an attractive profile with a straight nose and even chin. She always exhaled as he approached and inhaled as he passed by, smelling cedar and moss, or sometimes a trace of wood smoke or spicy winter apples.

Coty disappeared into tall winter grass near the top of the hill and Maya focused on her own reflection in the kitchen window. "We're both here to help Aunt Elly and that's all." She was determined to not make anything more of it than that. Her divorce from Benson was too recent and the wounds too painful to think about starting another relationship. She shuddered, picturing how it would feel, telling Coty about herself.

The anxiety, the OCD, the Lorazapam.

Coty was nothing like Benson. Benson had phoned the day after their first date. He sent yellow roses and an embossed card with lilacs and goldfinches on it. At first Maya was flattered, but that same evening her mother phoned.

"Maya?"

"Hi Mama. What's up?"

"I'm wondering how your date went the other evening."

"It was okay."

"Just okay? He sounded like such a gentleman when he phoned me yesterday."

"Benson phoned you?"

"He said I must be a very special mother to have raised such a wonderful girl. Isn't that sweet?"

"Really? He said that?"

"He asked me what your favorite flowers are, and what kind of cologne you like, and what kind of candy."

"And what did you tell him, Mama?"

"Yellow roses of course, and I told him you love goldfinches."

"I do like yellow roses, but lilacs are my favorite flower."

"Lilacs? Well . . . I don't remember you ever saying that."

"What else did you tell him?" Maya asked.

"L'Air du Temp cologne."

"I haven't worn that since college, Mama."

"Well for petesake, Maya, what do you wear then?"

"Gai Mattiolo. That's all I've worn for the last ten years."

"Well." Mama said again. Her words sounded clipped and irritated.

"I'm wondering what kind of candy I'm going to have to pretend I like," Maya said.

"Maya, I thought I was helping. He seemed so determined to impress you."

"He impressed you, Mama. I'm not blaming you, but . . . he did call you? You didn't call him, right?"

"I didn't call him. Do you still like chocolate covered caramels?"

"Love them."

When Maya thought about those early days with Benson, she realized there had been warning signs, like the way he treated waiters in restaurants, or slammed the receiver down on charity fundraisers. He threatened a neighbor's Shih-Tzu when the little dog dug under the fence. The neighbor repaired the lawn and then sought a restraining order after Benson threatened to kill the dog. Maya was relieved when the neighbor moved away because it was one less thing to worry about. She'd never told her mother about Benson's anger. Mama always praised Benson and Benson could put on a great act. He was in sales, after all.

• • •

Tony Bradley phoned and Maya glanced at the calendar. It was Wednesday, four days since he'd joined them for dinner. That was a respectable length of time.

"Did Elly say it was okay for me to tramp around and appraise her farm?" he asked.

"Elly said it's fine with her. Are you coming over today?"

"No. I'm leaving town on business for about a week. I'll phone when I get back."

"Talk to you then."

"Who was that?" Elly asked.

"Tony Bradley. He wants to explore the farm sometime soon, to get an idea of its value."

"He's a handsome devil, isn't he?" Elly said. "I almost remembered, the other day, where I've seen him before. It didn't quite come back to me, but it eventually will."

"He also suggested having your garage sale closer to Graceville. He said he manages an empty warehouse near the River Lodge Cafe. Lots of parking and a roof in case it rains. He gave us a number to call when we're ready. I wrote it down on the tablet there."

"That's thoughtful of him, but we'd have to move all the stuff over there. That might take a lot of driving back and forth and there is so much stuff."

"Tony said he has a truck and a driver and he'll transport everything for you."

"My goodness, Maya. He must be smitten with you."

"I don't think it's that," Maya said. "I think he's anticipating a return on his investment."

"Give it time, baby girl. I knew Harlan for twenty years before we got married."

"Tony Bradley isn't my type, Elly. He's too suave. I can't picture ever marrying someone prettier than me. I think he's more interested in you and this property."

Elly stared at Maya with squinted eyes and open mouth. "Who?"

"Tony Bradley."

Elly's voice dropped a full octave. "Who's Tony Bradley?"

Through the window Maya spotted Coty striding down the driveway. She wanted to open the door and call him inside. When Coty stood beside her she felt more able to deal with Mr. Elly.

"Nobody important, I guess," she said.

● ● ●

Maya searched her bedroom for her wristwatch. She changed the sheets on the bed and flipped the mattress, dug through her empty luggage, the bedside drawer and even under the braided oval rug. She sifted through the ashes in the fireplace and ran her hand inside every pocket of her wardrobe. Nothing. If the watch had been a gift from Benson she wouldn't have cared but she'd bought it with her very first paycheck. It was a nice watch, with one tiny diamond at twelve o'clock. Watches made Maya think of time and time made her think of her father and how quickly life passed by.

"I've got to phone Mom today, Elly. I haven't spoken to her since I arrived here." Maya dreaded a conversation with her mother. "She'll probably start interrogating me."

"Interrogating you how, honey?" Elly asked.

"Asking me when I'm coming home, or if I've talked to Benson. She'll want to know if I've found a job yet. Things like that."

"I'd tell her to kiss my hinny."

Grinning, Maya climbed the stairs to stand beside the morning glory window, ready to enter her mother's phone number. Her grin faded as she recalled her mother's judgmental tone when Maya mentioned the classes she had chosen for college.

"Art? Will an art degree get you a good job, Maya?"

"A degree in anything helps. It proves you have perseverance," Maya said. Every job since graduation, however, had been a financial disappointment and her mother was always eager to point that out.

"Another receptionist position, Maya? At a car dealership?" And two years later, "A word processor? Isn't that just a typist?" The word processing job lasted seven months before Maya found a job as an office manager for a book distributor. "I hope this job pays better, Maya." A year later, when Maya was hired as manager at the art gallery, her mother said, "Now we'll see what effect your art degree has on your income." When Benson insisted Maya stop working and stay at home, Maya's mother approved. "Now, your job is to support your husband. Behind every successful man is a wife with social skills. A supportive wife can make a big difference in a man's career."

Where was Benson at that very moment? Maya leaned against the wall beside the lavender window, glancing twice toward the door at the far end of the hall. She pictured Benson in the hospital, legs hoisted in a metal framework. Or was he recovering at home already? With both legs and one arm in casts, he would need help with just about everything. Perhaps his mother, Peggy, was there with him. Every time Benson screwed up, Peggy arrived to bail him out. Maya figured Benson had 'borrowed' over ten thousand dollars from Peggy in the last seven years. He'd never paid a cent of it back.

Maya tapped her mother's number into her cell phone. It rang several times. Maya was ready to leave a brief message when her mother answered.

"Hi, Mama. It's Maya."

"Of course it's you, dear. No one else calls me Mama."

"How are you?"

"Great. My realtor just called. Someone made a full offer on the house. Apparently there were multiple offers. There might be a bidding war. He said I could get a lot more if I wait."

"I don't remember you saying where you planned to live after selling the house, Mama."

"I plan to travel a bit. I've always wanted to spend a month or two in Italy."

"Italy?"

"And Spain. Maybe Portugal too."

"Alone?"

"No, not alone."

"Who are you going with?"

"You wouldn't know this person. The two of you have never met. Oh, someone else is calling, dear. It might be the realtor. I'll call you back."

"You don't have to, Mama. I'm going out for the day anyway. Talk to you in a day or two."

"Okay. Love you, Maya."

"Love you, Mama."

Maya entered the upstairs bathroom and stared at her reflection in the medicine cabinet mirror. She didn't want to move back in with Mama. The idea of living with her mother, for even a short period of time, made Maya's heart flutter with anxiety. Not even for a brief transition between jobs would she consider that.

I'd live at the YWCA before I moved back in with Mom.

Even so, Maya had happy memories of the house where she grew up and of the neighborhood. She smiled, picturing her father reading the newspaper in his big armchair with sunlight coming through the window behind him. She held fond memories of how he looked, tinkering in the garage, pruning the rose bushes out back, or replacing a pane of glass in the enclosed back porch. But those memories were like old photographs, the colors fading, the details blurring, the occasions hazy. What she remembered most often was her father's smile and the sound of his laugh, even though his laugh was a rare thing.

Maya remembered every item in her old bedroom. The twin canopy bed and bedside table were secondhand, given to her by Mama's sister, Ruth. It was white with hand painted pink roses across the headboard. The quilted pink bedspread and curtains were a set Mama ordered from J.C.Penny, and the white, fluffy rug from Montgomery Ward. Maya's father hand-built a trunk for her toys, although there were very few of those. Maya wedged her one, lonely doll, Sally, between the pillows on her bed, and her tricycle and bicycle stayed in the garage. Even so, of all the things Maya cherished, it was that trunk, built like a pirate's treasure chest with wide bands of brass and a brass lock with a brass key. Maya'd kept the key in her jewelry box, under the ballet dancer that pirouetted when she lifted the lid. The trunk now sat in the back of her closet in Aunt Elly's house. The doll, Sally, rested behind netting in the arched lid.

The thought that the house where she grew up would now belong to someone else felt amiss. Tears stung Maya's eyes. She blotted them with her sleeve. There was no longer the option of moving back home. For the first time ever, she felt homeless. Until now, she'd always felt as if the decision were hers. Reality, however, shouted it wasn't her decision after all and it made turning thirty years old even more painful. She'd never considered how turning thirty would feel, until it happened. "Home hasn't been home for nineteen years anyway. Not since Daddy . . ." Maya couldn't say the word, *died*. "Not since Daddy—left," she said.

• • •

The yard-garage sale took place on Thursday, Friday, and Saturday. The concrete block warehouse had a corrugated metal roof and it held ten long banquet tables. Four of the tables were piled with items from inside Elly's house. Seven more tables displayed tools and equipment from sheds and barns. A six-foot long clothes rack held all of Harlan's clothes. Almost everything on that rack was outdated but in excellent condition, as if he had seldom worn them. One leather jacket looked new.

Six early shoppers arrived while Maya and Elly were still setting things up for business. They wanted first peek at the goods, they said, but Elly shook her head no.

"Come back at nine o'clock, like the sign says. I'm not giving you first crack at anything."

"I'll give you top dollar," one man said. He dug a wad of bills from his pants pocket, held together by a sturdy blue rubber band. He held the bundle of bills up high, as if tempting a dog with a meaty bone. He wore pristine Cole Haan shoes, a cashmere sweater and summer weight wool slacks. He had pulled up in a classic old red Ferrari and parked it sideways in front of the warehouse doors, as if to block others from entering.

Elly spoke up. "Your money is no greener than the next fella's. So get out, or I'll turn the Dobermans loose."

Maya giggled as the man climbed into his Ferrari and drove away. There were no guard dogs, Doberman or other breeds. She was about ready to compliment Elly on her method of scaring the man away, when she realized Elly's voice had changed again. Mr. Elly was showing up more often lately. One minute it was Elly's high-pitched voice and a minute later it was Mr. Elly's growl. It wasn't the voice change that concerned Maya. It was Mr. Elly himself. It was as if he slept for days at a time and then he'd wake up, demanding to know what was going on, furious at things he saw. Mr. Elly seemed to disapprove of almost everything, but especially the fact that Maya and Coty were living on the farm. When Maya called him Elly, his face changed. He squinted, frowned, drew his brows together over his nose and focused his deep-set eyes on her. It was frightening when he glared at her like that, more frightening than Benson's face when he tried to strangle her. At least Benson was there, behind those eyes. With Benson, there was a light on. Mr. Elly was temporary. Where did he go when he left?

• • •

"Elly, your yard sale was a success," Maya said. "Almost everything is gone, and what's left has SOLD tags on it. Those buyers better get back here for their stuff before we close up shop."

Elly opened the cash box beneath the counter and counted the money.

"Eleven-hundred-forty dollars. Is that good?" Elly asked.

"That's excellent, and that antique dealer said he'd give you four thousand for the furniture at the farm. I'm sure he'll double that when he sells it later."

"You think he's cheating me?"

"No. He has employees and taxes to pay. Plus, he has to haul everything away and that takes labor and gas money. I think his offer was fair." Maya hesitated and then added, "But you could phone him and tell him you've changed your mind if you think you could get a better price somewhere else."

Elly shook her head. "Nah. I'm too old and tired to negotiate anymore. I just want to be done with it. It's time to move on. Harlan will understand."

I sure hope so, Maya thought. "How old was Uncle Harlan when he died?"

Elly looked thoughtful for a moment. "He was—my goodness, seventy-six, the same age I am right now. I hadn't realized that until just now when you asked."

"So, if Uncle Harlan were still alive, he'd be about eighty-one, eighty-two?"

Elly nodded. "Harlan would be almost eighty-two. He's been gone . . . heavens . . . over six years already."

Harlan takes over Elly's thoughts, her emotions, her body . . . but she doesn't realize it while it's happening. Does Harlan not realize he's dead?

A sudden rain shower danced in puddles outside the warehouse. Moments later, three cars pulled up and ten people climbed out. Talking and laughing as they entered the warehouse.

"Do you still have that glass, bubble-milk lamp?" One woman asked. "I asked you to hold it for me."

Elly motioned for the woman to follow her. Two people paid Maya cash for their items and loaded their treasures into their cars. When all three vehicles drove away, the last banquet table was bare and the cash box held over twelve hundred dollars.

"Shall we close up shop?" Elly asked. "It's three-forty-five and we said we'd close down at four o'clock. This is close enough isn't it?"

"After this next guy leaves." Maya recognized the man from earlier in the day, the man with the wad of bills. He now wore faded blue jeans and a black sweatshirt. Instead of a red Ferrari, he drove a brown Chevy Malibu.

"Howdy, ladies," he said. "Hope I'm not too late."

Maya smirked. Elly wasn't the only person whose voice changed. His Texas drawl sounded faked.

"I was here earlier," he admitted. "You had some oil paintings against the back wall. Still got'em?"

"I'll walk back there with you," Maya said. "I know the paintings you're talking about and yes, they're still there."

Side by side they headed toward the back of the warehouse.

"You related to that old shrew?" he asked, dropping the accent.

"Did that old shrew scare you away the first time?" Maya asked. "Is that why you came back in disguise?"

He smiled. "Yup."

"Are these the paintings?" Maya halted in front of three framed oils. She pointed to the first one. "That one's the best of the three."

"How much do you want for it?" he asked.

"Six hundred dollars."

"That seems steep, considering . . ." The man leaned close and squinted at the name in the bottom right corner. "I don't recognize that artist's name."

"Doesn't matter. It's a fine painting."

"And you'd know that because?"

"Because I know. That's why."

"I'll give you five hundred for all three paintings," he said.

"I want twelve hundred for all three paintings. Otherwise I'll keep them myself."

He stepped back. "You're not from around here, are you?"

"I'm from Tacoma, where I managed the Michael Sherridan-Smith Gallery for five years."

Without another word the man counted out twelve hundred dollars into Maya's palm, picked up the paintings and left. Maya strolled back to the warehouse entrance and handed the money to Elly.

"Now, we can close up," Maya said. "Twenty-four hundred dollars is a very successful garage sale, Elly."

Minutes later the Goodwill truck arrived and hauled away the remaining items, including some of Harlan's clothes and two sets of old mechanic's tools. Maya and Elly slammed the warehouse doors closed and attached the big padlock Tony Bradley provided. They climbed into the Ford Edge and headed for home.

"Those paintings were valuable?" Elly asked.

"Yes. Where did you get them?"

"Harlan painted them."

Maya tried to remember the signatures. Why hadn't she paid more attention?

"Uncle Harlan painted?" Maya asked. "You never mentioned that."

"When he was younger. He painted those when we lived in Chicago, many years ago."

"I didn't know you ever lived in Chicago."

"Well, that was long before you were born, Maya. Harlan and I lived there after we got married and he drove a delivery truck, but after a while Harlan said he couldn't breathe. He said he had to get away from those people and that city, so we moved west. He swore he'd never move east again."

"It was a stressful job?" Maya asked.

"I'll tell you about it sometime."

"I'd love to hear it."

"You might, you might not." Elly lowered her window. She leaned back, her gray head against the headrest. "How odd. I had no idea those painting were worth anything. I almost threw them away."

"They were done in a primitive style. It's difficult for adults to achieve such freedom when they paint, but small children often can. Somehow, we lose our ability to paint the things the eye craves. Colors. Shapes. Shadows. Instead, we get caught up on details. So many artists try to make their paintings look like photographs. It's a common mistake."

"Imagine that," Elly said. "Never heard of a primitive style before."

Chapter Twelve

PINE NEEDLES CRUNCHED UNDERFOOT as Maya climbed the trail leading up through the evergreen forest. This was Maya's second time up the trail. The warm day made it felt steeper. Sweat beaded her lip and forehead by the time she reached the meadow with the log cabin. The cabin's moss roof had sprouted spring grass, waving like fine, green baby hair in the sunlight.

The meadow grass had also grown taller in the past two weeks. It brushed her knees as she circled the old cabin. Where the door clung to the frame by one rusty hinge, Maya spotted something blue through the rubble. She stepped closer and spotted a stained glass window in the rotten door. It was about an eight-by-ten-inch window and she was amazed that it'd never broken as the cabin surrendered itself to the meadow and the mountain. She was surprised hikers had never taken it, or that harsh winters hadn't fractured it. Would that ancient glass survive another winter? Would it survive being pried from that old wood?

Maya appreciated the simple flower design . . . a yellow tulip with four green fronds and a background of sky blue. The outer edges were clear panes of bubble glass. Maya was tempted to pull the entire door away from the house, but was afraid she would damage the window. She decided to come back later and bring tools. Maybe Coty would come with her.

Around the cabin, the earth felt soft and spongy and, with every step, Maya struggled to haul one hiking boot upward while her other boot sank deeper. Staggering, she lost her balance. She went to her knees and the toes of her boots dug in deep. It felt as if the earth beneath her shuddered. Her knees sank into a depression; the prairie was now at eye level. Elly's nightmarish description of the earth swallowing the farmhouse flashed through her mind, and then she remembered Coty's warning of sinkholes.

Splintered, rotten boards protruded from the earth now along with the corner of an old step. It was an ancient porch. The weather and the meadow had taken their toll. The meadow was reclaiming everything, inch by inch, including the cabin, the porch, the steps... and now her?

Maya leaned back and grabbed a giant dandelion with one hand and a large stone with the other. The stone was smooth with rounded corners, like those used in old foundations.

"Help!" she yelled. She gathered more air in her lungs and yelled again. "HELP!"

The spongy earth inched downward again. Her left boot broke through and dangled inside open space.

Maya dug her fingers deep into the roots around the dandelion and held on. The clump made a tearing sound and pulled free, dirt and dandelion roots sliding into the sinkhole with her. Seconds later she was up to her waist, both legs dangling in an open space below ground.

"Help!" she screamed gain. She glimpsed the yellow tulip and the sky blue glass before the earth collapsed and she dropped through. Seconds later she landed in fir needles and a pile of brittle sticks. The sticks snapped under her weight. In the dark, something scuttled through the sticks.

The air smelled musty and stale. It reminded her of the dirt floor basement under Elly's house.

Overhead, gray clouds floated across the opening at least twelve feet above her. She leaned back against a stone wall, checking for injuries. *I'm okay. I'm okay. Nothing broken.* "I'm all right," she said aloud.

Maya tested the stone floor with one step and then a second. The floor held. The stone walls were curved. This was an old well, a dry one. It could have been full of stagnant water and she could have drowned. She searched her pockets, hoping for a flashlight and knowing she would find none, but she found a small box of wood matches from the River Lodge Café. She lit one. The well was six feet across with spidery roots and pale vines clinging to its walls. There was a black hole straight across from her, down near the floor. At some time in the past, three stones had fallen to the well floor leaving a hole big enough to insert her head and shoulders. She held another match inside the opening but a gust of cold air blew it out. She lit another and reexamined the well's floor again. The sticks were gray-white and piled up at the base of the wall. The sticks had broken her fall. A round, white stone had rolled to one side and Maya took a second look. It was not a stone. It was a skull, and the pile of brittle sticks surrounding it included a femur, a clavicle and a section of vertebrae. She saw toe bones, with a long arch and a broken heel. Nearby, she spotted the bones of a wrist, hand, and fingers.

The pile of bones shifted. A rat's head poked through, its black marble eyes reflecting the match light. Maya stumbled back, crashing against the wall behind her. The rat squealed and dove, its long pointed tail rattling down through a ribcage.

Maya blew out the match and lit another. The bones had been there a long time. She spotted a second skull. It had a small hole in the temple and a much larger hole on the opposite side. Dread crawled through her. Entrance and exit wounds? An execution?

"Help!" Maya screamed. She lifted her chin and screamed again. She screamed until she was too hoarse to scream anymore. She coughed and gagged. She fought back tears and lit another match. She protected it from the draft with her hand, knelt and held it inside the opening. It was a low tunnel. Ten feet inside the tunnel was very dark and it looked narrow. If she tried crawling through she might end up trapped there, unable to move forward or back. Buried alive. Maya retreated into the well, jaw quivering.

In addition to her anxiety and OCD, Maya had a dread of small, enclosed places. Such places made her mouth go dry and her heart pound. There was no way she could crawl into that tunnel. No way. It would be like sticking her head into the jaws of . . . she imagined the wide gullet of something massive and hungry. She imagined the sound of something gulping, swallowing. There was no guarantee the tunnel led to freedom. She might crawl into an even worse situation. *Is there a worse situation?*

Tears streaked Maya's face and she wiped them away. She heard the scuttling sound of the rat again. She and the rat had made eye contact. She pictured herself dying of thirst four days from now. Was she the rat's next meal? Would her bones and clothes be used for a new nest?

Overhead, the sky had grown darker already. A solitary cloud floated by, a cloud with absurd, cheerful, pink edges. Night was near. Total darkness would soon fill the well. Rats were nocturnal, weren't they? More active at night? More aggressive?

Maya lit another match, leaned down and peered into the tunnel again. She smelled something familiar in the gusting draft. Along with the smell of damp earth and musty air was the smell of cedar and fir—and pine pitch. The smell was faint, but it was there. The draft meant there was an opening to the outside.

The rat raised its head from the bones. Its black eyes glistened. Brazen, it twitched its whiskers. Maya crawled into the tunnel, her heart hammering against her ribs. She fought the urge to vomit. Her hair raked against the dirt ceiling as she inched forward on her stomach. Dirt sifted down and she prayed the tunnel held. The draft continued to gust on her face carrying the smell of pitch. She arrived at a Y and lit another match. Left or right? Would the rat follow? One way, she believed would lead to freedom and the other, perhaps a cave-in. She could be buried alive, sucking dirt into her lungs. Never found.

Maya pictured Benson's face. What would he say if he saw her there, twelve feet underground, trapped in a tunnel or wild animal's burrow, forced to choose left or right. Door number one, door number two?

"Benson," Maya whispered. "I hate you." She struggled forward.

"Stay with me." The whisper came from behind her. "Don't go," it said. It was a scratchy plea, and desperate sounding, as if the speaker had screamed himself hoarse.

"Hello?" Maya said. "Who's there?"

She paused, listening. She heard another scratching sound, like someone crawling through the tunnel behind her. She pictured the rat, a much larger rat than the one in the well. A human size rat.

"Hello?" she called, louder. The crawling stopped, and then a second later, "Wait for me."

"Who are you?" Maya shouted.

Maya waited but heard nothing until the crawling sound started up again. It sounded like the crawler was gaining on her, no more than thirty feet behind now. She pictured the pile of bones, reassembled, the rotten clothing dragging, the skull leading the way, the bone fingers clawing the dirt, straining to grab her ankles, to pull her back. She remembered the creature on her mother's front porch, and crawled faster.

Another Y. Cool air puffed against Maya's face. She turned and crawled into the tunnel to her right. It narrowed and she dug at the walls, scratching at the roots and the earth, shoving handfuls down alongside, kicking, forcing it back with her knees and boots, trying to close off the passageway behind her. She squeezed through and into a space where she could sit up. She lit another match. Something pale caught the flickering glow of the flame through the opening behind her, something round and gray.

Ahead, the tunnel divided again, this time in three directions. Maya continued straight ahead until she felt the floor of the tunnel sloping downward. The dirt felt muddy and slick. She heard water dripping. The sound echoed. She lit a match but saw only darkness ahead. She flipped a rock into that darkness and almost five seconds later heard it splash.

Maya scrambled backwards into the three-way intersection. She lit another match and saw a skeletal arm stretched through the opening behind her. She dove into the right side tunnel, panic driving her forward. She lost the rhythm of crawling and fell flat, her chin hitting dirt. Dirt coated her tongue and ground between her teeth. She crawled again, bumping her head on a rock and scraping her knees on another. Roots caught the toes of her boots. She strained, pulled free. Her fingers stung. They were sticky with blood. Maya crawled faster.

The tunnel curved left and then right. It rose higher. She climbed. She felt a whimper of hope vibrate in her own throat.

Dizzy and gasping, Maya paused to catch her breath. She felt something tickling her face. She lit another match and discovered white roots trailing down all around her. Only three matches remained.

She heard the muffled scream of a chainsaw and crawled forward again on stinging knees and hands. She spotted a speck of light up ahead and scrambled forward. She reached the opening. It was too small for her head. Dusky light glowed on the other side, but the hole was a mere crevice between two boulders. She stuck one arm through, waved and shouted. "Help!" She withdrew her arm and peered through the opening. The chainsaw sputtered and died. She saw nothing but tree branches, as if the crevice was on a hillside. She yelled again and heard her own, pathetic, scratchy voice. Her shout wouldn't carry far.

A moment later she heard the rev of a truck engine and then gears shifting.

"Wait, don't leave me here! Don't go!"

She heard the truck drive away, its rumble fading. She slumped against the boulders, tears spilling down her face.

"Wait for me." The crawler was close, just around the corner, four or five feet away. Maya dove ahead and spotted another light, another opening, larger but still not large enough. She clawed at dirt and roots with bleeding fingers. Rocks tumbled outward crashing downward through undergrowth. The crevice widened and she shoved her head and shoulders through the opening, scraping her ribs and hipbones as she squeezed through and landed on grass. She lay gasping on an embankment, tasting outside air and crying unashamed.

Below were ferns and a white rail fence. Beneath the trees it was already as dark as night. Maya scooted down the bank. She knew this place. She'd seen it before. The fence marked the property line where Mr. Elly claimed to have seen the llamas— this was the Schaff property line.

Above her, the escape hole was black and gaping and she pictured something squatting inside, concealed by shadows, watching her with its dead eyes.

Maya crossed a patch of rough ground and leaned against the fence. She was at least a quarter mile from the Fedder Prairie homestead. Her hands wore gloves of dirt and blood. Her knees and elbows burned. She was coated with grit from scalp to toes.

On the other side of the fence were tire marks in the grass. Eight trees had been cut down and dozens of rounds were piled up and ready for splitting. The smell of a two-cycle motor floated on the air. She had never smelled anything so wonderful. *Chainsaw smoke.* She draped herself across the top of the fence and sobbed with relief.

Chapter Thirteen

An hour later Maya staggered across the driveway and grabbed the doorknob of Elly's kitchen door.

"Hey!" The gruff voice came from behind. She turned to find Coty striding toward her across the driveway.

"Can't talk now," Maya said. "I need a bathtub, some soap, and twenty gallons of hot water."

"Can't talk, hell! Where have you been? Elly's hysterical. You'd better get inside and let her know you're okay because she was hollering about someone named Benson and threatening to drag a big-ass gun out from under her bed to go hunting."

"Oh jeez." Maya stepped inside.

Coty followed her into the kitchen. "So, where've you been?" he demanded.

Maya glanced down at her muddy clothing. She heard grit sifting from her hair to the shoulders of her jacket. A clod of dirt rolled from the waistband of her jeans and landed on the kitchen floor. She tasted grit between her teeth. She wanted to strip down right there in the kitchen the way Elly said she used to do, and to toss the filthy things into the basement.

"You were right," she said. "There are abandoned wells around here. I found one."

"Hell," Coty said. "Where?"

"Right next to that old log cabin in the meadow. This should provide me a lifetime of nightmares." She tried to sound amused but her voice sounded shaky.

Elly rushed into the kitchen through the pantry hall, reddened eyes glittering with tears. "Baby girl."

"I'm sorry, Aunt Elly. I went for a walk and fell in a hole. It took a while to find my way out."

"A hole?"

"An old well," Coty said.

"Are you hurt, honey?" Elly asked.

"Nothing serious. Just dirty, mostly, and a few scrapes and lots of bruises. Some torn fingernails."

Exhausted, Maya headed toward the stairs. "Luckily, it was a dry well and not a deep one. Let me clean up and then I'll tell you about it. We need to phone the sheriff, too. He'll want to know what I saw down there."

"Coty's been searching for you," Elly said. "He was gone for hours and when it got dark he came back cussing and swearing. I was just going to phone the sheriff myself."

"I've got to get out of these clothes." Maya sniffed her sleeve and grimaced. "Phew."

Coty exited the back door without another word.

"He's mad at me," Maya said. "I suppose I was foolish, exploring around that old cabin."

"I'll make you some hot soup," Elly said. "You've been gone a long time, honey."

Maya glanced at the clock. It was midnight? She heard a cooking pot slide across a burner as she climbed the stairs, one aching foot in front of the other. She halted on the landing and stared upward. At the top of the stairs swirled the green boy with the tattoos and the facial piercings. He held his hands forward in a pleading gesture. She heard him scream as if from a great distance,

"Please help me!" He sounded like a wounded animal, his voice rough, hoarse and desperate. He floated back, past the bathroom and then down the hall, vanishing into the closed door at the far end.

It seemed like an entire day had passed since Maya screamed those same words, her voice growing hoarse in that pitch black well, screaming until she gagged. No one heard her, though. If she'd been injured and unable to crawl, she would still be at the bottom of that old well. She'd seen human bones in the well, in the flickering glow of a single match. One foot bone had a broken heel. From trying to climb out and falling back in? That could have happened to her. It would have, if she hadn't worked up the nerve to crawl into the small tunnel. She might have tried to climb the well walls and fallen back in, landing wrong, breaking an arm or a leg, or something worse, and months later the rat would have piled her bones with all the others. Its treasure pile. The rat would have gnawed them clean and added her clothing to its nest.

No one heard me calling for help. Then Maya remembered. *Something* did hear. *Something* followed her through that tunnel. Maya entered the bathroom and peeled off her clothes. She turned on the faucet, filling the claw foot tub with hot water and the room with steam. She piled her filthy clothes in front of the door. They were too dirty for the hamper, too dirty to wash. Too dirty to ever, ever, wear again.

Chapter Fourteen

"Bones, you say, Mrs. Hammond?"

"I've petitioned to have my maiden name back, Sheriff Wimple. It's Pederson. Please don't call me Mrs. Hammond."

Sheriff Wimple was the same height as Maya. He was bone thin and she suspected he weighed less than she did, even wearing his jacket and leather boots. He reminded her of Mr. Trippe, her high school science teacher. Mr. Trippe and Sheriff Wimple both had straight brown hair parted on the right side and they both wore wire-rimmed glasses. They could have been brothers.

"The bones looked like they had been there a long time," Maya said.

"How so?"

"They were in a pile, and all disconnected."

"Disconnected?"

"All connective tissue was gone and the bones were piled up against the base of the wall."

"How do you know they were human bones?"

"I saw a hand and a foot, and two human skulls. Anyone would recognize those."

The sheriff shrugged. "Sounds like you're describing the old Fedder Prairie cabin. You say the well was close to the cabin?"

"The well was below the porch. I saw a stained glass window in the cabin door. That's what caught my eye and drew me closer. The door has pulled away from its frame. It leans back, under the corner of the roof. It's almost covered by wild grass and moss. When I stepped closer, the earth gave way and I dropped into a hole. Luckily, it was only about twelve feet deep and the bottom was covered with leaves and pine needles . . . and those bones. The pile of bones broke my fall."

"How'd you get out?"

Maya shuddered. "There's a narrow tunnel in the bottom of the well. I crawled through it and came out beside Karl Schaff's property, by a white rail fence where someone has cut down trees. It was quite a ways to crawl."

"Manmade tunnel, or natural?"

"I'm not sure. All I had for light were matches. I almost used them up."

"I'll call and have my deputy and a volunteer take a look-see. We'll need to fill in that well after we recover the bones. We can't have dangerous holes near a popular hiking path."

"Heavens no," Elly said. "I had no idea there was an old well there."

"Quite a ways is right, Ms. Pederson," Sheriff Wimple said. "The Schaff property line is a quarter mile from the Fedder Prairie cabin." Sheriff Wimple tapped the brim of his hat. "Ladies." He returned to his car. A moment later he coasted down the driveway, a drizzling rain blurring his brake lights. From the living room Maya watched his car crossing the bridge and climbing the hill to the road. She wanted to go back to the old well with him, to hear him admit the bones were human, but Sheriff Wimple didn't invite her.

"For petesake, Sheriff," Maya grumbled. "I saw the bones with my own eyes." She returned to the kitchen. *He must think I'm stupid.*

"Sheriff Wimple is probably excited to finally have some real investigating to do. I've lived here a long time and this is the first time I've heard of human bones being found." Elly entered the kitchen with a wide roll of paper in one hand. She spread it across the table, weighing it down with the blue vase, her teacup and salt and peppershakers. "I found this old map in the closet under the stairs. It shows the property lines and neighboring wells," she said. "The Fedder Prairie well isn't shown here, but then, that place was already falling down when Harlan and I bought this farm. I never even thought about a well being there. Maybe I should've. Harlan bulldozed over the old outhouse, though. I do remember that. There wasn't much to it."

"If he had bulldozed the cabin he would have destroyed the well under the porch," Maya said.

"There's a lot to be said for hindsight," Elly said. "Oh, and I found a picture of Harlan." Elly slipped a black and white photo from her shirt pocket and dropped it on the table. It was small and faded and trimmed with wavy edges the way photos were developed in the forties. Maya leaned closer.

"That's him?" Maya pointed to a tall lanky man at the end of a row of five people. "Uncle Harlan?"

"Oh heavens no," Elly said. "That's Frank Zoubek, one of Harlan's bosses. This is Harlan." She pointed to a slender man at far end. He was a foot shorter than the other men.

"Uncle Harlan's face is shadowed by his hat." Maya sighed, disappointed.

"I'll keep looking for more photos. I remember one in particular that shows his face real good."

"Elly, do you think the wells that Uncle Harlan bulldozed over need to be filled in, to make them safe?"

"I don't know, honey. Sheriff Wimple said the county will take care of that."

Maya nodded. "Guess I'll get busy in the skylight room now."

Three hours later, the knotty pine wood paneling in the skylight room glowed from cleaning and polishing. The carpet in the center of the room was shampooed and even though damp, appeared three shades lighter.

"There's an odd smell in that room," Maya told Elly. "Maybe it will fade as the carpet dries."

"Odd smell?"

"Yeah, sort of musty. I don't know, a little like garden soil mixed with a wet dog smell." She wrinkled her nose. "But at least that rug is clean. Even the shelves are clean. We sold all the books and knickknacks at the garage sale so the cupboards are empty too. There's nothing in there. Not a thing. I climbed the stepladder and checked all around the skylight, thinking there might be a leak and that smell could be mold, but I didn't find anything. If you'll ask Coty to clean the moss and the pine needles off the skylight, it will brighten up that room quite a bit."

Elly nodded. "Will do."

"What's the matter, Elly? You look sad."

"Nothing important really. I just keep thinking about Harlan. Cleaning up around here, moving things out, selling things he used to look at . . . things he bought for the farm . . . things he touched . . . they bring back memories. Not all memories are good but a lot of them are. I sure miss him. We were happy together."

"Want to talk about it?" Maya asked. "Talking helps. I have someone to talk to when I'm feeling low."

"Yeah, sometime soon, honey. Not now though."

"It can't be easy, leaving your home after so many years, but try to think about the good things ahead, like living in that retirement complex with your friend, Judith. You're looking forward to that, aren't you?"

"Yes. Judith is a good friend, and she has other friends there too. We might have fun, all of us."

Maya nodded. "It looks like the rain has let up and the sun is coming out again. Maybe I'll go for a short walk."

"Stay away from old farmsteads," Elly said. "Stay on the trails."

Maya put away the cleaning supplies and set the rented rug shampooer on the back porch. Coty had offered to get it back to Ace Hardware before the end of the day. She washed her face and hands, pulled on her boots, gloves, and slipped on her hooded jacket.

"Back in an hour." Maya entered the basement. She sprinted to the outer door with its opaque window. She held her breath, not wanting to inhale the mausoleum odor. Outside, the big leaves were soggy with rain, beaten down into the corner of the foundation, a slimy pile of brown and green. Maya strode across the yard and then followed the slope to the driveway where it entered the trees. There, the driveway dropped down into the giant firs. Her boots clomped along the side of the driveway, between the grassy center strip and the giant ferns, salal and huckleberry. She planned to walk all the way out to the road and back again, three quarters of a mile each way.

Nearby, a red-winged blackbird sang. Maya often spotted them where cattails grew, the showy birds clinging to the fluffy cattail heads with the sun reflecting off their indigo-black wings, their shoulders resembling bloodstains. The only other sounds was that of enormous water drops falling from high branches and hitting lower leaves or the muddy driveway with heavy *splats*. The air smelled washed. It had been a cool May so far, but Maya didn't mind. She paused and inhaled before she continued walking.

The previous day's incident with the well and the crawl through the narrow tunnel seemed more like a bad dream now that the sun was shining so bright and the birds were singing. Maybe all the effort she put into cleaning the skylight room would ensure she slept well later this evening, instead of having to rely on sedatives. She needed to check her med journal again, to keep track of how often she dipped into the prescription, just to cope. She also recorded in the back of the notebook, everthing she and Elly accomplished each day and things they talked about.

She paused again, the dark image of the well and the tunnel flashing through her mind. She heard the words of the crawler who had followed her. She had not mentioned him to anyone. No one would believe it anyway. Was this the kind of thing that had driven her father to do what he did? Had he seen things like that? Things that can't possibly be real? "Does Elly?"

Like everything else in her life, the farm visit was flawed. Her expectations had been high and she was somewhat disappointed. Also, she worried about Elly. Maya had arrived only three weeks ago and in that time Elly had exhibited some bizarre behavior. Especially her sudden, occasional, personality change. Maya and Elly were blood relatives. If her aunt saw Harlan in the house five years after his death, did that explain why *she* saw a green, glowing, tattooed boy in the upstairs hallway? Was Benson right? Was she nuts? Her own father had committed suicide in an asylum. Elly, her father's older sister, was disturbed, no question about that. Maya shook her head and continued her walk.

"Damn you, Benson. I hope you do kick down Elly's door and I hope she blows you away with her shotgun, and I hope I'm there when it happens." Maya's boots splashed to a stop in a puddle. She slapped her palms over her mouth. "No I don't." *What a horrible thing to wish for!*

It was obvious by the smirk on his face Sheriff Wimple had doubted her story. Did he doubt there were bones at the bottom of the well, or did he doubt her ability to distinguish human bones from animal bones? Did he assume she imagined it? Did he think she was stupid—or crazy?

"Yeah, right, Sheriff. You and the horse you rode in on."

Maya spotted a gap in the undergrowth and narrow deer trail. She followed the trail with enormous drops of water hitting her hood and shoulders. Drenched ferns soaked the knees of her jeans.

She continued along the path until a glinting light made her blink. The sudden, bright sunlight reflected off something in the undergrowth, from beneath a pile of fir limbs and behind the cattails. The limbs had had been there a long time. They were a gray color and even though wet from the recent downpour, they looked brittle. Maya stepped closer but water leaked inside one boot. She stepped back. Between where she stood and the shiny object was a mushy pond clogged with tall grass. A few wild yellow irises glowed amidst cattails. Her boots would fill with pond water if she tried to cross.

Maya worked her way around the marshy pond, lifting blackberry vines from her sleeves and pushing away dripping hazelnut branches. She ducked under a vine maple and arrived behind the pile of dead limbs. She halted in surprise when sunshine glanced off rusted metal and chrome. She recognized the rear end of a gray car. The license plate and its frame were gone but she knew the shape of that trunk. It was a 1942 Ford two-door coupe. Back in high school a friend of Maya's had spent all his time and money restoring one just like it, except his had been candy-apple-red.

A pile of branches blocked any view of the car's dark interior. Maya stepped closer but icy water trickled into her boot again. She backed up and returned to the farm. She banged on the bunkhouse door but Coty didn't answer. Maya pulled her boots off on the back porch and entered Elly's kitchen in wet socks.

"Already back from your walk, sweety?" Aunt Elly stood in the dining room entrance, her tiny silhouette framed by the bay window.

"I came across a car in a pond and came back to get Coty. Maybe he can see if there's anyone inside, but he wasn't in the bunkhouse. Should I call Sheriff Wimple?"

"Oh dear. I don't know." Elly put one hand to the side of her face. "Where is this car you found?"

"In a marshy little pond on this side of the driveway. The entire front end of the car is under water. Only the trunk sticks up, and most of that is buried under dead branches."

"Oh dear," Elly said again. "What will people say? Where again? Near the driveway?" Elly asked.

"It's right where the driveway drops down toward the stream, but I didn't see a place where a car slid off the driveway. I guess I should go back and look again."

Maya lifted her jacket from the back of the chair and grabbed her gloves.

"Let me get us both some dry boots and I'll go with you." Aunt Elly gathered outdoor clothing from the pantry wall and boots from the stairs closet and followed Maya down the driveway.

"The car must have slid off the driveway a long time ago, and down into the bog. I can't get close enough to see if anyone was inside," Maya said. "Just a step or two off the trail, the water is knee deep."

A minute later, Maya pointed to the side of the driveway above the pond. The dense undergrowth had grown back since the accident.

"This must be where the car went over," Maya said. "Elly, wait here while I go back down to where I spotted it from below."

Maya climbed around behind the pile of branches. She stepped to the car's bumper and then crawled across the car's roof. She stretched down and peered through the driver's side window.

"It's really dark inside, but I don't see anyone."

"Climb back here, honey," Elly said. "I don't want that pond to swallow the car while you're on top of it."

Maya returned to the driveway. "Should we phone the sheriff?"

"Maya, I'm not sure. Fedder Prairie is over a mile from here, so I don't care about what was found there, but I don't want Sheriff Wimple snooping around this farm. Let's wait a while before we tell him we've found a car in the pond, okay? That car has been there a mighty long time, maybe fifty years?"

"I suppose it doesn't matter if we wait a while."

Elly chewed her lower lip. "Let's give it until the end of summer, Maya. By then, maybe Coty'll spot it and he can be the one to phone the sheriff. Better Coty than you or me, don't you agree?"

It'd been less than twenty-four hours since Maya described finding the bones at the bottom of the well, and she didn't like the way Sheriff Wimple had looked at her, as if he doubted her intelligence. Or her honesty. She didn't want to explain a second incident so soon after the first. She nodded.

"Okay."

• • •

That night at bedtime, Maya locked the back door, unlocked it, and locked it again. She drew the curtains. The little stove window glowed orange from hot coals, but there were no flames. The kitchen was toasty. She counted six steps to the table and sat down, appreciating the silence. Silence was calming, even when she felt both exhausted and hyper from a day like today. She felt a muscle spasm in her eye. She rubbed her eye but it twitched again. Her left calf quivered, as did her little finger, and right hand.

Aunt Elly'd left the miniature lamp on in the dining room. Maya remained at the kitchen table for several minutes, appreciating the warmth and silence, and the lamp's soft glow. She pressed her twitchy eye every few minutes and stretched her calf muscles. The kitchen had become her favorite room. It was the heart of the house. There was heat, food, water—a clock.

Now her index finger twitched. Maya pressed her palms against the tabletop. When she released them, both fingers twitched again. She glared at them. "Oh, just stop it!"

Maya'd never been in any legal trouble, not even a parking ticket or a traffic violation. She'd been three minutes late to work once. Her boss patted her on the shoulder and said, "I've been late before, Maya. It happens sometimes. It's okay. Calm down." Were her anxieties so obvious? What did her coworkers see?

Maya passed through the dining room and counted the eight steps to the landing. Turned. Climbed fourteen more, dreading the green, glowing boy in the upstairs hallway. His pleading eyes and desperate whispers made her feel guilty for some reason. The way he held his hands out, begging.

She hated to admit it, but she wished he would go away. *I can't help him.*

When she arrived on the top step, the hall was empty. Maya washed her face and brushed her teeth in the bathroom because that's what she did every evening. The rituals were important. The rituals kept things normal. The rituals gave her a sense of control. They protected her, at least that's how it felt. Inside though, just beneath the surface, Maya knew they didn't help at all. Dr. Conover said, "They're simple performances, Maya, not magic."

"Crap happens," she told the wide-eyed woman in the full-length mirror. Even with the rituals and little ceremonies, crap happened—but what would happen if she stopped the rituals? How bad would things get if she abandoned the little ceremonies? Would she be under investigation by Sheriff Wimple because she'd found a car, maybe with human remains inside? Maya turned and studied her pale reflection in the medicine cabinet mirror and whispered, "I've never been a person of interest before."

Maya dotted her raw wounds with antiseptic and stretched clean bandages across her elbows and knees. She soothed her face and hands with moisture lotion, threw her clothes into the hamper, and pulled on her pajamas. At the last moment, she opened the medicine cabinet, grabbed the prescription bottle, and rolled a little white pill into her palm. She gulped it down with tap water before glancing at the clock on the counter. Twelve-thirty. Maya tiptoed down the hall and into her room. After locking the hall door she turned on the closet light, left its door ajar and then climbed into bed. She flicked off the bedside lamp.

There could be a sixty-year old corpse inside that 42-Ford, a corpse with his face and scalp eaten away by rats, his naked skull with a bullet wound, and bloodstains blackened with age on the driver's seat.

Why am I dwelling on that? There's no reason.

Maya dozed off and awoke with a start, hearing Benson's distant laugh. She listened again but heard nothing except a low whistle of air through the half-inch open window. With closed eyes she saw sunlight glint off old chrome fenders. She saw dead branches and dripping leaves. She felt her boots fill with icy water.

She opened her eyes. It had to be the wee hours of early morning. It was as if she had not slept at all. Her shoulders, thighs and calves ached, and when she straightened, her bandages pulled the scabs from her raw knees. She pulled the top sheet up and folded a cuff down over her chest. Her torn fingernails stung.

"Don't leave me here." The whisper came from the hallway, outside her door. "Help me. Please!"

Maya squeezed her eyes closed. "I'll try," she whispered. And then she said it again, louder, "I don't know how, but I'll try," and finally she slept.

Chapter Fifteen

"Harlan called my name again," Aunt Elly said. "Twice in the middle of the night."

Maya handed Elly a mug of black tea before refilling the kettle and returning it to the wood stove. "Just your name? Nothing else?"

"Nothing else."

The phone rang and Maya grabbed the receiver. "Hello?"

"Sheriff Wimple here. Am I speaking to Maya Hammond?"

"Maya Pederson."

"I stand corrected. I have some news regarding the bones at the bottom of the well—Ms. Pederson."

"Okay." Maya held her breath.

"As we suspected, they've been down there a long time . . . we're thinking forty-five, maybe even fifty years, and we're running DNA tests, but I doubt we'll learn who they are after this much time. If you recall anything else, anything you forgot to mention before, please jot it down and call me. Talk to you soon."

Maya heard an abrupt click as Sheriff Wimple hung up and Maya glared at the receiver. He had a way of insulting her without saying a word. "It's rude to hang up before I can reply."

Aunt Elly said. "I voted for him, ye know."

"He makes me feel like I've done something wrong. Like I am responsible for the bones at the bottom of the well. All I did was find them."

"Aw honey," Elly said. "Everyone is a person of interest until the case is solved. I heard that on CSI."

"It feels different when you're the person of interest, though" Maya said. "I don't like the way Sheriff Wimple looks at me. Like he's searching for something . . . anything . . . that proves I'm guilty. He even laughed at something I said, when I was completely serious. When I offered my opinion, he smirked. He either thinks I'm a killer or that I'm stupid. Maybe both."

"Don't take offense, honey. Sheriff Wimple told me that everyone's a sleuth these days."

Maya sat back down at the table and sipped room temperature tea. "I suppose everyone is."

"An amateur sleuth?"

"A person of interest."

Aunt Elly nodded. "Things are different now than they were seventy-five years ago. It's practically impossible to kill someone and get away with it these days. I watch Forensic Files too, ya see. There's ways of trackin' people now that they didn't have back when I was young. Ways of linkin' someone to a crime scene." Elly's head motion changed from a nod to a slow shake. "They have these lights that can detect old blood that's been washed and painted over, and radar that looks underground without anybody havin' to dig. Gracious. Pretty soon science will be solving crimes that happened hundreds of years ago."

"Thousands," Maya said. "They now know that King Tut had malaria, sickle-cell anemia and a broken leg. He suffered from a hereditary bone degeneration in one foot, a deformity that caused him so much pain he could hardly walk. Can you imagine? He was only nineteen when he died."

"That's what I mean about science," Elly said. "Killers don't stand a chance now days."

"A prosecutor still has to prove that the suspect committed the crime though, and that it wasn't an accident. Circumstantial evidence isn't enough."

"I'd rather be dead than locked up," Elly said. "I couldn't stand living in a cell."

"Me neither," Maya sipped her tea. "A prison cell is only eight by ten, isn't it? That's an awfully small space to spend the rest of one's life, isn't it?"

"Tup . . . tup . . ." Elly muttered.

"What? Elly?"

"Tup." Elly tilted to one side and Maya knelt and caught her before she hit the kitchen floor.

The back door opened and Coty stepped inside with a surprised expression. "What's going on?"

"Call 911. Elly's either fainted or had a stroke."

• • •

Coty drove. Aunt Elly sat propped up in the back seat of Maya's car, strapped in, with her lolling head supported by a travel pillow. Maya sat beside her, holding her hand and uttering encouragement even though she doubted Elly heard her.

The ambulance met them three miles away at the county highway and all of them headed toward the Olympic Memorial Hospital in Port Angeles. Maya and Coty followed the ambulance. Once there, Coty and Maya paced the waiting room for several hours before a doctor told them, "She's stable, but we want to keep her overnight. Go home. I'll phone when we know more."

Neither Maya nor Coty spoke during the first fifteen minutes of the drive home. The sky looked like it might rain. Coty broke the silence by clearing his throat.

"I need to confess something," he said.

Maya glanced sideways. Coty clenched his jaw. She waited.

"I've been investigating you."

"Me?" she said. "Well, find out anything interesting?"

"I didn't trust Elly's memory of you. I did a records check. Criminal history. Arrest records. You're squeaky clean. Your record is so clean it's . . . boring."

Maya leaned forward, frowning. Coty changed his grip on the wheel and continued. "I checked you out because I didn't know you from Adam, and Elly's judgment is questionable at best, especially lately."

"Questionable is a good word. Elly trusted a complete stranger just because he offered to fix her rotten porch."

"My point exactly."

"And I'm supposed to trust you?" Maya asked. "I don't know you from Adam either."

"But do you?"

"Do I what?"

"Trust me."

"Not so sure. Especially now."

Coty dug in his jacket pocket and pulled out a laminated card. He handed it to her.

She studied the card. "You're a private investigator?"

"Licensed and bonded."

"This card doesn't prove anything. Anybody could have this printed up."

"True." Coty grinned. "You can have me checked out if you like."

"Can you recommend a good private investigator for that?"

Coty smiled. "Several."

"Why are you at Elly's?" Maya asked. "Why did you come here?"

"It's a sad story and it might take some time to tell."

"We're an hour away from home. Is that enough time?"

Coty drummed his fingers on the steering wheel, back and forth like chords on piano keys. "My nephew, Danny, is missing. He had a big argument with his parents . . . my sister and brother-in-law. Typical stuff for a seventeen year old but they didn't think he'd pack his things and leave during the night. It's been four months and not a single phone call to let them know he's okay. My sister isn't sleeping. Not eating. She's living on sedatives."

Aren't we all?

"I tracked Danny to Port Angeles. Some street kids there recognized his photo. He hung out with them for a while and he had a part-time job cleaning a Texaco garage. Minimum wage—a place to sleep and wash up. The manager told me Danny was a reliable worker. He was never late and as honest as anyone he's ever hired."

Coty's voice cracked. He stared straight ahead, clenching his jaw again. "And by the way, my name isn't Coty. It's Wayne C. Matheson. You didn't notice that, on the card?"

"No, I just looked at the photograph." Maya lifted the card again and read the name. She twisted as far as the seatbelt allowed, leaning forward, eyeing his profile. "After calling you Coty for a whole month, I'm supposed to start calling you Wayne?"

"Elly was so convinced I was this guy named Coty, I just let her think it. Sometimes she'd call me Coty and I wouldn't answer; my mind already on something else. She must have thought I was rude."

"No, Aunt Elly thought you were either weak minded or hard of hearing."

"That goes along with my cover, I guess."

"You do realize, don't you? I can't call you Wayne, at least not when Elly is around."

"That's right. Just keep calling me Coty."

In silence, Maya stared out the passenger window for several minutes. She spotted a woman beside a rural mailbox who reminded her of her mother, and seeing the woman, reminded Maya she owed her mother a phone call. People often told her she resembled her mother. It was meant as a compliment, because Jennifer Pederson was a fine looking woman.

Will I look like Mama when I'm sixty? Or that creature on her front porch, wearing her clothes?

"You're awfully quiet all of a sudden. What are you thinking about?" Coty asked.

"I'm thinking about being boring."

"I never said you were boring. I said your record is. You're not boring . . . at all."

Chapter Sixteen

Maya heated a can of chili and she and Coty shared it along with leftover cornbread. It was ten-thirty P.M., the full moon lit up the driveway almost as bright as a hazy afternoon. Maya felt exhausted as she filled the sink with hot water and slid the dishes down through the bubbles.

Coty said, "I'd appreciate it if you'd keep my profession a secret, at least for a while longer. It makes my job easier if people think I'm an itinerant handyman. People stop talking to me if they discover I'm a private investigator."

"So I'm not a suspect anymore?" Maya asked.

Coty smiled. "Are you hiding something?"

"No. I couldn't kill anyone, not even if I thought they were a threat," Maya said, picturing Benson when he tried to strangle her. She washed and rinsed two butter knives and held them above the drain rack, trying to imagine driving them deep enough into someone's chest to hit something vital. She nestled them into the drainer, turned, and leaned against the counter with a sigh.

"Sure you could. We all can, under the right circumstances." Coty pushed his chair back. "You're probably exhausted after a day like this, so I'll head on out to the bunkhouse. Get some rest. I'll see you tomorrow morning." He let himself out and strode across the driveway.

Maya washed the chili pot, the bowls, bread plates and two spoons, and added them to the butter knives in the rack. Nine items, an uneven number. She took a glass from the cupboard and washed it, setting it beside the pot in the rack. Ten items. An even number. A safe number. A part of the ritual. Part of the ceremony.

"No. I don't do this anymore." She dried the clean glass and returned it to the cupboard. "It's time to fight the obsession. Time for the rituals to end."

She checked the lock on the back door and hesitated for a long second. "Walk away," she told herself. "You don't need to recheck it—a lock you just locked." She stepped back. Then forward again.

But can I climb the stairs and fall asleep without the lock ritual? She checked the lock on the basement door, sensing something wrong, and it wasn't because she was breaking the compulsive ritual. The hairs on the back of her neck rose. Her ears tingled. She shivered as a cold draft blew a dust ball from under the basement door. The dust ball trapped itself against the toe of one sock.

Maya turned the black enamel doorknob both directions, pulling hard. Testing was the only way to know for sure. The ritual. The ceremony. The doorknob felt freezing cold in her palm. Something was wrong. She withdrew her hand and glared at the black doorknob. She shuddered as the doorknob turned again, on its own—all the way to the left, all the way to the right. Something leaned hard against the door from the other side. The ancient wood groaned. The hinges strained. Someone stood on the basement's top step, inches away, putting his full weight against the door.

"Coty?" Maya pressed her ear against the door. The draft grew stronger, gusting through the half-inch gap at her feet. The door was so cold it made her cheekbone ache. She stepped back as the door's surface frosted over. The black doorknob grew a coating of ice.

"Who's there?" Maya asked.

"Open the door." It was a baritone voice—not Coty's. "Do you want your watch?"

My watch? Her voice quivered when Maya said, "Leave it on the steps. I'll get it in the morning."

Maya heard a sharp snap of old wood and the basement step groaned again. The draft reversed and sucked the dust ball back under the door. The ice crystals on the doorknob melted and dripped on the linoleum at her feet. A thin piece of ice slid down the face of the door. She ran to the kitchen window above the sink and parted the curtains. Coty's windows glowed with cheerful light. His shadow crossed from one bunkhouse curtain to another. He could not have run the length of the basement, out the back door, up across the driveway to the bunkhouse in such a short time. It wasn't Coty that made the basement steps groan. It wasn't Coty's voice demanding she open the door.

Maya stared at the yellow basement door for several minutes, her heart hammering against her ribs. With shaking hands she stoked the woodstove with a madrona log, the largest she could find in the woodbox. It was a dry, seasoned log. It would last until the wee hours. She inched the damper down. The log would burn slow and hot and leave a nice bed of coals for morning. It would keep the night chill away. What else would the flickering flame keep away?

Maya didn't like the thought of sleeping alone upstairs at the far end of the hallway. She filled the tea kettle and slid it across the surface of the wood stove. The wet bottom of the kettle sizzled on the hot surface. She would make a mug of instant cocoa before heading upstairs; a large, boiling mug of cocoa. It had never occurred to her she might spend a night or two alone here. Never once had she considered that.

Coty was thirty feet away, across the driveway, but calling to him meant unlocking the kitchen door. It meant opening it and stepping outside, alone. In the dark. Maya parted the curtains above the sink again, hoping to see Coty's silhouette. That would be reassuring, to know he'd hear her if she yelled, but now Coty's windows were dark. He was probably already asleep. He looked tired when he left. She wished she had thought to ask for his cell number.

The kettle hummed as it reached a low simmer, but Maya wanted it boiling hot. She hurried down the pantry hallway, through the skylight room and into the living room. Elly said the front door was always locked. No one exited or entered through that door in a decade, Elly said. The door led to a big outside porch and wide steps that dropped into an overgrown garden, a garden that sloped downhill toward pastures and a stream. Maya'd seen wild grass clogging the cracked walkway and moss bulging over the path's edges. Giant, lanky, rhododendrons touched tips from opposite sides of the path. She'd explored it not long ago. It was a jungle. An abandoned, overgrown garden. A neglected place.

Maya gasped at the sight of the safety chain hanging straight down. She rushed forward, grabbed the dead bolt and raked it downward, skinning her knuckles. She heard the sound of the bolt slamming in the mechanism. She turned the doorknob, pulled, and then pulled harder. It was locked tight. Her knees trembled. She fastened the chain. She wanted to test the lock again, but stepped away. Who had unlocked it, and when?

Now, all three doors were locked, the only entries according to Elly, but Maya suspected there was at least one other way in, somewhere. This was a big house and there were rooms she had never entered. There was the door at the end of the upstairs hall, two feet away from her bedroom door, a door that led to a steep flight of stairs with no railing. According to Elly. Sometimes Elly made sense and sometimes she didn't, and sometimes she became Mr. Elly. Who was Mr. Elly?

"Mr. Elly is—Harlan," Maya knew it was true the instant she said it. When under stress, Elly became Harlan. "She can't stand Harlan being dead. She can't let him go, so she brings him back the only way she can. She knows him so well, she can *be* him."

Tears stung Maya's eyes. Her aunt had been alone here for too long. Being alone the past five years had done something to Elly's mind. Twisted it. Warped it. And if Maya lived here alone, it would happen to her, too.

"But, I'm not going to stay here."

Maya returned to the kitchen. She spooned cocoa powder into a large mug and added boiling water, glancing at the basement door again. No frost. No ice. A couple small puddles on the linoleum was all. She turned off the light and headed upstairs. At the landing, something caught her eye. Something glimmered in the shadows. Her gold watch lay at the base of the sixth step, coated with dust as if no one had touched it in the four weeks it had been missing. Someone had to have put it there. Someone had to have touched it to leave it on the steps. How could they touch it without disturbing the dust?

Maya picked up her watch. It felt icy cold in her hand. The dust smudged her palm like damp ash.

Leave it on the steps…I'll get it in the morning. Her very own words.

She rubbed the watch against her sleeve as she climbed the stairs. Near the top, the green boy floated. She'd never seen his feet before. He wore baggy shorts down to the knees and below that, at the base of his gossamer legs, he wore Nike high-tops.

"Help me," he whispered. "Please." He floated back and dissolved into the wall behind him.

How long, Maya thought, had he been trapped in this house waiting for someone, anyone, to see him? To hear him calling out? How long? Decades? Is he even real? Or is it my sick imagination?

Twenty years ago kids didn't dress like that. They didn't have tattoos or nose rings. They didn't wear baggy, satin shorts and Nike high-tops twenty years ago.

Maya shivered as she undressed and dropped her clothes into the bathroom hamper. She bathed as fast as she could in three inches of hot water, dried off, grabbed her watch, and returned to the hallway wrapped in her towel. The door at the far end swung open without a sound. Maya's damp, bare feet squeaked to a stop on the hardwood floor.

The green boy appeared. He struggled against an invisible force and then his green glow was swallowed again by the black air of the stairwell. The door swung around and closed behind him and Maya ran into her room and locked the door behind her. She climbed into her pajamas. Trembling, she refastened her watch around her wrist. From now on she would only take it off when she bathed. She snapped the watch's safety chain. It would not get lost again. Somehow, having her watch on her wrist made her feel in control, as if she'd reclaimed a small part of her life, the strong part, the part before she ever saw a green boy or heard voices from behind ice-coated doors. Knowing the correct time put her in control of her schedule. Keeping to a schedule meant she was lucid. Cogent. Logical. Logical meant she was rational and that was the same as sane. It all started with the watch.

With her closet door ajar and its interior light painting a golden wedge across the hardwood floor, Maya raised her window shade all the way up. Moonlight reflected off the cedar shake roof outside. This was the third night in a row without rain. She propped herself up in bed and pulled the covers up to her collar bone.

Maya sipped her cocoa and felt the shivers subside. *None of this is real. None of it.* There'd been no voice at the yellow basement door. There'd been no frost on its painted surface, no ice on the doorknob. No puddles on the floor. She was imagining things again, that's all. Dr. Conover warned her about this. While under stress relapses were common. Just because she'd left her abusive husband and her dead-end life behind, it didn't mean all the symptoms would vanish overnight. Recovery was a slow process, a difficult process. It would take time to heal. It would take time to turn off the images and the voices. Time to leave the little ceremonies behind. She would put forth more effort, and she would win this fight.

"Give me a call, Maya," Dr. Conover had said. "I'm here for you." But Dr. Conover's office was in Tacoma, a three-hour drive away. She would phone Dr. Conover tomorrow, not so late at night. Tomorrow. That was soon enough.

Maya lifted the lace curtain. "No ring around the moon," she whispered. "No rain tomorrow."

Even though she felt weary and tired, it was after two A.M. before she dozed, and when she awoke in the morning, she recalled no dream. Without dreams, sleep was never satisfying. There seemed to be no passing of time without dreams.

Through her window the tops of the Douglas fir trees were tipped with golden morning light. She lifted her wrist to check the time, but her wrist was bare. Her watch was gone.

Chapter Seventeen

"Thought you'd want to know, I'll probably release your aunt tomorrow," Dr. Framish's voice sounded nasal over the phone, "I'll let you know early tomorrow morning. She's doing well, though. We want to run a few more tests because, apparently, your aunt hasn't visited a doctor since she was a child."

Maya changed the sheets on Elly's bed and vacuumed and dusted her aunt's room. Aunt Elly was recovering quickly.

Elly's closet door stood wide open. Maya stuck her head inside. The oval rug, the hamper and a tiny pair of pink satin slippers were the only things on the closet floor. Elly's clothes hung on a single rod down the left side of the closet. A shoe organizer with eight slots hung closest to the door. Four of the slots were empty. Maya slid one pair of shoes out. Size four. They looked like children's shoes they were so small.

Elly's wardrobe totaled two flowered nylon dresses and three pair of slacks—blue, black, and brown; and three blouses in white, blue, and pink. "That's everything?"

At the far end of the closet stood a tallboy dresser. On top of the dresser sat a miniature lamp with a mica shade. Beside the lamp was a satin envelope holding a pair of knee-high stockings. The stockings were folded flat and looked unworn.

The bottom drawer was tight and opened with a screech. It contained a dozen pair of wool socks and cotton underwear, folded in neat stacks on the left side. The right side of the drawer was empty. In the drawer above that lay three cardigan sweaters, all gray, all stacked on the left side. The middle drawer held two pair of pajamas and one nightgown, its bodice and sleeve ruffles yellowed with age. The drawer second from the top shrieked as Maya forced it open. It held one pair of men's slippers, seldom worn, a pair of men's pajamas, a pair of boxer shorts and one white t-shirt, all in one clear, zippered bag. Beside the bag were two, heavy flannel shirts, size small, folded. They looked almost new.

"You just can't let him go, can you, Elly?"

The top drawer refused to open. Maya checked all the way around the front and sides of the dresser but didn't find a release mechanism. She inched the dresser away from the wall and examined the backside. Nothing.

Maya rocked the dresser from side to side. She heard something solid and heavy sliding inside the top drawer. It sounded like two or three metallic things, sliding left and right. Tools? Shotgun parts?

"Maya?" It was Coty's voice, from downstairs. She shoved the dresser back against the wall and ran to the hall.

"Be right there, Coty." It was impossible to think of him as Wayne. She gathered up the sheets from the floor and hurried downstairs. Coty waited in the kitchen.

"Heard anything from the doctor?" he asked.

"Yes. Just a while ago. Elly can come home tomorrow, but we'll know for sure in the morning. The doctor said she's fine and didn't have a stroke."

Maya tapped the basement door with her toe and smiled at Coty. He opened the door for her and she threw the sheets to the bottom of the stairs before closing the door and locking it.

"Coty, do you know anything about lights that detect blood?" she asked. "Even old, dried blood, or blood that's been washed off or painted over?"

"Sure." He blinked. "Why?"

"I'm convinced someone died in this house," Maya said.

"Parts of this house were built a century ago. It wouldn't be unusual for someone to have died here at one time or another."

"Someone was murdered in that old well. I saw two skulls down there. I think one had a bullet hole in the temple."

"Sheriff Wimple is looking into that, but what makes you so sure someone died in this house?"

Maya chewed her lower lip. "Not just died. I think someone was murdered in this house."

There. I can't un-say it.

"Why do you suspect that?"

How would Coty react if she told him she heard voices? What would he say if she told him she saw a green boy in the upstairs hallway? Would he believe that someone—something—had crawled through the Fedder Prairie tunnel after her, calling to her, begging her to stay there in that underground burrow with him? She knew what to expect. She knew what would happen if she told him. She knew what Coty's expression would be, two seconds after she said the words.

Maya shook her head. "Never mind."

"No, tell me," Coty said.

"You wouldn't understand."

"Try me."

"No, because I told someone once, about something like this, and I know what happens."

"Really. You can tell me," Coty insisted.

"No. I told Benson, and he said I was nuts. I don't need someone else thinking that."

"But, I promise–"

"No, because you'll promise and you'll even mean it, but afterward you'd think to yourself . . . she's nuts. You might not say it . . . but you'd think it."

"You're seeing ghosts."

A moment passed before Maya asked. "Have you ever seen a ghost?" *That's evasive enough.*

Coty shook his head. "Nope."

"And no purple cows either, I suppose." She heard the irritation in her own voice.

"Purple cows? What? What are you talking about?"

"It means forget what I said. Forget about the blood light and about someone dying here. Forget everything I said."

"I'm not going to forget the possibility of murder."

Maya opened the stove's cast iron door and shoved a piece of pine inside. She wanted to tell Coty about the green boy, but couldn't say the words. Fear paralyzed her tongue. The two people she had told about hearing voices had turned against her, first Mama, and then Benson after they were married. Maya wouldn't make that mistake again. She wouldn't tell Coty anything.

"What does this ghost look like?" Coty asked.

"Green," Maya blurted. *Damn!*

"Green?"

"Transparent and . . . green."

Coty raised a brow.

They sat down at the kitchen table. "I saw my grandmother once, sixteen years after she died," Maya said. "I made the mistake of telling my mother. Afterward, Mom dragged me to a child psychiatrist."

Coty nodded.

Maya told herself to stop, right there, to say nothing more, but the words strew like marbles from a shattered jar. "I described my grandmother in detail, even how she called my mother by her nickname and what her voice sounded like. My mother's face turned white because she had never told me about my grandmother. I never saw my grandmother. Never met her. She died before I was born and my mother kept no photos of her. Mom never told me that her mother called her Maudy. Maude is my mother's middle name."

"So the doctor tried to convince you that you had imagined it, or dreamed it . . . that you hadn't really seen anything?"

"She's still trying."

"How often do you see this green apparition?"

"Four times so far."

"Male or female?"

"He's young. Mohawk hair. Nose ring. Brow ring. Baggy shorts and Nike high tops."

Coty stared at Maya for a moment, mouth open, looking as if he had a pinecone stuck in his throat. Then he leaned back in his chair, closed his eyes and sighed. "Aw hell." He dug in his back pocket, flipped open his wallet and held it across the table toward Maya. "Is this him?"

The photo was the exact image of the green boy upstairs, right down to those penetrating eyes. Coty's eyes. She recognized the family resemblance now.

"Your nephew?"

Coty nodded. "It's Danny, my sister's only child. After Port Angeles I tracked him to Graceville. Someone saw Danny hitchhiking on the road a half mile from here."

"I'm sorry, Coty. I wish I hadn't told you."

"I'm glad you did. I need to find out what happened, and why."

"How does one go about doing that?" Maya asked.

"Maybe we can start with that blood light you asked about."

"You have one?"

"No, but I know a hunter who uses one to follow wounded game."

"You don't have to have a permit to use one?"

Coty shook his head no. "Did Danny say anything to you?"

"The first time I saw him, his lips moved but I couldn't hear anything. Then later, in the middle of the night, he whispered, 'Don't leave me here'. Now, he usually just says, 'Help me.'"

Coty got up and leaned against the counter, staring out the window. His fingers gripped the sink's edge, the tendons in the backs of his hands bulging and flexing so tight his skin turned white and Maya wondered if he might pull the counter from the wall.

"If you see Danny again, tell him Uncle Wayne will find him and take him home." Coty stepped to the back door and opened it. He paused there, his back to Maya. "Okay?" Coty's voice cracked. He finished with a rough whisper. "Tell him I said that."

Chapter Eighteen

AFTER COTY LEFT, MAYA shoved Elly's sheets into the Maytag and pushed Hot / Large. The machine gurgled, filling with water. Steam floated up through the cool air. She added a scoop of soap and dropped the lid.

From the bottom step she studied the shadows in the back corner, far over to the right of the outside door at the end of the walkway. Over there the air was so black it looked like India ink. Unfathomable. Something gray moved in the murky air in that far corner. Something rustled, a sound like canvas against ice. Something sighed.

"Hello?" Maya called. She backed up one step. The step creaked beneath her foot. Behind and above, the flickering glow from the woodstove highlighted the top step and the open door. Overhead, the single light bulb flickered and dimmed. She called again. "Hello?"

Another deep sigh came from the shadows, along with the sound of something scratching and the sound of dirt dropping on dirt.

"Coty?" Maya backed up another step. She squinted into the blackness, at the gray thing, the thing bunching up on itself, round-backed, like a bear, digging, clawing, backing up and lunging forward. It looked bigger than before. It looked closer.

The flashlight was stuck to the side of the refrigerator at the top of the stairs. The flashlight would have helped but it was twenty feet away. Out of reach.

The basement's musty smell was trapped beneath the house by its mausoleum walls. The walls and floor held the stale, stagnant air motionless. Dead air. Imprisoned. Buried.

Nothing breathes down here. The only living things were rats, spiders and worms. Except for the concrete walkway the floor was all dirt. The worms were in the dirt.

What else was in the dirt? Who was that sighing? Who was digging over there? What was hunching its back, and lunging.

The smell changed. It smelled like fresh churned earth. It smelled like crops rotated and fallow fields plowed, like recent compost mixed with decayed crops, all returning to the soil, becoming soil, returning to what it was decades before.

Something was digging under the house. Did raccoons grow that big? What was that gray thing that bunched its back and rocked back and forth? That thing was bigger than a raccoon. It really was more like a bear, a bear caught in a trap and fighting hard to free itself, a bear thrashing and straining, ready to lose a claw or an arm in its struggle to escape. The bear moaned.

There was no way for a bear to get into the basement. The door at the other end was closed and locked. Maya was sure of that, having checked it yesterday and the day before that, from outside. She ran up the stairs and grabbed the flashlight. She pushed the button all the way to bright and headed back down, aiming the light into the shadows. Halfway down the stairs, she halted, open-mouthed. Her eyes widened.

The thing was not a bear. It was two people, pulling a third from the dirt. All three turned toward Maya's bright, flashlight beam, as if only then aware of her presence. They halted their struggle, staring over their shoulders, and Maya stared back—at skeletons, their bones stained by time and by their damp grave. Strips of rotten clothing clung to their shoulders and arms. Long, stained femurs stabbed the brown dirt floor. Three luminous skulls with empty eye sockets tilted left and then right, aimed in Maya's direction. The black sockets focused on her. A dull glow radiated from inside their craniums. The same dull glow exited their nasal slots and out through gaps in their teeth. The third skeleton struggled to pull his feet from the soil, flicking black dirt into the air. Clumps of dirt landed at Maya's feet.

Maya ran back up the stairs, dropping the flashlight on the top step in her haste. She slammed the door behind her and locked it. She heard the flashlight rolling and dropping, rolling and dropping, all the way down the eight wooden steps.

Maya ran upstairs to the bathroom. She grabbed the bottle of Lorazapam and rattled a pill into her palm. She tossed it into her mouth, leaned down, and gulped tap water straight from the faucet. She splashed cold water on her face and leaned, breathless and shaking against the sink.

"That didn't happen," she told her reflection. "You didn't see anything down there. Not anything real. Not anything."

● ● ●

"Mama?"

"Maya. It's good to hear your voice. How's things at the farm?" Jennifer Pederson's voice sounded cheerful, as if she had not missed Maya at all in the past month.

"Things are interesting. I thought Elly had a stroke, but apparently not. She spent two nights at the hospital, but she's coming home today."

"My goodness! That must have been upsetting. How are *you*, dear?"

"I'm fine, Mama." Maya crossed her fingers behind her back for telling a lie.

"Benson phoned," Mama said. "He wanted to know where you're at."

"Did you tell him?"

"I'm afraid I forgot that you asked me not to tell, so yes, he knows where you are. I told him you're helping your aunt get the place ready to sell." After a moment's silence, Mama added, "I'm sorry, Maya. It just flew out of my mouth before I stopped to think."

"That's okay. He would have found out eventually anyway. I've used my credit card twice. If he calls again, just tell him to forward my mail here."

"What does Elly have you doing up there at the farm?"

"Cleaning and painting mostly. She's getting rid of a lot of stuff, donating things to charities and we also had a yard sale. The house is almost empty."

"I'll need to have a garage sale pretty soon too."

"Any prospects on the house yet, Mama?"

"One couple has been back twice. So, maybe."

"Mama? Can I ask you something?"

"Certainly, dear."

"Did we ever have a kitten? Or did I just imagine that?"

"I don't remember ever having a cat, honey. Your father was allergic, remember?"

"Okay."

"I'm sorry, Maya, if taking you to Dr. Conover was traumatic. I didn't know what else to do."

"It's all right, Mama. Lately it seems like things are beginning to work themselves out. I've been able to tell the difference between what's real and what isn't."

"I'm so glad. When will you be coming home?"

"I wasn't planning on coming back to your house, Mama. I plan on getting an apartment downtown and looking for work within walking distance."

"That's logical."

Logical.

"Oh, I see Elly's handyman coming across the driveway, Mama. We're leaving now to go get Elly from the hospital."

"Call me again soon, Maya. Please?"

"Yes." Maya disconnected and opened the kitchen door.

"You ready?" Coty wore khaki slacks, a navy blue cotton sweater. His hair looked trimmed. He had nicked his chin shaving. A red dot marked the wound.

"Want to drive?" Maya asked. Benson always insisted on driving when they were together. It was a man thing, she guessed. The only time Maya drove was when she went somewhere alone.

"I'll drive if you don't want to," Coty said.

"Actually, I like to drive," Maya said. "You can drive coming back, okay?"

Moments later the Ford Edge rumbled across the wide wooden planks of the bridge and climbed the other side of the valley to the road. She glanced at Coty's attire.

"You look nice today." Her face burned and wished she hadn't said that.

"Thanks. I decided bringing Elly home is a bit of an occasion. Let's hope she remembers me."

Maya chuckled. "I'll introduce you if she doesn't."

Several minutes passed before Coty said. "You look nice too. First time I've seen you in a dress."

"Well, it is a special occasion."

Coty picked imaginary lint from his sleeve. "I have a confession."

Maya waited. "Another? What this time?"

"I lied when I said I've never seen a ghost. I've seen . . . things in the upper barn. They're difficult to describe, though."

Maya felt a sense of relief. She understood. There were no words to describe some of the things she had seen.

"You told me Danny looks green. The people in the barn are all gray. One guy's throat was cut from ear to ear. Blood-soaked shirtfront. Even his hands are black with old blood, like he tried to stop the bleeding by applying pressure. He scared the hell out of me. I ran all the way down the hill. Didn't sleep for forty-eight hours. All the others just look lost."

"When was this?"

"Two days after I arrived. Early February."

"Seen anything else since then?" Maya asked.

"Yeah, three Mexican men, standing outside the basement door."

"I was thinking—maybe you should come upstairs, around noon or midnight. That's when I see Danny. Maybe if he sees you, he'll communicate," Maya said.

"Okay." Coty sighed. "I never had nightmares before, and believe me, I've seen some bloody crime scenes in my day, but they pale in comparison to the stuff I've seen here, if what I see is real."

The memory of the three corpses pulling themselves from the dirt in the basement flashed before Maya's eyes. *I'm not going to try describing that.*

"Watch out!" Coty grabbed the steering wheel and they missed a mongrel dog by inches. In the rearview mirror Maya spotted the lanky dog loping, unscathed, along the shoulder of the road.

"He's okay," Coty said. "He looks like he's accustomed to dodging cars, and I'll be he knows exactly where he's going."

Maya drove for several minutes, her heartbeat finally returning to normal. "How much more work needs to be done around the farm?" Maya asked. "I mean repairs, before it can be sold?"

"The house is okay the way it is. I see no dry rot, no sign of termites. The place has good bones."

Maya grimaced.

"You know what I mean," Coty said. "The bunkhouse isn't worth saving except for the unit I'm in. It can be used as a guesthouse. The other four units are falling down. I'm done with repairs to the floor and toilet. The woodshed is okay, and so is the smaller barn. It's probably less than twenty years old. The upper barn though—" Coty shook his head. "It's rotting away, and as far as I'm concerned, it can be struck by lightning and burn to the ground. It's a nightmare up there."

Coty cleared his throat. "But as far as the farm in general, the well is fairly new. Nothing wrong with it. Elly had the water quality tested right after I arrived. The water's clean."

An hour out of Graceville, the clouds thinned to smears and the sun sent pillars of golden light into the surrounding forest. The Ford Edge hummed through a covered bridge, light flickering through the empty windows. Coty pointed at something up ahead.

"I haven't seen that in years," he said.

Two bald eagles tumbled, talons locked, wings and bodies in a falling dance until they were almost to the ground. At the last second, the two birds released each other and sped off in opposite directions. They perched in a pitchfork cedar snag forty feet from the side of the road.

"Beautiful," Maya said. "First time I've seen that in nature. I've seen it in films before."

The farther from the farm they drove, the more alive Maya felt, and more capable. She saw farmers working in their fields, children and dogs running across lawns. Flowerbeds screamed in primary colors. The farther away they drove from Aunt Elly's farm, the more unreal the ghosts seemed.

• • •

Dr. Framish met them on Level Four. "You're both caregivers?" he asked.

"No, but we both live at the farm with Elly," Coty said.

"I live inside the house with Elly," Maya explained. "Coty lives out in the bunkhouse."

"Bunkhouse? Like a cowboy?"

"It may have been a real bunkhouse at one time," Coty said. "But now there's no horses and no cattle. I do repairs and maintenance around the farm." Coty lifted one polished loafer. "No spurs."

Dr. Framish looked disappointed. "I understand you're related to Eleanor Pederson?" Dr. Framish fixed his gaze on Maya, crossing his arms. His thick spectacles made his gray eyes appear as if they hovered two inches in front of his face. His white hair was thick, wavy, and it covered his ears. His smile was a slit between thin lips, exposing on his short, upper teeth.

"I'm Elly's niece, Maya." Maya shook his hand. His hand was smooth, the fingernails short and flat with deep ridges. "Nice to meet you."

"I've signed her release papers. You can take her home. She seems a little unhappy and that's not unusual when someone is reminded they're mortal. Has she had something happen recently that's causing her stress? Some major change in her life?"

"She's made the decision to sell her farm and move into a retirement facility."

Dr. Famish nodded. "Quite normal then. It usually passes in a month or two. Keep her busy."

"I plan to stay with Elly until she's made the move. I'm helping her prepare the house for sale."

"Good, good." Dr. Framish slipped a card from his breast pocket and handed it to Maya. "That's my home phone and cell phone if you need to talk. A caregiver's job is exhausting."

"Thank you." Maya slid the card into her handbag.

"What's Elly's room number?" Coty asked.

"402," Dr. Framish said, pointing down the hallway.

"Thanks, Doc." Coty squeezed Maya's elbow and steered her down the hall.

"What's the rush?" Maya asked. "I wanted to ask him about Elly's home care."

"I felt like a big dumb fire hydrant, waiting for Dr. Framish to finish flirting with you. I'm sure Elly is eager to go home."

"Dr. Framish wasn't flirting."

"Are you kidding? Doctors don't give their home and cell numbers to people."

"It's for emergencies."

"Yeah, sure."

The door of room 402 stood wide open. Straight through was an oversize window. The room had a view of the bay and the Black Ball ferry as it arrived at the dock, shoving foam against the pilings.

"Hey there, gorgeous, you ready to go home?" Maya asked.

Elly turned with a smile. "I sure am, baby girl."

Coty picked up a blue folder from the bedside table. "Here ya go, Maya. Discharge papers and inside is a whole section on homecare." Coty handed the folder to Maya and then helped Elly to her feet. "You done harassing the doctors and nurses here?" Coty asked, grinning.

"I'll have you know I was as good as gold, Coty," Elly insisted. "But I've been worried about Harlan."

"Why? What about Harlan?" Maya asked.

"I tried phoning him but no one answered, even though I let it ring and ring and ring."

"You phoned the farm?" Maya glanced at Coty. He shrugged.

Elly nodded her cottony head. "Yes, but then Harlan surprised me with a visit, the sweetheart. He came to see me right here at the hospital," Elly continued. "He walked into this room in the middle of the night and kissed me on the cheek. It was so good to see him after all this time. I miss him so much."

Chapter Nineteen

Maya punched Dr. Conover's number while her hands trembled. She dreaded this call. Her connection dropped after the first ring. She tried again as she headed toward the second floor of the house. She halted beside the morning glory window on the upstairs landing. The window faced southwest, where two miles away a cell phone tower stood in the middle of a cow pasture.

She heard Dr. Conover's phone ringing and then the answering machine. Maya blurted, "Dr. Conover, this is Maya Hammond—uh, Maya Pederson. I'm having a few issues, same old stuff. You know . . . anxiety, sleepwalking . . . not sure about the sleepwalking but definitely nightmares. I need a refill on my Lorazapam. Can you fax it to the Bartell's in Graceville? I'm staying with my aunt here . . . she's seventy-six years old and needs my help so I'll be here for the summer, but—" The dial tone interrupted. Dr. Conover had a twenty-second time limit on her answering machine.

Maya slipped the phone into her cardigan pocket and leaned back against the wall. "She'll get the important part of my message."

Whenever she stood beside the morning glory window, she faced the door at the far end of the hall. She didn't fear Danny's ghost, but she didn't want to turn around and find him right behind her. That would be unnerving. She had not seen Danny since telling Coty about him four days ago.

It was now mid-June and Maya continued to wear sweaters or sweatshirts, unless she was in the kitchen. In the kitchen her upper lip beaded with sweat and she peeled off layers. When she passed through the dining room, she pulled the layers back on, shivering. Yesterday she saw frost on the china cabinet windows. She raised a finger and touched it. Her finger melted a hole in the frost.

"Or, did I dream that?"

The sound of a car in the driveway sent Maya racing back downstairs. She didn't want anyone banging on the backdoor with Elly napping on the living room sofa. Maya recognized Tony Bradley through the door window. He climbed from the car and waved.

"Hi," Maya said. "Come in."

"No, I'd better not. I've got my hiking boots on. Thought I'd tromp around the property if it's okay. I should have phoned first, but this was a spontaneous idea."

"I'm sure Aunt Elly won't mind. She's asleep right now or I'd ask her."

"Is she okay?"

"Doctor said it's stress. She's doing fine."

"Oh, glad to hear she's home already. I'll get going on my hike then and leave you both alone. I plan to head uphill first, to check out the view property." Tony pulled his cell phone from his pocket. "I'll take some pictures while I'm snooping around."

"Good luck getting a signal on your phone up there."

"I've had no trouble getting a signal there before. It's nice to see you again, Maya." Tony stepped back and zipped the front of his jacket up to his chin.

"Tony? Watch out for sink holes," Maya said. "There are some."

"I heard about that. Glad you're okay too."

Tony strode up the driveway toward the gate carrying a shovel in one hand.

Maya closed the door. "He heard about me falling into the old well?" What did he mean by, "Glad Elly's home already?" Did the whole town of Graceville know about Elly's stay in the hospital? Maya felt her face grow hot at the idea of being the subject of local gossip.

The old wall phone stuttered, and Maya jumped to answer it before it blared a complete ring.

"Hello?"

"Sheriff Wimple here. I have more news for you about those bones in the abandoned well."

"Okay."

"As I suspected, forensics decided they've been there for at least forty years. They're still unidentified at this point, but that tunnel you crawled through for a quarter mile is just one of a labyrinth of similar tunnels, mostly caused by erosion and the ground shifting. Most of them are dead-ends, only the one tunnel ends up where you found your way out. You were darn lucky, young lady. Darn lucky."

Crawling through that tunnel had been the most terrifying thing Maya had ever done, equal to Benson's hands around her throat. Equal to the skeletons in the basement. Some nights she had nightmares about the tunnel, the kind of dream that woke her up sweating and gasping and unable to sleep again until the sun came up. "I didn't feel lucky at the time, Sheriff."

Sheriff Wimple said, "We found another skeleton in one of the tunnels, someone who apparently tried to escape the well by crawling through like you did, but he never made it out. How'd you know which way to go?"

"I didn't know. I just guessed."

"Darn lucky, young lady, you were darn lucky." Sheriff Wimple hung up, again without saying goodbye.

Chapter Twenty

"**M**AYA?" ELLY CALLED FROM the living room where she napped on the sofa.

"You had a nice long nap, Elly. I walked out to the mailbox and back." Maya brought the new issue of Retirement Living and dropped it at Elly's elbow. "And here's a cup of chamomile tea."

"Thank you, baby girl. My mind feels sharp now, so maybe it's time I told you some things. You're the only person I'll ever tell these things to. It's best to do it while my mind is clear."

"Sure." Maya lowered herself into the big armchair beside the fireplace and balanced her tea mug on her knees. "You can tell me anything."

"It's about Harlan and me, about our life together. About things the two of us did. I was hoping no one would ever need to know any of this, but you need to know, and I need to tell someone."

"I know you loved Uncle Harlan," Maya said. "Practically all your life."

"Yes. I loved him. You see Harlan protected and defended me. When someone hurt me, he made them pay. He loved me."

"Someone hurt you?"

"Yes, but let me start at the beginning. It all began with a boy at school. His name was Grady Goode and he was meaner'n snot. He was a bully. Almost every day, Grady tormented and embarrassed me, starting in second grade when I was eight years old, not long after my mother died."

Maya gripped her hot tea mug and shivered. She recognized the familiar, cold expression on her aunt's face, the way Elly's upper lip hardened, the way it looked stiff and unmoving even while she talked. Like she talked through her bottom teeth.

"How did he embarrass you?" Maya asked.

"He called me Ugly Elly, always saying it loud so-as to make the other kids giggle. I knew they were afraid of him, and they were just trying to stay on his good side. Then, sometimes he'd shove me in the hallway. He'd come up behind me, reach around and knock things out of my arms. He poured a handful of sand down my dress at recess and rubbed some in my hair."

"He might have had a crush on you, Elly. That's how boys tease."

"It wasn't that, because when he pushed me down and I skinned my knees, he laughed. My knees bled and I cried, but he just laughed harder."

"Did you tell your teacher?"

Elly shook her head. "Nope. When she saw my skinned knees, I just told her I fell down. She sent me to the school nurse."

"What about your father? Didn't you tell him?"

"No, honey. He wouldn't have done anything. Instead, I told Harlan. One night after dinner, not long after the skinned knees happened, after I washed up the dinner dishes, Harlan appeared at the back door. I looked over and saw him on the back porch, all gray and sort of blurry looking through the screen door. It was dusk outside. He said, 'C'mon Elly. We're gonna pay Grady Goode a visit.'"

Maya didn't like the image of Harlan simply appearing at the back door. She almost told Elly to stop, but Elly said she needed to talk and Maya knew how that felt. Elly needed to share it, *and maybe I need to hear it*. Confession was part of the healing process. Nonjudgmental listening was an important part of any confession. Maya had never considered how often Dr. Conover heard distressing stories. *Stories that she'll carry around in her mind for a lifetime probably.*

"So, Harlan knew where Grady lived?" Maya asked.

"It was only a few blocks away. Harlan and me, we climbed over a picket fence and stood on a slope behind Grady's house, right beside a big maple tree with a rope swing. From there, we watched Grady through a window as he teased his little brother. His brother was only about four or five years old. He kept thumping his brother on top of his head with his knuckles. He kept it up until the little guy was in tears. I don't know where their parents were. Harlan asked me, 'Is that Grady?' I said yeah and then Harlan climbed the tree and untied the rope swing. He inched it about a foot to the left, behind the stub of a broken branch. After that, if someone grabbed the rope and ran and jumped with it, swinging way out over the steep slope, the rope reached that stubby branch and it flipped you right off, quick and hard, like the snap of a whip. Harlan showed me how it worked. He knew what would happen though, so when it flipped him off, he dropped straight down, landing on his feet because he was ready for it. But Grady didn't know." Elly paused and sipped her tea through a crooked grin. Her upper lip folded like a snarling dog.

"Did Grady get hurt?" Maya asked.

"Grady wore a cast on his left arm through all of October and November that year."

"That stopped his bullying then, right?"

"In December he started right up again. Even when I warned him he'd be sorry, he didn't stop."

"How long did this bullying go on?"

"Longer than it should have—until I was sixteen. Sometimes I managed to avoid him. I kept my eyes open. I'd walk clear around the school building, just to stay away from him."

Maya took another sip of tea but was afraid she would choke if she swallowed. She held the tea in her mouth, chilled by the direction the story was taking. Did she really want to know these things? Did she really need to know? She wanted to know about Elly, not Harlan. Maya wanted to learn about the bloodline. About heredity. Their family's history, but Elly started right where she left off.

"By then your father, Stephen, and Grady's little brother, had become friends. An odd coincidence, huh? I didn't like them being friends. I was afraid Grady would tease and torment Stephen the way he did me, but Stephen said he didn't. Grady kept after me though. I knew he'd never stop. I had to talk to Harlan about it again."

"To do what?"

"This is the part that's hard for me to talk about. It's gonna sound god-awful, I know, but I'm gonna tell you anyway, just the way it happened without leaving anything out. I have no excuses. I won't rose-color any part of the story. Remember, though, Maya, I was only sixteen. Okay?"

Maya folded her stocking feet beneath her in the armchair and wedged herself deep into the corner. She took a slow breath. "All right. Go ahead."

Elly closed her eyes. She also took a long, slow breath before beginning. "Grady's folks were often gone for days at a time. That's odd isn't it, to go off and leave two kids alone like that? Anyway, by that time Grady was sixteen like me, and his little brother's name was Gene. Gene and your father were both thirteen then, and they had gone somewhere together for the day, so Grady was home alone. Harlan and I climbed that same picket fence and we sat on the slope under that big maple tree. It was late May and it felt almost like summer. We sat there together, side by side, saying nothing for a long time, maybe an hour. I had already decided, whatever Harlan wanted to do, I'd go along with it. Harlan waited until it was dark and then he finally said, "Let's go." The back door wasn't even locked. We took off our shoes and walked right in, real quiet like. Grady was watching television, stretched out on the sofa in his underwear. Tidy whiteys, that's all he had on. I remember the soles of his feet were dirty, like he'd gone barefoot outside. He didn't see us coming, didn't hear us. He was facing the other way. Harlan walked right up from behind, leaned down, and slit his throat from ear to ear."

Maya sat straight up. "Elly!"

"I know. I know." Elly worried her hands in her lap, rubbing the thumb knuckles over and over until they were red. A minute passed. "I warned you it was an awful story. Awful—and what a mess. Grady grabbed his throat with both hands and rolled off the sofa. He scrambled to his feet and turned around, eyes bulging, choking and spitting blood. He pissed himself. I remember that. Then he dropped to the floor and thrashed around for a few seconds until I guess he passed out. There was a lot of blood. It soaked into the carpet, forming a wider and wider circle. Tan carpet, big red stain. 'Let's go,' Harlan said."

"You've never told anyone before? No one?"

"Who would I tell? Harlan was the only one I ever told my secrets to." Elly paused and rubbed her forehead. "Harlan insisted Grady got what he deserved."

"But what . . . I mean later . . . who found him?"

"Gene and Stephen came back from wherever it was they went. It was Stephen who actually found Grady's body. I didn't mean for that to happen, you know. My own little brother?"

"What did he say about it?" Maya asked.

"Stephen? He never said a word about it, not to me anyway. The police asked him a lot of questions. I remember Stephen had trouble talking about it. Trouble sleeping. He didn't eat for days. I was sorry about that. Harlan was too."

"Who else did Harlan kill?"

"Don't say it like that, Maya. Harlan made a few bad people pay for being bad, that's all. He never hurt nice people."

"But who else?"

"Two people who wouldn't pay him for the work he did, back when we were living in Chicago. Harlan made deliveries for Frank Zoubek and Frank Teisland. We called them, 'the Franks.' They sold things out of a warehouse in south Chicago. Harlan knew it was all stolen goods but he didn't care 'cuz he didn't steal nothin. He was no thief. He didn't even know what he was delivering at first, and didn't want to know. He kept his mouth shut and they liked him for that. And then one night Harlan made a delivery to a smelter, a big ore refinery, and that changed everything. He said he opened the back of the truck to help get the stuff out, and there was a big canvas sack leaking blood. Some men came out of the refinery, dragged the sack out of the truck and across a loading dock. "Go on, get out'a here," one of them said to Harlan, so Harlan hopped in the cab and drove away. He didn't hang around and ask stupid questions. He told me later, when he scrubbed out the truck, he puked. The blood had already turned black and it was slimy and smelled awful, and he slipped and fell in it, twice. He went to the Franks and told them he wanted twice what they usually paid him. They laughed. So he told them not to call him anymore 'cuz he was done with 'em. Zoubek laughed even harder and I guess Teisland stood there grinning like a fool, so Harlan grabbed Teisland by his fancy silk necktie and sliced him open from scrotum to sternum. Harlan always carried a knife on his belt, ya see, and he was good with it. Teisland didn't make a sound, Harlan said. He just stood there, gaping and staring at his pink innards spilling all over his expensive Italian shoes. Zoubek went for his gun but Teisland's holster was right there and Harlan grabbed it and shot Zoubek between the eyes. 'He dropped like a sack of shit' Harlan said. Harlan said he waited until Teisland quit twitching and gasping on the floor before he left the warehouse. I guess that took a while. Harlan said it was like watching a gutted fish flop around on the bottom of a boat. Afterward, a different man took over managing the warehouse and he seemed more open to discussion. His name was . . . oh, I forget right now. Doesn't matter anyway. He told Harlan if he wanted to quit it was fine, but he offered him a lot more money to stay. 'Just take care of the bodies,' he said. 'Dispose of them anyway you want, just don't get caught, and if you do get caught, keep your mouth shut.' He offered Harlan five thousand per drop. That was a lot of money back then."

"It's a lot of money now." Maya felt as if she was sinking into the armchair, like something heavy pressed her down into it. "What did Harlan do with all the bodies after that?"

"Most went to that refinery," Elly said. "I didn't ask Harlan and he didn't talk about it much."

"Why did you move from there to Graceville?"

Elly stared straight up at the ceiling as if pondering Maya's question. She adjusted her blanket and worried her thumbs some more. "A year later, in nineteen sixty, Harlan had a close call. His truck got pulled over by the cops. He explained to them, all that blood in the back of his truck was from a delivery of pig carcasses to a butcher on DiMaggio Street. Harlan said they stared at the blood a long time before one of them shrugged and closed up the truck and they sent him on his way. But that encounter really scared Harlan. After a few days he started talking about leaving Chicago and starting over someplace else. Someplace quiet and peaceful. He wanted to get out of the business, he said. We had enough money saved up and we bought this farm, all fifteen hundred acres. Harlan bought some animals and he built a shed for the cow and the horse, and a coop for the chickens. The chicken coop is now the woodshed. I helped him fence them all in. We had two, long happy years here, quiet and safe, until the new warehouse manager paid us visit—in person."

"He came all the way out here?"

Elly nodded. "They had what they called *affiliate* warehouses in Seattle, San Francisco, and L.A. It wasn't just that one manager who was the problem. It was the people he worked for back in Chicago. Once you're in that business, you're never really free of it. They're afraid you'll talk, so they keep a tight rein on you. They offer you more money, and more money, and if that don't work they threaten you, and you know they mean it. Harlan and me, we would have ended up buried somewhere under one of our own barns. Deep under. Harlan agreed to the new offer but he made that manager promise, only three drops a year. No more than that, he said. The people in Chicago had other drivers and other places, other people doing the same work. We weren't the only ones. The manager finally agreed, so we had a deal."

"Harlan was a closer?" Maya asked.

Elly frowned sideways at Maya. "No, honey. A closer kills people, we just buried 'em. Someone else did the killing. Harlan was a *cleaner*. He cleaned up other people's messes."

"How many?" Maya asked.

"You mean around the farm here?"

Maya nodded.

Elly studied the ceiling again. "Well, about three a year, for forty-six years. That's, let's see, one hundred thirty-eight? But there were a couple extras slipped in sometimes. The managers always called the extras, *spares*, and we were paid double for those. So, there could be something like, one hundred forty-eight bodies stashed around this farm. Maybe one or two more'n that." Elly shrugged. "After such a long time, I've lost track."

Maya forced a dry swallow. "Do you remember where they're all buried?"

Elly shook her head. "Heavens no. Harlan always told me to get inside the house when the deliveries arrived. I peeked though, sometimes. I know where some of them are."

"Under the house?" Maya asked.

Again, Elly glanced at her with a surprised look. She nodded. "A few."

"Two men and a woman?"

"How did you know that, Maya?"

"I saw them. I think they saw me too." Maya knew by the look on Elly's face, her aunt understood what she meant.

"Yeah," Elly said. "I've heard'em scratchin' around in the dirt while I'm stuffing laundry in the Maytag, but I get out'a there before they're finished diggin' their way out. Once you leave the basement, they're back where they belong, ya see. That's the way it works."

So Elly and I both see them. Did that make the ghosts real, or did that just mean that she and Elly were both crazy?

"What about the green boy I see upstairs?" Maya asked. "He keeps begging me to not leave him here, to come find him, to help him."

"To help him what, Maya? He's dead."

"I don't know what he wants, Elly. Maybe just finding him would give him peace?"

"Just leave him be, honey. Nothin' can be undone. There's no fixin' dead people."

"But he begs me—"

"No!" Elly sat up. "We're gonna leave 'em *all* right where they are. That's what Harlan told me to do and he always knew how to handle things."

"All right, Elly. All right."

Elly stretched out on the sofa again and pulled the blanket up to her chin. She sniffed like a scolded child. A tear spilled from the corner of her eye, following a deep wrinkle into the hairline above her ear. "Just leave 'em be," Elly muttered. "We'll just leave 'em *all* be."

So there were over a hundred graves around the farm. More than Maya suspected, but this was not the time to insist Elly recall dates and numbers. Elly was too fragile, too emotional after her recent anxiety attack. Maya knew what those were like. There would be days ahead when they could talk about this again. This was only mid-June. There was all of July and August and part of September. There was time.

Maya struggled from the chair, the invisible weight rolling from her lap like a boulder and dropping to the floor without a sound. In the kitchen Maya rinsed out the tea mugs.

Outside the kitchen window, Sheriff Wimple's car pulled up and parked in front of the bunkhouse. Coty opened his door as the sheriff climbed out, talking and gesturing. Coty nodded, stepped inside, and the sheriff followed. The bunkhouse door closed behind them. *Oh, to be a fly on the wall.* Maya wished she knew what Coty and Sheriff Wimple were talking about.

Sooner or later, Maya knew she would tell Sheriff Wimple about the bodies, the deliveries, and about Harlan's job as a cleaner and about Elly's involvement. Elly was guilty too, by association. Elly was Harlan's accomplice. Maya felt the heaviness return, deep in her chest, like icy, skeletal fingers squeezing her heart. Poor little Elly, Maya thought. What would happen to her? What would the courts do to a tiny, seventy-six year old woman with a deadly history?

• • •

Maya dwelled on the graves outside. Her mind refused to let them go. There were so many. She imagined bodies everywhere. Whenever she looked out a window she saw graves. That spot, right there, mounded up with the big rhododendron growing from its center. Was someone buried there? Over there, where the ground was uneven, another grave? In the orchard, between apple trees? In the old vegetable garden, where the rhubarb grew so tall with such massive stalks and table-size leaves? Maya turned away from the window. So many fallow fields around this farm, fields that had been plowed under and returned to a natural state. Overgrown. Abandoned. Forgotten.

Some of Elly's story made sense and some of it sounded exaggerated. Some of it sounded like she made things up as she went along—or maybe Elly avoided some details by saying she couldn't remember, or 'Harlan took care of that.' Harlan must have been a harsh man. An impatient, angry soul, but Harlan had somehow convinced Elly they were doing the right thing. They were just cleaners. They were not responsible for the deaths. They cleaned up messes other people made. Forty-eight years of cleaning up messes. One hundred fifty bodies. Maybe more.

Maya took the basement stairs one step at a time, hesitating on each one for several seconds.

She sat down two steps up from the bottom and focused on that distant, dark corner. After a moment the scratching sounds began, rustling sounds, like canvas against ice, and the rocking motion of a rounded shadow, like a black bear struggling to break free of a cruel trap.

"I know you're down here," Maya said. "I'm going to help you, I just don't know how yet. But it's all going to end. I know what happened to you, and what happened wasn't right. I'm sorry."

She lifted the flashlight, flipped it on bright and aimed it into the thick shadows. There was no one there. Maya turned off the flashlight and returned to the kitchen.

They heard me.

Chapter Twenty-One

Maya phoned Bartell's Pharmacy in Graceville. Dr. Conover had phoned in the prescription and it was ready for pickup. Maya hated needing the drug but she hated anxiety attacks even more. She hated the way the people at the pharmacy always seemed to make a point of acting uninterested and nonjudgmental, as if they had no idea what the medication was for. They knew. She felt their eyes studying her as she walked away. *They think I'm one step away from being institutionalized, but I just need help with anxiety and nightmares.* And the whispering voices in her head, voices that never finished a complete sentence or said anything of consequence—bits and pieces of meaningless talk—like interrupted conversation through a wall—

. . . *but what did they find after* . . .
. . . *especially if they knew* . . .
. . . *if he had tried harder he might* . . .

Maya was relieved Dr. Conover hadn't insisted she schedule an appointment before authorizing the refill, because of the three-hour drive back to Tacoma. It wasn't as if she needed to have blood drawn or her blood pressure checked. *It isn't physical, it's emotional.* Surly, if Dr. Conover needed to talk, they could do that over the phone, couldn't they?

Sometimes Maya suspected Dr. Conover had lost interest in her. The anxiety attacks occurred less often now and she was sometimes able to suppress them without medication by confronting her reflection in the mirror and by whispering encouragement to the wide-eyed woman staring back. Sometimes she simply told herself, "You're okay." With only one pill left in the bottle, though, Maya froze at the thought she might run out. She wanted that refill. She needed that ninety pill reserve that Dr. Conover always authorized. Having them was a security blanket.

Maya parked the Ford Edge between the Ace Hardware and the front door of Bartell's on Main Street. She climbed out, locked the car doors and, clenching her jaw, walked away without double-checking the locks. She tossed the leather strap of her bag over her shoulder and squeezed the strap with both hands to control the shaking. She didn't look back and it felt like a small victory.

Graceville was a quiet, one-street town. There were no cross streets and, therefore, no intersection lights. It was noon on a sunny Friday and only three other drivers were parked along the sidewalk. Two old men with canes sat on a bench across the street near the Chevron station, solving the world's problems, Maya guessed, in typical old man fashion, with lots of frowning, gesturing and shaking of their grizzled heads.

It promised to be a warm day, approaching eighty. A sudden change in the weather like this always brought people out like bees from a hive. A golden lab strolled by, pausing to lift one leg to pee on a light pole. Dark swallows circled overhead in the blue sky. In a small, second floor apartment a shiny, new, air conditioner hummed as Maya walked by. It was now late June and summer was making promises she hoped it kept. It had been a long, damp winter.

The pharmacy counter was at the back of the store, straight down the candy aisle. She strode to the counter, presented her identification and shifted her weight from one foot to the other as the pharmacist searched for her prescription in a plastic bin. The pharmacist placed a small bottle on the counter. Maya picked it up and frowned at the label. Her hand shook.

"Just twenty pills?" Maya rolled the bottle back and forth in her hand.

"That was the amount your doctor prescribed," the pharmacist said.

"And—no refills?" Maya set the bottle back on the counter. Something inside her chest tightened, making it difficult to inhale.

"Do you want me to phone Dr. Conover and double-check?"

"Yes, please."

The pharmacist took several steps away and then returned. "I recall now, Dr. Conover said you need to schedule an appointment before she'll authorize more of that particular prescription. That's indicated on the label there, but I'll phone her if you still want me to."

Maya's breath was uneven as she finally exhaled. Her voice sounded weak. "No. I'll call her myself. Thank you." Maya left the pharmacy, her optimism shattered. She climbed behind the wheel of the Edge and tossed the prescription bag on the passenger seat. Enough pills for a month or two. "You'll be fine," she told the woman in the rearview mirror. "You'll be okay."

Maya started the engine. She fastened her seatbelt and did a traffic check over her left shoulder. She spotted a man rushing from the men's restroom at the Chevron across the street. His walk, his posture, his way of straightening down the cuffs on his shirt looked familiar.

Benson? What are you doing in Graceville? She shivered even though the Edge felt warm from sitting in the sun. The steering wheel was hot to the touch. She lowered her window and studied the man as he jaywalked toward her across the street. He glanced up just before stepping up to the sidewalk. It wasn't Benson. Maya released a long-held breath.

• • •

"Elly? You here?" Maya hung her coat in the pantry hall, dropped her handbag on a kitchen chair and peeked into the living room. Elly's blanket was on the sofa, but Elly was not there.

Maya headed upstairs—slow and hesitant. The green boy did not appear. The bathroom door was wide open and the light off. Maya stepped inside Elly's bedroom. She could see clear to the back of Elly's walk-in closet. Elly was not in there either, but the top dresser drawer was open, the same drawer that had been locked before. Maya entered the closet and peered inside the drawer. It was empty. Whatever had been inside, sliding back and forth, was now gone.

Maya returned downstairs. Inside the stove was a bed of hot coals. She stoked it again with alder.

Odd, she thought. Elly's farmhouse is either too hot or too cold depending on the room. It was almost eighty degrees outside, sixty-five inside. She struggled to open the kitchen window but it had been painted shut years ago, as had the dining room window. The big living room picture window wasn't designed to open. Opening just one window would have allowed some heat and fresh air inside.

Maya heard a tap on the back door and saw Coty through the parted curtains. She waved and he stepped inside and said,

"Sheriff Wimple told me to stay in the county."

"Why?"

"He wasn't exactly clear about that—maybe something to do with those bodies and those tunnels. I explained to Sheriff Wimple why I'm here. He seemed satisfied with that, but still asked me to hang around. If I need to leave the county, he said let him know first." Coty poured himself a mug of steaming water and dropped in a tea bag before joining Maya at the kitchen table.

"I thought I saw my ex-husband today," Maya said. "On Main Street in Graceville."

"Doing what?"

"I was picking up a prescription at Bartell's . . . oh, you mean Benson. It turned out to be some poor sap who just looks like him."

"I saw Tony Bradley snooping around the farm. He has a criminal record. Did you know that?"

"What kind of record?"

"Extortion mainly. You invited him here for dinner, right?"

Maya was uncertain how much to tell Coty. He claimed to be a private investigator and he had a laminated card to prove it, but the card could be as fake as her best strand of pearls for all she knew. Maya liked Coty, but she liked Benson once, too. She decided to reveal a few things to Coty and see what happened.

"Elly invited him. She wants to sell the farm and Tony Bradley, naturally, wants to list it through his company."

"His 'company?'" Coty snorted.

"Bradley Realty, there on Main Street," Maya said. "It's new."

"Bradley may have rented the building and stuck the sign in the window, but the door stays locked and there's nothing inside. Bradley hasn't even applied for a business license. I checked."

"What's in there, then?"

"A wooden desk with empty drawers and two chairs, a cheap lamp, and a legal tablet, a ballpoint pen, two filing cabinets that are both completely empty, and a bunch of dust."

"How do you know this?"

"Wait until three A.M. I'll show you how to pick a lock and you can check it out yourself, like I did. The place is just a front."

"I wonder what he's up to then?" Maya asked.

Coty leaned forward, chin on his knuckles wearing an unreadable expression. "Do you think Benson would ever hire someone to get rid of you?"

"He'd never spend money on it."

"You're positive?" Maya closed her eyes for a moment and then nodded. "I'm ninety-nine percent certain."

Coty tilted his chair back. "You got a picture of this ex-husband? I want to recognize him if he shows up here."

"Good idea." Maya dug the old plastic photo holder from the bottom of her purse. "This is his business photo, taken four years ago." She slipped Benson's 2x3-inch photo from the transparent cover and handed it to Coty. "Keep it," she said. "It's just stinking up my purse anyway."

Coty frowned at Benson's photo and slipped it into his breast pocket. "Anything else?"

"Can you get the window above the sink open?" Maya asked.

Coty glanced at the kitchen window. "Sure. Anything else?"

"Write down your cell number for me please."

Coty scribbled his number on the kitchen notepad. "That's it?"

Maya knew what Coty wanted. He wanted to know about Danny. He wanted to know if she had seen him again, if Danny had spoken to her. He wanted to know if she had told Danny his Uncle Wayne was there and would take him home soon. Maya cleared her throat.

"I haven't seen Danny since I told you about him."

Coty nodded but looked disappointed.

"Elly told me an unsettling story yesterday, about the farm. I find the tale difficult to believe. I don't want to believe it. I wonder if she's making some of it up, because it's just too fantastic. Too crazy," Maya said.

"I thought we weren't supposed to use that word."

"Far-fetched then," Maya said. "But I can't repeat the story, yet."

"Why?"

"The story isn't finished. Elly wanted to tell me the rest, but she was becoming visibly upset and I was afraid she'd decide I was grilling her. If she stops talking we'll never know what happened here, and I need to know. You need to know."

"Does it include Danny?" Coty said.

"I'm pretty sure Elly knows what happened to him. But remember, she doesn't know he's your nephew. She doesn't know who you are yet."

"If we went upstairs, right now, would we see Danny?"

Maya glanced at the kitchen clock. It was fifteen minutes after twelve. Noon and midnight were when she usually saw Danny in the upstairs hallway. "Maybe," she said.

Maya and Coty headed through the dining room. "Have you seen Elly outside anywhere, Coty? Because when I got home she was nowhere to be found."

"No, but she can't have gone far." Coty halted at the top of the stairs. He squeezed the railing so tight his knuckles turned white.

Maya followed the direction of his gaze. The green boy floated at the far end of the hallway, his back to the last door. She whispered,

"Is that Danny?"

Coty nodded and continued forward until he stood less than ten feet away from the boy.

"Danny?" Coty said.

The green light spun, as if Danny was a slow whirlwind, transparent and glimmering the way a distant star flickers.

"Help me!" Danny appeared to be shouting but his voice sounded far away.

"Where are you, Danny?"

"It's dark!" Danny's face contorted inside the green glow. "Can't move. Help me!"

"Where?" Coty repeated. Danny shrank back toward the end of the hall, like a swimmer in an undertow, his glow fading.

"I'll find you, Danny." Coty shouted. "And I'll take you home."

Maya stepped up beside Coty. "He never stays very long." Coty's face and hands were pale.

"You okay?" Maya asked.

"No. I'm not." Coty headed downstairs where he slumped into a chair at the kitchen table. "Why wouldn't he tell us where he's at?"

"Maybe he doesn't know," Maya said.

"I tracked him all the way here, thinking I'd take him home to his parents, but I'm too late." Coty rested his elbows on the table and rubbed his eyes but Maya knew he was hiding angry tears. His shoulders drooped. "I have to find him, but where do I start? He could be anywhere around here. Anywhere! There's five hundred acres to search."

"We'll find him," Maya said. "Because inside this house is the only place I ever see him. Upstairs in the hall. He's in this house."

"Damn! What the hell happened here? Who would hurt a seventeen year old kid?"

"Give me more time. Elly is starting to open up, but I have to be careful. She's defensive when it comes to Harlan. If I push for more information, that's when Mr. Elly shows up, and he scares me."

Coty placed his tea mug in the sink. "I'm not afraid of Mr. Elly. I'll choke the information out of that scrawny throat if I have to." He opened the back door and crossed the driveway to the bunkhouse without another word.

Maya wanted to help Coty but she wasn't sure how. Behind her, the floorboards snapped. Maya felt the hairs on the back of her neck rise.

"Look what I found, baby girl." Elly maneuvered her way through the dining room, her arms loaded with photo albums. She carried them into the kitchen and dropped them on the table.

"Where have you been?" Maya asked. She hoped Elly hadn't heard what she and Coty were talking about.

"In the attic. Way in the back."

"I was looking for you and getting a little worried. What do you have there? Any photos of Uncle Harlan?" Maya asked.

"Yep," Elly said. "The one I told you about. It shows my sweetie's face." Elly slid a faded blue album from the bottom of the pile and flipped it open to the middle. "Right there, see?" She pointed to a black and white photo in the lower right corner of the page, held in place by black paper corners.

"But it's just his profile." Maya was disappointed. "And he's wearing a hat that covers his eyes."

"Well, yes, but you can see most of his face," Elly said. "And then, there's this photo too." She flipped several more slick, yellowed, pages and pointed to another black and white photo. "There's Harlan, right there."

Harlan sat on the hood of a delivery truck. Behind the truck were two big metal doors and above the doors hung a sign, CHICAGO ORE AND REFINING.

"That's so typical of Harlan," Elly said with a grin. "He was a bit of a showoff in those days."

Harlan wore denim coveralls and a checked shirt with the sleeves rolled up to his elbows. His painter's hat tilted forward, shading his eyes, but visible were his nose, his cheeks and smirking mouth and chin. The heels of his dirty work boots were jammed into the front grill of the truck. His left arm rested on one knee and his index and middle finger held a cigarette.

"I still can't see his eyes very good," Maya said. "Don't you have a wedding photo anywhere?"

"Justice of the Peace married us, baby girl, and there was no official wedding photo. No tux, no white dress, no bouquet, just Harlan and me and a clerk who volunteered as a witness. We were so happy that day."

"Elly?"

"Yes, baby girl?"

"What was Harlan's last name?'

"...last name?'

"You kept your maiden name, Pederson, but what about Harlan? What was his last name?"

"Jones."

"Elly? Who took this photo?"

"Of Harlan on the truck there, smoking that cigarette?"

Maya nodded.

"I did." Elly sounded proud. "I took that photo."

Chapter Twenty-Two

"Follow me."

"What?" Maya sat up, flipped on her bedside lamp and glanced around the room. She saw no one. "Who said that? Who's there?" She kicked away the covers. Seconds later she stood in the moonlit hall. Danny floated beside the morning glory window. He shimmered inside his spinning green light, as if he had been expecting her. He glanced over his shoulder, eyes dark and hollow as he floated toward the stairs. Maya followed, barefoot. She glanced through the bathroom door as she passed by. Both hands on the clock's glowing face pointed straight up. Midnight.

The hardwood floor felt like ice beneath her bare feet and she shivered. Why hadn't she grabbed her robe? It was right there on the foot of her bed, and her slippers, right there on the oval rug. Maya remembered pushing back the covers but she had no memory of opening her bedroom door or stepping into the hallway now. She glanced back at her open bedroom door. The doorway was dark. She was certain she left the lamp on.

"Follow me," Danny's voice sounded like a distant echo, or as if it was inside her own ears, not in the hall.

Maya followed him down the stairs, her toes growing numb on the cold wood. Her breath formed clouds in the air of the stairwell. The clouds rolled into the gloom overhead. When she reached the bottom of the stairs she saw a dull yellow glow. The glow came from the dining room. Maya looked around for Danny but he was gone.

Maya felt the floor *thump* beneath her feet. She grasped the newel post and sucked frigid air through her lips while sweat beaded her upper lip. A shiver traveled the length of her spine. She stepped forward, toward an opaque plastic curtain that blocked the entrance to the dining room. A shadow crossed the curtain. Maya lifted the edge of the plastic. Inside the dining room more plastic sheeting covered the window and the floor. Plastic sheets draped the china cabinet and the buffet and a giant blue tarp covered the dining table, almost reaching to the floor. The chandelier was gone. Instead, a six-inch hook hung from the chain. The yellow glow emanated from a double candelabrum on the buffet where ten candles flickered. On the floor stood a bucket, filled to the brim with a glossy red liquid, a thick, dark, red liquid almost as black as the bucket.

• • •

Maya steps into the room and the plastic curtain rustles closed behind her. It's even colder in the dining room than on the stairs. She blinks. It's difficult to focus on things in this room. Everything looks dim and blurry. The light is weak and the room's corners are thick with shadows. Something shiny gleams on the table. Maya squints, focuses. The gleam comes from polished metal. She steps closer and sees knives, a saw, and a cleaver. Their black handles glisten, slick and red with blood. She blinks again. On the table lay a man's body, face down, the bottoms of his bare feet face her. His flesh is stark white.

Another man rises up from between the buffet and the other end of the table. He is short and thin and wears a gray plaid shirt, the sleeves rolled up to his elbows. His arms are lean and sinewy. His shirttail is jammed into baggy jeans. He grabs the cleaver in one bony hand and seems to study the tool, turning it back and forth in the dim light, as if admiring the flashing blade.

Maya blinks again. The scene is like an aged newsreel, quick and jerky. When the man pauses, it looks like an old photograph, the reds having faded to sepia. He lifts the cleaver to eye level and brings it down. Whack. One foot falls into two pieces, sliced through the arch. No blood oozes from the wound. He picks up both pieces and tosses them into a black trash bag.

Whack. An ankle and heel follow.

Maya steps back, slips on something and looks down. Her legs are transparent, her feet gone. She has no body. She lifts her hands but sees nothing there. She is invisible.

I'm dreaming. Wake up. Wake up!

Whack. The cleaver flashes in the dim light again and another ankle and heel are thrown into the trash bag. The sepia man bends down again, below the table. A cupboard door squeals open and then clossd. He holds a serving platter—Elly's rose pattern china. He sets it down on the corner of the buffet. Whack. A man's head settles with a plop in the center of the platter, a man's head with silvery blond hair and thick dark smears across his forehead, cheeks and ears. A thin trickle of dark blood pools around the man's head. The man's face wears no expression. His eyes are closed. He frowns in his bottomless sleep.

Maya shivers. She feels herself trembling with cold. How can I be cold if I'm not here? I'm dreaming…just dreaming. Wake up! Wake up!

Blood drips from the edge of the tarp to the plastic sheet on the floor. Tap. Tap. Tap. It trickles, glistening and red toward Maya's feet and she steps aside before it reaches her invisible toes. She leans forward. She wants to see the sepia man's face, but he turns his back, his shoulders hunched. He drops the slick, red cleaver on the table and tosses two knees into the trash bag. His hand searches behind him for the saw. Finds it. Lifts it. The gleaming steel teeth sparkle in candlelight. Maya leans closer, determined. The butcher turns his back again and drags the bulging trash bag into the middle of the kitchen. He wears black boots. They make a sticky sound on the linoleum and leave a trail of smeared, red footprints.

On the dining room table are parts of the man's body, naked, so bloodless the flesh is blue-white. Like a side dish, both blue-white hands rest alongside the head on the platter. The legs have been separated from the torso at the hips.

Something brushes Maya's feet. She looks down, sees a bony hand blotting up a crimson puddle with a blue towel. The butcher has returned without a sound, without a footstep. He's swabbing up the blood. She steps back. He doesn't see her, she doesn't see herself.

How can he not see me? Why can't I see myself?

The sepia man carries the blood-soaked towel through the kitchen and tosses it through the open basement door and down the stairs. It lands on the bottom step with a wet slap.

In the middle of the kitchen stands a small freezer chest, the lid wide-open, inner edges bulging with thick frost. The butcher enters the dining room again, picks up two thighs and carries them to the freezer. He wedges them deep into the bottom, returns to the table and lifts the lower torso. He drops it straight down into the freezer, adjusting it to fit alongside the thighs and returns for the chest and arms. The torso lands with a meaty whump in the freezer. He folds the arms around the sides, fitting the elbows into the corners. There is a hollow in the open diaphragm beneath the ribs, below the heart. The head slides from the platter and into the freezer. The butcher fits the head into the hollow. He wedges the hands in tight alongside the head, covering the ears. The butcher pauses to grin at the image, nodding. He pats the head's silver hair and slams the freezer lid shut. He fastens a brass padlock and gives it a yank. The padlock holds.

Maya backs away toward the plastic curtain, slipping in traces of slick blood. She lifts the edge of the plastic and glances back toward the kitchen. The sepia man grunts as he tilts the freezer and rolls it across the linoleum. The freezer's small wheels crawl over the doorsill.

Thump, thump, thump. The freezer batters each step as it's rolled down into the basement.

• • •

Maya sat up in bed with a gasp. She turned on her bedside lamp. The lace window curtain lifted in the draft from the window. A breeze puffed into the room along with the smell of pine and moss. And early morning moon peeked through the tops of the trees. It was cool in her room, but not freezing. Her breath left no clouds in the air. Her toes were warm beneath the quilt, not numb with cold. She slipped one foot from under the covers. No blood.

"Danny?" Maya whispered. She waited.

Somewhere in the forest an owl hooted but Danny said nothing.

Chapter Twenty-Three

THE PHONE RANG. "MAYA Pederson? This is Dr. Framish. I have the results of your aunt's tests. Is she available?"

"She's asleep. If you'll wait I'll wake her."

"No. You're her caregiver. I can tell you."

"I'll write down what you say and I'll tell her later. Go ahead. I have a pen and paper," Maya said.

"It's good news. As I suspected, there was no stroke. Her blood calcium and cholesterol levels are excellent, and her cardiac catheter test shows that her arteries and veins are clear. Her blood pressure is normal. Her EKG came well within acceptable range, and I might add, she is surprisingly strong for a woman her age. In fact, all her tests came back in the upper five percent for her age group. She is as healthy as an active fifty year old."

"But then, what happened? She was incoherent and unresponsive to our voices."

"I'm guessing an anxiety attack. Is there a family history of neurological disorders?"

"Uh, yes . . . her brother . . . my father."

"Anxiety?" Dr. Framish asked.

"My father had serious clinical depression."

"She didn't exhibit signs of depression while she was at the hospital. Do you think she's depressed now?"

"No, but she gets stressed about things. She worries. She's been dwelling on the past lately. She gets upset easily. I suspect she's imagining things, maybe confusing her dreams with reality, and she sleepwalks. She said she spoke with her husband but he's been dead for five years. I don't know. Maybe that's anxiety?"

"She mentioned a visit from her husband while at the hospital. I knew he was deceased. Your aunt is on no prescription drugs, though, right? From any previous conditions?"

"None that I've discovered and none that she has mentioned. The medicine cabinets were both empty when I arrived here back in early May. I've never seen her take anything. Not even vitamins or an aspirin."

"If you inherit your aunt's genes, you'll probably live a long time," Dr. Framish said. "But I can recommend a good psychologist for her, if you'd like."

"I don't think she'd agree to see one."

"I understand. I'll have these test results sent to you. You should receive them in a week or two. I'll enclose a business card for the psychologist, just in case, all right?"

"Thank you."

"How are you doing, Ms. Pederson? Are you overwhelmed? Caregivers often find themselves exhausted. It's not an easy job."

"I'm okay. Thank you for asking though."

"Please call me if I can help in any way."

"I will."

"You still have my card?"

"Yes."

"Have a good afternoon, Ms. Pederson."

"You also."

Maya stared at Dr. Framish's card, impaled on the wall above the phone with a long straight pin. She might call him if Elly needed something, but she wouldn't phone him for her own concerns. She had Dr. Conover for that.

Chapter Twenty-Four

Maya called up the stairs. "Aunt Elly?"

Overhead, the upstairs hallway floor groaned. "Yes, baby girl?"

"Dr. Framish says you'll live to see a century. No stroke, just a bit of stress."

"Thought so," Elly said. "Something like that happened once 'afore, when I was young. I just slept it off."

"What did Uncle Harlan do? Did he phone for help?"

"Naw. He just let me sleep."

"For how long?"

"Almost a week. I woke up thirsty as a camel, but I was just fine after that."

The upstairs floor snapped and groaned again and Maya spotted Elly's shadow on the landing wall. "The phone rang twice. Who else called?" Elly asked.

"Before Dr. Framish, it was Tony Bradley," Maya said. "Tony's on his way over right now. He said he's received an offer on the farm and wants to discuss it with you." She climbed the eight stairs to the landing and looked toward the second floor.

Elly appeared at the top, rubbing her hip and frowning. "We talked about selling, but I didn't sign anything. If I was eager to sell I'd have phoned some big-time realty office, not Tony Bradley. I spotted a couple realtor signs from my hospital window. But, we aren't ready for that, are we Maya?"

"He might have gotten that impression by something I previously said. I'm sorry."

"That's okay, honey. I'm just grumpy 'cause my hip is aching "

"Do you want me to call Tony back and tell him not to come?"

There was a moment of silence and then Elly said, "Nah. Let him come. I'm curious what he has to say."

When Elly clipped her words and sounded annoyed like that, Maya guarded her words. She wouldn't accuse Uncle Harlan of anything. Elly had a quick, defensive temper when it came to Harlan.

Twenty minutes later Tony parked his silver Audi outside the kitchen window. He wore a silk shirt the same color as his aqua eyes and pressed, cream-colored trousers. His blonde hair had been trimmed within the last day or two, revealing a pale line along his hairline. Wherever it was he'd traveled to the previous week, it had tanned his face. Maya opened the door before he knocked.

"Elly and I were just about to have lunch. Care to join us?" she asked.

"I just had lunch at the River Lodge Café," Tony said. "But I wouldn't mind a cup of coffee."

"Is tea okay?"

He shrugged. Maya steeped a pot of tea and set out three mugs. "So, who is this buyer you mentioned?"

"A super nice family from the Midwest," Tony said. Maya thought he answered too quickly, as if he had anticipated the question and had practiced his answer.

"Is it a good offer?" Elly stood in the entrance to the dining room. Her expression looked hardened and for one uncomfortable moment, Maya was afraid it was Mr. Elly standing there.

"Hello, Elly." Tony carried his steaming mug to the table. He pulled out Elly's chair and she acknowledged his courtesy with a nod before joining him at the table.

"It's a fair offer, considering the economy these days." Tony sat facing the bay window, one polished tan loafer resting on the opposite knee.

Maya slid Elly's mug and a plate of homemade cookies on the table. "Oatmeal chocolate chip," she said.

"Don't let me keep you ladies from lunch. I'm happy as a tick on a hound with my tea and one of those cookies."

Maya frowned. She believed Tony was putting on a redneck act, as if he thought she and Elly would appreciate it. Did he consider them hicks? She scooped gazpacho into two bowls and set them on the table along with a plate of crackers and cheese. "What do you consider a 'fair offer'?" she asked.

Tony glanced from Maya to Elly and back again over the rim of his mug. He swallowed and cleared his throat. "Three hundred thousand."

Elly swallowed a spoonful of gazpacho before resting her elbows on the table and her chin on her knuckles. "We're talkin' five hundred acres, year-round stream, two barns, three sheds, a bunkhouse, carport, and three-story house with basement, for three-K? I don't think so."

"Most of the structures on this property are rotten, Elly, and like I said, it's a tough economy right now. This might be the best offer you receive." Tony sipped his tea again, twice. "Maybe the only offer." His voice lost any hint of friendliness.

Elly shook her head. "I can divide this farm into nine hundred half-acre lots, develop them myself and sell them off one by one. That ridge up there above the Fedder Prairie homestead, the one with the view? It's worth three-fifty all by itself. I'm not stupid, you know, and I won't take one cent less than one million."

Tony grinned. "That's the Elly I've been expecting. I knew you'd surface sooner or later. Shrewd, cutthroat, greedy little Elly. You probably have the first nickel you ever earned." His unidentifiable accent was gone, replaced by something much more east coast. Maryland? Pennsylvania?

"What did you say to her?" Maya grabbed the mug from his hand before it reached his grinning lips again. The tea spilled in his lap and he jumped to his feet.

"Damn! That's hot."

"I remember you, Fritz," Elly said. "I remember the first time you ever came here—and I remember the last time you were here. It wasn't so long ago, was it? Seven months maybe? You brought an unscheduled delivery—a spare—after I told you I was done with the business and to not *ever* bring another. Things didn't go so well, remember? You drove off and left me with a nasty little problem. So get the hell out of my house and don't ever come back or–"

"Or what, you stingy old bitch? You'll drag out your shotgun? Can you live up to your infamous reputation? When was the last time you talked to Felix, Elly? It's been quite a while since you heard from him, right? Felix can't protect you anymore. He's probably dead by now, or close to it. He wasn't doing so well last week when I saw him. He was hooked up to tubes and a machine that breathed for him. He couldn't even hold a pen or scribble his name. He's blind, almost deaf, half paralyzed and drools like an old dog. If I'd been alone with him in that room, I'd have crushed his windpipe." Tony snapped his fingers. "Like that."

Elly picked up the cheese knife and dragged it across the top of the kitchen table, gouging a deep groove. Orange wood and pale green paint curled up behind the blade. "You came here not long ago, dragging a shovel. I saw you. I know what you were looking for, but you didn't find it, did ya' Fritz?" Elly grinned. "And you never will, you stupid bastard."

Tony stepped back, eyeing the knife in Elly's hand. "Think you can take me, Elly? You could have once, twenty-five years ago when I was just a kid and you were in your prime, but not now. Not–"

"Now, I'm here too," Maya said. "And like Elly told you—get out. Now."

Tony glanced over his shoulder. His grin faded when he spotted the butcher knife in Maya's hand.

"Shit," he said. "Another Pederson loony."

"You've got ten seconds, Fritz, and then I gut you like a trout." Elly moved with remarkable ease, tossing the cheese knife from her right hand to her left and back again. "You know I can."

Tony kicked his chair away. It skidded against the refrigerator. He backed toward the door, opened it and paused. "Let me know when you're ready to negotiate, Elly. But remember, if Felix is dead the deal you made with him is just smoke, along with your stipend. There are people in Chicago who'll pay big-time to learn where you're hiding. I can sell them that information. Give me a call when you're ready to talk, but don't wait too long because I need cash." He left the door open.

A moment later Tony's silver Audi headed down the driveway into the trees. Elly and Maya crossed through the dining room and into the living room. They stood in front of the big picture window as the Audi climbed from the driveway to the blacktop and disappeared over the hill.

"He'll be back, won't he?" Maya said.

"I'm counting on it." Elly headed toward the kitchen. She traced the deep gouge in the table with the tip of her index finger. "Won't take much to sand this down and repaint it."

"What does Tony want, Elly?"

"Money, of course. But don't call him Tony. It's Fritz . . . Fritz Pulitano. He's originally from North Carolina but I met him in Chicago. I can't believe I didn't recognize him that night at the River Lodge Café."

"So, there isn't really an offer on the farm?"

Elly shook her head. "No honey. He wants three hundred thousand to keep his mouth shut, but if I give it to him he'll just demand more. He also wants the farm. That would be included in the deal. He wants this farm so he can search it, inch by inch. I won't ever let him take this farm, though. I'll burn it to the ground before I let him have it."

"So, there are people in Chicago who want to find you?"

"Yes, two families in particular. The Sonosa family . . . and the Zoubeks."

"Why?" Maya asked. "What would they do if they found you?"

"I'd be dead in a snap, honey, for things Harlan did—things Harlan was paid to do. Those people want my head 'cuz they figure I helped Harlan. And, well, I did help him, didn't I? They won't ever forgive or forget that."

"What does Tony . . . I mean Fritz . . . think he'll find here? And who is Felix?"

Elly sighed. "Fritz thinks there's millions of dollars stashed around this farm. And Felix? Well, that's another long story, baby girl. Let's clean up from lunch and then I'll tell you about it from the beginning."

Chapter Twenty-Five

"I MADE A PITCHER OF lemonade. Want some?" Maya asked.

Maya and Elly carried their lemonade into the living room and settled into their usual places, with Elly stretched out on the sofa and Maya in the big armchair beside the fireplace. Outside, sunlight shimmered off leaves in the overgrown front garden. Blood red rhododendron blossoms glowed along the fence line and at the bottom of the lower field the surface of the stream glimmered like sequins.

This day was too beautiful, too warm and sunny for one of Elly's nightmarish stories, but she began without hesitating.

"Felix Olsen was my father's first cousin and they were also best friends. Felix was . . . connected. You know what that means, honey?"

Maya nodded. "Friends in powerful places."

"Yes. Felix was almost two years older than my father. He convinced some higher-ups to give my father a job. At first, Dad just repaired trucks. That was his trade. Dad was a master mechanic and he taught me everything he knew. If I had all the parts I could build a truck or a car from the tires up. Anyway, Felix convinced those higher-ups to use Dad for other jobs, small stuff. Nothing big—nothing that would have sent him away for too long if he'd'a been caught. It was deliveries mainly, or after-hours break-ins and burglaries at a few small jewelry stores. Dad and Felix were both so good at that, the store owners didn't realize they'd been robbed until they took inventory and that was sometimes two weeks later. This was back before security systems were common. Dad and Felix did an armored car heist together once. Every time they told that story, I'd almost wet my pants laughing. It was like listening to the Three Stooges, except there were just the two of 'em. They were so careful and they planned things out so well in advance they never hurt anyone. The clumsy armored car driver got a concussion, but that was from tripping over his own feet as he ran away."

"This was back in Chicago?" Maya asked.

"Yep, before Harlan started delivering for them. When Dad was dying Uncle Felix promised he'd look after me. At first Uncle Felix wouldn't even consider using me for a driver. He'd just hand me some money and say, 'Let me know when that runs out, Elly girl.' But I cornered him one day and explained how there wasn't anything I couldn't do with cars or trucks, their engines or transmissions, and how I knew what made vehicles tick, inside and out. I knew the routes Dad had driven because we talked about them. I knew where all the stops were. Uncle Felix laughed and said, 'Elly girl, you have no idea how dangerous deliveries can be. The job is tough, raw, work. The people waiting for the deliveries can be mean sons-a-bitches.' I told him I already knew that. But I also told him, they won't expect trouble from an eighteen year old girl, and they won't expect a girl to have a gun strapped behind her ribs, or a knife in her boot—or expect her to know what to do if things go south, or how to keep her mouth shut if she screws up and gets caught. Give me a chance, Uncle Felix, I said. He looked at me for a long minute and then said, 'Let me think about it.'"

"How long did you have to wait?" Maya asked.

"Just two weeks. One of the other drivers was caught selling goods to someone on the outside and pocketing the money. I don't know what happened to him. I never saw him again. No one did, and because of that, Uncle Felix was a driver short that week and something was on the must-deliver list. There were six big wooden crates, each about four feet square and too heavy to move without a forklift. They were already loaded into the back of a truck. I didn't know what they were, but things went as slick as buttermilk. I backed the truck up to a warehouse door like I had been told to do, and the door opened and I heard men's voices in the back. Then the truck jostled and I heard three knocks on the back of the cab. After a couple seconds there were two more knocks. That meant, **go —*drive away***. I heard the back doors slam and I put the truck in gear. When I got home, Uncle Felix handed me five hundred dollars and he said there'd be another delivery in about a week. And that was the start of it all. I was a driver. Then later, I introduced Harlan to Uncle Felix. So actually, I was the one with the connection. I was a driver before Harlan was."

"Harlan took over your route?"

"Yeah, he didn't want me driving anyway. He said big money meant there was big risk. He talked to Felix and Felix hired him to replace me. I don't know what was said. I wasn't even consulted about it."

"You didn't drive for very long then?"

"Only about a year, but even after I quit driving, Felix paid me anyway, as part of his promise to my dad. It was a relief to stop making those deliveries. I didn't like the way the other drivers treated me. Felix gave me the easy jobs—easy compared to theirs. The other drivers called it favoritism, and I suppose it was. I remember the looks they gave me, and how they'd clam up when I walked by. I knew they were talking about me. Harlan took to the job like a fish to scales, and the other guys respected him. If they didn't respect him they kept it to themselves or found work elsewhere—or Harlan made them respect him. Nobody messed with Harlan. He didn't even need training. He just seemed to know what to do."

"You never knew what you delivered?" Maya asked.

Elly studied the ceiling for a moment and then glanced toward Maya. "That story is for another time."

Chapter Twenty-Six

WITH A MODEST DEGREE of satisfaction, Maya noted the gap in her medication journal. She had not taken any Lorazapam for two weeks now. Since the recent refill was much less than usual, she needed to save them for full-on panic attacks and would have to deal with stress or sleeplessness with exercise. Maya suspected Dr. Conover wanted to wean her away from the addictive drug. The thought scared her. Lorazapam was the only thing that halted an anxiety attack and ensured sleep without nightmares. It was a matter of time before the nightmares overwhelmed her again.

And the sleepwalking... and my inability to distinguish between dreams and reality.

Sometimes it took several hours before she could dismiss a nightmare. They seemed so real. Too real.

The last pill from her old prescription was now gone. Maya recounted the pills inside the new bottle. Twenty. She picked up her cell phone, planning to call Dr. Conover, to remind her that her refills had always been ninety pills—she punched in the doctor's number, heard the phone ringing and the answering machine pick up, but instead of leaving a message, Maya hung up. Dr. Conover knew how many pills she normally prescribed and she was also aware of how many pills she had prescribed this time. *She doesn't need to hear me whining about it.*

"Baby girl?" Elly called from the front of the hall.

Maya closed her journal and stepped from the bathroom into the upstairs hallway. At the end of the hall, Elly stood with her back to the morning glory window, her petite silhouette surrounded by a violet-blue glow.

"I have an appointment tomorrow in Graceville," Elly said. "I want you to help me choose what to wear. I need to look as business-like as possible."

"A doctor's appointment?"

"No, I'm meeting with my lawyer. I see him once a year to discuss investments, taxes, and such."

Maya followed Elly into her bedroom. Two dresses were tossed on the bed along with a small black purse. A pair of low-heeled black shoes sat on the oval rug, and an off-white cardigan lay folded on the rocking chair.

"Which dress do you think I should wear, honey?"

"The mint green dress looks more summery. The brown one seems more like autumn," Maya said. "Especially with those little flecks of orange."

"Green it is, then." Elly hung the brown dress back in the closet and took out a polyester slip and the envelope with the stockings from a drawer. "It's been over a year since I wore any of these things. I never did like wearing dresses. Pants are more sensible, don't you think?"

Maya smiled. "I wore dresses when I worked at the art gallery, and didn't really mind, but when I quit it felt good to get back to wearing jeans."

"When I was a girl, we were required to wear dresses to school. Things have changed since then. These days I see girls dressed like boys, or worse yet, like whores, and the boys now days—heavens, they dress like homeless people."

The image of Coty's nephew, Danny, flashed before Maya's eyes. Baggy shorts, hoody, facial piercings, tattoos. Homeless people didn't have a typical look. There were some well-dressed panhandlers on streets these days. Some wanted a job, some just wanted a handout. It was difficult to tell them apart. Some people who used to have good jobs were now homeless.

I'm homeless.

"Elly? What will you do if the farm doesn't sell?"

Elly closed the drawer and returned to the side of the bed where she took the green dress and draped it across a chair by the window.

"Then, I guess I'll just leave it to you." Elly set the purse on the folded sweater and the shoes beneath the chair. The slip and stockings went beside the purse. "There," she said with a nod. "I'll take my bath this evening and wash my hair so it won't take but a few minutes to get dressed in the morning. Do you mind driving me into Graceville, honey?"

"Not at all. What time is your appointment?"

"Nine o'clock sharp. He said to allow a couple hours for our meeting since we have a number of things to discuss. So you can do some shopping in Graceville or come back out to the farm if you want. I can phone you when we're finishing up."

"The weather channel said it's supposed to rain tomorrow, so I'll take an umbrella and walk up and down Main Street. There are several stores I want to check out."

"Sounds good, sweety," Elly said.

Maya turned, gazing at the furniture in Elly's room, at the dresser in the back of the closet, at the rocking chair in the corner. She focused her eyes through the lace curtains, at the big barn on top of the hill. The farm would be left to her? She would own it? She would own all that came with it? Everything that stayed here after Elly left . . . it would all be hers. All the graves.

Later that morning, it was warm and humid as Maya painted the pantry hallway. Elly said she didn't care what color, so Maya chose her favorite. Creamy white. It was such a dark and narrow hallway and the white paint brightened it. She managed to pry open the small window between the bookshelves in the skylight room, and she opened the window above the kitchen sink that Coty had pried loose. The cross-breeze pushed gentle air through the pantry.

Maya relaxed. She enjoyed painting, especially something easy like these flat cupboard doors and simple wooden doorknobs. The job required no masking except around the hinges.

Maya spread old newspapers over the yellow linoleum and got busy with the project. The creamy white semi-gloss gleamed as her paintbrush spread it across the wood, filling in old nicks, scratches and gouges . . . covering all flaws.

"Maya," Elly said. "I'm going out to the bunkhouse to ask Coty to clean off the skylight and the front porch roof. That wind we had dropped pine needles and little cones all over the place."

"Fine. I'll be right here in the pantry," Maya said.

The back door opened and closed and Maya heard Elly's footsteps crunching across the driveway, and then silence. She felt an immediate drop in room temperature. The pantry grew shadowed and the quiet felt loud…as if it screamed silence into her ears. She heard a faint ringing in her ears.

Maya sat down on the newspapers. The first time she saw Elly's house, the day she arrived and paused beside the mailbox out on the county road, she remembered how the front of the house had resembled a face, its two upstairs windows glaring outward across the valley like black, angry eyes. The big living room window looked like a wide-open mouth in the midst of a mute scream, and the chimney resembled an off-center scar, almost like the raw gouge in the kitchen table. Maya lived inside that house now, in the very throat of that mute scream.

Maya rested the paintbrush on the rim of the can. To her left, sunlight fell through the skylight turning the back room a mustard color. A second later a cloud passed overhead, filling the room with shades of gray. To her right, the kitchen flickered as more clouds raced across the sky. Through the bay window the fields blinked, first with sunlight and then with gliding shadows, as if someone turned an overhead light on, and then off—on and off.

Maya stood and entered the kitchen, She filled the teakettle and set it on the electric stove. This day was too warm for a fire in the woodstove. Moisture on the bottom of the kettle sizzled and popped as the burner grew hot. Another shadow raced across the fields and enclosed the house. The kitchen grew almost as dark as night. The temperature dropped even more. Maya shivered. She saw her breath.

To her right, the basement steps groaned. Maya pictured someone reaching for the door at the top. She ran to the basement door. It wasn't locked! Her hands shook as she twisted the lock closed. A second later the doorknob turned white with sudden frost. The surface of the door crackled as a layer of ice crystals formed, from the bottom up and to both sides. The door resembled a wall of ice.

"Open the door," a voice growled.

Maya stepped back. It wasn't Coty's voice. Coty stood in his open doorway across the

driveway. Coty and Elly stood there together, chatting and gesturing, often smiling and nodding, even chuckling. Maya saw them both between the parted kitchen curtains.

I can call out to them. The kitchen window is open.

She could hear part of their conversation—a word here, a word there. If she shouted they would come running, and if they came she could point to the ice crystals on the yellow door. Maybe they would hear the top step groan the way she did. Maybe. Maybe not.

Maya shuddered at the thought someone stood on the other side of that door, but she was even more afraid that Coty and Elly would rush inside, and see nothing. No ice. No frost. What if Elly opened the basement door and there was no one there?

What if I'm seeing things again? Hearing things? What if I'm getting worse, not better?

What if Elly opened the door and there *was* someone there? Who would it be? What would happen?

Elly had admitted seeing *things* in the basement and Coty admitted seeing the green boy in the upstairs hall, but only she had seen the yellow basement door freeze over. Only she had heard that chilling voice from the basement side. Was the voice real or was she imagining it?

Maya stepped closer to the door. She leaned close. "What do you want?" she asked.

"Out."

Maya whispered, "Who are you?"

No reply.

"Hello?" Maya said.

On the other side of the door the wooden steps groaned again and the ice crystals began to melt. Tiny slivers of ice slid down the old yellow paint. Like slush they dripped to the old linoleum.

Splat. Splat. Splat.

"Are you still there?" But Maya knew he was gone, down the stairs, across the dirt floor, into the deepest, darkest corner. Down into the dirt . . . down into the buried freezer chest with the thick white frost and the brass padlock.

Outside, sunlight flooded the fields again. A chickadee sang in the hedge. Maya heard Elly's laugh and then her quick footsteps on the gravel driveway. The back door opened.

"Coty said he will get to it before the end of day," Elly said. "Oh good, Maya. You already have the tea kettle on." Elly paused in the middle of the kitchen, her eyes on the linoleum t the foot of the basement door. "Spill something, honey?"

"Just tea water." Maya wiped up the melted ice with a paper towel before returning to the pantry hallway. She picked up the paintbrush with trembling fingers.

Six weeks ago this farm had promised refuge, a place to escape from Benson, a place she had wanted, with all her heart, to visit since the age of five. A place where she could start a new life. Now, the thought of being alone here made her shiver with dread.

CHAPTER TWENTY-SEVEN

IT WAS NOW JUNE twenty-eighth, eight and a half weeks since Maya first arrived at the farm. Early that morning, she noticed the vintage electric clock on the kitchen wall was stuck at six minutes after twelve. Maya lifted it from the wall, guessed at the time and adjusted the hands to 9:37 and plugged it back in, but it remained stuck. She unplugged it, slapped the clock with the palm of her hand and plugged it in again. Dead. With a shrug, Maya scribbled "new clock" on the shopping list and set the old clock in the counter beside the sink. She rubbed her wrist where her watch used to be. No unseen hand had left her watch on the steps a second time, or returned it to her bedside table from where it first disappeared. As of that moment, the only working clock was in the upstairs bathroom.

Maya took the stairs two at a time. The face on the bathroom clock was dark. Its electric cord dangled over the edge of the counter like a flat-headed snake with brass fangs. Elly must have unplugged it at exactly six minutes after twelve last night. *Odd, that's when the kitchen clock stopped.* Maya jammed the plug into the wall and spun the hands to 9:40. The clock's face lit up and the second hand ticked forward. She placed it on the counter facing the door.

A green glow reflected in the full-length mirror at the far end of the bathroom. Maya recognized Danny's swirling image hovering there, his eyes deep and shadowed. She turned to face him through the open door. He was arriving at other times now, not just at noon or midnight.

"Danger." Danny's voice sounded distant, as if he strained to be heard.

"What danger?" Maya asked.

Danny drifted back toward the far end of the hall. He appeared to be struggling like a swimmer against a strong current. His glow dimmed and then flickered.

"Wait, Danny. Talk to me. What danger?" Maya asked.

"Sonosa."

"What's a sonosa?"

Danny's voice faded away as the door at the end of the hall swung open. The darkness beyond seemed to extend out, like black smoke into the hallway. It enclosed him, pulled him back through the door. The door swung shut.

Maya ran down the hall and opened the door. "Danny?" The narrow stairs dove steep and straight into black air. The stairwell smelled sour, like fermenting beer. She remembered Elly's warning about the stairs being steep and how there was no railing. She took two steps down, her fingertips against the opposite wall. "Danny?" High above the overhead fixture was missing its light bulb. Ahead, the air was the color of India ink and Maya squinted into its depths. A cold, sudden, draft rose up from below, lifting Maya's bangs. She backed into the hallway and closed the door.

The sound of the kitchen door opening and closing announced Elly's return from the garden. Maya hurried back along the upstairs hallway, down the stairs and through the dining room. She found Elly at the kitchen sink, the faucet running. "I picked us the last of the spring rhubarb," Elly announced. Thought I'd make us a pie."

Maya shuddered at the thought of eating rhubarb from a garden where bodies were buried. In the sink, inside the colander, slender stalks of red rhubarb glistened like blood covered bones.

Elly nodded at the clock on the counter. "I see you've started a new shopping list. That old clock must be over sixty years old. I think the manufacture date on its back says nineteen-forty-two. It was on that wall when Harlan and I moved in."

"I thought I'd pick up some battery powered clocks the next time we're in town. Something that doesn't depend on electricity."

"Good idea," Elly said. "I like those new kind, with the big glowing numbers. You can see what time it is from clear across the room."

"Digital." Maya eyed the basement door. *Locked.* "They're called digital clocks."

This house plays mental games with me, Maya thought. First my watch and now the clocks. Why does the farm want to keep the correct time a secret? Why does it want to keep Danny from talking? Maya sat down at the kitchen table. "Aunt Elly? Do you know what Sonosa means?"

Elly's hands halted under the running water. She lifted her eyes to the open window behind the sink. "Oh, baby girl. I haven't heard that name in a long time."

"It's a name?"

Elly nodded. "Remember when I was telling you about the new warehouse manager? The manager who took over after the Franks? The guy who showed up here one day, insisting Harlan and I agree to a new contract? That's him. Angel Sonosa. I had forgotten his last name." Elly wiped her hands on a checkered towel. "It's time we had another talk, I guess, but to tell it right I have to go back in time again. Way, way, back, like I did before." Elly turned off the faucet. "Let me get this rhubarb diced and sprinkled with sugar. Then we can sit down and I'll tell you about Angel."

• • •

Ten minutes later Elly settled herself against the back of the sofa. "Thank you Maya, for listening to the ramblings of an old lady. I felt better after telling you that memory the other day, things I've never told anyone else. Sharing my memories is like a heavy weight lifting from my shoulders."

"You're Daddy's sister. Of course I'll listen."

Elly sat straight this time, resting one hand and wrist on the rounded arm of the sofa. "Have you ever known someone so mean you thought they were sent by the devil?"

"Well, Benson has a definite mean streak," Maya said. "But Benson is just ordinary mean."

"Oh, I'm not talking about an ordinary type of mean, Maya. I'm talking about someone who enjoyed hurting others. Someone who loved to terrify people. Someone who lived for it."

"No. I've never known anyone like that," Maya said.

"You couldn't judge Angel Sonosa by first impressions. My father and Uncle Felix took me to a Christmas program when I was about seventeen, about six months before my dad died. That was the first time I ever saw Angel Sonosa—in a big church in downtown Chicago at Christmastime. He looked like he glowed, and he sang like . . . well, like an angel. What a voice! The entire choir sang backup for him, that's how good he was. He sang *Oh, Holy Night* and the notes he hit gave me chills. I'm not kidding. Goosebumps raced up my legs and spine.

"This was back when the Franks were still managing the warehouse and Angel ran the loading dock." Elly paused and shook her head. "The Franks closed down the warehouse every Christmas Eve and everyone who worked there met at the church to hear Angel sing. I think people were afraid not to go. They were afraid of insulting Angel, and he wasn't someone you ever wanted to insult. There was a big glossy poster in a frame on the front stoop with his photograph and there were news reporters there. We entered a little side door and sat down in the back of the church just as the choir filed in and lined up across the front. A hush fell over the congregation and then Angel came in last, like a celebrity. I remember how the women and girls in the congregation started smiling and giggling. You'd think with a name like Angel Sonosa he'd be dark and exotic, wouldn't you? But Angel was blond and blue-eyed. He was vain about his hair. It was thick and wavy and he combed it in a, I don't know what it was called, but it was high and round in the front like Elvis used to wear his."

"A pompadour?"

"I don't know. I thought it was silly looking, but I heard other girls say it was dreamy. But Angel could really sing. I thought anyone who could sing *Oh,*

Holy Night like that, had to be a good person, right?" Elly's expression changed from awe to disgust. She frowned and swallowed, like there was a bad taste in her mouth.

"Worse than the Franks?" Maya asked.

"Oh yeah, much worse. If I told you everything he did it'd give you nightmares, but you need to know why Angel Sonosa was like the devil himself."

Elly changed position on the sofa, lifting her sock covered feet to the cushions and sitting criss-cross. "I need a minute though, to decide where to start because there's so much to choose from."

"Start with your first memory after the church. And don't worry about the nightmares. You can tell me everything."

"Okay." Elly's eyes were fixed on nothing particular. She stared into her memory. "When Uncle Felix told the Franks I was hired, the Franks stared at me for a moment like they thought it was a joke. "With full pay," Uncle Felix added before he walked away, and the Franks stood there looking like they were waiting for a punch line. I shouted, "Thanks, Uncle Felix," and then they understood it was no joke. I was a real driver. Best of all, I was the boss's neice. Can't argue with that."

"Well, let's show you around then," Frank Zoebek said. "Come this way, sweetie."

"My name is Elly Pederson."

Teisland said, "Touchy little broad ain't ya?"

"Uncle Felix said to let him know if I encounter any problems. Either one of you guys gonna be a problem?"

"Shit," Zoebek growled. "We just get rid of one crazy-ass driver and we're already stuck with another one. You're sure you know how to drive a rig, *Elly Pederson*? A real, full-size rig?"

"I can drive cars, trucks, tractors, loaders, cherry-pickers and bulldozers, and I can make repairs if they break down. But Uncle Felix said trucks are all I need to know for this job."

"How'd you learn truck repairs?"

"My father. He was a mechanic here–"

"Your father worked here?" Teisland asked. "Pederson. Oh, yeah. The guy with crotch cancer."

"Well, okay," Zoebek said. "Here's where you clock in. You're employee number six and that's all you'll need to know. We don't use names on the books or records. If the Feds show up, you wouldn't want 'Elly Pederson' written down anywhere.

"This here's the garage. All six trucks go in and out this one door. After every delivery, you bring the truck back here, clean it up from top to bottom and park it inside, stall number six of course. The cleaning routine is posted over there on the wall. Follow it to the letter. Wear the rain gear hanging on the wall hooks, including a mask, rubber gloves and goggles because the chemicals are strong. There's a watchman on duty at all times to open up the doors and allow you in and out. His name's Ed. Honk twice, wait and honk twice again."

"Ed is here twenty-four-seven?"

"As far as you're concerned, yes," Teisland said. "The watchmen's name is always, Ed, no matter what he looks like. Got it?"

I shrugged. "Okay."

"Ed's the only one without a number. Always wear gloves while driving. No fingerprints inside or outside the truck. Got it?"

"Yes."

"Over here, through this door, is the loading dock. Your truck will already be loaded when you arrive. If it isn't, wait until it is. You never do the loading. When you arrive at the delivery point, there'll be more men to unload it for you. Stay inside the truck. Got it?"

"Yep."

"Come back here. Clean up the truck. Park it in the garage and get the fuck out. Okay?"

"Yeah, I said, and they stared at me, like they were waiting for something. I remember thinking there was something they weren't telling me, like I was the one who should be waiting for the punch line."

"Hey, Angel!" Zoubek shouted. "C'mere. Meet the new driver!" And Angel Sonosa strolled over, eyeing me like a petite filet at the deli. He was well over six feet tall and it was obvious he lifted weights or worked out. He moved like a boxer in the ring. You familiar with the way they walk?" Elly asked Maya. "Boxers?"

Maya nodded. "I went to some boxing matches with Benson, before I realized he was betting on them."

"Well, Angel moved like a boxer. Not really dancing so much, but rolling up on the balls of his feet when he walked, springy and quick, like he was ready to jump one way or the other. He sauntered up to me and stopped less than a foot away. Too close, you know? Looking down at me like . . . I don't know . . . like he didn't care if God knew what he was thinking. 'You're old enough to drive?' he said. 'What are you, fifteen?'"

"Eighteen."

"Hmmm," Angel said. "When Felix told me he might hire a female he didn't mention she'd be a spinner."

Elly shrugged. "I'd never heard that term before and didn't know what it meant. He patted me on the head like a dog, and then he slid his hand down the side of my face, pausing on my cheek and then down my neck to my collarbone. I shoved his hand away and he laughed."

"Sweet," he said. "I heard you know your way around a cherry picker."

"Careful," Teisland said. "She's Felix's niece, remember?"

"Angel just grinned like he didn't care who my uncle was."

"Come on, Miss Pederson." Teisland tapped my shoulder. "We'll get you a jacket, boots and coveralls and show you where your locker is."

Maya frowned. "I've known guys like that, Elly, free with their hands and so certain they have already impressed you, just by breathing."

"It was more than that, Maya. Now, I'd recognize what he was. He was a predator. If I met Angel Sonosa today I'd kill him on the spot."

"Aunt Elly!"

Elly looked tired. "It's true, honey. If I'd killed Angel that first day, maybe things would have turned out better than they did. Maybe Harlan would have been a happier person. I know I would have been."

"But what did Angel do that was so horrible?"

Elly tilted back, rested her head on the rounded arm, and stretched her legs out. "Anything he felt like doing. For instance, one rainy morning I arrived early, before my truck was loaded, so I went inside to wait. There was a man inside, leaning against the wall, smoking. I didn't recognize him and I knew all the other drivers. Angel came around the corner and the man yanked his hand out of his pocket and handed Angle some money. Angel said, "Next time, asshole, you pay first." The guy squirreled out through the door before it shut, but I heard him shout, "There won't be a next time, Sonosa. Your goods are dirty." Angel caught the door and yanked it open. "Hey, Mariccello! What the fuck do you expect for ten bucks?" Angel hadn't spotted me yet. I was sitting on a stool between the time clock and the office door. A few seconds later a storage room door opened and another guy came out, tucking his shirt in and zipping up his pants, and I got this awful feeling, a sick feeling. Behind him, in that storeroom, it was dark but I saw something on the floor. Something pale, something moving, and then the door closed. That guy nodded toward Angel and headed out through the warehouse. Angel walked over and opened that storage room and stood there, long enough for me to see the edge of a mattress on the floor. "You saved some for me didn't ya, honey?" he said, and the door closed behind him. I heard someone crying, so I got up and I ran over and yanked that door open. Angel was kneeling on the mattress. There was a girl there, cowering in the corner and she couldn't have been more than sixteen years old. I told Angel I had already called Uncle Felix and that he was on his way. It was a lie, of course, but Angel jumped up, pulled the naked girl to her feet and shoved her toward me. "Take her with you then, bitch. Let her go outside'a town somewhere. Your rig's ready." I grabbed some coveralls from a hook on the wall and tossed them to the girl. She pulled them on. Her right eye was swollen shut and there was blood crusted around her mouth. She limped and I saw a dozen burns on her toes and the tops of her feet. They looked like cigarette burns. We climbed into my truck and I drove away. I asked her what her name was, but she just stared straight ahead. I asked her where she wanted to go but she didn't say anything. I said, hospital? Police? She didn't say a word, but about a mile away at the first intersection, I stopped at a red light and she opened the door and jumped out. I never saw her again. I never heard what happened to her."

"What did your Uncle Felix say about it?" Maya asked.

"I didn't tell him."

"Why?"

"I was just an eighteen year old girl, scared out of my mind by what I saw. And embarrassed. I should have said something, but I didn't, and I've always regretted that. It was one of my worst mistakes, an unfixable mistake. I could have told Uncle Felix—should have—but I chose not to and I felt guilty. That poor girl was the first person I thought of when Angel showed up here all those years later."

Chapter Twenty-Eight

"Right here, Maya. This here's the place." Elly pointed to a recessed door in a two-story stone building at the south end of Graceville. "You can come upstairs and wait for me if you want, but my lawyer doesn't have much of a waiting room. The magazines are all old and the coffee is awful."

"I'll just walk around Graceville. I'll get a couple clocks at the hardware store, check out the bookstore and Jim's Mercantile. Those can be fun places to browse. I spotted an antique shop too. I love antique shops."

Elly opened the passenger door and stepped out. "I'll be looking for your car around eleven o'clock then," she said. "He said it'd take two hours and he's always right."

Maya parked the Ford Edge in front of Ace Hardware, locked it, and went inside. She picked up a shopping basket and headed up and down the aisles. She found the digital clocks on the fourth aisle and bought three. She picked up extra batteries and another big flashlight. As an afterthought, she bought a dozen plumber's candles, because, if Elly's old house could mess with electrical clocks, it could mess with battery operated clocks too. After paying, she placed the sack on the back seat of the Edge and locked the doors again.

A light rain fell as she hurried down the sidewalk toward the bookstore, regretting that she'd forgotten the umbrella. Her footsteps slowed as she passed Bradley Realty. She paused and peered through the front window. Coty was right. It looked abandoned. A taupe-gray dust coated the chairs, the desk and the filing cabinets. The photos of local properties had been ripped from the front window, leaving spots of tape residue.

Maya dashed from the shelter of one store awning to the next and finally to a third before reaching the bookstore. The door opened with the ring of a brass bell.

"Hello," the woman behind the counter said. "Looks like you just escaped the rain."

"Just barely," Maya said.

Outside, the black clouds opened up and flooded the street and sidewalks. The torrent lasted for a full minute and then let up as suddenly as it started, leaving the gutters rushing like little creeks, pouring into the corner drains.

"I just made a fresh pot of coffee," the woman said. "Help yourself."

Maya's mouth watered at the smell. On a small table chugged a Krups coffeemaker, a pitcher of cream, and a bowl of sugar packets. Behind the sugar bowl stood an old café-style napkin dispenser and a stack of paper cups. She poured cream into a cup and filled it the rest of the way with coffee. "Thanks," she said.

"Are you looking for anything in particular?"

"I'm curious about the history of Graceville," Maya said. "Have anything like that?"

"Yes, up there in the front right corner area of the store. Originally, Graceville was a fort. Later, the town grew up around the logging industry. There's a map on the wall, too. It shows the location of that fort, the wood mill, the hospital, the company store and the old cemetery."

Maya headed toward the map.

"Are you familiar with the area?" the woman called.

"Not much," Maya said. "I've only been here eight weeks."

"Are you a writer?"

"A writer? No. Why?"

"I thought maybe you were a new member of the writer's group. They meet here every Wednesday. They should be showing up any time now. They sit over there at that big table and do timed writings."

Maya glanced toward the table and six chairs at the back of the store.

"Only two of them are real writers—published I mean," the woman said.

"What do they write?"

"Lillian is writing her memoirs. She's an old maid and mainly writes about gardening and canning. There's a romance writer. Her name is Camille." The bookstore clerk frowned and shook her head. "Silly stuff. And then, believe it or not, there's George, who writes awful stories about dead people."

"Oh, biographies?"

"No, it's fiction."

"Ghosts?"

"No, the kind of dead people who are falling apart but keep walking?"

"Zombies?"

"Yes! I can't imagine even thinking about such things, but I find myself eavesdropping, whenever he reads his stuff aloud. Another guy is writing about Graceville. You might want to talk to him. He knows a lot of the history of this town. The other two women are writing mysteries I think."

"I'll check out that map you mentioned," Maya said.

"It's right over there on the wall above the newspapers," the woman said. "Speak of the devil, here come the writers."

The brass bell clanged and six people filed in. She expected to see men wearing rain hats and smoking pipes, or sweaters with leather elbows and the women to have long, graying, untrimmed hair, dressed in ankle length denim skirts with clogs on their feet, but they looked like anyone Maya might pass on the street.

One by one they dropped stenography or yellow legal tablets on the big table before gathering around the coffee machine. They stuffed dollar bills into a tall paper cup.

"Kill anybody else off since last week, George?" One of the women asked.

"Nope." A man grinned.

Maya studied the big map on the wall. It took a minute to identify landmarks. She spotted the river, the quarry, the old hospital which had been torn down, and the fort. Maya's eyes settled on the legend and measured a square of land three miles from the northeast corner of the fort. The script writing labeled the square, Cemetery.

"That can't be," Maya whispered.

"Hello." It was a man's voice.

Maya felt someone touch her sleeve. It was one of the writers. "Hello," she said.

"Linda told me you're interested in Graceville's history." Close up, he looked older than his thick hair suggested. Crow's feet starred the corners of his blue-gray eyes.

"Who is Linda?" Maya asked.

"The woman at the counter," he said.

Maya glanced over his shoulder and spotted the woman he called Linda gawking in their direction. "Well, I am confused by this map," Maya said. "This shows the cemetery much closer to town than it really is."

"That's the old cemetery. It was moved about sixty years ago, every grave and headstone dug up and relocated to a level piece of property three miles farther out."

"Why was it moved?"

"That was a mystery for a while, but I finally dug up the old city records—pardon the pun. It seems the river has changed course several times in recorded history. Some people felt that the graveyard was too close to the river to begin with and ... how can I say this tastefully ... residue from the graves was leaking into the stream. People were terrified at the thought, since quite a few draw their drinking water from that stream. Can't blame them for worrying."

Maya offered her hand. "I'm Maya Pederson. I'm new here."

He nodded. "I'm Hal Neil. Are you a writer?"

"No."

"Too bad," Hal said. "I was hoping for another non-fiction writer for our little group. I'm the only one, unless you count Lillian. And I strongly suspect her memories are embellished. I'll deny I said that, though."

"Your friends are staring at us," Maya said. "I'm probably holding things up."

"No, I am." Hal dragged his wallet from his hip pocket, flipped it open and slid a business card out. "If you have any other questions about Graceville, just call. I've been reading and writing about this town for the last ten years. I'm on my second book, and there isn't much I don't know about this place."

"Thank you, Mr. Neil," Maya said. "I might do that."

"Please, it's just Hal."

"Thanks, Hal."

He returned to the table and sat down. "My turn to draw the first start line, right?"

"Yes. It. Is," someone answered in an impatient tone.

Hal drew a small, folded piece of paper from a yogurt container in the center of the table. He unfolded it and read aloud. "The dirt road was the color of blood."

"Aw jeez. Another one of George's start lines," someone said.

One of the women set a timer on the table and everyone around the table attacked their

tablets with ballpoint pens. Except for the occasional cough or squeak of a chair, the store was silent.

Maya leaned closer and studied the map again before spotting a table against the next wall, loaded with paperbacks. 'All Books $1' the sign said. Maya spotted a book by Victoria Holt, a gothic mystery with the original copyright date. It was in excellent condition, so she picked it up, paid for it at the counter, and exited the store. She tossed her half full coffee cup in the garbage at the street corner and checked the time on the old street clock. Ten-fifteen. She jaywalked at an angle, spotted a CLOSED sign in the antique shop window and entered Jim's Mercantile instead. Inside, the place smelled old. The wood plank floor angled upward toward the back. The wide planks groaned and snapped as she perused the aisles.

"Let me know if I can help you find something," the clerk called.

"Thanks. Just browsing."

He went back to reading his magazine.

Forty minutes flew by and Maya paid for a bottle of lilac bubble bath, a couple light bulbs, and a new Krups coffeemaker. She hurried back to her car, stashed her purchases in the back, and pulled up to the lawyer's office door at exactly eleven o'clock. Elly ran across the sidewalk and opened the car door as enormous raindrops hit the windshield. She slid inside the car and said, "I won't need to see him again for a whole year. Hey, I see sacks on the back seat. Buy anything fun?"

"I'm going to treat myself to a bubble bath and I also bought us a coffeemaker."

"Let's stop at the Red Apple and get us some fresh ground coffee then," Elly said.

"Good idea."

Chapter Twenty-Nine

SHERIFF WIMPLE DROPPED HIS hat on the kitchen counter and himself into a chair at Elly's table. "Thought I'd catch you up on some things," he said. "And I'm hopin' you've thought of some details to fill me in on, too. How's that sound?"

"Fine," Maya said, and made the immediate decision to not tell Sheriff Wimple about Harlan's dark past, nor Elly's dark history. Not yet anyway. When she knew more, maybe then. "Would you like some coffee?" she asked.

"Plain black, please," Sheriff Wimple said. "I've spoken several times recently with your estranged husband, Mrs. Hammond."

"I'd appreciate being called either Maya or Ms. Pederson. My lawyer has assured me it's just a matter of hours before my maiden name is re-established."

"I'll try to remember that, Ms. Pederson."

"I haven't seen or talked to Benson since I left Tacoma," Maya said. "That was over eight weeks ago. If you plan to tell me that Benson is involved in something shady, it won't surprise me." Maya shoved a mug of steaming black coffee on the table and Sheriff Wimple sniffed the steam. "Ahhh. Starbucks?"

"Millstone." Maya studied Sheriff Wimple as he sipped, remembering her first impressions of him. She had been wrong about him. He wasn't milquetoast nor was he timid. He certainly wasn't stupid. Close up, the lines around his eyes gave him a serious or wise appearance. She had not noticed that that before. His habit of clenching his jaw made him appear determined. Sometimes small men were tougher than people expected. She would have to guard her words around him. She wasn't ready to tell him anything about Aunt Elly, not until Elly was done telling everything she knew about Danny.

"Is your aunt going to join us?"

"She's napping. You got a gun under that denim jacket, Sheriff?" Maya asked.

Sheriff Wimple glanced up before setting his mug down on the table. "I do. Does that make you uncomfortable?"

"Not at all. I was just wondering what caliber and whether or not you're a good shot."

"It's a thirty-eight and I usually hit my target."

"You had a talk with Coty a few days ago," Maya said. "He told me the two of you came to an understanding—about what he's doing here."

"We did, yes, but I'd already had him checked out, so I knew what he was telling me was the truth. He is a licensed and bonded private investigator from Seattle. His nephew, Danny went missing over six months ago. Coty isn't his real name though, it's–"

"Wayne C. Matheson," Maya finished his sentence for him. "He told me. But Elly still thinks he's Coty, her best friend's nephew. Elly was expecting this nephew to show up here, and Mr. Matheson's arrival coincided, so he just went along with it because it was a convenient cover."

"I'm not sure it's the right thing to do . . . keeping his identity a secret from Elly, but Mr. Matheson isn't breaking any laws by doing so, and as long as he performs the duties she has hired him to do, and if Elly is informed after his investigation is over, I have no problem with his alias."

"That's how I feel, too," Maya said. "Right now, Elly seems happy to have a handyman around the farm, and Coty . . . I mean, Mr. Matheson, is quite handy with tools and making repairs. If Elly's happy, I'm happy."

"Nothing else new?" Sheriff Wimple said. "About your estranged husband or Tony Bradley?"

"Sheriff, what I know about both men could easily fit inside a thimble. However, Coty told me that Tony Bradley's real estate office is just a front."

"Possibly, although I haven't yet decided what scam he's playing. Mr. Bradley was advised to remove his signs from the front door and the realty photos from the windows or apply for a business license. I'd like to talk to him again, but he seems to have made himself scarce. He's not answering his cell phone and the land phone in his place of business never was connected."

"If I see Mr. Bradley, do you want me to call you?" Maya asked.

"That would be helpful, Ms. Pederson. I'd appreciate it."

Maya smiled. She wanted to like this country sheriff but something about him made her uncomfortable. She didn't know why exactly, but she didn't completely trust Sheriff Wimple.

"When your husband, pardon me, ex-husband and I last spoke, I asked him about his arrest record."

"What did he tell you?" Maya asked.

"He claimed all of the domestic violence charges were due to anger issues and that they were your fault, Ms. Pederson. That's typical. Most husbands who assault their wives claim that. It was his most recent arrest I was curious about, though. He seemed hesitant to discuss it at first, but after a bit, he opened up."

"Benson was arrested after I left?"

"You don't know?"

Maya said, "How would I know? Benson doesn't keep me informed of his activities."

"Seems he used a glass cutter to gain entry to his mother's back door and was in the process of helping himself to her jewelry when she woke up and confronted him. I guess he thought she wouldn't notice the missing jewelry because, as he said, 'It was just old stuff that she doesn't even wear.' I guess she informed him that it was her mother's jewelry, and just because she didn't wear it didn't mean she didn't want it."

"Benson gambles. You probably know that," Maya said. "And sometimes he borrows from one unscrupulous person to pay off another unscrupulous person."

"You mean loan sharks. Yes, I know. That's in his file too."

"Benson may be desperate for cash, Sheriff. He has a good job and earns good money, but he never seems to have enough to support his edgy lifestyle."

"He'll cross the wrong person sooner or later. Guys like him always do."

"Can I give you a refill on your coffee, Sheriff?"

"No thanks. I'll be going now." Sheriff Wimple rose, swiped his hat from the counter and opened the back door. "I'll talk to you again soon."

"See you, Sheriff."

Chapter Thirty

"I'll do the laundry this time, baby girl. That basement doesn't intimidate me like it does you." Elly stood in front of the yellow door with an armload of dirty clothes. "You got anything that needs washing?"

"I'll run upstairs and get my things from the hamper."

"No need to run. I'll put these things in and get them going, and then do your things next." Elly descended into the basement.

Upstairs, the beveled glass in the morning glory window painted a prism on the hardwood floor. The upper landing glowed with sunlight. Light reflected in sharp angles and distorted shapes on the opposite wall. Maya paused there, expecting Danny's green glow to appear, or for the door at the end of the hallway to glide open, exposing its black throat. She felt as if the house was holding its breath. She suspected it was watching her.

"Danny?" Maya whispered. "Are you there?"

The bathroom clock said eleven A.M. A little early for Danny, but he was showing up more and more often, no matter what the time. Sometimes it was brief flashes of Danny's green glow or whispers in the night. He kept trying to tell her something, but something or someone was holding him back. At this moment he was elsewhere. He said nothing.

She stepped into the bathroom and gathered up her things from the hamper. When she returned to the hallway, she halted. Her breath caught in her throat. A gaunt man stood with his back to the morning glory window. His face was sheer and gray and daylight penetrated his entire being. His clay colored hair was dull and straight, sticking out in wisps around his ears. His face was a blur with deep, circular shadows where his eyes would be. His neck was wrapped in a tangled, striped cloth and the cloth hung down across his chest toward his knees. He wore a faded, red striped shirt. He was almost invisible from the waist down but his legs appeared to be bare. He held out one hand and Maya recognized that hand and the gesture.

"Daddy?" Maya stepped closer.

He lifted both hands, as if warning her to stay back.

"Maya." His voiced sounded strained, as if he shouted from a great distance.

"Daddy." Maya took another step toward him.

"Leave here, Maya. Get away . . . today . . . today!"

A second later a cloud blocked the sun and he was gone in an instant. The soft prisms were gone. The angles of light on the wall were gone. The hallway felt cold.

Maya dropped her laundry and ran to where he had stood. She searched the spot with her hand and arms. "Daddy?" She stepped into the space where he had stood. Nothing.

She waited for several moments but he didn't return. Maya picked up her laundry and hurried down to the landing, paused there, hoping her father would appear again, but he didn't. She raced through the dining room and into the kitchen. She heard the sounds of the Maytag chugging and sloshing through the open basement door. The sight of the open door made her throat go dry. And then Elly appeared on the threshold. "I need to show you something," Elly said. "Come with me please?"

"You mean, into the basement?"

"Yes." Elly waved for Maya to follow. "Don't be afraid. There's nothing happening down there right now, nothing except laundry."

Maya carried her laundry down the stairs behind Elly.

"See right here?" Elly crossed eight feet of dirt floor and stopped. She pointed with her toe to a square of plywood at her feet. "When the time comes, tell them to dig here."

"What do you mean, when the time comes?"

"When I can no longer make decisions myself. You know what I mean."

Maya nodded.

"And also over here." Elly moved further away, into the deep shadows in the far corner. "I've put another piece of plywood down here too." Elly tapped her toe on the board. "Tell them to dig here too."

Maya nodded again. "All right."

Elly stared at the plywood for a moment and then said, "One more thing. See this board over here against the wall behind the furnace?" She crossed to the concrete walkway and halted in front of the furnace. She pointed to the gray foundation.

Maya shoved her dirty clothes on the laundry counter and joined Elly on the walkway. She had not been this far into the basement since the door had frosted over and the doorknob grew a coating of ice. She glanced behind, at the small square of plywood, almost expecting skeletal arms to appear and to see bony fingers clawing up through the dirt. She pulled her gaze away and followed the direction of Elly's pointing finger.

"Yes, I see the board," Maya said. "What's behind it?"

Elly frowned and turned her back to the furnace, as if she wished she had never mentioned the board. "It's the opening to a tunnel."

Maya felt something icy touch the back of her neck. She shivered and crossed her arms over her chest. She buried her freezing hands beneath her arms. "A tunnel?"

"It's an escape route, for people Harlan and I hid here."

"You hid people?"

Elly nodded. "Sometimes the deliveries were alive, Maya. Sometimes Felix sent people here to escape from the police."

"Criminals?"

"Sometimes, but not always. Sometimes they were witnesses . . . or the family members of witnesses. Sometimes witnesses don't want to testify, Maya. Sometimes they're afraid to testify. Sometimes there are consequences if they testify."

"Because they're afraid of the people they're testifying against. Sometimes, families are kidnapped until the witness forgets everything he saw, right?"

"Yes, but sometimes testifying means you were guilty too. You've heard of that before, right?"

"You mean when people incriminate themselves, but they get protection from the authorities for telling what they know."

"Unless the cops are crooked too. Felix had friends in the police department. He bought them off. He paid them a lot, so sometimes witnesses disappeared before they could testify. But sometimes a witness was family or an old friend, and those people were sent here and Harlan and I hid them until it was safe to get them out of the country, or to a place where no one would ever think to look for them."

"They stayed down here . . . ?" Maya glanced behind her, into the shadows.

"No, in the attic. The tunnel was just in case the Feds showed up without warning. We were served with a warrant once. They never found this tunnel though. Behind the plywood are concrete blocks. No mortar, so the blocks are easy to move and replace, but if you knock on that plywood it sounds like a solid wall behind it."

"Where does the tunnel lead?" Maya asked.

"Straight out, beneath the driveway, under the bunkhouse and up toward the barns."

"You mean, under the hillside?"

"Yes."

"Elly, was the tunnel already here when you moved in?"

"No, just the house, the big barn and a couple outbuildings. Harlan and I enlarged the living room, built the skylight room and extended the pantry, but . . . " Elly nodded toward the deepest, darkest corner. "First we extended the basement, to support the extended house. Harlan said we needed a foundation to support that much weight. You should always start with a strong foundation."

"When are you going to tell me about those people buried under that board?"

"Oh Maya, the story doesn't start with those people. I can't explain without starting at the beginning. If I told you it was because it was so cold outside . . . that sounds so callous, so uncaring. But it wasn't an ordinary cold winter, honey. We had blizzards that year, and Harlan was very ill, and I had to handle things all by myself. Down here it was dry at least, instead of ice and snow. The dirt is soft and the digging was easier. Let's go back upstairs, get comfortable and tell I'll you about it."

"How about I make us some coffee?"

"Yeah. Okay."

They climbed the stairs. In the kitchen Elly checked the new digital clock on the counter. "It's ten-forty," she said. "Yes, make some coffee, but we have to have everything cleaned up and put away by noon. No coffee pot on the counter, no grounds in the garbage, no dregs in the cups. Harlan can't tolerate the smell of coffee."

"Uncle Harlan is dead, Aunt Elly."

"I know." Elly leaned against the counter with a blank expression. "And that's what makes it all the more baffling when he complains about such things."

Maya filled the new coffee maker with cold water and measured out the ground beans into a paper filter. "When was the last time you saw Uncle Harlan?" Maya plugged in the machine, unplugged it and plugged it in again. Her hands felt cold as she pressed BREW, even though the kitchen was warm.

"Stephen used to do the same thing you just did there, with appliances," Elly said. "He did everything twice. He said it was for luck."

"I never noticed Dad doing that."

"I think he got over it by the time you came along. Your mother used to fuss at him about his little rituals. She called them little ceremonies. If anything, she made things worse by nagging at him all the time. Anyway, I saw Harlan just the other day, when I got back from seeing my lawyer. He was sitting in my rocking chair upstairs, waiting for me."

"In your bedroom?"

Elly nodded. "He wanted to know what the lawyer and I talked about. Harlan's always been bullish and stubborn. He doesn't like me making decisions without him."

Maya couldn't help smiling. "Maybe he should have gone to the lawyer, instead of you."

Elly giggled. "That's funny, because that's what I suggested he do while I was changing clothes."

"What did he say?"

"Nothing. When I came out of the closet he was gone."

"Smell that?" Maya said. "I love the smell of fresh brewed coffee."

"I think the smell reminds Harlan of something that happened to him a long time ago. I seem to remember that he was scalded by hot coffee when he was young. He had a red burn scar on his shoulder."

Maya said, "I understand that. I've never been able to tolerate the smell of cigarettes. I used to get carsick when Daddy smoked, even though he always cracked the window. I still feel sick when I smell cigarettes."

"Guess it's a good thing I gave up smoking," Elly said.

"You smoked?"

Elly paused, two large mugs in her hands and the cupboard door open. "I have a memory of smoking, briefly. But it was a long time ago and maybe I just dreamed it. Sometimes I have a hard time telling a dream from what's real. Doesn't everyone?"

No. Not everyone. Just you and me.

In the living room Elly set her mug on the coffee table and stretched out on the sofa. She took a deep sigh and eased into the memory.

"Felix sent four Mexican men to dig the tunnel for us. None of them spoke English. They were here over three months and all we had to do was feed them. They stayed out in the bunkhouse."

"They never talked to you?"

"No, just to each other, and I couldn't understand a word they said. One of them ordered the others around so I guess he was the boss. The other three called him, Coatl."

"That's an old Nahuati name," Maya said. "Ancient Aztec."

"Whatever they were, they worked awfully hard," Elly said. "From dawn to dark. It was a warm summer, so they washed their own clothes and bathed in the stream."

"I'm going to ask you a question, Elly . . . and I hope you don't think I'm mean. I know nothing about Felix except what you've told me—that he helped you, that he gave you a job, but, would Felix have killed those men rather than pay them?"

Elly stared into the empty fireplace as if searching for an answer in the soot and ashes. She frowned. "Maybe. When the Sheriff's men found another skeleton in those tunnels, and you found two at the bottom of the old well . . . the same thought occurred to me. Those bones might be those Mexican tunnel diggers. I never saw them leave. One morning when I got up, they were just gone."

"We don't know for sure that's what happened," Maya said. "DNA testing would tell us a lot. We can ask Sheriff Wimple about it."

"If it's true, it was a rotten thing for Felix to do, wasn't it? Just thinking about how he might have done something like that makes telling this story easier," Elly said. "And the story needs to be told."

Elly reached down and pulled the afghan up over her feet and legs, even though the room felt warm and stuffy to Maya. Elly closed her eyes and was quiet for a moment before she began.

• • • *

"Some of the money for this farm came from Felix. Harlan and I used all the money we had saved up as a deposit . . . half the price of the property, and Felix made quarterly payments to the bank after that, but somehow he got the impression this place was his. We had words about it once and he backed down. I guess he remembered his promise to Dad, to take care of me, but sometimes he'd remind me of all the money he'd given me over the years. Eventually though, we called it even. We didn't talk about it anymore after he agreed the farm was ours, but I think he always believed I owed him something.

"Felix phoned one day and said he needed to store something in our attic. I said, sure. He said he was sending four men and that they'd be here for a while. He said for Harlan and me to feed them and to give them someplace to sleep out of the rain. I said, okay. About a week later those four Mexicans showed up. Coatl handed me a roll of paper . . . drawings . . . plans for the tunnel, along with a note from Felix, saying what he wanted them to do in our attic."

"What about the attic?"

"First, they reinforced the flooring up there and then they put down pads and runners of thick carpeting everywhere. After that, the attic floor didn't creak or groan at all. People could've danced up there and it would've been dead quiet down here. Then those dormers were boarded over and black canvas nailed up. Not a trace of light shows from the outside."

"Because people were going to stay up there? People you were hiding for Felix?" Maya asked.

"Yep. One guy hid out there for two months before Felix sent a car for him. Felix said they got him into Canada and set him up with his own small business."

"A legitimate business?" Maya asked.

"Probably, since they didn't want any more trouble. About a year later Felix sent next two more people, a man and his wife. Poor souls. They were scared out of their minds. They never said one word to me in the three weeks they were here. Not one word. I'm not certain they spoke English. I'd send a tray of food up through the dumbwaiter, and an hour later, clean dishes would come back down. There's a sink and toilet up there, but I never once heard the toilet flush or water running."

"There's a dumbwaiter here?"

"I've never shown you, have I? It's inside the utility closet in the pantry. If you look up, you'll see a bent nail sticking out in the corner of the ceiling. The ceiling of that closet is actually the bottom of the dumbwaiter. Pull down on that nail and the dumbwaiter lowers. The pull cords are behind the mop handles in the corner. They look like wound up clothesline. Anyway, that man and woman were probably the easiest people we ever had here. They never asked for anything, and then Felix sent a car for them and he told me later they ended up in Amsterdam."

"They didn't end up . . . in the basement?"

"No, no. I'm getting to that." Elly opened her eyes wide and stared straight up at the ceiling. "That basement episode happened one winter . . . and it was such a terrible cold winter. It was January. The warmest day that whole month was twenty-five degrees. Most days it never got above ten. Some nights it was down below zero. We had eighteen inches of snow for Christmas, and the snow turned to ice. The ground was frozen solid. I could have buried them inside the upper barn, but there were already so many buried up there and it would've been hard getting them up the hill by myself. Like I said, Harlan was sick." Elly turned her head and blinked at Maya. "Remember, Maya, about the upper barn . . . when it's time.

"I was afraid to go very far from the house with Harlan so ill. I had forty chickens in the coop to feed and water, a cow to milk twice a day in the shed, and Harlan to nurse upstairs. The driveway was really bad. I slipped and fell just trying to cross it and I wouldn't have tried driving across that bridge down there for anything. It was coated with two inches of ice. So we were stuck here, and then out of the blue Fritz shows up. How he managed to get that truck across the bridge and up the driveway, I don't know. Maybe he and the devil really are friends.

'Got a spare for ya, Elly,' Fritz said. Hell Fritz, I said, take it someplace else, cuz' Harlan's sick and the ground is frozen. 'Not my problem,' he said, and he had those three bags out of the truck and on the driveway before you could scat a cat. Then he hopped in that truck, turned it around, and headed down the driveway. I watched him from the pasture gate, hoping he'd slide off the bridge and down through the ice, but somehow the bastard made it back to the road. He left that delivery for me to handle all by myself. There I was, sixty-eight years old with arthritis setting in, and he just laughs and drives away.

"So I dragged them one by one, down the driveway, around the side of the house, and in through the basement door. Let me tell you, honey, you might think it feels cold down there right now at fifty degrees, but compared to twenty, that's practically balmy.

"First, I checked on Harlan. He was sound asleep, so I went back down and started digging. The last bag moved a little after I rolled it into the grave. It was the woman. She was in bad shape with a hole in her forehead and her eyes rolled up under her lids. I pressed my fingers against her throat and felt a faint pulse. I went upstairs and got a wool blanket, folded it and put it over her, and then I sat down beside her and waited. I put a few drops of water on her lips, but was afraid water would drizzle into her lungs—she wasn't swallowing—so I stopped doing that. I checked her pulse again. It was weak and fluttering. I went up and checked on Harlan again. He was sleeping just fine, so I stretched out beside him and dozed off. When I went back down to the basement, she had no pulse, made no breath on a mirror and her skin was cold to the touch, so I closed up her bag and buried all three of them, side by side. I figured they'd want to be together.

"If there had been just one, I would have dug down six feet, but there were three of them. A four-foot deep hole was all I could handle. It was horrible, baby girl. It was just awful.

"And when I'm gone, baby girl, dead and buried . . . or whatever . . . I want you to make up for some of the things that happened back then."

"How?"

"You'll know what to do. You're smart. And you have a kind heart. After everything calms down and people are done snooping around and asking questions, you'll know what to do. I'm so glad you're here and that you listen to me. I'm glad you understand."

Elly thinks I would have done the same thing? That I would have allowed the woman to lie in a cold shallow grave as her life slipped away like a wisp of smoke—before shoveling dirt over her? Maya leaned back into the armchair with a numb feeling. *No. I wouldn't have done that. Couldn't have. No.*

"Goodness! It's eleven-fifty." Elly threw back the afghan and ran for the kitchen. She rinsed out the carafe, wound up the cord and stored the coffee maker in a bottom cupboard. Maya dumped the coffee grounds and the filter into a grocery bag and dropped the bag into the garbage can outside the door while Elly washed the mugs and dried them. As Elly fanned the kitchen door, wafting fresh air into the room, she giggled. "Harlan will never know."

Maya shuddered. *Five minutes ago Elly described sleeping beside Harlan while a woman lay dying in the cold dirt of the basement—and now she's giggling.*

Chapter Thirty-One

"Thanks for meeting me here. This place has the best desserts in Graceville." Hal Neil opened the door for Maya. Inside Louisa's Bakery, the smells of fresh bread and apple fritters filled the air. Six small tables and chairs lined the wall opposite the display counter, where cakes, pies, donuts, cinnamon rolls and maple bars lined up on trays behind the glass.

"Why doesn't your writer's group meet here?" Maya asked. "Look at all the treats."

"Our group did meet here at first, but Lillian complained she gained fifteen pounds that year, and Camille is diabetic so we moved to the bookstore. What would you like?"

"I'm partial to maple bars," Maya said.

Hall waved at the man behind the display case. "Two maple bars and two coffees please, Bill." Hal slid a chair out for Maya at a window table. From where she sat she had a view of Main Street, all the way up to Ace Hardware.

"I've been thinking about that map at the bookstore," she said. "It looks like the cemetery used to be–"

"Where you're currently living?" Hal nodded. "You're right. Elly Pederson's house was a mortuary and the ten acres surrounding it was the old graveyard. Some of those graves were Native American dating back over two hundred years. Special permits had to be obtained before they could be moved, and the graves handled with honor and ritual to satisfy the local tribes."

A man approached along with the smells of maple sugar and coffee. He slid the edge of a tray on their table followed by two steaming mugs and two giant maple bars. "Let me know if I can get you anything else." He smiled and hurried away.

"Thanks, Bill," Hal said. "Bill makes the best maple bars in the state, and I'd know because I'm sure I've tried them all."

Hal sipped his coffee and said, "On the phone you said you have a question about the Pederson farm."

"You answered it already. Sounds like my aunt and uncle bought an old cemetery."

"They must have got a heck of a deal on it. It had been on the market for quite a while without any takers. If you want, I can find out how much they paid for it."

"I don't need to know that, but the graves had already been relocated when they bought the place, right?"

"Oh yeah. Years earlier."

"Every single grave?"

Hal smiled. "That would have been my first question, too. Actually, I can't imagine buying an old cemetery and living there. I know it's just dirt and I'm not superstitious, but the whole idea—it's just not something I would consider doing. I don't think I'd be able to sleep in a house where bodies were prepared for burial, and surrounded by ten acres of empty graves. Moving them a mile or two away wouldn't have satisfied me."

"I want to know where the boundaries of that old cemetery were, the original property lines. Was it from the top of the hill down to the stream, or from the house over the hill to the Schaff property? And what about that old barn? It's practically falling down it's so old. It must have been there back when the cemetery was there."

"Yes, it was there according to the records," Hal said. "It was built the same time as the house. The cemetery included the top of the hill, but not clear to the Schaff property line. The
graveyard was ten acres in size, all the way from the top of the hill down to the river, although I don't think there were graves in all ten acres. "

"Aunt Elly told me she and Uncle Harlan added on to the house."

"I don't recall reading about a Harlan Pederson."

"His name was Harlan Jones. Aunt Elly and Harlan were married, but she kept her own name," Maya said.

"Interesting. Thanks for the info."

"This is the best maple bar I've ever eaten, and this coffee is certainly better than that stuff at the bookstore."

Hal chuckled. "Linda doesn't drink coffee herself, and that probably explains why the stuff she makes tastes like boiled boots."

Maya spotted Coty standing on the sidewalk outside the window. They made eye contact before he turned and walked away.

"Do you know him?" Hal asked. "He looked kind of upset."

"That's Coty, the handyman at the farm. Elly hired him back in February to fix the roof and the bridge because she plans to sell the place." Maya finished her coffee. "I wonder why he's upset."

Hal shrugged. "Just a thought about selling the old cemetery farm. Potential buyers will find out the history behind that property, so selling the place might not be so easy."

"That's what I was thinking, unless someone wants a lot of acreage at a reduced price. But there is that view property up there on the ridge. That's got to be worth something."

"Yes, that view is outstanding, but there's no road up to it," Hal said. "No power, no sewer, no water. It's not developed. That reduces its value, unfortunately."

Chapter Thirty-Two

TWO DAYS LATER, MAYA knocked on the bunkhouse door and listened for the sound of footsteps. Earlier that morning she had knocked on Coty's door and also the previous evening, with no luck. She hadn't seen Coty since having coffee with Hal Neil at Louisa's Bakery. She tried the doorknob. The door opened.

"Coty?" Maya stuck her head inside. The lights were off and the room felt cool. The little window on the potbellied stove was black. The bunk against the wall was unmade, the sheets and blankets in twisted lumps and the pillow was on the floor. Maya backed out and closed the door. She returned to the kitchen. "I haven't seen Coty in two days, Elly. Have you?"

"Not since morning before last. I wonder what he's up to," Elly said.

"He mentioned his nephew is missing. Maybe he's visiting his sister and brother-in-law."

"Could be," Elly said. "But you'd think he'd tell us before leaving, wouldn't you?"

Maya nodded.

Elly washed and Maya dried the dinner dishes.

"Time for a clean dish towel." Elly opened the basement door and tossed the used towel and dishcloth to the bottom of the stairs. She left the basement door open behind her as she opened a drawer and selected another towel.

Maya closed the door. She locked it, unlocked it, and locked it again. She tested the lock. It held, and she rubbed her hands together to stop them from trembling. She feared the day Elly forgot to close that door, a day when she wasn't around to close it and lock it herself. Who might climb those stairs, and what would he do if he came inside?

"Are you okay, Maya? You look pale, honey."

"I'm chilled," Maya said. "I can't seem to get warm."

"Go up and take that bubble bath you mentioned. That'll warm you up."

"I meant to do that last night," Maya said. "But was too tired and just took a quick shower instead."

"Well, go take that bath now. There's nothin' like a hot bath to warm your joints."

Ten minutes later Maya stretched out in the big claw foot tub with lilac scented bubbles crackling beneath her chin. Her neck and shoulders relaxed. The cramps in her calves eased and her hands stopped aching with cold.

Discovering this house had at one time been a mortuary and the surrounding acreage an old graveyard didn't bother Maya as much as she expected it would. Hal Neil said it would keep him awake nights, but graveyards didn't frighten her. Graveyards had never frightened her. Cemeteries were peaceful places, like walking trails and public parks. She had grown up within walking distance of a graveyard. Graves were hallowed ground, sanctified and blessed. Prayers were murmured over graves. It was the one hundred-fifty or so, unnamed, unmarked graves surrounding Elly's house that bothered her, because no prayers had been spoken over those graves. Those were tainted by murder. Maya had made a promise to those people buried in the basement. She had promised she would help them. And she would. "But how?" Maya slid lower into the tub, until hot water touched her lower lip, and the scented bubbles crackled in her ears.

"I know where you are," she whispered. "And I won't forget my promise to you."

When perspiration tickled her upper lip, Maya pulled the bathtub plug, rinsed off with the hand-held sprayer and stepped from the tub. She heard the phone ring downstairs in the kitchen.

"Hello? Yes," Elly said. "Coty, is that you? Well . . . wait a minute. Let me check and see if she's out of the tub yet."

Elly's footsteps tapped across the linoleum, the hardwood floor in the dining room and then her voice carried up the stairs. "Maya? Coty's on the phone."

"Be right there!" Maya wrapped herself in her robe and slid her feet into her slippers. She ran downstairs and grabbed the phone. "Coty? Are you okay?"

"Maya, sorry . . . sorry." It was Coty's voice but he sounded drowsy. His words were slurred.

"Coty, what's wrong?"

"I'm hunky dory. How are you?"

"Where are you?" Maya asked.

"River Lodge."

"Café?"

"Nope. I'm in'da bar."

"What's going on? Do you need help?" Maya asked.

"Dey woon't gimme my car keys."

"You need a ride home?"

"Yeah. I guess so."

"I'll be there in fifteen minutes."

It sounded like Coty dropped the receiver. It banged against the wall or the floor before he hung up.

"I'm pretty sure he's drunk," Maya said. "I'll go get him."

"Want me to come with you, baby girl?" Elly asked. "Drunks can be hard to handle."

"No, you stay and read your new magazine. I won't be gone long. I'll have my cell phone."

Upstairs again, Maya slipped into clean jeans and a shirt, grabbed her wallet and keys and ran outside to the carport. Once inside the Edge, she coasted down the driveway, across the bridge and then climbed the other side of the valley. It was a mild evening, warm enough to drive with the windows wide open. How odd, she decided, that she had been so chilled and achy earlier. Now the air felt muggy and warm.

She headed straight toward a bright full moon above the tree line. Maya pulled into the River Lodge parking lot and spotted Coty on the big front porch. He sat on one of the rustic benches near the front door, leaning back against the wall of the restaurant with his legs stretched out in front of him. She parked alongside the front steps, leaned over and opened the passenger door.

"Hey," she called. "Can you walk?"

"I walked in by myself." Coty stood, swaying from side to side. "Didn't I?" He staggered to the stairs and then stumbled. His knees folded like a wooden puppet's and he grabbed the log railing and held on while his legs and feet continued down the steps.

"Aw jeez." Maya climbed from behind the wheel, ran around and grabbed Coty's free arm. "What's the occasion?"

"I tol' my sister Danny's dead."

"Oh."

"Sis said she already knew. She dreamed it, she said."

Coty stumbled again and leaned heavy against Maya. "Fuck," he said. "Oops. Sorry. Took French in high school."

Maya propped him up. "You're not going to throw up in my car, are you?"

"Nope. I can hold my liquor."

"I can tell. Can you climb in?"

Coty nodded and crawled into the passenger seat. He fumbled with the seatbelt until Maya snapped the buckle for him and then fastened her own.

"Home, James." Coty said. "Or maybe, home Jane." He chuckled at his silly joke.

Maya headed out of town, the moonlight glowing through the back window. "I'm sorry about your nephew," she said.

"He wasn't a bad kid, ya know, just in trouble all the time. He did a short stay in Juvie."

Maya had no idea what to say or how to console Coty. *Just let him talk, I guess.*

"Looks like I fell off the wagon," Coty said. "Damn. After seven years sober too."

"You're a recovering alcoholic?"

"Wuz recoverin' more'r less." Coty slapped his knee and chuckled again. "Right now it feels like less." He leaned close to the open window and inhaled. "It's nice out, isn't it?"

"It's a very nice evening."

"How was your date at the bakery? Yummy?"

"What?"

"Is it a good bakery? I saw you there . . . with that guy."

"His name is Hal Neil. He's a local writer."

"Oh, a real smarty-hearty pants, huh? All educated and stuff?"

"I don't know. I suppose he is. He said he's working on his second book."

"Did'ja kiss him?"

"What? No. He writes history . . . about Graceville. I had questions for him about Elly's farm. We talked about how Graceville used to be an old fort with a hospital and a cemetery. Hey! Why would you ask me something like that anyway?"

"Cuz' I saw how you were looking at him, smilin' like women do when they're flirtin'."

"I was not flirting."

"Well, maybe not. You sure haven't flirted with me."

Maya pulled to the shoulder of the road. "What's wrong, Coty? Are you accusing me of something? If so, be specific."

"It's Wayne C. Matheson . . . member?"

"I have a hard time remembering because you've been 'Coty' all this time–"

"And yet," Coty waved a scolding finger in the air. "You 'spect every'n to call you Maya Pederson instead of Maya Hammond. Dubble standard, dubble standard."

"That's different."

"How is it different?"

"All right," Maya said. "I'll try to remember to call you Wayne from now on."

"Let's hear it, den."

"Your name?"

"Yeah. Say it."

"Wayne C. Matheson."

"Again."

"Wayne C. Matheson."

"I like the way you say it. Sounds nice."

Maya sighed. "Let's go home before you pass out and I have to carry you inside."

"Wait." Coty leaned across the console, grabbed her arm and pulled her closer. "Gotta do dis now, or it'll never happen." He held her face with both hands and kissed her.

Maya almost pushed him away, but Coty's lips were warm and gentle and his eyes were closed. He was hurting and vulnerable. His nephew was dead. He fell off the wagon. Right now he was convinced he was a failure. She knew that feeling.

Coty settled back into the passenger seat. "What I'm 'bout to do, has absolutely nuthin' to do with you, so doon't take it personal." He released his seatbelt, opened the passenger door and dropped to his knees on the shoulder of the road. Holding the door with one hand, he vomited, twice. "Oh hell," he said. "Sorry."

Maya smiled. "Better now than two minutes ago. Are you done?"

"I think so." He wiped his mouth on his sleeve and climbed back into the Edge. "I hope so anyway."

"Let's get you home." She fastened Coty's seatbelt again, checked the rearview mirror and pulled out on the road. Five minutes later the Edge idled in front of the bunkhouse door. Coty rolled out again, but managed to stand on his own.

"I owe ya," he said. He leaned against the front door of the bunkhouse, fumbling with the doorknob.

"Wayne?"

"Yeah?" He glanced back toward the Edge.

"It was a nice kiss."

"Jeez," he said. "I wuz wonderin.'"

Chapter Thirty-Three

"WHY ARE YOU SITTING here in the dark, Aunt Elly?"
"Just remembering stuff—doing some thinking."
"About what?"
"I'm thinking about when my father died and Uncle Felix ran the warehouse."

It had been over a week since Elly had talked about the early years with Harlan and Felix and the Mexican workers.

"Need to talk?"

"Yes, but would you mind making me a cup of chamomile tea first, Maya, while I go upstairs and get into my robe and slippers?"

Maya nodded and headed for the kitchen. She heard Elly climbing the stairs. Maya checked the lock on the basement door. Locked. She tested it, tested it again, and then again. She filled the kettle and waited, gazing through the kitchen window above the sink. Outside, the fir branches above the bunkhouse were black-green lace in front of a deep purple sky. The window was open and the curtains hung straight down. It had been a hazy day, clearing as the sun set behind the hill. A frog called from the forest and another answered from under the porch. She checked the wall clock. 9:00 PM.

Earlier that day, Maya had answered the phone when it rang. She heard a man say, "This is Milo's truck driver. What's the biggest truck we can get up your driveway?"

"It's the antiques dealer." Maya handed the receiver to Elly.

"Yeah?" Elly said, and a few seconds later, "The bridge will hold a ten ton with tail lift. Nothin' heavier or you'll break through and end up in the river." Elly hung up with a frown. "They're on their way."

An hour later a moving truck pulled up to the back door and three burly men wearing gray overalls with blue oval patches that read, *Milo's Resurrection* climbed out and tromped inside.

The shortest man halted at the bottom of the stairs. He eyed the living room and then turned around and frowned at the dining room. "What about all this stuff in here?" He pointed to the big table, the china cabinet and buffet while flipping through papers on a clipboard.

"Nothing there," Elly said. "Leave all that."

"You're sure, lady? Milo said all the furniture except the kitchen and a couple bedrooms upstairs."

"I'm quite sure." Elly sounded irritated, her words clipped short. "As you can see, the cabinet is still full of my china and crystal. Don't touch it. Don't touch anything in there because I'm taking it with me when I leave."

"Fine," he said and entered the living room. "But this stuff goes, right?"

"Yes. Sofa, chairs, tables, bookshelves. Take it all," Elly reached down and claimed her stack of Retirement Living magazines from the coffee table. "You can empty the bedrooms upstairs, except for the two rooms with their doors closed. Don't even open those doors."

Two hours later, the truck rumbled away and Elly lowered herself into a chair beside the kitchen table with a sigh. "Let's sit here and talk, Maya. All those bad memories I shared with you before has made the living room a depressing place for me. And there's no place to sit in there anyway unless it's on the floor, and I'm too stove-up to do that."

Elly flipped on the kitchen light and sat down with her back to the dining room. Maya faced the dark bay window. A three-quarter moon had risen high enough to peek through the upper branches of the evergreens where the fields sloped down toward the stream. There were no clues, no hint that the field has once been a graveyard. It was covered with willowy field grass. The grass waved like pale feathers in the breeze and glowed like pale hair in moonlight.

Maya pulled her gaze away from the field and glanced toward the big barn. With a tight feeling in her throat she lowered her eyes to her steaming tea cup. She and Elly sipped without talking for a few more minutes. Finally, Elly spoke.

"Have you seen Coty since you hauled his drunk ass home?"

Maya smiled. "I saw him late yesterday afternoon, sitting on the chopping block by the shed, sipping bottled water and looking kind of green around the gills."

"I got drunk once. It wasn't worth the hangover, and besides, Harlan doesn't approve of spirits." Elly grinned. "No pun intended."

"Have you seen Uncle Harlan again?"

"Not since the day you drove me into town, and that's been, what, a week? I think Harlan is peeved with me about talking to the lawyer. He won't stay mad, though. He never does."

Maya rubbed the warm bottom of her mug with the palm of her hand. She wanted to make small talk, to discuss the weather or the grocery list on the counter. Or they could list the things left to do around the house before phoning a realtor. Maya wanted to postpone hearing another of Elly's secrets, but she hesitated too long and Elly dove straight into the story.

• • • *

"Angel Sonosa gave Harlan a wide berth around the Chicago warehouse, but then, everybody did. Uncle Felix used to say, 'Harlan is a short fuse with explosives at the other end.' Felix gave me an odd, cautious look when he said that, like he expected me to react.

"Nobody gave Harlan guff twice. He didn't chat with the other drivers or brown-nose management. He did his job, took his pay and came home to me. I'm the only person Harlan ever really talked to. I'm the only person he trusted.

"There was this one time, Harlan was sick with some kind of—despair or melancholy—something to do with his childhood. I think it was something that happened when he was five years old, about his shoulder getting scalded, but he never wanted to talk about it, so I showed up at the warehouse to drive his route for him. I remember clocking in two minutes late, and I remember the way everyone stared at me and how they all stopped talking as I walked by, and the way they grabbed their coats and scattered like I carried the plague or something. They were gone in seconds."

"Hey Elly, is that you?" Angel asked. "I'm never sure if it's you or Harlan from behind."

"Harlan's sick," I said. "He's not coming in, so I thought I'd drive his route for him."

"Well, Harlan's truck is already gone, Elly. I gave it to Henry 'cuz Henry was here and Harlan wasn't. Them's the rules. But, I got Harlan's paycheck. It's in the office if you want it."

"Sure, I said, but I should'a known something was wrong. I should'a known something was fermenting in Angel's sour brain. He opened the office door for me and I stepped inside. He closed it and locked it and turned off the light. He grabbed me around the neck with one big hand, and shoved me down on the floor behind the desk. I hit my head on the foot of the chair and I landed so hard on that floor it knocked the wind outta me. The bastard fell on me like a collapsing wall and he didn't let me up until he was finished. I've never told anyone before . . . not even Harlan." Elly set her mug down. "I didn't want Harlan trying to *fix* that. There was no way to fix Angel raping me. I just needed to get away, far away, before he thought about hurting me again.

"It wasn't really Harlan who wanted to leave Chicago, it was me, but Harlan agreed. He'd had that close call with the bloody truck and the cops, remember? So when I said I wanted to leave, he said, let's go right now, Elly. That night we packed up our old forty-two Ford and early the next morning we headed west. We didn't stop for anything except gasoline and restrooms until we reached the Montana state line. We ate and slept in the car and took off again the next morning—made it all the way to Bremerton Washington in two days. We slept in the car again, near the beach outside a little town called Tracyton and we bought a newspaper that listed cheap acreage. We drove up here to Graceville and found this place and we've never left. I phoned Felix and told him where I was and he promised he'd keep that news to himself.

"We had four years of peaceful farm life before Felix talked Harlan into doing some more work for him. Sweet Harlan would never have agreed to the new contract if he'd known what Angel did to me. When Harlan told me we were going back into the business, I got terrible sick and even ran a fever. I swallowed nothin' but water for three days but then I finally snapped out of it. One day Harlan said he had to drive to Seattle to see where the new warehouse was and to get a delivery truck. I stayed here to take care of the chickens, and Bossy the cow, and Morris the horse. That's where I was, out there milking Bossy when Angel drove up. 'Well if it isn't my little Elly,' he said. He was driving a new blue Cadillac with lots of chrome. 'Want to go for a ride, Elly? This baby has automatic everything, even the windows. Look at this.' He raised and lowered his driver's window twice, showing off. I can't, Angel, I said. I got animals to care for. "What animals?" and he snorted like that was the stupidest thing he'd ever heard. He turned off the engine and got out of the car. 'Where?' he said. A cow and a horse, I said, and forty chickens. I pointed to the coop and the shed and Angel pulled his gun from his back holster and he walked straight toward the shed, dragging me because I was hanging on his sleeve. What are you going to do, Angel? Wait, I said. Stop! But he threw open the shed door and he shot Bossy and Morris, right through their ears. Shot 'em dead, right there in front of me, and while I stood there crying, he went back and got a gas can out of his trunk and he doused the chicken coop and set it on fire. Oh, Maya, you've never heard such a terrible sound as those chickens going up in flames. Poor things. There were chicks in that coop too. That's what Angel was like though. He enjoyed hurting people and animals alike. I remember him describing one time, how he almost drove off the road trying to run down a neighbor's dog, and he was pissed because it got away, and he was planning to go back and hunt for that dog.

I stood there in the driveway and screamed at Angel. Harlan won't like what you've done, I said. Harlan's going to be angry.

Angel grinned. 'Well, Crazy Harlan knows where to find me, Elly. Felix had me move out here from Chicago to manage the new warehouse in Seattle. I'm your boss again, Elly, and you know what I think is so funny? You and Crazy Harlan both work for me, but I only have to pay one of you." He laughed so hard I thought he would choke.

So, I walked around the front of his car, through rolling smoke that smelled of scorched feathers and burned chicken, and I opened the passenger door and slid inside. I remember the ashtray was full of butts and ashes. It didn't smell like a new car. It stunk. There was an empty cigarette pack on the floor and an empty beer can and a Charleston Chew candy wrapper. Isn't it odd how I remember those things? I can still see them plain as day. He opened the driver's door and dropped in behind the wheel with a smile and said, 'You've missed me, haven't you Elly? That's why I made this first delivery myself. It's in the trunk." I said, it smells like it's been there a bit too long. And you know what, Angel? I haven't missed you at all. I was just hoping you'd show up here someday. I leaned against him and stroked his neck with my left hand for a second while I slid my ankle stiletto out with my right hand and drove it straight and deep into his ear. I pulled it out and sliced his throat wide open with it. Didn't take more'n three seconds to do all that."

Elly dragged her gaze away from the dark bay window and stared straight at Maya. There was an odd, familiar light in Elly's eyes. Probably, Maya thought, the same light Angel Sonosa saw as his life pulsed into his lap.

"I couldn't believe Angel Sonosa just sat there in my driveway, dying like any mortal dies. I could tell he was shocked at what I'd done. He couldn't believe he was dying. His eyes were bulging, and his tongue slid out through the gash in his throat. I leaned back and watched him choke and sputter. Blood went everywhere. It spattered the windshield and all over the dashboard . . . even some on me. He grabbed his throat—they always do—and blood throbbed out between his fingers and down his arms and shirtfront. After a few seconds his lap was shiny with blood and his pants and the upholstery were soaked red. I leaned closer, looked him in the eye and I said, 'thanks for making the first delivery in person, Angel. And don't you worry . . . no one will discover it for a very long time. I'll take care of everything, like I always do.'

"I realized afterward, that I could have saved Bossy and Morris and the chickens if I'da acted sooner, but Angel took me by surprise. So then, doesn't it seem right for me to have taken him by surprise too? I think so. I don't think I've ever seen anyone look more surprised than Angel Sonosa did that day, right out there in the driveway."

Chapter Thirty-Four

Heart pounding, Maya ran from the skylight room into the pantry hall. She halted in front of the utility closet. She heard a loud thump from inside and opened the door. The closet was empty. It smelled sour and moldy inside, even though it gleamed with fresh, white paint. No mop or broom leaned in the corner, no bucket sat on the floor. Again, *thump*. The closet ceiling vibrated with the sound. The dumbwaiter cords shook. Maya reached up and pulled the nail and the dumbwaiter slid downward. She saw brown, bare feet, nicked, bloody shins and frayed cut-off jeans. A stocky man squatted on the floor of the dumbwaiter. His eyes were dull. He stared straight ahead. His calloused hands lay in his lap like two raw steaks. His mouth hung open, drool trailing from the corners of his mouth to his tattooed chest. The tattoo was that of a phoenix.

Maya jumped back as the dumbwaiter landed hard in the bottom of the utility closet. The man tilted forward, rolling out at her feet. The back of his head was gone. A patch of black hair, white skull and pink brains lay in the bottom of the dumbwaiter.

"Elly! Elly!" Maya ran into the kitchen and halted by the sink as the back door opened and Harlan stepped inside. His brows were cinched together over the bridge of his nose and he wore his usual scowl. His long gray hair was braided and the braid hung down over his collar and across the front of his red plaid shirt.

"Found him, huh?" Harlan said. "Finders-keepers—you found him—you bury him. The shovel's in the basement, girl."

The yellow basement door stood wide open and on the threshold squirmed a mismatched, collection of body parts. A man's profile bulged outward from between a portion of abdomen and armpit. The jaw clenched and the teeth snapped. Maya dove through the open window above the sink and landed on the driveway. Coty and Elly turned from where they stood arm-and-arm at the bunkhouse door. They frowned at her and from the shed came the sound of an engine's growl. Coty's Dodge truck coasted forward and down the driveway toward her with no one at the wheel. Maya leaped toward the bunkhouse but the wheels turned and the truck followed her. When she backed up, the tires turned again. She ran back to the kitchen door, but Harlan slammed it shut. She heard him turn the key and heard the door lock. She heard him test the lock. He grinned at her through the window. Behind him squirmed Angel's writhing collection of fleshy chunks, his teeth grinding, his eyes pearly gray, like those of a long-dead fish.

Maya heard the porch railing splinter behind her, the wood ripping away. The porch floor buckled, one plank after the other like keys on a piano. Maya jumped away from the truck, toward the rhubarb garden, landing waist deep in steaming, green mud. She heard Elly and Coty laughing as the truck continued the length of the porch, tearing away the posts and collapsing the roof. The truck swerved back to the driveway and continued down into the trees. All around Maya in the mud were arms and legs and feet and hands. A skull bobbed to the surface and sank again, its jaws chewing green mud.

Maya sat up in bed, drenched in sweat, her breath was ragged.

The nightmares are back.

"I should take a pill," she whispered, and then added, "No. No pills." The thought of drugged sleep was more terrifying than her fear of nightmares. She wanted to be alert, to awaken easily. She needed to hear if her bedroom doorknob turned. She needed to hear footsteps in the hall, or the sound of whispers in the night—the sound of something crawling across the floor toward her bed.

The closet light threw a golden wedge into her room, until a shadow blocked the light. It was the shadow of a man with half his head blown away. He pushed the closet door all the way open and fixed his dry eyes on Maya.

Maya sat up in bed with a painful gasp. Before, she had only dreamed she was awake, but this time she turned on her bedside lamp and slid her bare feet to the cool floor. Moments passed while she waited for her heart to calm.

"Danny?" she whispered. "Are you there?"

Danny said nothing. He had not shown himself for two weeks. Was he staying away, or was someone keeping him away?

It's Angel. It's Angel, keeping Danny away.

CHAPTER THIRTY-FIVE

COTY KNOCKED ON THE kitchen door before sticking his head inside. "We . . . we need to talk," he said.

"I'll let Elly know we're taking a short walk."

"I'll wait outside," Coty said. His boots sounded even and determined on the wood porch.

Maya found Elly in the skylight room, staring out through the little window between the bookshelves.

"Coty and I are going for a walk, Elly. You need me to do anything first?"

"No, I'm fine, honey. Enjoy the walk," Elly said. "He's not drunk again is he?"

"Seems sober as a judge." Maya slipped a denim shirt over her tank top and joined Coty on the driveway. "Which direction?" she asked.

"Uphill," Coty said. He opened the wide gate at the end of the driveway and together they climbed the back pasture. Maya glanced behind the shed as they passed. Coty's charcoal gray Dodge truck was parked beneath the cedar shake roof.

"Are we going inside the barn?"

"No. I just want to get away from the house." Fifty yards from the barn, Coty halted. "I've got a confession, okay? That day at the quarry, when I grabbed you and scared you . . . and later I apologized and told you I didn't mean to scare you . . . that was a lie. I meant to scare you. I wanted to scare the hell out of you. Scare you back into your car and away from this place. I wanted to snoop around with no one but a crazy old lady to deal with . . ." Coty sighed. "Sorry. I mean a confused old lady to deal with. She assumed I was her friend's nephew and that mistake gave me free reign to snoop and to search every building and every square inch of this property, which I've almost done. Elly's neighbor, Parker Haynes recognized Danny's photo when I showed it to him. He told me he saw Danny hitchhiking along the road. He said he saw a blond man in a delivery truck pick Danny up about a quarter mile from Elly's mailbox. Mr. Haynes said the truck entered Elly's driveway, so I know Danny made it to her place before he disappeared. That's why I came here. That's why I'm still here. Well, that's part of the reason I'm still here."

"Okay. And what's the other reason?"

"You. I knew when we met in Elly's kitchen that first day, you'd be trouble."

"Me? Why am I trouble?"

"Because I like you and I don't want anything bad to happen to you."

"I like you too, Coty . . . I mean Wayne."

"Let me finish, Maya. I didn't realize how much I liked you until I saw you with that guy at the bakery. Seeing you there with him was like getting gut-kicked by a horse. That's why I was gone for two days and needed a ride home from the bar. But I should've known better. Alcohol never fixes anything . . . it only adds another problem . . . two if you count the hangover. So I owe you a double apology. It seems I'm a real screw-up when I'm around you."

"But, I already explained to you what Hal Neil and I talked about," Maya said. "The history of Graceville, the old fort, the hospital and the cemetery? Hal is researching the property lines for Elly's farm and the cemetery—they seem to overlap. Hal said he'll . . . "

"I know, I know. You don't need to repeat everything the two of you talked about. I'm not going to confront Mr. Neil. I don't plan to knock his teeth out or anything"

"I hope not!" Maya kicked a clump of grass with the toe of her tennis shoe. "You know, you said Dr. Framish flirted with me at the hospital, and the other night you accused me of flirting with Hal Neil. Do you have a jealousy problem?"

"Never did until now."

"You have nothing to be jealous about. I can't stand my ex . . . and I don't care for Dr.

Framish. Hal Neill is barely an acquaintance. Got it?"

"Got it," Coty said. "Did you mean what you said about my kiss being good?"

Maya smiled. "Considering the condition you were in."

"You mean, drunk on my ass?"

"Yeah. Do you remember throwing up?"

" . . . I threw up? Before or after I kissed you?"

"After."

Coty closed his eyes and ran his fingers through his hair. "Hell. How about we try it again, stone cold sober and with teeth brushed?"

Maya smiled and wrapped her arms around him. He held her close, lifting her off the ground. His lips tasted like apples. He smelled like coffee and like the wind from across the grassy field. Maya's neck and ears tingled. The sensation traveled from the nape of her neck to her toes and back. He released her and her cheeks burned.

"Not bad. Not bad at all," she said.

"Got a surprise for you," Coty said. "Look behind you."

Maya turned. Along the fence, near the shadow of the trees, three llamas grazed on Elly's land.

"Should we tell Elly?" Maya asked.

"Oh, hell no . . . because she'd tell Harlan and who knows what he'd do. Let's keep this to ourselves."

Laughing, they headed back down the hill toward Elly's farmhouse.

Chapter Thirty-Six

"I'VE ALWAYS ENJOYED A walk to the mailbox," Elly said. "It's even better when you find mail there." She sounded happy. Her cheeks were pink. She smiled as she dropped envelopes on the kitchen table. "There's something there for you, Maya."

Maya sifted through the mail until she found a manila envelope with her name on the label. She opened it. "Oh," she said. "Finally. It's your medical records from Dr. Framish. I wonder why he addressed it to me."

"Probably because he thinks I'm scatterbrained," Elly said. "I told him about Harlan coming to see me at the hospital. That was a mistake. You should've seen his expression."

Maya chuckled. "Doctors and scientists—if it can't be proven mathematically, it can't be real, right?"

"You and I are alike." Elly poured boiling water into her tea mug.

Maya studied the back of Elly's head. *No we're not. At least, I hope not.*

"So, what's the verdict? Does Dr. Framish think I should be locked up?"

"Just a second," Maya said. "I'm reading the medical part right now. According to this, you're quite healthy. Normal blood pressure, no cholesterol problems, no signs of cancer, kidney function is excellent . . . there is nothing checked in the abnormal column at all. My goodness, that was your first mammogram Elly?"

"And my last. They're not meant to be pancakes, even if they're small."

"Your colonoscopy report is excellent. Not a single issue there."

"I don't remember much about that," Elly said. "They gave me something they said would help me relax, and I slept right through it."

"Down here in the comments, Dr. Framish says your physical strength is equivalent to an active woman in her fifties. That's great, huh? He does recommend that you visit a psychologist, about things that worry you. He recommends a Dr. Divan. That's funny, isn't it?"

"Why?"

"Because most psychologists have sofas or divans so their patients can recline, and relax."

"I don't need a psychologist. I have you to talk to, Maya. I don't need some stranger digging into my private thoughts."

"There are counselors at retirement homes, if you decide to talk to one of them. Dr. Conover has been good for me," Maya said. "And whatever you tell them remains confidential."

"You're not going to tell Dr. Conover the things I've told you, are you Maya?"

"Nope. I won't say a word to her about any of it. It's none of her business and it has nothing to do with me, so she doesn't need to know."

"After I'm gone, I don't care, of course," Elly said. "After I'm gone, you can tell anybody anything you want. Then, they can dig me up and hang me."

Maya said, "Let's not talk about that. It makes me sad."

"All right, baby girl." Elly lifted a business envelope from the pile of mail. "This one is from my lawyer." She ripped open the envelope and removed two smaller envelopes. "This copy is for you, Maya. Keep it in a safe place but please don't open it until I'm gone. It lists my final wishes, how to take care of . . . everything."

The envelope was pale blue, letter-size, with her full name, Maya Caroline Pederson (Hammond) on the front. In the upper left corner was the lawyer's name and address.

"I'll keep it in the back pocket of my medical journal," Maya said.

"Maya, have you seen that boy upstairs again? That green boy?"

"Not in a couple weeks. Why?"

"If you do see him again, tell him . . . tell him I'm sorry."

"It's almost noon. You could tell him yourself. He usually shows up around noon."

Elly shook her head and frowned. "No."

The phone rang and Maya grabbed the receiver. "Hello?"

"Mom died."

Maya was speechless for a moment. "Benson? Is that you?"

"Yes, who else would it be?"

"Your mother died?"

"You understand what that means, don't you?" Benson said.

Maya nodded at her reflection in the kitchen window. *Yes. It means you no longer have someone to bail you out when you get yourself into deep shit.* "Not sure you and I are thinking along the same lines, Benson. Sorry about you mother. Tell me what you think her death means, because I have no idea."

"Everything is mine now. The house, the cars, the beach condo in Hawaii, the savings account, the investments. It's all mine, and all I have to do is sign this document from your lawyer, and you're out of the picture. I don't have to share any of it with you, Maya."

"Knock yourself out, Bens."

"Two million in cash can stretch a long ways."

"The way you gamble, it'll be gone in a year," Maya said.

"I'm not gambling anymore."

"I have to hang up, Bens. You take care now." Maya slammed the receiver down. She paced the kitchen several times and then opened the back door and stepped outside. She took several deep breaths of cool air. "What did I ever see in him?"

"I thought you handled that well, Maya."

"No. I shouldn't have even talked to him. I should have hung up as soon as I recognized his voice. He has a way of twisting my guts into knots."

"Let's go for a drive," Elly said. "There's something I want to show you and it'll take your mind off Benson. It isn't far."

It was a hazy, mid-July afternoon. The two of them walked to the end of the bunkhouse and climbed into the Edge. Maya drove down the driveway and halted at the edge of the blacktop. "Which way?"

"Left, and then left again after a quarter mile." Elly pointed to the road sign. "I wonder how long that sign will stay up this time. The city was putting it in when I walked out to get the mail."

The sign read, Cemetery Road. The mound of dirt around its base looked like a fresh, round grave. Maya followed a narrow strip of blacktop up over a hill and coasted down the other side, under overhanging branches. Sunlight flickered through the leaves and the windshield. She lowered her visor, blocking the glare.

"Why are we going to the cemetery," she asked.

"I decided I should tell you about it. Years ago the farm used to be the cemetery," Elly said. "The city relocated all the graves clear out here, farther away from the stream. Farther away from town."

"It didn't bother you, to buy property that used to be a cemetery?"

"Nah. and Harlan said it was perfect for us anyway. Harlan said any graves or bodies found on our property could be explained away if the place used to be a cemetery. Also, people who can't afford a funeral or burial plot have been known to sneak into cemeteries late and night and bury their family members in secret. Did you know that?"

"I've never heard that before."

"Harlan caught somebody doing that once. The city was done relocating the old graves, but some people came in the middle of the night and put their grandmother in a grave that hadn't been filled in yet. They were shoveling dirt over her when Harlan caught 'em. Scared the bejeebers out of them."

"I'll bet he did."

"Harlan told them to get Grandma up and out of there, and to take her to the new cemetery because he wanted to plant three acres of corn there, not Grandma." Elly giggled. "But if any bodies had been found on our farm, we could've claimed that's how they got there."

"I doubt the authorities would believe one hundred fifty people snuck into an old cemetery to avoid burial costs."

"Ah, well, the authorities would've never found all the bodies," Elly said. "Felix used to send bags of lime with the deliveries."

Maya parked in one of the vacant parking spots shaded by giant maple trees. A three-foot-high rock wall with an ornate iron gate surrounded the twenty-acre cemetery. "It's pretty here," she said.

"And so nice and level. I've wondered why our hillside was ever considered for a burial ground in the first place. It slopes right down to the stream."

"I heard the hilltop was originally a Native American burial site," Maya said.

"Yeah, those old graves were up near where the old barn is. It was the settlers and the soldiers from the fort who started burying people further down the hillside."

"And the house, before you and Uncle Harlan added on . . . it was a mortuary."

"How did you know that?"

"I talked to a history writer at the book store, that day I drove you into town to see your lawyer. The writer knows a lot about Graceville."

"Does that bother you, Maya? Knowing that about the house?"

"No. It doesn't worry me at all . . . their spirits don't prowl the house and startle me in the middle of the night. They don't call to me, or whisper in my ear."

"Like the green boy?"

"Like the green boy."

"What does he say to you, Maya?"

"He says, 'Help me. Don't leave me here.' And one night he led me downstairs into the dining room. I've never been certain if that really happened or if it was a bad dream."

"What about the dining room?"

"There were sheets of plastic hanging like curtains all around," Maya said.

"And you saw Angel on the dining room table?" Elly's voice sounded flat.

"Parts of him."

"What else did you see?"

"I saw Harlan, packing those parts into a freezer in the kitchen. Everything looked dim and hazy, the way old photographs look, but Harlan was dressed in a checkered shirt with the sleeves rolled up. He had knives, a saw and a clever on the table. He put Angel's head on your antique rose serving platter, and he set the platter on the corner of the buffet."

"Guess I need to tell you the details regarding that," Elly said. "You need to know, but let's wait until when we're done for the day. I want to gather my memories together first."

• • •

For dinner, Elly heated vegetable soup and they took kitchen chairs, bowls, napkins and a box of crackers to the back porch and ate dinner outside. They didn't talk except to agree it was a pleasant evening in the shade of the tall evergreen trees. Afterward they washed and dried the dishes, and then they returned to the porch.

"That wasn't Harlan. That was me hacking up Angel on the dining room table. I wore Harlan's clothes that night. They already had permanent stains on them anyway, and besides, Harlan was gone, remember? To Boise."

"What did you do about Bossy and Morris?" Maya asked.

"I hiked up to the old barn and got the little backhoe. I dug a deep trench under the burned-down chicken coop and rolled Bossy and Morris into that trench. I covered 'em up and packed the dirt down and cleared away all the charred wood. The following spring, Harlan and I built the new wood shed over it all. That's the same one that's still there today."

"What did Harlan say about the dead animals and the chicken coop burning down?"

"I told him vandals did it in the middle of the night. He said, 'bastards.'"

"Why didn't you bury Angel in the ditch, along with Bossy and Morris? Wouldn't it have been easier?"

"Yeah, but they were good animals. Practically pets. Morris loved to have his nose rubbed, and Bossy would close her eyes and let me pick seeds and grass out of the little hollow behind her horns. They deserved a clean grave of their own," Elly said. "Not a place contaminated by Angel's filth. And you know, the strangest thing happened a few days after that. I spotted three hens running loose in the pasture. I guess they got out before the flames got'em. Every once in a while I still see a hen with her chicks out there. They must've found themselves a rooster if they laid fertile eggs. Maybe it's Schaff's rooster. I never kept roosters myself. They eat up the grain and start crowing too early in the morning. I had a beautiful rooster once, though. I called him Glamour Boy, but one day he lowered his head and stretched out his wings and ran at me, so I wrung his neck. Harlan and I had chicken and dumplings, and soup made from his skin and bones.

"I don't know why I decided to bury Angel in the basement. I should've buried him out there in the open field somewhere in a deep, deep grave and a whole bag of lime. He doesn't belong down there, with those other people. Especially that poor woman who struggled to live for so many hours before she finally quit breathing."

While you took a nap with Harlan.

"I guess I was just tired. Tired of blood and bodies and digging holes. Tired of deciding what to do and when to do it. It's not an easy business, Maya."

CHAPTER THIRTY-SEVEN

A TEENAGE BOY AT THE Red Apple loaded their sacks of groceries into the back of the Edge and closed the hatch.

"Thank you, Fredric." Elly handed the boy a five-dollar bill. He jammed it into his jeans pocket with a quick glance at the front of the store. He smiled and jogged away pushing the cart.

"The store doesn't allow tipping," Elly said. "But he's delivered groceries to the farm before in the pouring down rain. He deserves a good tip."

Maya climbed behind the wheel of the Edge and started the engine. "Let's stop for a donut at the bakery."

"Oh yes, let's do that," Elly said. "That sounds wonderful."

There was a vacant parking spot right outside the front door of Louisa's Bakery. Inside, Maya and Elly sat down at the same table where Maya sat with Hal Neil a week earlier.

"Welcome, ladies," the baker said.

"Two maple bars and two coffees please," Maya said. "With cream."

"Gotcha," Bill said.

A moment later, the door to the restroom opened and Hal Neil exited, wiping his hands on a paper towel. He looked up and met Maya's gaze. "Hey, Maya. Good to see you again."

"Hal, this is Elly Pederson, my aunt. Elly, this is Hal Neil, the writer I told you about."

"Hello," Elly glanced up and then out the window. "Maya, I have a headache. Let's get our donuts to go, if you don't mind."

"I'll handle it," Hal said. "Bill, their order is to go, please."

Bill bagged up the two maple bars and poured the coffee into tall paper cups with lids. Hal brought them to the table.

"It's on me," Hal said.

"Thanks, Hal." Maya led Elly outside and into the Edge. "Do you feel okay,

Elly?"

"I just want to go home."

"Does this have something to do with Hal?"

"How well do you know him, Maya?"

"I don't really know him at all. We just talked once at the bookstore and once at the bakery. Why?"

Elly shook her head. "I think he's from Chicago."

"Why would you think that?"

"Just a feeling."

"Don't worry. I won't be inviting him to the farm."

"Don't drink the coffee or eat the donut, Maya."

"But..."

"I'm serious. If he is from Chicago, he's looking for me. And now he's found me."

At the farm, Maya dumped the coffee down the kitchen sink and threw the maple bars to the crows. Four hours later the crows were still circling the house, begging for more.

"Looks like the maple bars weren't poison, Elly. The crows are alive and well."

"Better safe than sorry," Elly said.

• • •

Maya spotted Coty through the kitchen window. He sat on the gate to the upper pasture, the toes of his western boots jammed behind the lower rail. He looked up and smiled as she exited the back door and headed toward him. Sunlight glinted off his dark bronze hair.

"I introduced Hal to Elly at the bakery today and she's convinced he's from Chicago.

Apparently there are people in Chicago who want Elly's head on stick."

"Let's have coffee in the bunkhouse," Coty said. "I need something more than chammomile tea for conversations like this."

Inside Coty's quarters everything was tidy. Instead of a twisted wad of bedding, the blankets and the pillow were smooth and straight. Across the room dishes had been stacked to drain beside the sink. He pushed the curtains open and sunlight flooded the room.

"I have two percent, but no cream," he said.

"Milk is fine."

"Tell me about the people in Chicago."

"I'll start at the beginning," Maya said. "We have some serious catching up to do."

"Anything about Danny?"

Maya shook her head. "For some reason, Elly is dragging her feet on that."

Coty set two mugs on the counter and the coffee pot on a glowing burner. He opened the door of the little refrigerator and poured milk into one of the mugs. "Sorry, I don't have tea."

"I only drink tea with Elly because Harlan doesn't like the smell of coffee." Coty shook his head. They sat down at the little table by the front windows.

"This is where you were sitting the day I drove up, wasn't it?" Maya said. "I saw this curtain move and suspected someone was watching me."

"You made a great first impression."

"I tried to convince myself that you looked mean and scary."

Coty grinned. "That takes practice, you know."

The coffee pot hummed on the burner and steam gusted from the spout. The first leap of amber liquid chugged into the glass dome and the aroma filled the small room. Coty hurried over to slide the pot to one side of the burner to allow it to perk gently. He picked up dishes from the draining rack and stowed them in a cupboard behind a striped curtain. He draped the towel on a wire rack above the sink and then returned to the table.

"Coffee takes about five minutes," he said. "Go ahead. I'm curious to hear this story."

"It's Elly's story, and it's a long one. She grew up in the Chicago suburbs. Her mother died when she was eight. Her father was a mechanic, a very good one apparently, and he taught Elly a lot about engine repair," Maya said. "Elly's little brother, Stephen, was my father."

Maya told him about Elly driving a truck for Felix. She said the deliveries were often stolen goods. She didn't mention the bodies. She talked about Angel and how everyone was afraid of him, about Angel raping Elly, and about how he showed up at the farm one day and how Elly cut his throat and buried him under the house. Even though she kept some details secret, it took over an hour to tell Coty the story.

• • •

Later that afternoon, Maya returned from a walk and found Elly asleep on the living room floor where the sofa used to be. Elly was curled up beneath the patchwork quilt with one of her bed pillows under her head. Her eyes flickered open. "Maya?"

"What are you doing on the floor?"

"I've always napped here," Elly said. She closed her eyes again and was snoring in seconds.

Maya climbed the stairs, feeling guilty for revealing some of Elly's secrets to Coty. *But he needs to know. He has a right to know. And I needed to tell it to him while I still remember it.* She would tell him the rest of the story later. It was all written down in the back of her medication journal.

Maya expected to see Danny hovering in the upstairs hallway, but he was elsewhere this afternoon. The upstairs landing was aglow with violet-blue sunlight through the morning glory window.

Maya halted in Elly's bedroom doorway. The closet door stood wide open.

Maya glanced behind her, down the stairs. She listened, heard nothing, tiptoed across Elly's room and flipped on the closet light. Overhead were tiny hairlines in the ceiling. The lines formed a four-foot square. She had missed seeing that before. A nylon cord stretched from a small hole in the square to a hook by the door, and from the hook the cord dangled straight down. Maya pulled the cord. A trapdoor swung downward. Stairs unfolded with almost no sound. She climbed the stairs into the attic. Maya felt her way around until she stubbed her toe on the leg of a chair. In front of the chair was a table and above the table she found a light cord. She pulled the cord and a single, hanging bulb glowed.

The attic ceiling was low and the room was L-shaped and long. It started above Elly's closet and continued around a corner to the opposite end the house, somewhere above Maya's room. Beside the table and chairs were cupboards and an open door leading to a toilet and laundry sink. Around the corner were four, twin iron beds, the headboards against the dormer wall. They looked like old hospital beds from the late thirties or early forties, painted white. Striped mattresses covered the sagging springs. Thick black canvas had been nailed over the three dormer windows and carpet runners formed paths between the beds and along the inside wall. Beyond the beds lay empty space and at the far end of the room stood a single door. Maya strode the length of the room and opened the door. She stared into charcoal gloom. Stairs descended through a narrow gap between trusses, and then between unfinished walls further down. She searched but found no light switch. *It's the escape route to the tunnel . . . but it's also a way into the house from under the house.* She closed the door. There was no lock.

Maya backed away from the door. *No lock.*

Anyone in the basement could enter and climb those stairs. They could enter the attic. From the attic they could drop the folding stairs and climb down into Elly's closet and from there they could find the hallway, and down the hallway to Maya's bedroom at the far end.

At least my door has a lock.

"Stop it," Maya whispered. "Don't do this to yourself. Dr. Conover said not to feed your paranoia . . . so, just stop it."

Maya wanted to run from the attic. She wanted to return to the lower floors. Instead, she returned to the table, pulled out a chair and sat down.

She studied the stark room, imagining the people stashed here years ago. She pictured them tiptoeing and whispering, afraid to make any sound, afraid to ask for food or water. She pictured them trying to trust the strangers in the house below. Elly and Harlan. Harlan!

"It would have been impossible," Maya whispered, "to trust Harlan."

Were any of those people Harlan hid up here, still alive? Had anyone really survived up here, long enough to escape from the law? Or was Elly's memory faulty? Was that simply how Elly *preferred* to remember things? It was impossible to decide. Elly admitted having trouble distinguishing between real and imagined. *It runs in the family.*

Maya slid the chair back beneath the table before descending the stairs into Elly's closet. She crossed the upstairs hall and entered the bathroom. Inside one of the lower drawers she found one of the new flashlights. She carried it back to Elly's closet and retraced the route into the attic and through the long, L-shaped room to the door at the far end. She opened the door and smelled the gloom again. It was musty and silent in that stairwell. Maya flicked the flashlight on and descended, feeling her way along a cold wall.

The stairs were as steep as a ladder, each step barely wide enough for her foot. The stairwell narrowed as she descended. There was no railing and soon there was no wall, nothing but a straight drop on either side into a black air. Finally, she stood on the last step, a foot above a dirt floor. All around her was dirt, the walls were dirt, even part of the ceiling was dirt. The tunnel led off to her left. Elly said the tunnel crossed beneath the driveway and the bunkhouse and continued deep beneath the hillside. The walls were scarred with shovel marks, grooves from pick axes and pry bars. Maya pictured the Mexican men, sweating, digging, carting the rock and soil outside to the fields and gardens, returning to dig more. Had they been paid or had they been thrown to the bottom of the well and left there to die? Had it been one of the Mexican men's spirit who crawled through the tunnel that day, following her, calling to her? What would he have done, had he caught up to her?

Elly said they didn't speak English. But was the story true at all?

To Maya's right sat a dozen concrete blocks, the blocks Elly said concealed entrance to the basement beside the furnace. Maya aimed her flashlight left again, into the gaping tunnel. The bright beam penetrated a short distance and then lost its strength, as if hitting black velvet. Overhead, wood beams supported the tunnel every ten feet or so, like crooked arms. The dank smell of the tunnel reminded her of her crawl through the hillside. She shuddered, remembering the crawler's voice behind her, "Don't leave me here." She remembered the skeletal hand reaching for her, the dull gray cranium with its empty eyes and the scratching sounds it made as it followed her. Coatl?

Maya took the stairs two at a time toward the attic, toward the open door at the top. It was a long, straight climb from the basement to the attic. She arrived breathless, closed the door and descended the folding stairs into Elly's closet. She paused in the bedroom doorway and listened for sounds of activity downstairs. With relief, she heard Elly snoring.

Chapter Thirty-Eight

T HE NEW CLOCK NUMBERS glowed in the dark. It seemed Maya woke every morning now at 2:22 AM.

"Who are you?" The voice came from the hallway.

"Danny?" Maya turned on her bedside lamp. She pushed back her covers, tiptoed to the hallway door and grabbed the doorknob.

"Don't open the door," another voice said. "He's out there . . . in the hall."

"Who is out there?" Maya's heart pounded. Her ears pulsed with the sound of blood rushing through her veins. She looked behind her, expecting to see the green boy.

"Angel is out there."

The closet door swung open and Elly stood in the opening. Her eyes were wide open but she seemed to be looking straight through Maya.

"Elly?"

"Angel is out there. Don't open the door."

"I won't." Maya led her aunt to the side of the bed.

Elly sat down. "What are we doing in your room, Maya?"

"You were in my closet. You must have been sleepwalking."

"I was dreaming of that green boy." Elly headed for the door.

"You told me not to open the door, Elly. You said Angel was in the hallway."

Elly pressed and ear against the door before she opened it. She sighed as if relieved. "Of course he's not there. Of course not. Sorry, I must have scared you."

"A little bit, yeah. Want me to walk you back to your room, Elly?"

"Nah. You go on back to sleep, baby girl. I'm sorry about this. It was just one of those dreams that seem much too real."

Maya said, "I'm going downstairs to get a drink of water. The pizza we had for dinner made me thirsty." Maya followed Elly to the bathroom door, and then she continued downstairs. As usual, the dining room felt icy cold as she passed through. Her breath made clouds and then the heat in the kitchen felt as if she stood in front of an open oven door. She filled a glass with tap water and sat down at the table.

Moonlight poured in through the kitchen window, forming a golden square on the linoleum floor. Something glistened there. Something gleamed outside the basement door. She turned on the light and found a puddle of water. A sliver of ice slid down the face of the yellow door and another floated on the surface of the puddle. Another, smaller puddle had formed a foot away, and a third puddle just beyond that—foot shaped puddles, heading toward the dining room. Maya shuddered. *Angel was here.* This time . . . had he managed to get beyond the basement door? Had he crossed the kitchen? The yellow door was unlocked? She tried the lock. *Locked.* She followed the footprints into the dining room where the puddles became thin smears. How far had Angel gone? Upstairs? Maya searched the stairs for wet spots but found none. Had Elly seen him, even though she slept? Had Angel stood outside Maya's bedroom door?

Maya checked the basement door again. She unlocked it, and locked it again. She wiped up the puddles with paper towels. She listened for the groan of footsteps on the basement stairs, for the sound of breathing, for Angel's whisper. She heard nothing.

The wet footprints had been small, very small. Elly was barefoot. She must have come downstairs, sleepwalking. She must have stepped in water.

Stepped in melted ice? It must have been Elly's footprints across the linoleum.

Maya checked the locks on the backdoor and the living room door before returning upstairs.

Chapter Thirty-Nine

THE FOLLOWING MORNING, ELLY had no memory of sleepwalking, and no memory of their pre-dawn conversation in Maya's bedroom.

Coty tapped on the kitchen door and stuck his head inside. "I'm heading into town to get some supplies. Want to go?"

"I can't," Maya said. "Elly asked me to dismantle some old iron beds in the attic and haul them down to the back porch. The Salvation Army truck will be by this afternoon to pick them up."

"Heavy beds? Maybe I should do that," Coty said.

"No, they aren't heavy. It means several trips up and down the stairs, but I can handle it. You go ahead and do your shopping. I'll talk to you when you get back."

Coty almost closed the door and then stuck his head inside again, and whispered, "Seen Danny?"

"No. Sorry."

Coty looked disappointed as he closed the door. A minute later his truck rumbled down the driveway and into the trees.

Maya finished washing and drying the breakfast dishes. She eyed the calendar as she draped the towel across the drying rack. Today marked exactly nine weeks since she had arrived at the farm. She had anticipated a happy summer here. A joyous adventure. She remembered being five years old and longing to see this place. Her father had talked about the farm many times. He had visited Elly here once, but Maya's mother had stayed home. *Why would Daddy visit Aunt Elly and leave Mom home?* According to her mother, it was after his trip here that his emotional problems began.

The old porcelain sink was in vogue again, but not with those rhubarb stains in the bottom. Maya searched under the sink for stain remover. She found it behind a red, plastic squirt bottle, the kind normally used for ketchup.

"Ketchup? Under the sink?" Maya pulled off the miniature cap and sniffed. *Gasoline?*

Maya scrubbed the stains and then climbed the stairs. "Aunt Elly?"

"Up here, baby girl. Up through my closet," Elly said. "I found some more photographs."

Maya pretended to climb the folding stairs for the first time and tried to look surprised at the attic room. "Wow, it's big up here."

"I expected it to be dustier than it is. Once we get it emptied out, I'll run the vacuum around and dust the cupboards." Elly sat at the square table, rifling through a pile of photographs inside a shoebox. "Most of these are from before I graduated from high school. Not a one of Harlan, doggone it."

"Coty just left for the store. He'll be back in about an hour." Maya halted at the corner. "Are those four beds the ones you want me to take apart?" Maya crossed the room and stood between two of the beds. "Should we take down all this old black canvas, too?"

"Yes. I don't want people wondering why we had this room so closed off from the outside. When Coty gets back I'll talk to him about taking down that door at the far end of the room. I'll want him to sheetrock over it, tape and mud it. No one will ever know it was there."

"Is it a closet?" Maya felt guilty pretending not to know.

"No. It's an old stairwell, and it leads to that tunnel I told you about. The escape route, remember? Nowhere anyone would want to go now."

Maya said, "I brought tools from the kitchen drawer, because if those beds have been sitting here a while, they might be stubborn."

"Good thinking, Maya. Let's get started."

An hour later, Maya hauled the last headboard down through the trapdoor, down the main staircase and through the kitchen. Finally the attic was empty.

"I'm glad they were just twin beds," Maya said. "I don't think I could have managed bigger mattresses."

The attic furniture was now on the porch, up against the outside of the house between the kitchen window and the end railing. The square table and four chairs were included and so was a cardboard box with old dishes, cups, and stainless ware from the attic room.

"I never allowed anyone to do any cooking up in the attic." Elly sat down at the kitchen table with a tired sounding sigh. She glanced out the window toward the barn. "I was afraid they'd start a fire. That's why I cooked and sent things up through the dumbwaiter."

"The beds, the table and chairs, and the dishes, didn't make as big a pile out there on the porch as I expected," Maya said. "Have you noticed how the house sounds hollow now that it's empty?"

"That's how it sounded the first time I came here," Elly said.

"I can start painting again if you want me to."

"Nah. The new owners will probably paint anyway. People usually do, don't they? All we need to do is keep this old house clean," Elly said. "The two of us can do that, with it empty and all."

Maya washed the dust and grime from her hands. "What's this bottle of gasoline for, Elly?" She held the ketchup bottle up for her aunt to see.

"Ahhh, let me think. I used it for cleaning something, something greasy and corroded, but I can't recall exactly what it was now. Just leave it there please, Maya. I'll remember eventually and maybe need it again."

Maya returned the ketchup bottle under the sink. "Dad came here once, didn't he?"

"Stephen? Yes. But that was before you were born."

"Did Dad and Harlan get along?"

Elly shrugged. "Neither one of them ever said anything to me about the other."

"Why didn't Mom come?"

"She didn't like me, remember?"

"Seems strange that she wouldn't come, though. I continued living with Benson for three years after I decided I didn't like him."

"You'll have to ask your mother why she didn't come, Maya."

"Dad always said the farm was such a pretty piece of property."

"He said that?"

"He said it was awfully big though, for you to take care of. Dad never mentioned Harlan, but he said you talked about Harlan a lot."

"Mainly, I just kept the house clean and organized. Harlan was usually outside, from morning to night. He didn't want the animals, but I did and I talked him into getting them. The fields required regular plowing. Some years we rented a combine harvester and sold hay to local farmers. You have to keep your fields down, otherwise trees take over and you end up living in the middle of a forest, and then your roof turns to moss. We wanted open fields. We wanted to be able to see all the way out to the county road, and up to the barn."

Maya set plate of cookies on the table. "Elly, where is Uncle Harlan buried?"

". . . buried?"

"In the new cemetery?"

Elly gazed out the window with an unreadable expression. "Oh dear," she said.

"What's the matter?"

"I . . . I can't remember."

"It'll come back to you. It'll just pop into your head when you're not even thinking about it."

"But that's so odd, isn't it? That's just so—odd—to forget something like that. Why can't I remember?" Elly buried her face in her hands and shook her head.

"Don't cry, Elly. I'm sorry I asked."

Elly sniffed. "I can't believe I've gone and lost my sweet Harlan."

"I can ask in town," Maya said. "There should be records . . ."

"No, baby girl. Don't do that. I'll ask Harlan the next time I see him. Harlan will know."

A black cloud appeared, growing in size behind the upper barn, taking on the shape of a fist with gnarled fingers. A moment later it stretched its fingers toward the house. The fields and fences blurred. Maya took her first bite of raisin cookie as the first blast of rain hit the windows.

Chapter Forty

IT WAS NOON, THE last Sunday in July. Maya had been at the farm for eleven weeks. Earlier that morning several prospective buyers had phoned and arranged to visit the farm in response to Elly's ads in the Port Angeles Herald and The Seattle Times: FOR SALE – 225 acre farm – two hilltop view lots – 6,500 sq ft house, five bedrooms, two full baths, 1/2 bath in bunkhouse, 3 fireplaces, year-round salmon/trout stream, two barns, chicken coop, woodshed, carport and new furnace – fenced fields – serious buyers only – DIY Reality 555—469 – 1313.

In addition, over thirty realtors phoned, hoping to list Elly as their exclusive client. She said no. She would sell it herself.

Elly answered another call and then hung up. "That's the twelfth one to ask about the view lots. No one seems to be interested in the farm. I wonder if some of them found out this place used to be a mortuary and the fields were a graveyard. Cowards."

Maya and Elly finished emptying out the kitchen cupboards. They threw out the remaining food items that were nearing their pull dates along with chipped, cracked, or broken, bowls and cooking pots with lose or missing handles.

"Harlan always planned to repair these," Elly said. "This here cooking pot is one of the first things I ever bought for the farm."

Maya dragged the filled cardboard box out to the back porch before returning and scrubbing out the emptied cupboards with hot bleach water, followed by a wipe down with a damp towel. She left the cupboard doors open to dry.

"Coty did a good job of removing all that black canvas in the attic. Next I'll have him remove that door. I'll have him pry open some windows around here too," Elly said. "Most have been painted shut for at least fifty years."

"I'll clean out the wood stove," Maya said. "Where's the cinder bucket?"

"Basement."

"Oh." Maya glanced at the basement door and then took the big, new flashlight from the counter. "Is it near the stairs?" she asked.

"It's over by the furnace," Elly said.

"Why so far away?"

"When we bought this place the furnace was a big, wood burning thing, so that's where the ash bucket sat. And even though I had the new oil furnace put in, I've just always left the bucket sitting there in the same spot."

Maya hesitated with her hand hovering an inch above the doorknob.

"I'll go down an get it, baby girl."

"No," Maya said. "No—I can do this." She opened the yellow door. The flashlight came to life with the click of a button, lighting up the basement stairs. She took five steps down and then paused and aimed the beam of light toward the distant corner. She saw nothing except for the square of plywood Elly had placed there a short time ago to 'mark the spot.' *Tell them to dig here, Maya.*

Maya continued down the stairs, noting the snaps and groans of the aged wood. She halted at the bottom and once again aimed the beam of light into the darkest corner. Still nothing.

The dirt in the basement was the color of dust. Down there everything smelled old, the way antique shops and junkyards smelled old, abandoned cars, condemned buildings, barns, sheds, musty attics and mausoleums. That thought always came to Maya when she entered that basement. Mausoleums.

Her mother had taken her to a mausoleum once. "My mother is in this drawer, right here."

Maya remembered exactly how her mother said, *drawer.* She thought it seemed odd, to put someone in a drawer, even if they were dead. Maya remembered her mother's slender, manicured fingers as she stroked the smooth marble face of the drawer. She remembered her mother tapping on the polished gray stone with a red, enameled fingernail. "Mother? Can you hear me? Are you still in there? I brought my daughter with me this time. We have something for you."

With a cynical smile, Maya's mother pulled a long-stemmed rose from a slender brown sack. She slid the stem of the rose into the small brass vase fastened to the front of the drawer. The stem was too long and the rose tilted forward, top-heavy, threatening to topple. Maya's mother lifted the rose from the vase. She snapped the stem in half and placed the blossom back in the vase. "There, Mother. That's for you."

The rose was brown and crisp. Maya had been with Mama when she bought it two months earlier, but now its blood red color had drained away. Its five leaves were the color of dirt and they curled up like dead bird claws, so fragile one broke off and dropped to the granite floor. It shattered. Maya's mother ground it into powder with the sole of her shoe.

"Maya?"

Maya jumped. Her heart felt like it had leaped into her throat making it difficult to breathe. She fumbled with the flashlight, almost dropping it. Elly stood silhouetted in the open door at the top of the stairs. "You okay, baby girl?"

"I see the cinder bucket now." Maya strode down the concrete walkway as far as the sleeping furnace. She grabbed the handle of the bucket, turned and hurried back toward the stairs. To her left the dirt beneath the square of plywood, bulged, its rounded peak trembled. The top of the mound cracked and crumbled. Clods of dirt broke away and rolled to the bottom. More dirt rose through the center of the mound, darker, damper dirt. Something underneath was thrusting upward from below. Digging upward. Struggling.

Maya reached the stairs. Breathless, she halted, looked back and whispered, "No. Stop. It isn't time yet. But don't worry. I haven't forgotten my promise. Just wait. Wait."

The bulging halted. The mound smoothed out and the clods and crumbles settled back into place. The dirt was flat and smooth again.

Maya took the stairs two and a time, reached the kitchen and locked the door behind her, releasing a long-held breath. Her hands shook as she knelt beside the wood stove and opened its little door. "I'll clean all the soot off the little window, too," she said. She heard the tremble in her own voice.

"You're such a blessing, Maya."

"Back in early April, your invitation to spend the summer here was like the answer to a prayer, Elly. I was desperate to get away, and I had always wanted to see your farm. It sounded so perfect."

"I don't know how I would have gotten all this work done without you, Maya" Elly said. "I probably wouldn't have. You've been a wonder, and I've enjoyed having someone to talk to for a change. Ever since Harlan died I've been mighty lonely. I almost don't want your visit to end."

"What did Harlan think of Angel Sonosa? He must have said something about him at some point."

"Harlan said Angel was an SOB. He liked playing pranks on Angel. He was the only one of us brave enough to do something like that."

"Pranks?"

Elly nodded. "Harlan knew Angel was mean. Angel liked promising someone a day off, and then changing his mind at the last minute—after that person had made plans or bought tickets to a baseball game. Things like that."

"Why did your Uncle Felix let Angel get away with that?"

"Uncle Felix was caught between the rock and hard spot, honey. Angel had connections. He had a brother real high up in the organization. Uncle Felix said that the brother wanted Angel to stay away, and the warehouse was a nice, long distance away."

"Away from what?"

"Away from that brother. Angel and his brother hated each other, but you know how family can be. I'll bet that brother probably had to answer to another family member who loved Angel for some reason. You know, some old grandmother or maiden aunt? I remember seeing you just after you were born, Maya. You were a tiny little, perfect doll-baby, all rosy and pink with big eyes and a rosebud mouth, and soft baby hair. I loved you the instant I saw you. I imagine some old person in Angel's family felt that way about him, you know? So, Angel had that job for as long as he wanted it, unless Uncle Felix really wanted to push the issue, and when you're in that business, you don't ever want to push the issue."

"What kind of pranks did Harlan play on Angel?"

Elly giggled. "I'll tell you about one – just one. It's the best one anyway."

• • • *

It started out like any prank starts, sort of by accident, a spur of the moment thing. That's how you discover someone's weaknesses. Their Achilles heel. Their vulnerabilities, you know? You find out what scares them.

Harlan just happened to be outside Angel's open office door one day when the bookkeeper got fired. Angel was giving that poor slob a real ass-chewing. Pardon the French, but that's how Harlan always described it. Lots of JC-ing and GD-ing and such. You know? Language I'd never use, and neither would Harlan.

Anyway, after the name-calling and cussing and swearing wore itself down, Angel threw an envelope across his desk and said it would be the last f-ing paycheck that f-ing bookkeeper would ever f-ing get from him. He said to take it and get the f-out, and to not ever come back. The bookkeeper stood, picked up the envelope and stuffed it in his shirt pocket. He turned toward the door, spotted Harlan and gave Harlan a wink – all this while he slid a Zippo lighter from his pants pocket with his right hand, and a little firecracker from his other pocket with his left. He lit the fuse before he reached the door and then tossed it behind him as he exited. Funny thing is, according to Harlan, the firecracker landed in Angel's wastebasket, and the wastebasket was full of waste paper. Harlan said he stepped back, not knowing what to expect—and nothing happened. Not for almost a whole minute anyway. Just as Angel stood up and opened up a file cabinet drawer, that firecracker finally exploded and Angel dove to the floor and covered his head. He started screaming, I'm sorry Morton, Morton! I'm sorry. I swear I'll never do it again, Morton! Don't! Don't hurt me.

A moment later when Angel realized there was nothing really going on, and looked up with a face so white he looked ready for the grave. That's what Harlan said.

Who is Morton, Harlan asked him. None of your fucking business, Angel said. Where's that fucking bookkeeper? I'm gonna kill the little bastard. Harlan told him the bookkeeper was already driving down Main Street by then. Angel's face turned beet red then, I guess. He could've started a fire with that damned prank, Angel said. A fire in this warehouse would be the end of us all. You realize that? Do we want the fire department showing up? Snooping around? Checking our licenses and restrictions? Checking to see if we're up to code? Not to mention some of the chemicals we have stored here, explosive chemicals.

Harlan said Angel was shaking as he poured a thermos of coffee into the smoking wastebasket. I've seen a warehouse fire before, Angel said. The whole place went up in a matter of minutes. Two men didn't make it out and the rest of us could hear them screaming. And then, Harlan said, Angel dropped to his knees, leaned over and puked in the waste basket.

"Who'd'a ever thought?" Elly said. "Seems Angel wasn't just *afraid* of fire. He was terrified."

Chapter Forty-One

ELLY SAID SHE'D CHANGED her mind about selling the farm herself and phoned a realtor in Sequim. "He said he'll be out to look at the place tomorrow, and, judging by my description and the size of the property, he said it's worth between eight-hundred and nine hundred thousand. That's a lot more'n the ninety thousand Harlan and I paid for this farm fifty-five years ago."

"I'll make us some lunch." Maya sensed another story on the horizon and braced herself for more of Elly's nightmarish secrets.

Elly eased down into the kitchen chair that faced the back door. From there she also had a view through the bay window to her left. She always sat in that spot, as if she expected to see someone standing in the door of the big barn, as if she needed to keep her eyes on that barn and the grassy hillside in between. There was always an expression of dread in her eyes.

"I've been thinking a lot, Maya, and remembering things about Harlan and Angel and Felix. It was a dark business Felix chose for himself, and then Harlan chose it too. And once a person chooses a job like that, there's no going back. There's no way to un-do things. It becomes a part of your past. It's your history. It's you.

"I used to think great things would happen in my life. I used to think I'd do something worthwhile, like drawing or painting . . . like Harlan did. Or maybe I'd help people who were in trouble, like I'd be a volunteer at a church. Somethin' like that. Somethin' respectful, but I chose Harlan and Harlan chose the business. I've often thought that if I had given Harlan an ulti . . . ulti . . . what's that word, Maya? It means if I had made him choose between me and the business?"

"Ultimatum?"

"Yeah. Ultimatum." Elly closed her eyes. A silent moment passed. "But I loved Harlan more than he loved me. I knew that from the beginning. He would have chosen the business over me."

"Aww, Elly. I can't believe that. I mean, Harlan came to your rescue numerous times, right?"

Elly nodded. "Yeah, but he always expected me to follow him no matter where he went, and he expected me to listen and to nod my head and to never question him. He expected me to obey him and stay out of his way once he decided how to handle a situation . . . as if I were too stupid to solve my own problems. He never knew I solved my worst problem without him, though." Elly's smile was bitter. "I solved my problem with Angel, and I did that by myself." She spun around in her chair, eyeing the dining room and the lower stairs, as if she expected to see Harland standing there, listening. Apparently satisfied Harlan wasn't eavesdropping, she turned back around with a sigh.

Maya nodded toward the yellow basement door. *Locked.* "I'm not convinced you solved that problem, Elly, not entirely anyway. Angle is still a threat."

"Somewhat, but Angel has limitations. He can't seem to . . . gather himself together. Heh heh heh. It's like he lost the ability to organize his thoughts after I chopped him up. Maybe plopping his head down on that rose pattern platter is what did it." Elly giggled. "I suppose Harlan would have handled things differently."

"How so?"

"Harlan wasn't nos . . . nos . . . Damn! Another word I can't think of. It means melancholy."

"Soup's ready." Maya wanted to change the direction Elly's story was taking. Discussions of heads on dinner platters made her feel ill. "Nice to have a cooler day for a change, isn't it?" Maya asked. "Too many hot sunny days in a row and I get headaches. Today is cloudy and cool. Perfect for a bowl of soup."

"I don't pay much attention to the weather anymore. Harlan was the one who grumbled about hot days, rainy days or icy cold days. Weather made working outside difficult sometimes."

"Nostalgic! That's the word I was trying to think of. Harlan wasn't nostalgic. He never bought something just because it was pretty, or because it reminded him of his childhood, or because he knew I'd like it. I sometimes wonder if he was one of those people who don't care about anyone except themselves, those people who can live fairly normal lives but if they decide to do something vicious or cruel . . . they never regret it. They never feel remorse."

"I think you mean a psychopathic personality, but now days it's called an antisocial personality disorder," Maya said.

"Whatever the experts call it, I've come to realize that Harlan and Angel had a lot in common. They both thought their behavior was acceptable. They treated others like they were just things, things to be used. Neither one of them hesitated to tell a lie if they thought it would benefit them. They both had short tempers but long memories. Whenever they appeared compassionate or kind, it was just an act. They'd both get so angry over little things, but something that would shock you and me . . . they just shrugged it off. Hardly blinked.

I remember how Harlan blamed Grady Goode for what happened that day. Remember? Grady might have grown up and learned how to be a nice person. Maybe. I don't know, but he deserved the chance, didn't he? He was just a kid. But Harlan had no patience. No tolerance. Didn't matter what I thought. One scowl from Harlan and I knew to shut my mouth.

"Harlan and Angel were both those antisocial people you mentioned, Maya. They both had that disorder—probably born that way. They didn't look alike, but they could've been brothers.

"Remember when I told you how Harlan was real upset after the police pulled him over and they found all that blood in the back of the truck, and Harlan told them it was pig blood from a delivery to a butcher shop on DiMaggio Street? He was so upset afterward, he agreed to leave Chicago when I said I wanted to go, remember? Well, he wasn't upset about the blood or about delivering bodies to the ore refinery. He was just scared because he almost got caught. That's all."

"You can add Benson to that list of people who don't care about anyone but themselves. I never realized it before, but Benson fits the description too."

Elly took a sip of soup and smacked her lips. "At least I'm not one of *them*. They were incapable of love, but I loved Harlan with all my heart. And I love you too, Maya."

Maya patted Elly's shoulder. "You and I are family, Elly."

"Harlan told me that you're okay, Maya. Just like he decided Bossy the cow and Morris the horse were okay. Remember me telling you he didn't want any animals? But I talked him into having Bossy and Morris and those forty chickens. After a while Harlan kind of liked them."

I'm just like the horse and cow. Maya smiled at her cup of steaming tea.

"I remembered something else this morning when I first got up," Elly said. "That's when memories come flooding back as if a dam has burst. That old car you found in the pond? I remember the car now, and I know how it got down there. Gracious sakes alive, that was fifty-five years ago. It's the forty-two Ford that Harlan and I drove here, all the way from Chicago. You don't need to worry about it Maya, cuz' there's nothing in that car. Harlan said we needed to hide the vehicle, because those Chicago people we were trying to find us and they would have recognized that car. Harlan rolled that old Ford down into the gully and covered it up with branches. There was no pond back then. It was just a deep, weedy ditch with a little stream trickling through it. That old Ford has been sitting down there under those trees and branches all this time, just rusting away. I suppose it's been a home to some mice, maybe some raccoons or possums and such. Nice to think that it's provided shelter to something."

Maya sighed with relief. There was nothing horrific about that old Ford. The sheriff wouldn't be finding any human remains in the driver's seat. No bones in trunk. No black, moldy bloodstains on the rotted upholstery.

A burst of sunlight turned the lower fields amber. A flock of chickadees darted along the fence line, chirping and chattering.

"Good vegetable soup," Elly said. "That was the last container in the freezer, wasn't it?"

"Yes."

"No sense in making any more soup from what's left in the garden, then. There's a half row of beets, a dozen or so carrots and one head of cabbage. After we've eaten that up, we'll have to buy fresh vegetables at the Red Apple."

"Oh, this farm is going sell soon, Elly. And you'll be partying with Judith by September."

"I hope you'll come and have lunch with Judith and me."

Maya said, "I look forward to meeting Judith. She sounds like a good friend."

• • • *

"Maya?"

". . . Mama? What's wrong?" Maya turned on her lamp and checked the new digital clock on her beside table. "It's two in the morning. Has something happened?" Maya held her cellphone, not remembering hearing it ring nor answering it.

"Oh dear. Is it 2:00 A.M.? I'm sorry, Maya."

"What's wrong. Where are you?"

"I'm at home. I have trouble sleeping lately. Seems to be happening more and more. I was watching an old movie and it brought back memories of when you were little and your father was still here and still happy. Oh, Maya. I just lost track of time. I'm so sorry."

Maya slid her feet and legs back beneath the covers and pulled the sheet up to her chin.

"So, you're okay, Mama?"

"Yes, I suppose, although the offer on the house fell through. I guess the people who made the highest offer didn't qualify for the loan. I might take the second best offer."

"That's too bad. What about your trip to Italy? When do you leave?"

"That's been cancelled."

"Oh?"

"My traveling companion has decided he'd rather not go."

"Oh."

"Yeah."

Maya was surprised to hear her mother use the word, yeah. She'd never heard Mama utter that word before. It was always, yes. Never uh-huh, yup or yeah. Always—always, yes.

"Was this traveling companion someone you were dating?"

"Uh huh."

"Well. There are other fish in the sea, Mama."

"I know, but we really did seem to hit off at first."

"What caused him to change his mind?"

"This is embarrassing to admit, but I think he was looking for financial gain."

"It's not like you're a millionaire, Mama."

"No, but . . ."

"You can tell me. I'm not going to be judgmental. After all, I'm the one with the problems, remember? I'm the one who chose to marry a sociopath."

"Benson did have a mean streak, didn't he? I didn't want to admit that I suspected it, Maya, because I was the one who encouraged you to develop that relationship. I insisted Benson was a real catch, remember?"

"I didn't have to agree with you. I could have said no."

"Aren't we the pair, though?" Mama said.

"Some lessons are learned the hard way, Mama. Why did you decide your gentleman friend was after money?"

"He proposed marriage. When I suggested a prenup, he became *terribly* offended."

"Oh."

"He kept asking how much I expected to get for this house when it sells. That was a red flag. Then he wanted to borrow my car one day, saying his was in the shop. I don't know why, just an odd feeling, so I said no. It was after that he decided to cancel the trip. He hasn't phoned in three weeks."

"Sorry, Mama."

"I feel better, just hearing your voice, Maya. How's things going at the farm?"

Maya tried to stop herself, but her sudden burst of laughter felt cathartic, the same way crying felt when a burst of tears was involuntary.

"You wouldn't believe it, Mama. Remember what you said about Elly?"

"You mean, that she isn't *right*?"

"Yes. And you were correct. But even though strange things are happening here, I'm handling it just fine . . . and without the drugs. I haven't had a Lorazepam in twenty-eight days."

"Maya, that's wonderful."

"I've decided to stop the little rituals too. You know? The little ceremonies?"

"What happened to cause these changes, Maya?"

"I think it was finally deciding that the drug doesn't really change anything. If something's wrong I need to deal with it, not drug myself. Confronting the issue feels so much better than taking a pill and sliding into a stupor. Besides, if something happens, I want to be completely awake so I can deal with whatever it is."

"I'm happy to hear this, Maya. You sound strong."

"And the rituals—I just don't *want* them anymore. I've decided—I don't *do* those anymore."

"I think you're right. I think confronting a situation is so much better than pretending it doesn't exist. And, you know what? I'm sorry I woke you, but I'm glad we talked, because I feel so much better," Mama said.

"I do too, Mama. I think this is the best conversation we've ever had."

"It is, isn't it? Go back to sleep, Maya. Call me in a day or too, okay? I'll have dealt with my own issues by then."

"I will. I promise."

"Good night, Maya."

"Good night, Mama. Talk to you soon."

Chapter Forty-Two

COTY LEANED AGAINST THE back porch railing. When Maya stepped outside and closed the kitchen door, he whispered, "What's Elly doing?"

"She's asleep. She complained of a headache, so I gave her an aspirin and snuck one of my sedatives into her chamomile tea. She'll be out for a few hours."

Maya and Coty headed up the driveway toward the big barn. It was 10:18 AM and the morning sun struck the face of the barn straight on. The barn's once red stain had faded—bleached to a rust color. The white trim paint was peeling like sunburned skin. White strips hung from the doorframe and windowsills and tiny bits lay in the scruffy grass like dandruff.

"Tell me what we're going to see," Maya said.

"We might not see anything, but if we do, I want someone else to see it too. I need to know I'm not going batshit crazy."

Maya smirked. *Like I'd be any judge.*

When they arrived at the barn, Coty opened the narrow side door and they stepped into a shadowed interior. Maya stood on compact dirt beside an empty horse stall. Thick dust covered harnesses, stirrups and ropes on hooks fastened to the outer wall. A saddle with splitting seams sat on a sawhorse inside the stall. It took a moment for her eyes to adjust to the darkness, and then she looked up and saw sunlight slicing through cracks in the upper levels. Every ray of sunlight danced with dust motes. The dust particles swayed left, right, up and down. The smell was musty. This building was filled with memories. Maya's nose itched from the dust.

"Over here," Coty said. "Follow me."

He led the way between more stalls, alongside hay bales that were nothing more than piles of mold with snapped wires. An old saddle blanket lay in a wad at the bottom of a ladder. The ladder climbed toward a loft where more rotten hay draped the edges. Maya paused there, looking up, feeling eyes on her.

They were not alone in the barn. She felt something scrabble across her toes, glanced down and spotted a brown rat dive beneath the frayed horse blanket. She shuddered and hurried after Coty.

They passed a workbench. On the bench were dust covered tools, including a small hammer, several cans of salve with faded paper labels, disintegrating cardboard boxes filled to overflowing with brushes and mane combs. Four shovels hung on hooks by another outside door. There was a smell here. Ammonia? Fertilizer? Bat droppings? Whatever it was, it was strong.

Coty passed through an open gate and turned down another passageway. Here, the smell grew even stronger. He halted beside a set of double doors and glanced back at Maya. Without a word, he shoved the doors apart. The doors separated on wheels, squealing on lower and overhead tracks. Straight ahead Maya saw a dust-covered tractor, a flatbed two-wheeled trailer resting on its long tongue, and behind the trailer was a large mound in the corner covered by an over-sized gray tarp.

Coty crossed between the trailer and the tractor, around to the mounded tarp.

"What is that?" she asked.

Coty lifted one corner of the tarp but then seemed to hesitate. "Maybe this was a bad idea."

"What's a bad idea?" she asked.

"Bringing you up here. I'm accustomed to seeing things like this. You're not. I think we should go back down to the bunkhouse and have a cup of coffee. I bought some half and half just for you."

"No," Maya said. "Show me. I want to see what's under the tarp."

Coty wore a pained expression as he dropped the corner of the tarp. He shook his head and stepped away from the mound. "No, really," he said. "Bad idea. Let's go." His hands trembled as he stuffed them into his jeans pockets.

He's afraid.

Maya grabbed the corner of the tarp and pulled. Dust boiled up in a brown cloud, filling the air like smoke.

"No!" Coty shouted. "Wait!"

Maya dragged the tarp several feet away and dropped it. Blinking and coughing she pulled her handkerchief from her pocket and covered her nose and mouth. She squinted, blinking at the dust cloud, and as it slowly settled she said, "It's a car."

Coty nodded. "A 1960 Cadillac. Loaded. Must've cost someone a year's pay."

Dust continued to float and settle, covering the entire top of the vehicle, but the sides were bright blue with lines of chrome. The whitewall tires were rotted, flat and streaked with mold.

Maya stepped up to the passenger side door and grabbed the handle.

"You sure you want to do that?" Coty asked.

Maya opened the door and leaned closer. The smell was very strong there.

Almost overwhelming. This was where the smell originated. This was what she had smelled when she first entered the barn. Thirty years ago the smell would have been intolerable. It would have been at its rotten peak, its most putrid. It would have driven her away.

This is what Elly had described, this fancy blue Cadillac with all the chrome and the interior that resembled the cockpit of a plane. "Automatic everything," Elly had said. "Angel was such a show-off."

The dashboard was smooth blue metal with louvered vents for heat and defrosting. The clock, the speedometer, the temperature and fuel gauges, were all intact, their round glass faces framed in chrome. The seats were tufted white leather except for where blood had pooled and dried. Those spots were black. Black dots and streaks decorated the windshield and dashboard. The open ashtray full of butts, had soaked up a cupful of blood and then dried into a cracked cake. Blood had dripped from the ashtray to the white carpet. Blood had splashed across the bench seat toward the passenger side. Where Elly sat.

Elly's clothes caught those sprays of blood.

Maya closed the door and strode around the massive chrome grill to the driver's side. She opened the door and saw where Elly had dragged Angel's body from the car, back when it sat in the driveway. Blood had stained the side of the driver's white leather seat, the narrow strip of carpet below and had filled the grooves of the chrome step.

"It's been here a long time," Coty said. "I'd say thirty-five, maybe forty years."

"Fifty," Maya said.

"How do you know that?"

"It's part of Elly's story."

"Has she said anything about Danny yet?"

"All she said was that, if I see him again, to tell him she's sorry."

"Sorry for what?"

"I don't know yet."

Coty sighed. "I'm required to report murder scenes like this, to the authorities."

"How soon?" Maya asked.

"The minute I find Danny."

"I'll try to get Elly to talk more. She really doesn't want to discuss Danny though. She feels guilty about him. I just don't know why yet."

Coty lifted his shoes, one after the other, and checked their soles. He raked them against the edge of a piece of plywood. The plywood was free of dust. It had been there but a short time.

After Coty stepped off the board, Maya lifted it with the toe of her boot. Beneath, the soil appeared loose as if roughened by a shovel and then smoothed again by the weight of the board. There were no decayed wood chips or sawdust beneath the board like everywhere else in the barn.

When the time comes, the authorities should dig there, too. Maya stepped over the plywood.

Coty seemed anxious to leave, but he covered the old Cadillac with the tarp again. As they walked away, he glanced over his shoulder several times before they reached the door.

"No gray man this time?" Maya asked.

"Maybe he's not around between ten and eleven o'clock in the morning."

"Is that offer of coffee still good?"

Coty latched the outer door and then wrapped his arm around Maya's shoulders.

"It's going to be a scorcher today, but right now, hot coffee sounds like just the thing, especially with you there."

"Tell me about the gray man," Maya said.

"He's about my height, slender, parts his hair on the left side. He has deep-set eyes and a gentle face. He looks sad, like he's looking for something, or someone. He looks between forty and fifty years old. I get the feeling, he's a tragic victim here. I get a terribly sad feeling when I see him."

"What time of day is it when you see him?"

"The first time it was sun-up. February, so that's around eight o'clock in the morning."

"Maybe we should go back again sometime, around eight o'clock. Maybe this gray man has something to tell us."

"Maybe."

Chapter Forty-Three

WHILE ELLY NAPPED UPSTAIRS, Maya finished wiping down the shelves in the closet beneath the main staircase. She pulled on rubber gloves and used hot bleach water and an old towel. She scrubbed away decades of dust and grit from the shelves, ceiling and walls. She was undecided what to do about the old carpet remnant on the closet floor. It was almost worn through.

Before the garage sale, this closet had been jammed with old magazines, books, a moth-eaten green afghan, and stacks of 33.3 and 45 rpm records from the forties and fifties. The records had been among the first things to sell. Several old wool jackets had hung on hooks to the right of the angle-topped door along with a rubber raincoat that fell apart when Maya lifted it down from a peg.

The closet was empty now. It took less than an hour to scrub down the interior of the six-by- eight closet. On her knees, Maya wiped the lowest corner in the back, under the stairs. The carpet remnant was short there, exposing an inch of oak hardwood beneath. She pulled back the carpet and found a small trap door, about two feet square with tarnished brass hinges and a slot large enough to insert three fingers. She inserted her gloved fingers and lifted. Three photo albums rested in the recess, wrapped in clear plastic. Maya sat down on the floor of the closet, her back against the wall and the albums in her lap. She peeled off the rubber gloves and opened the first album. A yellowed label at the top read, Chicago 1943. The first black and white photo was of Elly behind the wheel of a truck. The driver's door was wide open and she sat with both hands on the steering wheel, a smile on her young face. She wore her light hair short and wavy. Behind the truck were shelves filled with five-gallon plastic containers. The containers were filled in varying levels of liquids and hoses dangled from overhead pipes. It looked like the place Elly had described, where she and the other warehouse drivers cleaned their trucks, removing any trace of where they had been or what they had delivered.

A man sat further back, on the corner of the counter. In the photo, he looked straight at Elly, not at the camera. He was muscular and blond, very handsome in a harsh way. A cigarette drooped from his smiling lips.

"Angel," Maya whispered, and a chill ran the length of her body.

There were three more photos on that first page, all of the warehouse and of the street lined with other warehouses. Several men wore hats, as was common in the forties and fifties. Their trousers were cuffed. They wore ties and button-front jackets, most of them loose and baggy.

Maya thumbed through the album to the end, spotting several more photos that included Elly, one where she stood beside a tall, thin man in the door of an office. A sign over the office door read MANAGER. It had to be Elly's Uncle Felix. Behind Felix stood another man, younger and shorter, but with a strong family resemblance. Elly's father, Maya decided. *Not long before he died.*

She continued turning the heavy felt pages until she had seen every photo in all three albums. She saw no one who resembled Harlan until the very last page in the last album. Maya halted there, not quite daring to touch the photo. Harlan wore the same clothing as in the photo Elly had shown her before, where he sat on the hood of a truck, his face shadowed by his hat. In this photo, he was one of six men standing side by side along the front of the loading dock. Harlan stood at the end on the left. He was the shortest. It must have been autumn when the photo was taken because their coats and jackets looked windblown. Two of the men were balding, their thinning strands of hair trailing off to one side like loose yarn. Harlan held his cap in his hands and Maya leaned closer and squinted at his face.

"Aww rats," Maya said. His features were too small, too distant for her to see him well.

Maya jumped at the sound of footsteps overhead. Elly was awake. Maya closed the albums, wrapped the plastic back around them and lowered them into the cubbyhole. She closed the trap door and smoothed the carpet back over it, pressing it down into the corner. Then she stood, picked up the scrub bucket and rubber gloves and stepped out of the closet just as Elly reached the bottom step.

"Perfect timing," Maya said. "I was going to get some lemonade. Want some?"

"What have you been doing in there?"

"Got it all scrubbed out. Dust and grit are gone. What do you want to do about that old carpet, though? Should we shampoo it or replace it with something new?"

"I don't know," Elly said. "It's just a closet."

"I saw carpet remnants at Ace Hardware," Maya said. "Under ten dollars each."

"Do you think you can find something exactly four-by-eight?"

"If not, I'll get something larger and cut it to fit."

"That old carpeting never did fit exactly right," Elly said. "And that always irritated me."

"I'll make it fit," Maya said.

"Lemonade sounds good, baby girl."

Maya headed toward the kitchen, leaving Elly standing beside the open closet door. She saw Elly bending down, eyeing the back corner, as if checking to see if the carpet looked disturbed.

What would Elly do if she knew I found her cache of photo albums? The thought gave Maya a fearful ache in her stomach. *She needs to trust me, long enough to tell me about Danny. Elly says she loves me. Blood kin, she says. I hope she does. I hope Elly loves me.*

Chapter Forty-Four

"Sheriff Wimple phoned while you and Coty were out walking," Elly said. She stood on the threshold of the basement door, a loaded laundry basket in her arms. She kicked the basement door shut behind her. "You were right about the those Mexican workers—those workers who dug our tunnel all those years ago? Their DNA indicates they're from an ancient southwestern tribe. Aztec, the sheriff said. He said forensics decided one of them died of a gunshot wound to the head and the other one, they think he probably died of dehydration. That's just their guess, though the sheriff said, since the only damage to the other skeleton was a broken heel bone. Poor sap just laid there at the bottom of the well and died a slow miserable death."

"Aunt Elly, why are you limping?"

Elly set the laundry basket on the kitchen table and rubbed her left hip. "My back is acting up again. Sharp pains in my lower spine. I remember Dr. Framish saying I have a slight herniated disk. He said it's common in women my age, bless his heart. Stairs are getting to be a challenge though."

"I'll take care of the laundry from now on," Maya said, before remembering it meant going down into the basement.

"I'll be fine tomorrow. It comes and goes," Elly said. "Don't worry about it, baby girl."

"I brought some muscle relaxant with me," Maya said. "Taking one might help."

"Nah, I'll just take a hot bath. I don't want to take drugs. Harlan might find out."

"Harlan is . . . gone, Elly."

"Yes, but somehow he still finds out about things. I'll go upstairs right now and fill the tub. Will you bring the laundry basket up for me?"

Maya lifted the basket and followed, noting how Elly leaned against the handrail most of the way and then stumbled on the top step. Maya caught Elly before she toppled backward. The laundry basket tumbled to the landing below, the clean towels and sheets spilling out.

"Let me help you into the bathroom, then I'll come back for the laundry."

"I'm okay, baby girl. I can make it the rest of the way now that I've reached the top. It's just stairs that give me problems." Elly limped into the bathroom and closed the door. Maya heard the tub faucet turn on and pictured the steam rising and filling the long, narrow room.

Maya gathered up the sheets and towels and shook each one before tossing them back into the basket. She carried everything up the stairs and into Elly's room, and stood at the foot of Elly's bed refolding the items and stacking them in neat rows. Finished, she parted the window curtain and gazed out across the fields to the upper barn. From there she had a clear view of the barn's bleached face, its open loft, the double carriage doors and the side door she and Coty and entered. She turned her gaze toward the stream at the bottom of the hill. The dark water glistened as it slid under the bridge.

Maya's attention was drawn to a shadow in Elly's dresser mirror. Her breath caught in her throat—someone sat in the rocking chair in the corner. Maya felt paralyzed with an icy dread. The shadowy figure was thin and small and wore a plaid shirt with the sleeves rolled up to the elbows. She felt Harlan glaring at her.

Elly was wrong. Harlan doesn't like me. He hates me.

Maya turned to face him. The chair rocked back and forth ever so slightly, but it was empty. She drew a shaky breath and checked the mirror for his image again. Harlan was gone. Maya rushed from the room. She leaned against the wall beside the morning glory window, its lavender panes of glass casting a hazy, blue glow in the afternoon light. She stood in the exact spot where she had seen her father's shimmering image a month ago. She had seen him only that one time. He had tried to tell her something. He mouthed the words, "Leave here. Get away . . . today!".

"Daddy?" Maya whispered. No answer. She crossed the hall. "Aunt Elly? You okay in there?" Maya tapped on the bathroom door.

"Yes and no," Elly answered. "I climbed into the tub just fine, but I can't seem to get back out."

"I'm coming in." Maya opened the bathroom door. Thick, white steam rolled like storm clouds, so dense the window and the full-length mirror at the far end were obscured. A few feet away Elly sat in the draining and gurgling oversized tub, her lower lip quivering, her pale, bony hand gripping the side.

"Oh, sweety," Maya said. "Let me help you up."

With Maya's help, Elly stood and Maya wrapped a thick, white towel around her.

"Getting old isn't at all what I expected," Elly said. "I just thought I'd get bony, wrinkled, and stooped, but this pain in my back has been coming on for some time now, and I can't seem to do much of anything anymore, not even give myself a decent bath. It's embarrassing."

"It's what I came to do, Elly. To help you, remember?"

"Yes, but a bath? I just never expected to be this way."

"When you're in the retirement place where Judith lives, there will be showers built for people with physical limitations. You won't have to step over anything, or climb in. You just stand behind a curtain and sit on a little stool, and you can use a hand-held spray attachment. You won't even have to get your hair wet if you don't want to."

"That's good because I want to take care of myself. Don't want some stranger helping me."

"How did you get this scar, Elly?"

The scar was speckled, like a patch of rough freckles. Between the freckles it was snowy white, and cutting straight through the scar were stringy twists of pink tissue.

"What scar?"

"On your shoulder here."

"Oh that. My mother spilled scalding coffee on me when I was small." Elly glanced at her shoulder with a frown. "It used to be red but as I've gotten older, it's faded."

Maya soon had Elly dressed in a clean nightgown, slippers and robe.

"Did the bath make your back feel better?" Maya asked.

"Good enough to go down and have a bowl of that vegetable soup I made earlier, sweety."

Maya heated the soup in a saucepan and ladled it into two bowls. She opened a tube of saltine crackers and they sat down at the table facing the bay window.

"What did Dad do, when he came to visit the farm?"

"Do?"

"Mom told me you asked Dad to come help you with something. I'm just wondering what that was."

"Hmm," Elly ate two more crackers. "That was a long time ago. Stephen and your mother had been married about ten years and they thought they'd never have children. Stephen said they'd been trying, You were a bit of a surprise, Maya."

"So I've been told."

"Well," Elly took a spoonful of soup and savored it for a long time before finally swallowing. Maya suspected Elly was purposely delaying her reply. *Thinking up a story.* "That was when Harlan was gone to Seattle, making a delivery down in Boise. He transferred a truckload of cigarettes." Elly chuckled. "*Transferred* means hijacked."

"Uh huh." Maya wanted Elly to keep talking. This was no time to interrupt.

"Anyway, right after Harlan left, Uncle Felix phoned and said he was sending someone over to stay in our attic. I wouldn't've dared tell Uncle Felix no, but I didn't want to receive any strangers here by myself. So, I phoned and asked Stephen to come over and help me."

"Dad knew about you and Harlan hiding people from the law?"

"No, not until he got here and saw them for himself."

"Mother told me that Dad never had emotional problems until after that visit."

Elly grimaced. Her face turned red. "Your mother is a liar. Stephen had problems ever since . . . well, since Harlan handled that situation with Grady. You remember what I told you about Grady, don't you?"

Maya swallowed the last of her soup. "Grady, the school bully."

"Yes, and it was after your father found Grady in that pool of blood that he started having a hard time dealing with stressful situations. He'd have long good spells and then sudden bad spells, and as he got older the bad spells lasted longer. I know I'm responsible for some of that, but then, who knows? Stephen might have gone kookoo anyway. Life is like that."

"Kookoo?" Maya felt a white-hot, angry heat ignite deep in her chest. She took of sip of her ice water before saying, "After all the things you've seen and after all the things you've done, I'm surprised you haven't been . . ." Maya focused on the double doors of the big barn on top the hill. She swallowed again, holding back the words, trying hard to not blurt them out.

"Surprised I haven't been what, baby girl?"

Maya spotted a patch of freshly turned dirt, where carrots, onions, and beets had been growing just yesterday, was now a rectangle of churned dirt, three feet wide by six feet long. For a few seconds she feared her soup and crackers would come back up.

"You're surprised I'm not what, Maya?" Elly repeated a wary gleam in her eyes.

Maya had almost said, *locked up in Western State Hospital*, but she didn't dare say that, not now, not after all the things Elly had revealed about her past.

"I'm surprised you're not emotionally scarred," she finally said. "I mean, Grady, Angel, the Franks, the people buried in the basement. Those would have wounded me emotionally. Haven't they wounded you at all?"

"Of course they have, but there's nothing I can do about the past is there?"

"But did anything tragic happen while Dad was here visiting you? Back when he came to help you with the people in the attic?"

"Not that I recall," Elly said. "I'll think about it, though. Sometimes memories fly back into my brain like a wasp, buzzing and darting and stinging. I'll think about it, Maya, but I don't want to think too hard or too long. Because sometimes remembering causes things to happen."

"Causes things to happen? Like what?" Maya pulled her eyes from the sight of the grave shape in the garden. She studied Elly's face, almost expecting to see the sweet, gentle old face morph into someone else. Mr. Elly.

Elly's expression had lost its red flush of anger about Maya's mother. Instead, Elly was staring at something over Maya's shoulder, at something behind her, and Maya remembered with a sudden flash that the basement door was unlocked. Neither of them had locked it after Elly climbed up from the basement with the laundry basket, and that was over an hour ago.

Maya was almost too afraid to look, but was terrified not to. She turned in her chair. The basement door had already frosted over. Crystals of ice spread from top to bottom across the ancient yellow paint. The black doorknob was already white with ice. Something black appeared in the gap beneath the door, something liquid and shiny. It trailed across the old linoleum toward the kitchen table.

Elly whispered, "We forgot to lock the door, baby girl."

Maya stood, took four quick steps across the kitchen and twisted the lock. A half second later the icy doorknob turned left and then right, crystals sparkling. The door groaned from the weight of something leaning against it from the other side.

Maya stared down at the black liquid pooling around her bare feet. It wasn't black. It was the deepest, darkest red Maya had ever seen.

"Elly." That deep, familiar voice came from behind the door. "Elly."

Elly rose from her chair. She limped across the floor in her slippers, stepping over the coiling, snaking trails of blood. She halted a few feet from the yellow door.

"You'll never touch me again, Angel," Elly said. "Go back down. Back where you belong. Now! Or I'll make good my threat."

The frosty ice coating the yellow door, melted, as if the door had grown warm from the heat of Elly's voice. Islands of ice slid down the ancient, blistered paint and out onto the floor, diluting the black blood and turning it a brighter red. The blood halted its progress across the linoleum, stopping an inch from the feet of Maya's chair. There, it halted. It gleamed, its scarlet edges catching streaks of light through the kitchen window—then it retreated, slithering back through the crevice under the basement door. It left no trace of its journey across the floor and back again.

Elly sighed. "He keeps trying, more and more often, but if Angel ever makes it through that door, I have another surprise waiting for him."

Chapter Forty-Five

"That's odd," Aunt Elly said. "Lookit that."

Maya followed the direction of Elly's gaze but noticed nothing. "What?"

"The pantry light is on, the little one on the ceiling outside the utility closet."

"Maybe I brushed against the switch while putting the mop away," Maya said.

Elly shook her head. "That light only turns on from the attic. It means something is in the dumbwaiter. It means the guests are done eating and their dishes are coming back down."

Maya entered the pantry and stared up at the small light. It was a 25-watt, recessed bulb. She flipped the switch on the wall beside the utility closet and the light in the center of the hallway flashed on. A second later the small yellow light went out.

"Someone's in the attic," Elly said.

Maya and Elly stood side by side, staring up at the kitchen ceiling, listening for sounds of movement overhead but the house was silent.

"Maybe it's just a short in the wiring," Maya whispered.

Elly shook her head no.

Maya stepped across the kitchen and slid open a drawer. She lifted the butcher knife and followed Elly through the dining room to the foot of the main stairs. There, they paused to listen again. After another moment Elly led the way to the second level and leaned around her bedroom door. Maya peered over Elly's shoulder. The closet light was out and the closet was dark.

"Let me go first." Maya rushed across the bedroom, reached inside the closet and flipped the light on. A warm glow filled the space and she released a long-held breath. There was no intruder in Elly's closet. She felt her knees shaking and wondered what might have happened if she had confronted someone. Her reaction would have been involuntary. Maya rotated the handle of the butcher knife in her sweaty hand and took another breath. Everything inside the closet was in order; even the thin veil of dust on the shelves was undisturbed.

"He wouldn't have come through here," Elly whispered. "He would have come in the other way."

"What other way?"

"Remember the place I showed you in the basement? Where the concrete blocks hide an opening in the wall beside the furnace? He either went through there, or . . . he came through the underground tunnel."

"Who did?" Maya asked.

"Fritz."

"Oh, you mean Tony Bradley? What's he doing here?"

"He thinks I have millions of dollars stashed here somewhere, the damned fool. That's why he showed up here that time with the shovel."

I thought you were asleep when he drove up.

Maya reached for the trap door cord, but Elly shook her head no. Elly tiptoed to the tallboy against the back wall of the closet, grasped the two knobs on the top drawer and turned the left one counter-clockwise and the right one clockwise. Maya heard a click and then Elly slid the top drawer open. It made no sound. Elly reached inside and lifted out a double-barrel shotgun. The barrels were sawed off. Elly lifted an open box of ammunition from the drawer and loaded the chamber. With a nod, she closed the drawer and returned to where Maya stood. Elly whispered,

"Fritz has made a big mistake coming back here. If he's armed, and I'm sure he is, he won't be leaving here on his own."

"Elly, please don't shoot anyone."

Elly smiled. "For your peace of mind, baby girl, I'll use discretion."

Discretion? Until that moment Maya would never have suspected Elly knew the meaning of the word. This was the same woman who could not recall the words ultimatum and nostalgic.

Maya turned off the closet light and pulled the cord. The trapdoor eased open and down with a soft, brushing sound. Just as silent were the unfolding stairs and Maya followed Elly into the attic.

At first Maya saw nothing. She halted on the second step behind Elly. They stood there listening. Finally Maya noticed a hint of light from around the corner.

"It's the bathroom light," Elly whispered. "Someone's in there, with the door ajar."

The door squeaked as it opened and the light brightened before it went out. Darkness surrounded them again.

Elly climbed the last step into the attic, reached up and yanked the light cord above the table. The single one hundred watt bulb flashed on. At the same instant, Tony Bradley appeared from around the corner. He wore charcoal coveralls, Adidas sneakers and a black stocking cap over his silvery blonde hair. He looked startled.

Elly lifted the shotgun and aimed it, but he was gone in a second. Elly ran after him, shoving a chair out of her way as she rounded the table. Maya rushed after them both. When she reached the corner, Maya spotted Tony jumping into the dark stairwell at the far end of the room. The door slammed behind him. His footsteps pounded as he descended into the underground.

"Fritz!" Elly had no limp now. She ran like a young woman. She flung the door open and disappeared into the gloom behind him.

"Elly!" Maya ran and then halted in the open door. She stared into the black air below. She had no flashlight this time. This stairwell had no railings and there was that gap between the steps on both sides and the wall. One misstep and it would be a long, straight drop to the basement.

"Elly?" Maya called again.

A light came on at the bottom of the stairs. Elly stood there, looking up, shotgun aimed downward and braced against her ribs. Elly nodded for Maya to follow. Maya headed down, her left hand sliding along one wall, her eyes on every step. At the bottom she asked, "Where did Tony…Fritz go?"

Elly pointed to a set of footprints in the dirt. They led straight to the wall of concrete blocks. Six of the bottom blocks had been pulled away, leaving a gaping hole. Elly chuckled. "He's in the basement. He can't get out. The kitchen door is locked. The outside door is padlocked and its window has been boarded up from the outside. Fritz is trapped."

"He came through the tunnel?" Maya asked. The thought made her shiver.

"Yes, but apparently he didn't want to return by the same route. He decided to kick down the concrete blocks—his second mistake. Now we've got him."

"We're not going in there after him, are we?" Maya asked.

"The basement? Aww, hell no." Elly leaned down beside the hole. She called out, "While you're in there, Fritz, be sure to say hello to Angel. He's been dying to see you."

Elly straightened. She slid her palm across the wall and pressed something, leaning into it, and from overhead came a *snap* sound and then a rumble. A thick sheet of metal slid down from above. It lodged into place on the dirt floor, covering both the concrete blocks and the dark opening.

"He's not getting out now," Elly said. "Come on, baby girl. Let's get back to the kitchen. This should be interesting."

"Interesting how?"

"You'll see." Elly flicked the light off and they headed back up the long, straight flight of stairs toward the open attic door.

"Are you going to phone Sheriff Wimple and have Fritz arrested for breaking and entering?"

"Nope."

"You just going to leave him locked in the basement?"

"Yep."

"For how long?" Maya asked.

"Forever." Elly closed the door at the top of the stairs and continued around the corner to the trap door. Maya descended into the bedroom closet behind Elly and raised the folding stairs. One minute later they were downstairs.

In the kitchen Maya stood in the center of the room, her knees shaking.

"What about his body, Elly? Won't it be . . . a problem when people come here, interested in buying the farm?"

Elly poured coffee into two mugs. Smiling, she added half and half and stirred them with a spoon. The spoon made a cheerful *ping-ping-ping* sound against the mugs. The shotgun rested on the table.

"There won't be a body after Angel finishes with him. I've been waiting for this a long time, Maya. Fritz has finally made a fatal mistake."

Maya shivered in the July heat. She raised the window above the sink and propped open the back door with the rock painted like a ladybug. The kitchen felt cooler with the air coming across the driveway from under the fir trees.

"Harlan painted that ladybug doorstop for me when we first moved here." Elly sipped her coffee and stepped toward the basement door. She leaned close but didn't touch it. "Any time now," she said.

"What's going to happen?" Maya asked.

"Don't exactly know really, but I know Angel hates Fritz."

"What are you talking about, Aunt Elly? Angel is dead. He can't do anything—can he?"

"You saw what happened to the door, Maya. You saw the ice and the blood. You don't think Angel can *do* anything?"

"But, you said Fritz is probably armed."

"You can't kill a dead man with a gun, baby girl. Shhh, listen. Maybe we can figure out what's happening by the sounds they make."

A moment later footsteps pounded up the basement steps. Maya held her breath as the doorknob twisted left and right, left and right. The door shook in its frame.

"Elly? You in there?" It was Fritz's voice. "Elly! Open the door!"

"Maybe the money's buried down there somewhere, Fritz. Dig around. There's always the chance you'll find it." Elly slapped her knee and laughed. "There's a shovel by the furnace."

"Elly! Open this door!" A few seconds passed. "Elly! Please!"

Elly's grin faded. Her expression changed and she sounded awestruck. "Angel is coming, isn't he, Fritz? Can you see him? Ain't he a sight? No telling what he's gonna' do." Elly stepped away and a second later three bullets tore three holes in the yellow door, splintering the wood.

"Elly! Elly!" Fritz yelled. "Please!"

Maya rushed toward the yellow door. "Maybe we should let him . . ."

"No," Elly blocked Maya. "Once he was free, Fritz would torture you, forcing me to tell him where the money is."

The door strained against the doorjambs, the aged wood snapping and popping. The hinges screeched an the door bowed, but it held.

"Elly! Please!" Fritz yelled. "Elly!" He pounded on the door. He kicked. The last sound he made was an inhuman scream. His scream became a gurgle and the gurgle was cut short. Something heavy rolled down the stairs. A second later the black doorknob twisted left and right again.

Maya stared open-mouth at the twisting doorknob, expecting frost and ice to form on its surface, but Elly stroked the blistered enamel, smiling. No ice formed. The top step snapped and heavy footsteps descended. Elly pressed one ear against the door, and then she shrugged.

"What happened?" Maya asked.

"I can't see through doors any better than you can, baby girl." Elly crossed the kitchen, lifted the coffee carafe and filled her mug again. "I'll take a look-see down there tomorrow morning. 9:00 AM has always been a safe time to open up that door." Elly's dialect had returned.

"Why did Angel hate Fritz?" Maya asked.

"That's another story, honey. You want to hear it?"

Maya didn't want to hear any more of Elly's memories, not unless they explained what happened to Danny, but Elly stood there, smiling and waiting. Elly wanted to share the story.

"I guess so," Maya said.

• • • *

"Ye see, Fritz was hired by someone high up in the organization, even higher up than Angel.

Someone phoned one day and said he was sending a guy over who had been given a job. I was outside the office when Angel got that call. I remember Angel's expression. He was annoyed.

"'Shit,' he said after he slammed down the receiver.

"About an hour later, Fritz arrives and Angel must have realized he had serious competition in the looks department. Not only that, but someone high up . . . really high up, apparently liked Fritz better than they liked him. That can't feel good for someone with ambition, can it?

"So Fritz and Angel sit down in the office with the door closed. Nobody got to hear anything they said, but when they came out, Angel wasn't being the asshole he usually was. I expected Fritz to be given the regular tour, shown where the coveralls were hung, where the trucks were scrubbed down, stuff like that, but the two of them stood out there on the loading dock for a while and then they parted ways without another word. I knew then that Fritz had friends more powerful than Angel's friends.

"I've told you before how most of the other drivers and I never talked much. Sometimes they quit talking altogether when I walked by. But on occasion, when the news was juicy enough, I was included in the scuttlebutt. Seems

Fritz was an inspector. He came by once a month or so, without warning, and snooped wherever he wanted to snoop without so much as a howdy-do. The law would say, without due process. Heh. I guess he was sort of a spy for upper management.

"Angel became obsessive about how things were done around the warehouse, and how clean it was, and how on time we all had to be, and how the books were kept up to date. Not the public books, just the ones the higher-ups were interested in. The real books. Angel was on the bookkeeper's ass day and night after that. That's when that first bookkeeper up and quit and set Angel's wastebasket on fire. Remember that story? Heh.

"The second bookkeeper was there about a month before he quit and then Angel hired a twenty-two year old redhead. Her name was Lyla. She apparently couldn't work every day but Angel hired her anyway. She only worked two days a week because she had another job that paid more than bookkeeping, but still not enough, I guess.

"I don't know for sure, but I heard the other drivers say she was a stripper three nights a week in some club on the west side. I didn't care. She didn't flaunt her looks. She dressed nice enough, professional even. Know what I mean? Office attire. Proper. Not too much makeup either. Who'da thought a stripper would show class like that?

"Angel must have had a thing for redheads. Either that or she just plain had what it took to reel him in. We'll never know.

"Lyla was divorced, but her ex-husband stayed protective. Some people are like that. They love each other but can't get along. Anyway, Angel tiptoed around her like she was hot coals and he was ice cream in danger of melting. He arranged for flowers to be delivered to her office every Monday morning, and he was there to make sure they were nice flowers. He picked out a pink donut with sprinkles and set it on her desk on a napkin every morning because she said those were her favorites. I was amazed Angel could pretend to be nice for that length of time. The other drivers were entertained, too. I saw their expressions. I heard their comments. That's when I first heard the term, pussy-whipped. Figured out on my own what that meant.

"Strangely enough, Lyla was there almost six months before Fritz discovered her. Their schedules didn't jive until then. Angel spotted Fritz arriving and tried to ambush his visit. Tried to keep him away from Lyla. Tried hard but failed. Heh. There were quite a few of us trying to appear busy while we followed Fritz and Angel around. Angel offered to take Fritz to lunch. Didn't work. Angel wanted to show Fritz the newest truck. Fritz frowned and shook his head. The recently tarred roof? Even I laughed at that.

"Like I told you before, baby girl, Angel had a cruel handsomeness. I'll give him credit for trying hard. Since Lyla's arrival, Angel started showering daily, and wearing clean clothes and shaving and getting regular haircuts. I think he even started getting manicures. But he was no spring chicken. He was probably in his late-fifties. And Fritz . . . well, Fritz was in his mid-twenties back then. You've seen him. He's now the same age Angel was back then, but Fritz was in better shape."

Elly paused there and stared at the yellow basement door for a minute before she continued.

"Fritz was always in great shape right up until today. Until now. Heh.

"Have you ever realized how feeble most women are, Maya? Compared to men we're scrawny things. Even if we're at the top of our physical strength, we don't have the weight behind us, and I mean muscle weight. We can haul off and plug a man in the face . . . maybe break his nose if we're lucky . . . maybe keep him down long enough to run if we kick him in the nuts first . . . but in a real confrontation, we're pathetic. Maybe that's why God made men so vulnerable when it comes to sex. Men are helpless if they're smitten. Sex is their Achilles heel. Watching Angel stumble around trying to impress Lyla was downright comical. When she looked up from her desk and made eye contact with Fritz that first time . . . there was instant chemistry. It was like electricity in the air. Angel felt it too. He looked like a balloon with a slow leak.

"A week later, Lyla resigned. She just up and quit—walked out the door. One of the drivers told me she had already shacked up with Fritz. A month after that, her ex-husband shot and killed her outside the strip club. Angel had pursued Lyla, but he lost. It was after that he turned really mean. After that was when he hurt me. Angel hates everybody . . . but he especially hates Fritz."

• • • *

"Hated," Maya corrected. "Past tense. Angel is dead, Aunt Elly."

Elly pulled her gaze away from the bay window. "Yes, he most assuredly is, baby girl, and Fritz is probably dead too. Fritz is either dead or praying death takes him soon, but neither of them are done hating. Angel and Fritz—they'll be down there together in that basement a long time, maybe forever . . . or until this farm is nothing but a pile of rot."

Chapter Forty-Six

COTY'S MIDNIGHT-BLUE DODGE RAM rumbled by the kitchen window. He parked behind the shed under the overhanging shake roof and turned the engine off.

Back in April, when Maya first arrived at the farm, there had been two cords of firewood stacked in that very spot. Back then Coty had parked behind the woodpile and tossed a brown tarp over his truck, but it had been a cold, damp, spring and she and Elly had used up most of that firewood. A half row of wood remained. That half row leaned against the back of the shed, and Coty was no longer splitting and stacking firewood. He was no longer forming bundles of kindling. Maya and Coty hoped to have Elly moved into the retirement home by the time it turned cold enough to need firewood again. Coty said, "The new owners can split their own firewood."

Coty rounded the front side of the shed with a Red Apple grocery sack in his right arm and the handle of a small, brown leather case in his left hand.

He spotted Maya at the kitchen window and smiled. Maya stepped through the open door.

"Is that it?" she asked. "The ALS thing?"

"Yeah. Is this a good time?"

"Yeah, Elly's asleep. She should be asleep for at least a couple hours. I slipped a Lorazapam into her lemonade at lunchtime."

"I wish you could have convinced her to go shopping in Graceville instead of her staying at the farm," Coty said. "I'm uncomfortable with her being here at all."

"I tried hard to convince her to go, but she doesn't shop anymore. 'I don't need anything,' she said. What are we going to say if she wakes up and finds us using this thing in the upstairs hallway?"

Coty kicked open his bunkhouse door. "We'll say, Elly, we're just searching for traces of old blood. You don't mind, do you?"

Maya grimaced. "Not funny."

Coty set the grocery sack on the table and the ALS case on the kitchen counter. "Don't worry, Maya. I'll tell her it was all my idea," Coty said. "I'll say I talked you into it. I'll say I just wanted to try out my new piece of investigative equipment."

"Elly doesn't know you're a private investigator, remember?"

"Oh yeah. That's right. Well, maybe I can convince her that I just got my P.I. license and thought this thing needed testing. You just act dumb."

"She'd never believe it."

"Let's hope she doesn't wake up then," Coty said.

Coty shoved a six-pack of Beck's and a dozen eggs into the refrigerator, along with three honey crips apples, a small loaf of bread and a block of cheddar.

They hurried across the driveway and into the house. Maya halted in the middle of the kitchen, eyes closed, listening. Not a sound. She glanced over at the yellow basement door. Locked. She checked the clock. 1:30 PM. "Elly's been asleep a half hour. We've got to be done by 2:30, okay?"

"It won't take that long." Coty took the main stairs two at a time with Maya on his heels.

Elly's bedroom door was closed. Maya leaned close and listened.

"She's snoring," Maya whispered.

Coty placed the case on the floor of the upstairs landing and flipped open the latch. Inside the case were three glass containers and a plastic spray bottle. One container was labeled Luminol, the second contained potassium hydroxide, and the third bottle's label read, hydrogen peroxide.

"My friend, Walt, already mixed up a batch. All we do is spray the area we want to test,"

Coty whispered.

"Spray right here." Maya pointed to the place where Coty knelt. He looked down at the dark hardwood floor with a frown.

Coty sprayed a four-foot circle with the liquid. He stepped back. "Nothing," he said.

Maya almost gasped with relief. That was the spot where she had seen her father, where his gray image floated in the dusky hallway, his voice sounding miles away when he screamed, 'get away from this place.'

"You okay?" Coty asked.

Nodding, Maya swallowed the lump in her throat. She pointed down the hallway. "In front of that door at the end," she whispered. "Where we saw Danny."

They halted at the end of the hallway. Coty sprayed the entire area.

"Nothing."

"I don't understand. This is where I've always seen Danny. He floats in the air, right in this part of the hallway, and then he . . ."

"Then he what?"

"You saw him, Coty. It's like something pulls him away. Something drags him straight through the door, but when I open the door, there's nothing there but the stairs going down into the skylight room."

Coty opened the door. "Ever seen Danny in the skylight room?"

"Once." They descended the stairs. "Just once," Maya said, "not long after I arrived here, but after that, he's always been in the upstairs hall."

"What else?"

"What do you mean?"

"What else has happened to you in here? What else have you seen or experienced in this room?"

"I've already told you everything . . . well, except for the incident with my watch. It disappeared from my bedside table the very first night I was here. Later, I found it on the main stairs, coated with dust as if it had been there for months."

"I know you're not telling me everything, Maya."

"You're right, I'm not—but I will once we find Danny, and once we get Elly into the retirement home. I made Elly a promise to not tell some things . . . not until she's gone."

"Gone?"

"Dead."

"Hell. That crazy lady is healthy as a horse. That could be twenty-five years. Maybe thirty."

"I promised her."

It took ten minutes for Coty to spray the floor and walls of skylight room. When he'd circled the room twice, he halted at the base of the wood paneled wall. There, spots on the hardwood floor glowed blue.

"Do you see that?" Coty said. "Something happened here in the past, but it wasn't a lot of blood. A bad cut or scrape could have caused that much. This part of the house was an add-on in the fifties, with plenty of sawing and hammering. Accidents happen."

"I thought we'd find more than this. Are you sure this blood testing stuff really works?"

"Show me a spot where you know for sure, blood has been."

"The dining room," Maya said. "And the kitchen."

Coty strode around through the living room and into the dining room. He sprayed the floor between the dining table and the window. The entire floor glowed blue. He sprayed the tabletop. "Look at that! The whole tabletop is blue." He sprayed the floor all the way around the table. "It's like this room was painted with blood."

"Check the kitchen," Maya said. Five minutes later Coty said,

"The entire kitchen floor glows blue. What the hell happened here?"

"It's an old house. Things could have happened before Elly and Harlan moved in."

"Such as?"

"I've heard about farmers cutting up hogs and cattle in their kitchens during cold weather," Maya said. "Maybe some hunters cut up a dear. I don't know."

Maya felt guilty. Coty's narrowed gaze was an accusation. She turned her gaze out the bay window toward the garden. Coty knew she was hiding something. He knew she was protecting Elly. *Why am I protecting Elly?* Maya shook her head. *I don't know.*

"I'll tell you *everything* after Elly is gone," Maya said. "But, I'll tell you about Danny, as soon as I know anything. I think Elly's going to tell me about Danny pretty soon."

Coty glared at the old linoleum. "Your explanation doesn't add up," he said. "The hogs, the calf . . . dear hunters? Those animals are drained of blood outside, before they're butchered. They're not brought into the house to bleed-out."

"When Elly is gone I'll . . . "

"Why are you protecting that old bitch?"

"Don't call her that."

"She did something to Danny. I know it. And you know it."

"I suspect it, but I don't know it."

Coty placed the ALS case on the kitchen counter, opened it and jammed the spray bottle into its slot. He slammed the case shut and strode out the kitchen door. Maya held her breath as he crossed the driveway and kicked open his bunkhouse door. It slammed shut behind him.

"I knew I could trust you."

Maya jumped at the sound of Elly's voice. She twisted her head around and discovered Elly standing on the bottom step, on the other side of the dining room.

"How long have you been standing there?" Maya asked.

"Long enough to know you haven't told Coty anything important yet."

"I promised you I'd keep your secrets and I keep my promises," Maya said. "Coty's name is Wayne C. Matheson and he isn't Judith's nephew."

"What's he doing here?"

"He's looking for his nephew, Danny."

Elly stepped down and crossed through the dining room in her robe and slippers. "What time is it?"

"2:25 in the afternoon."

"Things are coming to an end, Maya." Elly sat down at the kitchen table as if she were exhausted.

"An end? What do you mean?"

"I've known for some time now. When I was in the hospital and they were running all those test on me? I knew then."

"But your tests all came back great. Dr. Framish said you're very healthy."

"Doctors don't know everything."

"Are you feeling ill, Aunt Elly?"

Elly shook her head. "No, I'm just tired. The only time I have any energy is when I'm angry, but that's not healthy."

"Angry?"

"Like when Fritz showed up. I had energy then, didn't I?"

Maya remembered how Elly chased Fritz through the attic room and down the long, straight flight of stairs. For a woman in her mid-seventies, Elly had moved with surprising agility.

"I don't want you to feel angry, Aunt Elly. Anger is as bad as fear."

"No, no. Fear is worse than anger. Fear is almost as bad as grief, but grief is the worst, because grief doesn't end. When I went to see Stephen, your father, in the institution, they told me there was very little chance he'd ever be released. Back then, Stephen was the only kin I cared about. Everyone else was gone. My father, my mother. I'd never met any cousins or grandparents. Uncle Felix . . . he was blood kin but I didn't love him, and Fritz said Uncle Felix is probably dead now anyway, remember? I believe Felix is dead. You're all I have left, Maya. You're all I care about."

Maya nodded. She had nothing to say. No answers.

"Want to know something I saw at the institution, Maya? Something so sweet and so sad, it broke my heart?"

"If it would help to talk about it, okay."

"After they told me Stephen would never leave that place, his doctor showed me a room where they kept some of the patients' personal belongings . . . things the patients brought with them, but that were taken away for one reason or another. Safety, I suppose. Belts and shoelaces. Drugs. Knives. Knitting needles. Sharp things." Elly sighed. Her eyes looked blurry. She rubbed her palms against her eyes and sniffed. "It was such a big storage room, filled with suitcases and trunks. The doctor—I can't recall his name—he showed me Stephen's suitcase. It was packed so neatly. Stephen was a tidy boy. His bedroom was always tidy. Not many boys make their beds every day like Stephen did. Men don't seem to care much about things like that.

"'We allowed him to have the photo of you,'" the doctor told me. "But we took the metal frame and the glass away, of course. He has his shoes, but not the laces. He wanted his bible and I allowed that."

"Dad had a bible?" Maya asked.

Elly nodded. "Stephen went to Sunday school as a boy. He went every Sunday until about the age of fourteen. He never said why he stopped going, but I suspect I know why.

"I guess the doctor allowed him his favorite pair of pajamas. Those were the ones he used . . . he tore them into strips and wove an eight foot long rope. Eight feet was just long enough.

"I still remember all those suitcases in that storage room. I dream about that storage room sometimes. There were so many suitcases propped open, displayed on the shelves for people like me to see. I don't think it was right, allowing strangers to see their personal things. Odd things. Unusual things. I remember one patient had a lot of baseball cards. Another had a whole box of broken, worn down crayons, like a little kid might have. One lady had beautiful scarves and some beaded headbands from the nineteen twenties. One had three pair of ballet shoes, well worn. One man had several military medals. Another man had a small trunk full of little, clear boxes and inside each box was a beautiful, hand-made fishing fly. There were over two hundred of them, apparently.

"I can picture those poor souls carefully placing each item, one after the other into their suitcases, along with the memory attached to it. Evidence of insanity? Not nearly. No. Just memories they couldn't stand to leave behind."

Chapter Forty-Seven

MAYA PAINTED BOTH THE upstairs and downstairs bathrooms, even though Elly said it wasn't necessary. Now, there was only one gallon of white semi-gloss remaining, having started with the pantry hallway and the big cupboards. Maya liked the way things looked when painted white. If not new, at least pristine—not yet corrupted by human touch.

"Want me to sand down and paint the basement door, too?" Maya asked. "That old yellow paint is blistered and peeling. I can putty over the bullet holes."

"Nope." Elly had said. "Go ahead and paint everything you want, except that door. I'm going upstairs to take a nap."

It was late afternoon when Maya stowed the brush, the roller, and the paint pan, inside the utility closet. She stood at the kitchen sink with her hands under warm running water, rubbing paint from her nails and fingers. She pulled her painting scarf off her head as a man strode up the driveway from the shadow of the trees.

With a frown, Maya opened the back door and confront him before he reached the porch. "What do you want, Benson?"

"We need to talk," he said. "May I have a drink of water?"

"I'm not letting you inside."

"May I have a drink of water though?"

"Stay right here." Maya closed the door. She took a clean glass from the drying rack on the counter and filled it from the tap. The kitchen door opened and Benson stepped inside. "I told you to wait outside," she said.

"It's too hot out there."

"Where did you park? I don't see your car."

"It's out on the road, by the mailbox," Benson said. "I didn't want you or your crazy aunt to slash my tires or take a baseball bat to the windshield."

Maya chuckled. "It's quite a walk in from the road, isn't it? You might as well start back now if you want to miss the line of traffic at the ferry. Or do you plan to drive all the way around the sound to Tacoma?"

Benson accepted the glass of water and sat down at the kitchen table. "Let me catch my breath, Maya."

"If Aunt Elly hears you, she'll be down here in a flash with her shotgun."

Benson grinned. "A real Annie Oakley, huh?"

"You'd be surprised, Bens."

"Nothing about your family surprises me, Maya. You come from a long line of loonies."

"Don't go there, Bens."

"Why are you so anxious for me to leave? Why don't you want me here? I just want to discuss something with you."

"Such as?"

"My inheritance."

"I don't care about that. Go ahead and sign the divorce papers and keep it all for yourself. I don't want you or your mother's money."

"Got your own money, huh?"

"No, but I can get a job when it comes time."

"I think you're lying, Maya. I think your crazy Aunt Elly is leaving you a fortune and you just don't want to share it with me. I'm being generous though. I'm willing to share my inheritance with you."

Maya smirked. "You think Aunt Elly has more than your mother? Didn't you tell me your mother was worth a couple million?"

"Yeah. How much is Elly worth?"

"I have no idea and I don't care. It doesn't matter."

"Sure it matters. If I sign the divorce papers now, you'll get nothing."

"Sign the papers, Bens. Sign away," Maya said. "Just go away and leave me alone."

Benson studied the kitchen. "Old places like this often had safes built into the walls, or even under the floor somewhere."

"I've been here since April, cleaning and scrubbing and painting, and I haven't come across any safes. Or money. Or jewelry. Aunt Elly is just an old farmer and she's ready to sell this place and move into a retirement home. I agreed to help her. End of story, Bens."

"Oh, it's here somewhere. I guarantee you. It's in the attic, a back bedroom . . . the basement."

"There's nothing in the basement."

"Is that so? You said that awfully quick."

"There's nothing of value in the basement. The Maytag washer and dryer are twenty years old. The furnace is five. And that's it. That's all that's down there."

"What about the attic?"

"The attic is interesting. Elly and Harlan housed farmhands up there during cold weather back in the fifties, because the bunkhouse was already rotten and falling apart. Want to see the attic? We'll have to tiptoe through Elly's bedroom while she's napping, though."

"Nah. I'm more curious about the basement."

"Why?"

"Because you're so determined to keep me out of it."

"No, I'm not. Really. It's just that there's nothing down there."

Benson rose to his feet and drained the last of his water. He set the glass on the counter and pointed to the yellow door. "That's it, right?"

"Don't go down there, Benson. I promise, there's nothing down there you'd want to see." Maya stepped toward the yellow door, blocking Benson's path.

Benson grabbed her by the arm and pulled her away. He shoved her backwards and she fell against the front of the cook stove, landing hard. He twisted the black enamel doorknob. He tugged. The door rattled but refused to open.

"It's locked," Maya said. "Just turn the t-shaped lock." She massaged her elbow where it had struck the oven handle.

The lock clicked and Benson opened the door.

"Is there a light?" he asked.

"To the right." Maya pushed herself to her feet as the basement light flashed on and the eight steps appeared. The top step was ecru with dust. The bottom step was half hidden in charcoal shadows.

"Coming?" Benson asked.

Maya shook her head.

Benson descended the stairs and halted beside the Maytag washer and dryer. He leaned down, palms on thighs, peering into the shadows. "Dirt floor. It's probably buried somewhere down here," he said. "Look at all the nice, dry, fluffy dirt."

"There's a shovel, over by the furnace," Maya said.

Benson strode down the concrete path, beyond the glow of the single lightbulb. She closed the door. Locked it.

"Yes, I come from a long line of loonies." Maya counted down from ten.

"Maya!" Footsteps pounded up the basement steps. "Maya!"

"I'm right here in the kitchen, Bens."

The black enameled doorknob twisted. The old yellow door rattled in its frame. "Open the door! There's . . . something down here." His voice sounded more like a squeal. "Let me out."

"What did you find . . . a safe full of money?"

"Maya! Open the door!"

Maya pictured the top step and Benson standing there, pressed against the door. She pictured something gray moving in the shadows below, something squirming in those shadows, inching toward the steps. Something pale. Something bizarre—an undulating pile of human parts—one arm where a leg should be, the other arm around a headless neck like a flesh scarf, one severed leg facing backward, the head carried in one bloodless hand, blond hair streaked with black, rancid blood, the scalp pulling away from the skull like cheap plastic, the eye sockets—round holes filled with pus.

"A thing. A man . . . a thing," Benson stuttered.

"Make up your mind, Bens. A thing or a man?"

"Open the door!" Benson screamed.

Two seconds passed.

"Maya!" Benson shouted. "He's . . . coming up the stairs."

"You said Elly and I were loonies, but you're the one who sees a *thing* in the basement."

Benson pounded on the kitchen door and then he screamed her name one last time.

"Ma-ya!"

Maya mopped up the little puddle that had formed on the linoleum in front of the yellow door. One small island of ice slid down and she caught it with a paper towel and threw the towel into the garbage under the sink.

"Is someone here?" Elly stood in the entrance to the dining room. "I thought I heard talking."

"Benson. He went down into the basement, convinced he'd find a safe full of money."

"I would like to have met him," Elly said. "You know . . . to put a face to the name. Too late now though, right?"

"Yes, I'm pretty sure it is."

Chapter Forty-Eight

"Sheriff Wimple is on his way over," Elly said. "He's said he has something he wants to discuss with me. I invited him to stay for dinner, but he said no. Guess he doesn't want to socialize with a suspect."

"I'm no longer a suspect," Maya said. "They decided those skeletons had been there since before I was born."

Elly said, "I'm the suspect."

"He said that?"

"No, but I could tell by his voice. He said he has a warrant to search this place. We both know what that means."

"That depends on what they're looking for."

"Doesn't matter what they're look for. There's a fifty-year-old corpse inside a freezer, buried in the basement along with the skeletons of three more people buried nearby—not very deep either."

"What should we do?"

"There's no time to do anything, Maya. If I was going to do something, I should have done it fifty years ago."

"What about Angel's Cadillac in the old barn?" Maya asked.

Elly's eyes widened. "You know about that?"

"Coty found it. I mean Wayne. He showed me. There's a lot of old blood in that car."

"I don't know why I kept Angel's car. I didn't need to. I've got Angel for a trophy, down in the basement."

"Elly?"

"Yes, baby girl?"

"You'd better tell me about Danny," Maya said.

Elly wore a defeated expression. She finally nodded and said, "Never even knew the boy's name. Fritz picked him up out there on the county road and brought him to help make that last delivery. Poor kid. Fritz never intended to pay him."

"But that was only six months ago. You said you weren't in the business anymore."

"I wasn't, and Fritz knew it, too. He showed up here anyway, because he had a spare in his trunk and couldn't find a place to get rid of it. He said he crossed the Agate Pass Bridge at 2:00 AM and thought he'd have time to toss the body over, but every time he opened the trunk, headlights appeared. One guy even stopped and asked if Fritz was having car trouble. So Fritz drove over the Hood Canal Bridge and pulled over to the side, but a Coast Guard boat pulled up and aimed a bright light on him, so Fritz drove on up here to Graceville. As it turns out, the body was a big one. Some guy who was swelling up from an entire week in the trunk. It took all three of us to drag him out."

"Where?" Maya asked.

"You mean, where'd I bury him?"

Maya nodded.

"Right where Coty's been parking his truck. Fritz and that kid, Danny, moved three cord of wood and I dug a hole with the backhoe. We rolled the body bag into the hole, spread the dirt back over him and restacked the wood over the grave. Fritz told the kid he'd give him a ride into town and they left while I finished restacking the woodpile. By the time I got back to the house, Fritz had suffocated that boy with a plastic bag. The kid was on the landing upstairs. I guess he had tried running through the house to get away from Fritz, but Fritz caught him. Take the kid with you, I said. But Fritz said, I *make* deliveries here. I don't *take* deliveries here."

"So *you* buried Danny?"

Elly nodded. "I tried to revive him first because I've always felt bad about that woman in the basement. Didn't want another one like her. And I thought the boy was breathing at first, but then I realized he wasn't. I waited until I knew for sure he was dead."

"Where is he? Where is Danny?"

"He's in–"

Sheriff Wimple's car rolled to a stop outside the kitchen. His engine was already off.

"Well . . ." Elly said. "He sort of snuck up on us, didn't he?"

Sheriff Wimple stood in the open door. "Hello Sheriff," Elly said. "Come on in."

"Here's the warrant." The sheriff dropped an envelope on the kitchen counter.

"What is it you're searching for?" Maya asked.

"Ask your aunt," he said.

Coty appeared behind the sheriff. "My nephew, that's what," he said. "He's here somewhere, isn't he, Elly?"

Elly stared at Coty for a long minute and then turned her gaze out the window. "Search all you want, fellas."

"Dammit, Coty. She was just about to tell me."

"She's been 'about to tell you' for three months now. I'm done waiting."

"What can you tell me about that forty-two Ford in the pond?" Sheriff Wimple asked.

"Which pond?" Maya asked. "There are several."

"Ms. Pederson, we checked your record out previously and you were cleared of doing any wrongdoing, but don't try to protect your aunt by lying or playing dumb. Don't involve yourself with Elly's activities or you could find yourself in a real mess," the sheriff said.

Elly said, "Maya has done nothing wrong, sheriff. Nothing."

Coty held the bottle of Luminol in one hand and the black light in the other. He and the sheriff crossed into the dining room.

"Distract them, Maya," Elly whispered.

"How?"

"Follow them. Pester them with questions. I just need a few minutes."

Maya leaned against the entrance to the dining room. The top surface of the dining table glowed blue. "This house is over a hundred years old. How can you tell if blood is old or new?" she asked.

"Forensics will know," Sheriff Wimple said.

"Well then, let's check that spot in the skylight room again, Coty," Maya said. "The one right up against the wood paneling. Remember?" Maya hurried through the living room and around into the skylight room. As she had hoped, they followed. She pointed to the spot on the hardwood floor. "Right there."

Coty nodded. "Yeah, but that wasn't much blood."

"No, but this room is relatively new. So the blood has to be new too. Samples from here can be compared to samples from other places in the house, right Sheriff?" Maya said.

"She's right," Sheriff Wimple said.

Coty sprayed the spot and under the black light, a spatter glowed blue.

"Where's your aunt?" Sheriff Wimple asked. He hurried back into the living room and around through the pantry. "She's not in the kitchen. Where did she go?"

Maya shrugged. "I don't know. I was in the skylight room with you guys."

Coty unlocked the basement door and shouted down the stairs. "Elly? Elly!"

Sheriff Wimple headed upstairs. His footsteps on the wood floors revealed his hurried travels through the second floor, room after room. His footsteps returned to the top of the stairs. "How do we get into the attic?" he shouted.

"Through a ceiling trap door in Elly's closet," Maya shouted back. "I can show you." When she reached the top of the stairs she found the sheriff already inside Elly's closet. "I doubt she's up there, Sheriff. I don't think she can handle the folding stairs by herself anymore," Maya said. "She's got a bad back, you know. She hasn't been out of the hospital that long." Maya was surprised at how easy it was to lie.

"I've spoken with Dr. Framish. He seems convinced she's capable of many things." Sheriff Wimple strode to the window and shoved the lace curtain aside. "Your aunt is up there on the hill! Hell! She's setting fire to the barn!"

Maya peered over the sheriff's shoulder. Flames were already thirty feet high and black smoke mushroomed into the sky. "Is she destroying evidence up there?" the sheriff asked.

"You keep asking questions, Sheriff. Again, how would I know? I've been cleaning and scrubbing and painting for three months now, not searching for evidence."

"I just phoned the fire department." Coty stood in Elly's open bedroom door. "That's where the old Cadillac is, in that barn, Sheriff!"

"How long have you known about the car?" Sheriff Wimple asked.

"Who, me?" Maya asked. "Coty showed me the car a few days ago. Why don't you ask Coty?"

"Actually, I *was* asking Mr. Matheson," Sheriff Wimple said. Coty stepped into the room.

"Maya, you said you knew it was old blood. Fifty years, you said."

"You took me to the barn, Coty, because you said you had seen a ghost there, back in February. The car was secondary. That's all I know, sheriff."

"A ghost?" Sheriff Wimple fixed critical eyes on Coty. "You didn't say anything about seeing ghosts, Mr. Matheson."

"Ghost. Singular," Coty said. "Doesn't matter, does it? I discovered the Caddy, recognized the bloodstains, and *then* saw something unexplainable. It doesn't change the fact that there's a bloodstained car up there and it's likely a crime scene."

"Ghosts. Plural," Maya said. "You also saw your nephew's ghost in the upstairs hall."

"Aw hell," Sheriff Wimple said. "Your testimony won't hold water in court if the defense attorney gets hold of that."

A sound like coyotes became sirens as they got closer. Maya headed downstairs to the kitchen, followed by Coty and Sheriff Wimple. Elly strode in through the back door at the same time.

"Who left the basement door open?" Elly said.

Maya's mouth went dry at the sight of the yellow door. It stood wide open and the black air of the basement yawned wide within the frame. Had Angel escaped this time?

Elly closed the basement door and turned the little t-shaped lock.

The sirens grew louder as two fire engines crossed the stream and the bridge and started up the driveway toward the house.

"Well," Elly muttered. "Look at that. The old bridge held more than I thought it could."

"What's in the basement?" Sheriff Wimple asked.

"Nothing, as far as I know," Coty said. "I've been down there many times and never saw anything out of the ordinary."

"We'll check it out later." Sheriff Wimple said as the two fire engines rolled by and up the grassy track to the barn.

The barn was aglow by then, a raging framework of ancient beams and timbers engulfed in flames. The roof collapsed and sparks and glowing ash exploded into the air. A boiling column of gray smoke rolled upward, higher that the tops of the tallest trees.

"She used an accelerant," Sheriff Wimple said. "That's a damn hot fire. Won't be any bloodstains left to test. But you said it's in the house that we'd likely find your nephew's remains, right?"

Coty nodded. "Upstairs in the hallway. At the far end."

"Don't leave this house again, Ms. Pederson," Sheriff Wimple said. He pointed directly at Elly.

Elly's smile was as sweet as a child's. "I don't plan to, Sheriff. Did I ever mention, I voted for you?"

A county car appeared outside the door. It halted beside the sheriff's vehicle. Two officers climbed out.

"Elly Pederson is under arrest for obstruction of justice. One of you men stay here and keep an eye on her. The other, come with me." Sheriff Wimple headed back through the dining room toward the stairs. Coty hurried with them.

"Destruction of what evidence, Sheriff?" Maya asked.

"The barn. The old Cadillac. The blood."

"All you have is Coty's story. There's no proof there was blood, and there's no crime in storing an old friend's Cadillac in your barn, is there? Elly told me an old friend stored it there, years ago."

"You wait here with your aunt, Ms. Pederson." Sheriff Wimple nodded at the young

officer. "Make certain the younger Pederson remains in the kitchen with the older Pederson."

"Yes sir."

Sheriff Wimple, Coty, and one young officer, climbed the stairs, rounded the first landing and headed toward the second floor.

Chapter Forty-Nine

"I CAN'T BELIEVE I KISSED Coty," Maya said. "He lied to me."

"Ahh, don't be angry with Coty, Maya," Elly said. "He's searching for his nephew. Can we blame him for wanting to find out everything he can?"

Maya stared at Elly. "That's very open minded of you, since you're the only one who knows anything about Danny."

"But I understand how Coty feels," Elly said. "That's his blood kin who's missing."

"It's noon. That's when Danny is usually in the hallway. There is a chance they'll find what they're looking for upstairs."

"They won't find anything upstairs." Elly lifted the teakettle and turned on the faucet. She smiled at the police officer. "Young man, would you care for some herbal tea? My niece and I always have some around noon."

"No thank you."

Elly set the kettle on a burner and then paused in front of the yellow door, stroking its cracked and peeling paint with her fingertips.

"Ms. Pederson, please come and sit down," the young officer said.

"I'll make the tea, Aunt Elly." Maya prepared two mugs with tea bags and set napkins on the table. "Cookies?"

"Oatmeal raisin, please." Elly's eyes were fixed on the yellow door. "I've lived here for almost fifty-six years now. It's been a good fifty-six years, especially when Harlan was alive. We were happy here, for the most part. Right up until Angel showed up, of course."

"This might not be the best time for an old story, Elly," Maya said.

"It's as good a time as any. This old farm is going to keep the police busy for some time to come."

"Why is that?" the young officer asked.

Elly chuckled and crossed her arms. He stepped back, his hand on his weapon. "Oh relax," Elly said. "I'm not going to do anything you need to worry about."

Overhead, the sound of footsteps in the hallway traveled back and forth several times.

"They won't find anything up there," Elly repeated. "No blood, anyway. Unless it's a bit of ancient menstrual blood in that old bathroom."

The young officer's cheeks turned red.

"You asked me something recently, Maya, about what your father did here. Remember? I was either interrupted or lost track of the subject, and never told you about Stephen's visit."

Maya set two steaming mugs on the table along with a plate of cookies. She sat down at the table across from Elly.

"That's right. You never told me anything about Dad's visit."

"The cookies aren't poisoned, young man, if that's what you're thinking," Elly said. "Maya and I eat them all the time. We get them at the Red Apple in Graceville for two dollars and ninety-nine cents. They're just the store brand, but I like them as much as those fancy cookies that come eight to a little sack and cost over four dollars."

"Thank you. No," he said.

"Suit yourself." Elly bit into a cookie, chewed a long time and finally swallowed. "I phoned Stephen and asked for his help because Harlan was gone on that delivery. To Boise and back. Gone four days."

Elly took another bite of cookie and chewed again. She swallowed and took several sips of tea before continuing. "It all started with my uncle Felix. That was the only time Felix came to the farm. He didn't even tell me he was in Washington State. I thought he was back in Chicago, like always, but there he stood, right in the driveway. He had some . . . guests . . . for me in the back of his delivery truck. They were healthy enough, but the truck hadn't been cleaned up since the previous delivery. You understand, Maya?"

"Yes."

"There were three men with Felix, and they were sick as dogs, covered in . . . pork trimmings from that previous delivery. They scrambled out of that truck and I hosed them off and led them around to the basement door. They had one suitcase between them. I told them to strip down, put on clean clothes and to drop the soiled ones by the washing machine. Then I went back out to talk to Felix. Felix said he'd be back for them in three days and he handed me five hundred dollars cash for food and expenses.

"Those three guests had changed into clean duds when I returned to the basement. I led them to the guest suite." Elly caught Maya's eyes, nodded, and then continued. "By the shortest route."

Maya nodded.

"Within an hour I had a tray of hot food on its way up to them, you know?"

Maya nodded again.

"When the dishes returned, they were licked clean, but had not been washed. I sent a note back, saying to wash them next time or there would be no more meals. Little did I know. there would be no more meals anyway. Felix returned the very next day and said he wanted to see them. So, I brought them back outside and Felix shot them dead in the driveway."

The young officer pushed away from the wall. "Ms. Pederson," he said. "I'm a witness here. I can quote you in a court of law, word for word, what you just said. A judge and jury will most likely believe my testimony over yours. You might want to talk to a lawyer before you admit to involvement in a murder."

"It was forty years ago, young man," Elly said.

"It doesn't matter if it was yesterday or a hundred years ago. A confession is a confession."

"Well forty years matters to me. I need to tell my niece what happened while there's time, so you just go ahead and listen and see if you can memorize all the details. It's a long story and you don't know any of the people involved."

The young officer leaned back against the wall, his gaze fixed on Elly as she continued.

"Felix shoved a thousand dollars into my hands, climbed into the truck along with his driver, and they were gone. That was the last time I ever saw Felix. Our only communication afterward was by phone. Those three bodies were there in the driveway, just about exactly where Sheriff Wimple's vehicle is parked right now—maybe a bit closer to the bunkhouse, not sure. Anyway, that was another cold winter's day. The ground was frozen. You follow, Maya?"

Maya nodded.

"I ran into the house and phoned Stephen. He wanted to know why he should drop everything and drive all the way over here, because back then there was no freeway, ya see. The highway stopped in Tacoma. From there on it was a two-lane country road, and, it was the middle of the week with commuters and all. Stephen had a job. He'd have to call in sick, he said. I told him it was terribly important. I told him I needed his help. He wanted to know where Harlan was. I told him Harlan was gone to Boise and wouldn't be back for three days. I could hear your mother in the background. 'Just hang up, Stephen. What does she want, Stephen? Tell her to leave us alone, Stephen.' You know how your mother can be, Maya.

"But finally, Stephen said he'd be over, and sure enough, he showed up just after dark. He asked a lot of questions, and I felt he deserved to know the truth, so I told him everything. Well, not everything, but enough, you know? He must have started thinking back to that Grady episode, from years and years ago when I first knew Harlan. Stephen probably put two and two together and drew his own conclusions. Bless him—even knowing what he knew, Stephen helped me. Together, we made several trips from the driveway to the barn, and then Stephen left. It was midnight as he crossed the bridge. I never saw Stephen again until he was hospitalized and visited him there."

"And you believe, it was because he helped you that Dad was hospitalized?" Maya asked.

"Yes. I don't think he was strong enough emotionally to deal with it. He was more fragile than me. And it was a particularly unpleasant job, that one. Felix must have been angry with those three men to do what he did to them. Numerous shots to the head and chest. Emptied both guns."

"Who is Felix?" The young officer asked.

"Felix is my uncle," Elly said.

"Where can we find your uncle?"

"In a hospital in Chicago."

"What hospital?"

Elly shrugged. "I didn't ask, but I strongly suspect Uncle Felix is beyond answering any questions. He's apparently hooked up to life-support, if he's alive at all."

"What about Danny?" Maya asked.

Footsteps sounded on the stairs. Coty, Sheriff Wimple and the other officer were returning.

"When it's noon and the sky is light," Elly whispered, and winked at Maya.

Sheriff Wimple rounded the newel post on the landing. Coty and the other officer followed him down the last eight steps.

"Find anything interesting?" Elly asked.

"There's a long flight of stairs leading from your attic to a tunnel under the hill," Sheriff Wimple said. "How long has that been there?"

"Since 1957. Uncle Felix had that built. He never said what it was for."

"You just let your uncle come here and dig a tunnel without questioning his reasons?"

"First of all, Uncle Felix didn't do any of the digging himself. He sent three Mexican men here to dig. The day after they finished the tunnel, those three guys took off for parts unknown. I never saw them again. Additionally, Uncle Felix wasn't the kind of person I'd have *ever* considered interrogating myself."

"The remains of two Mexican men were discovered at the bottom of the well by your niece, and a third in one of the old tunnels. Any connection?"

"I suspect there was. None of them spoke English. None of them ever spoke to me."

"Coty, did you see Danny upstairs just now?" Maya asked.

"No." Coty glanced twice at the yellow basement door. "We should check the basement, Sheriff."

"There's a specialized group on their way from Seattle forensics. They'll take a more detailed approach to the upstairs and the basement."

"Am I still under arrest, Sheriff Wimple?" Elly asked.

"Yes, and I'm having someone spend the night here to ensure you don't leave the house."

"That's fine. I don't sleep well except in my own bed anyway," Elly said.

"Whether you sleep or not, doesn't concern me," the sheriff said. "I want you where I can find you."

"I'll be right here, Sheriff. I'm not leaving."

"Jackson, phone Withers." Sheriff Wimple's gaze was aimed at the young officer who leaned

against the wall near the back door.

"Yes, sir." The officer slipped his cell phone from his pocket and stepped outside.

"Who is Withers?" Maya asked.

"Withers will be staying here tonight, to make sure you and your aunt remain on the premises."

Elly snickered. "Night crew, huh? I used to work for a trucking company in Chicago. We had a late-hours man, too. His last name was Friendless. Funny, huh? Everyone referred to him as the night crew."

Sheriff Wimple, Coty, and the two young officers stared at Elly like she had two heads.

"I overheard an incriminating story, Sheriff Wimple," the young officer said. "While you were upstairs."

"I'll ask you to write down everything you can remember, Jackson."

"Yes, sir. Won't be a problem. I recorded it all on my cell phone."

Elly smiled at Sheriff Wimple. "Got yourself a good officer there, Sheriff. He's smart."

"Aren't we going to check out the basement?" Coty asked.

"We'll be back in the morning." Sheriff Wimple picked up his hat from the counter, jammed it on his head, and exited. Officer Jackson remained while the other officer followed the sheriff out to the driveway.

"Maya, may I speak to you in private," Coty asked.

"No," she said.

"Now, Maya. Let Coty speak his peace. I'm going upstairs to lie down anyway. This is becoming a tiring afternoon." Elly stood, passed through the dining room and climbed the stairs.

Coty said nothing until Elly's door closed upstairs.

"I'm sorry, Maya. I've been searching for Danny for seven months! He was a good kid.

Don't you understand? I used to baby sit Danny. I changed that kid's diapers. I fed him strained carrots and broccoli and apple juice. I rocked him to sleep. I still remember how he smelled.

I remember how the fine hair around his ears curled. Maya . . . I loved that kid." Coty's voice broke. Tears filled the corners of his eyes.

Maya's voice was barely a whisper. "Elly told me what happened, but I don't want to tell you about it. It's too awful."

"I have to know," Coty said. "I have to."

"At least it wasn't Elly's doing. It was Fritz, a guy who used to make deliveries here. Deliveries, meaning bodies.

"For the cemetery?"

"No. Just bodies."

"I don't understand."

"Uncle Felix sent delivery trucks here once or twice a year, with bodies to be buried. Felix didn't care where they were buried or how, or even *if* they were buried, as long as they were never found. And Harlan never asked who the people were or where they came from. It's what Harlan did back in Chicago. The job followed them here, even though Elly tried to leave all that behind. Do you understand now? Elly found herself in the midst of a very dirty business, with no way out. Even after Harlan died, they wouldn't let her go. She said, 'once you're in the business, you're always in the business.'"

"Okay, but how did my nephew get involved?"

"Wrong place at the wrong time. Danny was hitchhiking on his way into Graceville and Fritz picked him up and offered him money to help make a heavy delivery. Fritz killed him afterward."

Coty said nothing for a full minute. "So where is Danny's body?"

"You guys came back downstairs a few seconds too soon. All Elly had time to say was, *when it's noon and the sky is light.*"

"What in the hell is that supposed to mean?"

"I don't know."

"It was always noon whenever you saw Danny upstairs, right? It was around noon when I saw him."

The kitchen door opened and officer Jackson stepped aside. "This is Mr. Withers. He'll be staying here with you tonight."

On the threshold stood a man wearing a brown denim jacket with frayed cuffs and gray jeans. His brown loafers were scuffed, the heels worn down in back and the threads broken at the toes. He stepped inside. Mr. Withers was thin, with a pale complexion and a nose like a parrot's beak. His straight hair was sparse, like strands of brown yarn glued across his scalp. His deep-set eyes were the palest, coldest blue Maya had ever seen. The fingers on his left hand were stained yellow-brown, as if from the constant grip of cigarettes, and the smell of an ashtray arrived with him.

"There is no smoking allowed in this house, Mr. Withers," Maya said.

Mr. Withers fixed his icy gaze on Maya and after a few second, he nodded. "I'll be stepping outside the kitchen door on occasion, then," he said.

"Take an ashtray with you. There will be no butts flicked into the driveway or into the shrubbery either."

He nodded.

Officer Jackson climbed into his squad car and drove away.

"Who are you?" Mr. Withers eyed Coty.

"I'm the handyman. I've been here for the past six months, making repairs and such. I'll be staying the night too."

Mr. Withers glanced around the kitchen. "I need to familiarize myself with the place," he said.

"Fine," Maya said. "Just don't open Elly's bedroom door at the top of the stairs. She's sleeping. You can meet her later. Stay out of my room too, at the opposite end of the hallway. Coty will accompany you on your sightseeing tour through the house."

"That's okay with me," Mr. Withers said.

"Meet you back here in ten minutes, Maya," Coty said. "Think about what Elly said."

"I'm going to heat up the leftover chicken, biscuits and green beans," Maya said. "Have you eaten, Mr. Withers?"

"I don't eat dinner. It makes me sleepy." Mr. Withers strolled away, down the pantry hall, passing by the big cupboards and pausing to open them one by one, and the utility closet door. Maya smiled when he missed spotting the dumbwaiter. He continued around the corner into the skylight room.

Noon, when the sky is light.

Skylight room, Maya thought. Noon.

Chapter Fifty

After his tour, Mr. Withers lifted a straight-backed chair from the kitchen, carried it into the living room and placed it beside the picture window. He sat down with the window to his right. From there he had a view of the driveway, most of the skylight room, the lower stairs, and all the way through the dining room and into the kitchen. Every thirty minutes, he rose, crossed through the dining room, opened the kitchen door and stepped outside. He took deep drags from a cigarette and a few minutes later, returned to his chair in the living room. It had grown dark outside with no change in his routine except for two bathroom visits.

"That guy's a box of broken crackers," Coty said. "Weird."

It was almost 10:00 PM when another car pulled up and parked near the kitchen door. Maya heard the familiar squeak of a car door. She hurried across the kitchen and parted the door curtains and discovered her mother, one hand was raised as if prepared to knock. She and Maya made eye contact through the glass, and Maya's mother slumped as if intolerable stress had been relieved. Maya opened the door.

"Maya, you promised to phone me. You haven't answered your cell phone in days. You said I'd be able to reach you on it. I've been calling you every few hours with no answer."

"I guess I forgot to recharge it. Sorry, Mama. It's been kind of crazy around here lately."

Her mother looked distraught, as if fighting the urge to cry.

"Mama, come inside. I'll make you some cocoa."

Her mother entered and paused in the center of the kitchen. She turned all the way around. "This place isn't at all what I thought it would be. It's so much bigger and . . . older."

"Yes, it's over a hundred years old," Maya said.

Coty entered from the pantry. "Hello. I'm Wayne Matheson."

"I'm Maya's mother, Jennifer. Most people call me Jen."

Jen? Really? Since when? Even Dad called you, Jennifer.

Elly arrived through the dining room, having wakened from a three-hour nap. "Well, Jennifer, I am surprised to see you here."

"Hello, Elly," Jennifer said. "Long time no see."

"Have you eaten?" Elly asked.

"I'm too upset to eat, but thank you for asking."

"I have something we can all use, out in the bunkhouse." Coty exited the backdoor and a moment later returned with a fifth of Black Velvet. He cracked the seal.

"Oh my," Jennifer said. "I never–"

"First time for everything, Jen." Elly collected four glasses from the cupboard and placed them on the table. Coty poured each glass half full.

"Apparently, you've met Coty already," Elly said.

"Who?"

"I introduced myself as Wayne," Coty said.

"Yes, I met Mr. Matheson," Jennifer said, "but who is that other man in the living room? The man sitting in front of the window."

"He's only here to keep everyone safe tonight," Elly said.

"Like a security guard? So, I guess he won't drink while on duty?" Jennifer asked.

"Yes," Coty said. "But mainly it's because this is my party and he's not invited."

"Where's your luggage, Mama?" Maya asked.

"I just brought my overnight case, Maya. It's on the front seat of my car. I'll be gone first thing in the morning. Now that I know you're okay, I'm okay."

"You'll have to sleep with me, Mama, because the guest rooms are empty. Elly sold almost all of the furniture."

Jennifer Pederson nodded. "I'm feeling pretty drowsy already. This Black Velvet stuff is relaxing, isn't it?"

"Nothing like it, especially on an empty stomach." Elly chugged the last of her drink.

"Mama, I'll take you upstairs now and show you where my room is, and the bathroom. Let me get your overnight case from the car."

Coty jumped up. "Allow me." He returned with the case a moment later.

Within twenty minutes, Jennifer Pederson was sound asleep in Maya's bed. Maya plugged her cell phone in to recharge it, closed the bedroom door and hurried downstairs.

"That was a surprise," she said. "Mama showing up here."

"No kidding," Elly said. "Jennifer swore she'd never set foot in this house."

"We all say things we're sorry for later." Coty made eye contact with Maya.

Maya no longer felt angry with Coty, the way she had earlier. Even now, he smelled like cedar and fresh coffee, and she remembered how his lips tasted like apples. She smiled at him.

Forgiveness is a good thing.

• • • *

It was almost 1:00 AM when Maya checked the lock on the basement door and followed Elly upstairs.

"I'll be here at the kitchen table," Coty said. "Got my laptop and plan to be here all night if you need me."

Mr. Withers kept his face turned toward the picture window as they passed by.

"Goodnight, Mr. Withers," Elly said. "Please, whatever you do, don't open the basement door. The basement door is the yellow one in the kitchen. It must remain locked."

Mr. Withers made no reply. He inhaled, exhaled with an impatient sound, leaned back in the straight-back chair and crossed his arms. Twenty-five minutes had passed since his last cigarette. His nicotine addiction was probably gnawing at him, Maya thought.

Maya changed into her nightgown in the bathroom before crossing the hall. She hesitated outside her bedroom door. What would she find on the other side of that door? Would it be Mama in the bed, or that moldy, skeletal creature she had seen on the front porch three months ago?

She braced herself and eased the door open. Jennifer was a small lump in the bed, taking up very little room. Her mother faced the open window. The curtains waved in and out on the breeze. The closet door was ajar and a slice of pale light angled across the floor. Moonlight turned the white lace curtains platinum.

Maya locked the door behind her and slipped into bed beside her mother.

Jennifer rolled over and pulled the blankets up snug to her neck, took a breath and said, "Maya, I must tell you something. I'm homeless."

"Homeless?"

"The house sold and the buyers wanted me out right away. I got a motel room, but felt . . . just awful there by myself. I tried calling you but . . ."

"But I didn't answer."

"And I started imagining all kinds of things."

"It's okay, Mama. We'll work things out."

"I can't believe I'm a homeless person. I feel ashamed."

"We'll be okay. We'll both be okay," Maya said.

• • •

"Maya! Maya! Wake up!"

Maya struggled to open her eyes. She found her mother sitting at the foot of the bed, staring at the door.

"What's wrong?" Maya asked.

"I heard a man yell, and then it sounded like a scuffle downstairs."

Maya grabbed her robe and shoved her feet into her slippers. "Wait here,

Mama. Lock the door behind me."

"No, I'm coming with you."

"There's one of Elly's old robes in my closet, but there are no slippers."

Moonlight had turned the hallway's pale walls a stainless steel blue. Maya and her mother ran past the bathroom and empty guest rooms. Elly's door stood open. Her bed was empty. Maya and Jennifer tiptoed down the stairs. Mr. Withers was not in his straight-backed chair beside the living room window. In the kitchen, Coty's laptop glowed on the table. His chair was upturned.

"That yellow door is open," Jennifer said. "Is that the basement?"

The basement door stood wide open and a man's voice rose from below.

"Help!" His voice sounded muffled. "Help!"

Maya ran to the door. The feeble light above the washer and dryer emitted a sickly yellow glow in the black basement air. At the foot of the stairs Mr. Withers struggled with mismatched, chalky-white arms and legs, a foot attached to a wrist. A lump of thigh wriggled and flexed by itself in the dirt while a pale hand protruded from a collarbone. The white hand squeezed Mr. Wither's face. His eyes bulged. "Help!" he screamed again.

"What is that . . . thing, fighting with him?" Jennifer Pederson asked.

Maya closed the yellow door and locked it.

"Maya?"

"What did it look like, Mama?"

"Mr. Withers was being attacked."

"By?"

"It was a . . . thing. I don't know what it was."

"Something *impossible*, Mama?"

"Yes. Something impossible."

"A thing that can't exist? It's just your imagination, Mama? Because, what else could it be? That kind of impossible thing?"

"You never told me you saw such things, Maya."

"Yes I did. That's when you dragged me to see Dr. Conover."

"But what should we do now? What about Mr. Withers?"

"We do nothing. It's too late to help him. I told him not to go down there." Maya stepped toward the pantry. "Coty! Coty, where are you?"

"Here." Coty appeared in the entrance to the skylight room. He leaned against the wall with a frown.

"Mr. Withers went into the basement," Maya said.

"To do what?" Coty asked.

"He's wrestling with something that defies description," Jennifer said.

"Like the something you saw in the barn," Maya said.

Jennifer nodded, "I saw it too."

Coty staggered across the kitchen. "Someone clobbered me from behind." He turned on the kitchen faucet and held his head under cold water. Red water swirled in the bottom of the sink.

"The back of your scalp is split," Maya said.

Footsteps ran up from the basement. Something crashed against the yellow door and Coty reached toward the t-shaped lock.

"No! Coty! Don't open it!"

The sound of another pair of feet plodded up the basement stairs, the old wood steps groaning under the weight. The black enamel doorknob frosted over and long, sharp islands of ice formed on the yellow paint.

"Wait," Maya whispered. "Don't touch the door."

Coty stepped away from the door without a word. From the basement side of the door came the sounds of bones snapping and a man's single, painful scream.

Chapter Fifty-One

MORNING. THROUGH THE BAY window beyond the fields, a pink cloud appeared trapped in the highest branches of the trees. The sky around the cloud was the palest blue.

Coty turned his kitchen chair upright and sat down. "I heard Withers talking to someone before I was hit. I think he was on his cell phone. I can't believe I was stupid enough to turn my back to him. Stupid!"

"Did you hear what he said on the phone?" Maya asked.

"I heard him say 'sheriff' and the word, 'basement.' At the time I didn't think it was important but apparently it was."

"Elly and I both told Mr. Withers to not open the basement door. He must have thought we were hiding something down there."

"*Is* Elly hiding something down there?" Coty asked.

"Not Danny," Maya said. "If that's what you mean."

"What in the world are you talking about?" Jennifer Pederson asked. "It's like you're speaking in code."

"It's a long story, Mama. A story you don't want to hear."

"Who is Danny?"

"My nephew. He's been missing for six months and I've been searching for him," Coty said.

"Maya, when this is all over and you're back home safe, I want you to tell me everything," Jennifer said. "Everything."

"You won't believe some of it, Mama."

"I believe there is a creature in the basement of this house, made up of severed, detached body parts, a creature that travels . . . somehow. I cannot have seen that, but I did, so I guess I can believe anything," Jennifer said.

"Detached body parts?" Coty repeated.

"I'll tell you about that, Coty. Later though. Right now we need to make plans for noon."

Elly told me we'll find Danny at noon, 'when the sky is light'. I think that means we need to be in the skylight room, at noon."

"Let's check out the skylight room right now." Coty shoved his kitchen chair back.

"We won't find anything," Maya said. "It's always noon when Danny appears."

"Appears?" Jennifer said.

"I wonder where Elly is," Maya said. "She's not upstairs."

"I think it might have been Elly who hit me," Coty said.

"Why would Elly hit you?" Maya asked.

"To get past me, and to make sure I didn't see where she went."

"Why did the basement door freeze over?" Jennifer asked.

"Because that thing you saw down there is pure evil," Maya said.

"But, I've been in the basement," Coty said. "Several times, and I've never seen anything like what you just described."

Maya said. "Were you ever there late at night, or before dawn?"

"No, only in the middle of the day."

"I think I hear a car outside." Jennifer crossed to the kitchen window and parted the curtains. "It's the sheriff's car."

Maya checked the time. 7:40 AM.

Coty opened the back door and Sheriff Wimple stepped through. "I got a call about an hour ago, from Withers. I need to talk to him."

"He's in the basement," Jennifer said.

"Who are you?" the sheriff asked.

"I'm Jennifer Pederson, Maya's mother. I arrived last night."

Sheriff Wimple opened the yellow door and aimed his flashlight down the stairs, cutting a wedge of white through the black air.

"Withers! You down there?"

"I saw him at the foot of the stairs," Jennifer said. "Just a few moments ago."

Maya nodded. "Mother woke me after she heard someone shouting and the sound of a scuffle. We came downstairs and heard Mr. Withers in the basement, but we're uncomfortable going down there."

Sheriff Wimple said, "Withers said he found something in the basement and for me to get over here, pronto. Any idea what he found?"

"He didn't say anything about that to us," Maya said. "All we know is someone hit Coty on the head."

Sheriff Wimple glanced at them one by one, with suspicious, narrowed eyes. He turned and entered the basement. He strode along the concrete path into the shadows. Maya closed and locked the door behind him.

"What's he going to find down there?" Coty asked.

"Old graves," Maya said. *Maybe Benson. Maybe Angel. Maybe the woman or the two men in the grave with her.*

"How many graves?"

"Not sure. Elly said four people. She didn't say how many graves exactly."

And the numbers have grown since then.

"Not Danny's?"

"Elly said Danny isn't down there," Maya said. "Wayne is a private investigator, Mama. Wayne C. Matheson."

"Oh, like Rockford?"

"No." Coty said. "Nothing like Rockford."

Something sounded like an explosion in the basement, followed by a second explosion a few seconds later.

"That's a shotgun blast," Coty said.

Maya yanked open the basement door. "Elly?" Maya called.

"Don't come down here, baby girl. Do you understand?"

Maya heard the sound of shoveling. She closed and locked the door again.

"Let's get out of here," Coty said. "Sounds like Elly shot Sheriff Wimple. I don't want to even think about who she'll shoot next."

Jennifer headed for the stairs. "Come on, Maya."

"I'll grab some things and be back to get you. We've got to get the hell out of this place," Coty said. "Hurry."

Upstairs, Maya dragged her trunk from the closet and tossed everything important inside, her medical journal on top. She grabbed her prescriptions from the bathroom medicine cabinet before she and Jennifer headed for the stairs lugging the trunk. Maya halted beside the morning glory window. Her watch glistened on the floor at her feet.

"That wasn't there before." Maya picked it up, looking left and right, hoping to see the transparent gray shadow of her father one last time. She didn't.

"Come on, Maya!" Jennifer looked up from the landing. "I hear Coty calling you."

They hurried down the stairs and through the dining room as Coty appeared in the kitchen doorway. He tossed Maya's trunk into the back of his truck.

From the basement came the sound of a third shotgun blast. The explosion rattled the kitchen window. Maya and her mother climbed into the truck and Coty dropped behind the wheel. He headed down the driveway and didn't slow down until they reached the parking lot of the River Lodge Café.

Inside, the place was empty of customers and the waitress told them to sit anywhere they wanted. Maya chose a booth near the window where the morning sun drew warm squares on the plank floor.

"Coffee," Coty said. The waitress nodded.

"What are we going to do?" Maya asked. "Should we phone someone?"

"I already did," Coty said, "When I woke up with a bloody scalp."

"Who?" Maya asked.

"A friend of mine at the F.B.I. He and his men will be here in an hour."

"It's almost ten o'clock." Maya said. "You should eat something, Mama. You didn't even have dinner last night."

Jennifer grimaced and shook her head as if the thought of food was revolting.

The waitress set four mugs and a full carafe on the table. Jennifer grabbed a mug and sipped, eyes closed. "I never imagined," she whispered.

"I've got to go back to the farm," Coty said. "This isn't over until I find Danny. I'll leave here at 11:30 and go straight to the skylight room. I've got to know."

"I'm going with you then," Maya said. "Elly won't hurt me."

"How do you know that?" Jennifer asked. "That woman is deranged. I've always said so."

"Elly told me I'm the only person she cares about, Mama. I'm her only blood kin."

"That doesn't mean she won't try to take you with her, wherever it is she thinks she's going."

"She won't hurt me. I know it. Mama, I want you stay here and wait for us."

"Oh, Maya. I'm so scared for you."

"We know our way around that farm," Coty said. "We know what to expect."

Maya felt a flutter in her stomach and tasted something sour on the back of her throat. She wished she hadn't told Elly about Wayne being a private investigator searching for his nephew. If anything happened to him it would be her fault.

"All right, I'll wait here," Jennifer said. "But I'm going to be a mess until I know you're safe, Maya. You'll have your phone with you this time, right?"

"Yes, but don't phone me, Mama. My phone might ring when I don't want Elly to know where I am. Understand?"

Jennifer nodded. "But you'll phone me as soon as you're safe. Right?"

"Yes."

They drank the entire carafe of coffee and a second carafe in the next hour. The waitress brought them three cheese Danish. "On the house," she said. "I warmed them up for you too."

"I didn't realize how hungry I was," Jennifer said after she finished eating.

"It's time, Coty." Maya slid from the booth and she and Coty exited.

"I'm going to park at the new cemetery," Coty said. "There's a trail that leads straight through the woods to the back of the farm."

A wind had picked up and overhead the giant maples rustled their leaves. The rows of granite headstones appeared first silver and then black as dense clouds dragged shadows across the lawns. Coty headed for a gap in the trees on the far side of the graveyard and Maya entered the woods on his heels as a light rain began to fall. Under the canopy of trees the rain never reached the ground. Fifteen minutes later they came out of the trees behind the shed. They stood under the overhang, catching their breath and eyeing the house. The kitchen door stood wide open. Everything appeared calm. It was silent.

Coty checked his watch. "It's eleven-fifty. Let's go."

They entered the kitchen. The yellow door was closed.

"But . . . it isn't locked," Maya whispered.

"Leave it. If Elly's down there she'll hear you turning the lock. And let's avoid the pantry too. It's too close to the basement stairs. She'll hear us."

They tiptoed through the dining room, through the living room, and into the skylight room. Sunlight blinked through the skylight as clouds raced overhead. A sunny square appeared on the carpet in the center of the room. Seconds later the room turned dark, the sunny square gone.

"The sky doesn't look very light," Maya said. "And we don't know what we're looking for."

They pressed their backs against the bookcase wall. From there they had a clear view into the living room to their left, and the entrance to the pantry to their right. A few silent minutes passed. Coty checked his watch again. "Eleven-fifty-eight," he whispered.

Maya stepped away from the wall and stood below the skylight. She looked up and saw fir needles scuttling around on the glass. A maple leaf landed in one corner and blew away again. She noticed a design in the glass she had never noticed before.

"The glass has a line in it," she said. There's a beveled line all the way around the glass."

Coty glanced up. "Yeah, I know." He checked his watch. "It's noon. Right now. It's noon."

They glanced around, eyeing every corner and listening for the slightest sound.

"What the hell," Coty whispered. "I don't see anything."

"I don't either. I can't figure out what Elly meant . . . wait. Look there." Maya pointed to a prism of light on the wood paneled wall. Sunlight hit the skylight window again and shot a colorful beam against the wood. It grew sharper and became a circle of orange, yellow and blue.

Coty touched the spot on the wall. He slid his finger back and forth. "Nothing there."

"Push it," Maya said.

Coty pressed the spot and Maya heard a click. Four wide panels slid to one side, revealing a narrow, upward-curving staircase, thick with dust. Coty climbed four steps up and halted. "Drawers," he said. "Built into the walls."

Maya leaned inside. "Where does this stairwell go? It must come out in one of the guest rooms? Or behind them, or, between them?"

They climbed to the end. Maya pulled open several drawers built into the back wall. "They're all empty. The stairwell stops here. It goes nowhere."

"this drawer wasn't empty," Coty said. "This drawer had this inside." He held up a one hundred dollar bill. "These drawers must have been packed with money. Where do you suppose it all went? "

"Over a million dollars," Maya said. "That's what Fritz was looking for."

"Did Elly shoot him too?"

"No. It was that thing in the basement my mother described."

"You saw it too? I thought your mother was just craz . . . imagining things."

"It's real. It's a thing made of body parts, all writing and twisting. Somehow it manages to travel."

They found and opened twenty-four drawers and carried them down into the skylight room. They stacked the empty drawers in the middle of the room beneath the skylight.

"Still no Danny," Coty said.

"Danny is somewhere in that stairwell," Maya said. "I just know it, because of Elly's clue."

Coty climbed the first four stairs again and halted. He felt along the curved back wall. "These boards are newer than the others. The nails are different, too. I don't think this stairwell always had a curved wall here. I suspect there is a corner behind it." He slid a knife from his pocket and pried at the crack between two boards. He inserted a finger and pulled. The board cracked and then broke loose with a loud ripping sound. Coty pulled a second board and then another.

"Aw, hell," he said. "There's a body bag in here." He grasped the uppermost edge of the bag and it toppled forward, along with dust and a flurry of hundred-dollar bills. The money was loose, as if it had been stuffed around the body bag like insulation. Coty caught the bag in his arms but it knocked him down. He went to his knees and the bag tumbled past him and into the skylight room. Coty followed and knelt by the bag. He unzipped one side.

Maya looked away, afraid to see inside the bag. "Is it Danny?" she asked.

"Yes."

"Take the boy and go." Elly stood in the pantry entrance.

Coty shouted. "He was only seventeen years old, Elly! Seventeen! And he was a good kid!"

"I didn't hurt him." Elly said. She looked ashamed and averted her eyes.

"But you let someone else hurt him."

A massive silhouette loomed behind Elly, growing larger as it grew closer.

"Elly!" Maya shouted. "Behind you! Angel!"

Somehow, Angel had reassembled in an almost-human form. His head sat at an angle on his jagged neck. His shoulders and arms were attached in correct order. His torso and abdomen faced backwards however, his thoracic and lumbar spine faced forward from his collarbone down. The three sections of leg—thighs, knees and calves were arranged in the natural pattern, but his ankles and feet pointed back, causing him to totter and wobble as he lurched forward, his bloodless, blue-white hands reaching for Elly.

"What the hell?" Coty growled. "Come on, Maya."

"Hurry. Go. No time left." Elly limped into the skylight room. She held the plastic ketchup bottle in one hand, the cap gone and the nozzle cut off short.

Coty dragged Danny in his body bag through the living room and out through the front door, down the steps into the overgrown garden. "Come on, Maya!" he shouted again.

"Elly. Come with us," Maya said. "Please, Elly?"

"It's too late." Elly stood in the square of sunlight beside the stack of empty drawers. A cloud darkened the room. The prism vanished. Elly's expression changed. Her brows drew together and the corners of her mouth curved down. Her shoulders bent forward, hunched and crooked. It was Mr. Elly who turned to face Angel.

Angel's tangled body lumbered to a clumsy halt. His pale, mismatched body parts squirmed, each part flexing on its own, his rotten hair, chalky, bloodless fingers and dry, milky eyes rotated this way and that. His mouth hung open and green spittle oozed from between his lips. "El…ly," he moaned.

Maya backed toward the open door.

"Elly says for you to leave now. She says you're to keep the money beca we worked hard for it, all those years." Mr. Elly's voice was the familiar gr "Go now, cuz I'm busy here." He aimed the ketchup bottle at Angle and do him with clear liquid. Angel lumbered forward, one hand reaching ou fingers clawing the dark, dead air of the skylight room. He knocked the k bottle from Mr. Elly's hands. Maya smelled gasoline.

Mr. Elly backed up. He pulled a lighter from his pocket, raked his t against the igniter and a small flame shot forward. He threw the lighter at but the flamed died and Angel batted the lighter away. It landed at May; He staggered, taking one awkward step and then another.

Mr. Elly yelled, "It's past time for you to burn in hell, Angel!" He do the monster's abdomen.

"No, Elly!" Maya wanted to save Elly from the monster. She so grabbed the lighter, flicked the switch and the flame shot forward. She it toward Angel, but he looked only at Elly. Angle wrapped his arms Elly. He took two off-balance steps, left and right. "El…ly."

Maya ran toward them, stumbled on the empty cash drawers, and landed hard, bit her tongue and tasted blood. She stretched out one l touched the flame to Angel's toes. The flame shot up his leg, up his b spine and to his hair in seconds.

Angel waved his arms, flinging fuel and flames against the walls Flames spread across the walls and roared across the ceiling. He stur then he toppled forward and landed on the floor with a thud, tra beneath him. He grabbed Elly's neck and then she was on fire too. engulfed them both.

Mr. Elly said nothing. His eyes were closed, as if he had gone aw where—and had taken Elly with him.

Angle's and Elly's nightmarish struggle was surrealistic and same time. Orange flames turned black and roared up the secret s' skylight room filled with thick, rolling smoke. The skylight shatte heat. Class particles rained down through the flames.

"Elly's gone!" Coty lifted Maya from where she had fallen, they ran out the front door.

Chapter Fifty-Two

WAYNE C. MATHESON FROWNED. "My mind can't seem to grasp it. One hundred-fifty-four graves in those fields! Four more in the basement! My mind froze up after they told me that."

Maya sat across from him in the restaurant atop the Space Needle on a sunny mid-October day. She had finally managed to think of him as Wayne instead of Coty. He nursed a near-beer and Maya traced lines in the condensation on her glass of lemonade. The color reminded her of the yellow door and how it froze over when Angel climbed the basement steps. She looked away, toward the star-faced mountain across the sound, not far from Elly's farm.

"So the lawyers decided the money is all yours," Wayne said. "That's a lot of money."

"Too much. Most of it's going to charity, with some going to your sister for Danny's burial expenses. "

"There's no proof the money came from criminal activity, Maya, if that's what bothers you."

"But it did come from criminal activity. The worst kind. I have no doubt about that."

"Remember me telling you about seeing a ghost, a gray man with a gentle face and deep, sad looking eyes?"

Maya nodded.

"I saw him again, as Elly's house burned down. You were in the grass crying your heart out, so I didn't say anything at the time, but he walked out of the flames and down toward the stream. It was like he was finally free."

"What was he wearing?" Maya asked.

"Odd. I think he was wearing striped pajamas."

Again, Maya studied the star-faced mountain. She swallowed and fought back tears.

Bye, Daddy.

"You've never told me about this guy, Angel," Wayne said.

"I can tell you everything now that Elly's gone," Maya said. "And more about Harlan too."

"What about Harlan?"

"Judith said Harlan was Elly's imaginary friend, clear back from early childhood."

"You mean, there never was a Harlan?"

Maya shook her head. "I watched Elly *become* Harlan . . . there in the skylight room, confronting that *thing* that came up behind her. There was no Harlan, but to Elly he was real. She couldn't accept being a killer . . . so she convinced herself that Harlan did it."

Wayne shook his head with a look of disbelief. "Little Elly killed Grady Goode when she was just sixteen years old, and she killed those two professionals, the guys she called the Franks . . . and then she killed Angel?"

"It was Elly."

"That's just plain crazy," Wayne said.

Maya nodded at the distant mountain across the bay. "I'm afraid I must agree."

ABOUT THE AUTHOR

SHERRY DECKER lives in Washington State and tries to write every day—but life gets in the way. Even so, she has written a collection of short fiction titled, *Hook House and Other Horrors* and a futuristic earth novel titled *Hypershot*. Her short fiction has appeared, or soon will, in publications such as *Cemetery Dance, Black Gate, Dark Wisdom, Best of Dark Wisdom,* and *Best of Cemetery Dance 2* to name a few.

One of Sherry's favorite stories, "Hicklebickle Rock" simultaneously won First Place in the North Texas Professional Writers Association and appeared in *Alfred Hitchcock's Mystery Magazine*. She has been a Finalist and year's-end Honorable Mention in *Writers of the Future*, and three-time Finalist in the Pacific Northwest Writers Association genre contest.

She also edited and published, *Indigenous Fiction ~ wondrously weird and offbeat* from 1997 to 2001. She can be found on Facebook, Twitter, and Linkedin.